Addicted To Trouble

In Ashwood, Volume 4

Kinney Scott

Published by Mosquito Creek Publishing, 2019.

ADDICTED TO TROUBLE

First edition. July 24, 2019.

Copyright © 2019 Kinney Scott.

ISBN: 978-1950800049

Written by Kinney Scott.

Also by Kinney Scott

In Ashwood
Inheriting Trouble
Trouble Brewing
Chasing Trouble
Addicted To Trouble

Watch for more at https://kinneyscott.com.

To readers who are unashamed of their addiction to romance books.

ONE

Lincoln watched from a stealthy distance while a stream of happy people gathered to chat up their small-town lives. Men shook hands, women wrapped each other in loose-arm hugs, and kids raced into the party ahead of their parents, hoping for a thick slice of cake. Lincoln huffed. *All this bullshit to celebrate an engagement. Why the fuck did anyone bother getting married anymore? A pathetic waste of time, except for the free booze at the open bar.*

New to town, he hadn't expected to score this invite. Shit, he'd only hired the guy who was getting hitched to knock out a quick remodel job. In Oakland, that slim business connection would have only earned him a lukewarm beer from a dirty cooler. Evidently, in Ashwood, a handshake agreement was enough to get in. But into what? A dull surprise party packed with uptight asshats.

Lincoln shook his head. *Nope. Not going.* There wasn't enough alcohol inside that old converted lumber mill to loosen up this stiff crowd. He'd seen enough. He didn't belong here and probably never would. Determined to leave, he shifted his weight, and his Harley's leather seat creaked beneath his butt. Why should he give two-shits? Making friends wasn't his priority—making money was.

Instead of wasting time here, he'd head over to the run-down building he'd just bought and knock down another wall. It would put him one day closer to opening Lincoln's Pizza. That temporary front would get him by until he transformed the restaurant into his real moneymaker—a marijuana shop. And when Cascade Cannabis opened with zero competition, he'd thrive in this isolated hole. Ashwood came loaded with plenty of young tourists—climbers, hikers, and whitewater rafters —who'd make up for all these well-dressed, smiling, annoying-as- shit locals.

1

He snagged his helmet from the tank, more than ready to leave these happy people to their happy gathering. Feet planted, he twisted the key and pressed the starter, sending a low, vicious growl from the pipes. The sound surged across the gravel lot and collided with a gorgeous woman wearing a blue skirt. Buoyant fabric floated, putting long legs on display as she spun his direction with a startled, wide-eyed jerk.

His sly grin spread when he spotted two bottles of Jack Daniel's tucked against her torso—one heavy liter in each fist. Fear held her taut, giving Lincoln time to measure her discomfort. Why did she look so fucking scared? Incrementally, his grin faded and his fingers tingled, wanting to smooth that distress away. But, damn, that alarm only enhanced her wild beauty—dark hair, silky as liquid chocolate, ruby lips worried by white teeth.

Defiant, she lifted her chin and held his attention as his bike growled beneath him. The machine vibrated, eager to leave, but Lincoln's boots drilled into the gravel, steadying the motorcycle.

A frigid gust whipped her dark hair and urged the long-legged angel into the party. With the grace of a dancer, she rushed away on flat silver shoes through the wide bay doors, melting into the sea of happy people.

Lincoln's hand released the Harley's throttle, and he silenced the engine. That woman gave him reason enough to stay, if only to learn her name. He pulled off his helmet, raked his fingers through his hair, and considered his options. Contemplating choices came easier with a smoke. He swung his leg over his bike and ambled toward the trees while fishing his lone cigarette of the day from a pack—that single cigarette kept a promise he'd made to his son to cut back.

He usually waited until after dark for the heady hit of nicotine, but he needed to think, and the familiar feel of a paper cylinder between his index finger and thumb helped. A quick flick ignited his Zippo, a silver rectangle that had belonged to his Dad. Sheltering the flame, his fingers smoothed over the worn camel embossed on the front. The tip lit. He inhaled, pulling heat past his lips while considering the stunning woman in the sexy skirt.

What had frightened her? And why was she packing two bottles of pricey whiskey into the party? The temperature dropped a few more degrees while he paced the edge of the massive gravel lot. Cooled by an early March wind, the air smelled a little like snow. Lincoln pulled another hit from his cigarette to keep warm. He'd already decided to attend the shindig, but he'd hold off until after a loud *'surprise'* trapped the engaged pair inside.

Eventually, the bright and shiny couple pulled up. Arm in arm, they walked unsuspecting into the massive building. A moment later, a cheer erupted and loud music echoed through the tall evergreens. Lincoln waited out three more songs before he wandered in from the cold, reeled in by the dark-haired angel wearing those sexy silver shoes.

*****

Watching Natalie melt into Seth's arms brought back too many memories—Iris vaguely remembered being held like that a lifetime ago. She sighed, brushed away a few tears, which were equal parts happy and sad. Maybe someday she'd have another chance at a love like that. But was taking that chance in a small town where she owned the local dive bar worth the risk?

"Can I get another pitcher of the IPA?" Kent's request brought her back to her senses. Even though he was one of her regulars, and almost ten years younger, he still flashed his sexy-as-sin grin. *Definitely not taking any chances with Kent.*

Iris smiled and lifted an eyebrow. "Pitcher of beer coming right up. Anything else? Maybe a Cherry Coke for Amanda?"

"Oh, sure, I guess." Kent swallowed hard when Iris leveled a look, letting him know she was keeping track of her underage guests even at an engagement party.

As Kent turned away, Wade leaned in. "Thanks for keeping an eye on my cousin. I'm afraid she's trusting the wrong guy."

"Don't worry about Amanda, she's got that poor guy tied up in knots."

Their eyes traveled to the dancefloor—girls spinning in high heels, wrapped in snug cocktail dresses, keenly aware of the power they had over the men in the room. Yet Iris noticed a few guys hovering near the bar, their glasses too full to need another round. They seemed held in orbit by an invisible force. She looked one way and then the other. Was she the one controlling the pull?

The DJ changed things up and she grinned as a 90s hit took her back to barefoot summers in Kansas, simpler times where a good day was defined by staying out late riding bikes and wearing cut-off jeans. *Slide* by the Goo Goo Dolls moved her feet, and Dillon stepped from the all-male asteroid belt near the bar and grabbed her hand, coaxing her onto the floor.

Hands over her head, Iris lost herself in the rhythm. When the next song began, Wade claimed Dillon's spot and kept her on the floor for another familiar throwback. Arms that easily lifted kegs wrapped around her, and she let him control the way her body rocked from side to side. Iris tangled her hands around his neck and Wade leaned in. "I love these songs but look around—it feels like we're dancing to the oldies. Would you go back and repeat your glory days if you could?" he asked with a grin.

She fought a shudder and laughed. "Not a chance." Iris kept a smile in place and spun, thankful she'd never have to repeat her past again. "There's a line at the bar," she said with a thumb over her shoulder.

"Keep dancing, I'd like to watch you from a distance." Searing heat in his voice scalded her senses, flushing her cheeks, chest, and center with unexpected heat. A cold drink seemed vital. Iris tried to follow Wade back to the bar, but her steps were suddenly halted by a cool, steady hand.

"Stay." A voice slowed her momentum and dark eyes held her in place. His tattooed arms were so chilly, he must have just come inside from having a smoke. A hint of tobacco still clung to his clothes, but on him, the scent enticed rather than offended.

If Wade's comment had felt hot, this man's presence incinerated, and she became steam in his hands. Iris blinked, barely registering that he'd already plastered her against his chest. Good thing, otherwise, she would have drifted away.

"Are you new to our small town?" she asked, staring into unfamiliar, captivating eyes. The rich auburn bands around his pupils reminded her of top-shelf whiskey.

"Yeah. I hope I didn't crash this shindig. Wade tossed me an invite the last time he dropped a delivery by my place."

"A delivery? B-Beer, I'm assuming," Iris stammered, ensnared in his tattoo-covered arms.

"Yeah. Bottles, not kegs. I'll never move the volume you do at Northside Grill."

Iris narrowed her gaze. "You have me at a disadvantage. Clearly, you know who I am."

His chuckle should have put her at ease, but he seemed to be mocking her. She stiffened in his arms, trying to gain some space. His hand flexed across her back, keeping her secured. "Iris, I'm Lincoln. I'm opening a pizza shop in town."

Her feet missed a step, and she wished the classic U2 song would end, even though *With Or Without You* was one of her favorites. Iris lifted her chin, synced her feet to the rhythm again, and steadied her gaze. "Great. I can't wait to sample the competition."

Lincoln's eyebrows lifted and his lips spread in a devilish grin. "Angel, I can't wait to give you a taste."

TWO

Iris shimmied into threadbare coveralls, yanked them over her jeans, and started to sweat. The strange racket coming from the big convection oven forced her to endure a hot layer of workwear in the scorching July heat. She crouched onto the floor, pulled out the racks, then stuck her head inside. With the gas off and the fan on, the oven rattled and clanked.

"Damn, that doesn't sound good at all." Her words still echoed in the smelly steel box when she sensed vibration beneath her knees. Crap. Someone was coming.

"She's back here somewhere." Her employee's voice floated into the cavern which concealed Iris' upper half. The vibration stopped too close, right beside the round butt she'd left on display. Whirling fast, Iris whacked the inside of the oven with her forehead, clanging the metal like a church bell. "Jeez." Crouched on her heels, she closed her eyes and gently rubbed her forehead, waiting for the pain to dissipate.

"Sorry, boss," Paige said from a few feet above her. "I didn't know you were still dealing with that blasted thing."

"Still dealing," she mumbled from her knees.

Two chuckles—one distinctly low and rumbly—echoed above her head.

Paige stopped laughing long enough to add, "Dillon's looking for you."

"Guess he found me." Iris rolled her head from side to side and mumbled, "Give me just one sec." She opened her eyes and found two leather boots a few feet from her hip.

Her gaze panned up and Dillon shrugged. "Sorry about that, Iris. Damn, that had to hurt."

7

She stroked her forehead. "It's not too bad."

Sweet as always, Dillon smiled, reached down, and carefully pushed back her hair. "Well, it left a bump."

"Did it?" Iris laughed, knowing she looked like hell with her hair shoved into a clip and baggy coveralls protecting her clothes. "What can I do for you, Dillon?" She grasped the hand he offered and straightened from her knees to her feet.

Reaching for the counter, Iris inhaled deeply and prepared herself for an inevitable confrontation. Paige gave her a knowing *good luck* shrug and exited the kitchen to handle the bar.

She'd anticipated a visit from Mosquito Creek Brewing, but Iris figured Wade would man up and come himself. That talented brewer, the dick she'd dated until two weeks ago, had sent a messenger instead.

What a coward. Wade's balls weren't as big as she remembered.

Dillon cleared his throat, shifted foot-to-foot, and half-grinned. "Um, well, I just came by to make sure your beer order was correct. It looks like you forgot to include the usual kegs of the stout, Barbed Stinger."

For years, Northside Grill's order had stayed consistent with Mosquito Creek Brewing. Iris always carried Wade's top four varieties on tap. After her boyfriend strayed, she decided it was time for a change.

"I didn't forget." When Iris broke the news, Dillon winced, concern distorting his features. Taking pity, Iris tried to find words that would soften the blow. "Well, you see, I've decided to feature another brewery—one from Olympia. I just need to free up one tap."

"Another craft brewer? Damn. Are you sure? I'm sorry about the way—"

Iris halted his words with a lifted hand. She wasn't about to discuss her latest failed relationship with Wade's best friend. "Hey, no worries. It's just business."

Nothing would alter her decision. When Wade Michaels' broke things off and started seeing Ravenna, Iris learned again that a man couldn't solve her problems. Hell, men usually made her problems worse.

Dillon stared at his feet. "Do you still want the IPA?"

"Of course." She squeezed his forearm, and he looked up. "I'm only replacing the stout. That beer doesn't move well in the summer months, anyway." She sighed, giving him hope. "Why don't we talk about the darker brews again in September?"

"Sounds good," Dillon agreed with a hesitant smile.

"If you have the rest of my order, I'll help you bring the IPA back."

Dillon nodded and spun for the door, seeming eager to get the keg inside before she had a chance to change her mind. Sweat trickled down Iris' neck, carried by a sliver of guilt and blistering heat. Sticky sweat settled between her breasts, soaking into one of her favorite demi bras. Her head swam as she added another worry to her list. Northside Grill's aging air conditioning system might be grinding toward a collapse—a repair she couldn't afford.

With his smile back in place, Dillon pushed a dolly loaded with Double Deet IPA toward the walk-in refrigerator. Iris opened the massive metal door and cool air rushed out, washing her skin with refreshing relief. A satisfied breath hissed past her lips as she soaked in the chill. "Just leave it right there." She pointed to the vacant spot next to two kegs of beer from a brewer one hundred and twenty miles to the north.

"Capitol Crest," Dillon mumbled when he saw the competitor's logo. "Good choice. Quality beer."

Iris stifled a grin, knowing how much this switch would piss off Wade. Even if the new line from Olympia didn't sell, the change gave her satisfaction. And fans of Mosquito Creek Brewery wouldn't suffer. They could still get their fill of Wade's beer a few miles down the road—that taproom hijacked more of her customers every damn day. She had to diversify and offer another choice—different beer to go along with tasty food, hard liquor, and a game of pool.

The fan kicked on in the massive refrigerator and Iris shivered. Dillon backed out, guiding the dolly toward the rear exit.

"Dillon," Iris called before he ducked out the door.

"Yeah?"

"Give me a call before your next release. I'll feature that beer with a special."

"That'd be great. I'll bring by a sample." Dillon's sweet grin was genuine, but not tempting. Too bad. Still, his terrific beer reflected his love for brewing and he was a good friend. No matter what happened in her small town, an easy give and take bound Iris to Mosquito Creek Brewing. She'd still maintain the business connection and do everything she could to promote Wade's new brews. Maybe someday karma would eventually tip an overdue favor her direction.

Hoping for a cool breeze, Iris followed Dillon out and watched him heft the empty dolly back into Mosquito Creek's truck. He climbed in and the diesel engine growled. The deep sound produced a thin crackle of fear as he pulled away. Dust billowed from the rig's tires and caught on the wind like a frightening thundercloud, blotting out a section of sky near the massive Cedar that shaded the back of Northside Grill. She chased that disturbing visual reminder and checked her weather app for summer storms developing east of the Cascade Range. As much as she dreaded flashes of lightening and terrifying thunder, she knew rain couldn't fall soon enough. All around her, forests were tinder dry.

Iris stopped in her office to change her sweaty shirt, then passed from the kitchen to the dining room. The place was quiet. She chose to blame the heat for her nearly empty bar. The Friday afternoon crowd at Northside Grill might be slim, but the music was still great.

Her feet followed the beat coming from the jukebox and her hips swayed while she sliced oranges, limes, and lemons for drinks.

As the night wore on, couples wandered in, and she relaxed when an entire table ordered a second round of expensive summery liquor concoctions loaded with fresh berries. The till filled, yet Iris noticed the vacant pool tables. She knew exactly where the younger crowd was—across town, drinking pitchers of beer, listening to the live band at Wade's taproom.

Well after the dinner rush, Maggie walked in and waved. "Hey, girlfriend," she said as she found a spot at the bar.

"Aren't you up past your bedtime?" Iris teased.

The owner of Goldfinch Bakery grinned. "It's not quite ten. I won't turn into a pumpkin for at least an hour."

"What can I get you?"

"A vodka tonic sounds refreshing."

Iris scooped ice into a glass, tipped her best vodka from a tall slender bottle, then added tonic and a squeeze of lime. "It sure was sticky today. I'm hoping that's why it's so slow in here tonight."

Twisting at the waist, Maggie scanned the bar. "It's not so bad. There's a couple of large groups in the dining room."

"Yeah, but the young crowd's missing . . . they're the ones who stay late, drink beer, and shoot pool. Hey, I could probably leave Paige in charge if you want to come over and watch a movie."

Maggie shrugged. "I'd only fall asleep. And I've got a wedding cake appointment in the morning. Why don't I bring the left over samples by tomorrow afternoon?"

Thinking of her hips, Iris kneaded her lip and hesitated.

Maggie's grin conspired against Iris' willpower. "You know you want a sugar fix," she teased.

With a shrug, Iris caved. "Sounds delicious." Her friend's buttercream frosting was a favorite addiction.

Leaning in, Maggie whispered, "If you have time, we could give our little project another try."

"I hope you've come up with something new. I'm not sure we'll ever figure out Lincoln's magic ingredients. I lose another pizza sale to that miserable man every day."

A sympathetic smile tilted Maggie's lips while she sipped her vodka tonic. "We're getting closer with each new batch of dough."

Northside Grill took an instant hit the minute Lincoln's Pizza opened its doors. But Iris refused to give up without a fight. She and Maggie went to work, determined to figure out why that man's food was so damn good. After several late-night sessions, they weren't any closer. No matter how many times they tweaked the recipe, their crust and sauce came up lacking.

Even if Lincoln's pizza was perfection, he certainly was not.

Rough, crass, and cigarette smoking, the biker had a ruthless edge. His tattoos, goatee, and dark unruly hair were more than sexy, but that man pushed every hot button Iris had. He left her so flustered that avoiding him was her only defense. And in a small town, that took effort.

With a twist of her wrist, Maggie spun the ice in her glass. "Do you want another?" Iris asked.

"I better not." She covered a yawn with her hand. "Look at me—I'm already turning into a pumpkin."

The door swung again, drawing Iris' attention. "Look who just walked in."

Maggie searched the mirrored wall behind the bar for clues. "Who is it? I can't turn around, that'd be too obvious."

"It's Jerrod Holden, and he's alone again."

"I haven't seen the sheriff's wife in weeks. I hope everything's okay." Sympathy softened Maggie's features, but she sat up straighter, sensing the man's quiet approach. He greeted Iris first, lowered his voice when he said hello to Maggie, then left a vacant stool between them as he sat.

When he ordered a beer, Iris knew he was off duty, and asked if he wanted something to eat. He ordered a burger, and Maggie lifted an eyebrow. *The man was eating alone. Again.*

After she turned in his order, Iris served Maggie a sparkling water with lemon and kept herself busy with another customer farther down the bar.

The pair chatted until Iris brought Jerrod's meal. He looked a little lonely when Maggie rose and said goodnight. Iris stayed close as he nursed his beer and her bar slowly emptied. When he began picking through the last of his cold fries, she offered a hot batch and another pint. The sheriff declined both, paid his bill, and left. When Iris put his payment and ample tip in the till, she took a quick glance under the cash drawer. The sight churned her stomach—her deposit would be even smaller than the one before.

Giving up wasn't an option, and she only had one shot this November. With a win in the local election, she'd secure a spot on the city council and use that position to force change. If she wanted to save Northside Grill, the marijuana moratorium had to go.

Without a local shop, her faithful clientele drove thirty miles south of town to pick up weed, most times grabbed a bite to eat, then bypassed local businesses and headed home to chill. A pot shop would benefit every business in town—Stop-n-Shop, Northside Grill, even Lincoln's Pizza. Iris knew it, and everyone with an open mind agreed. Unfortunately, the rest fought change.

THREE

Lincoln backed his bike to the curb, sat for a moment, and inhaled the clean air. Even after six months, it still smelled strange—nothing like Oakland. Lifting from his Harley, his long strides carried him toward City Hall. Jumping the steps two at a time, he was at a jog as he grasped the heavy door.

Bright sunshine reflected from the glass blinding him to everything on the other side. He gave the handle a yank, and Iris stumbled into his arms with a yelp. Lincoln steadied her with a firm hand at her waist, recalling just how good those curves felt.

"Sorry about that, darlin'," he said with a grin as his touch lingered on her trembling warmth. He wasn't sorry at all, and he wanted more of her heat on his skin. She pulled away, but not fast enough to escape the memory of last March—the night they'd danced, the few moments he'd had her trapped in his arms.

Iris clutched a large manila envelope to her chest like a shield. "Let go," she said, urgent and low. He released her and she bolted toward her car.

Still holding the door, Lincoln turned to savor the view of her ass wrapped in snug denim, propelled by a hurried gait. He settled his shoulder, looped a thumb in the pocket of his faded jeans, and studied her hips as she swayed toward her lime green VW bug.

"Fuck, she's gorgeous," he mumbled to himself. "But that woman has a stick shoved so far up her ass, she's got splinters in her throat."

No doubt, sensing the weight of his gaze, she kept her eyes on the Beetle's door handle. At the last moment, Iris tilted her head, daring fate.

His eyebrows lifted. *Hah. Made you look.*

Trapped, her lips pressed together and she narrowed her eyes, accepting his visual challenge.

Lincoln grinned. *Game on, sweetheart.*

Iris tossed the envelope onto the passenger seat, slid behind the wheel, and slammed the door with extra force, all while never breaking eye contact.

Chick's got talent. Lincoln smirked.

She secured her seatbelt, turned the key, and the motor purred. Her jaw clenched and her eyes widened as it dawned on Iris that she had to look away.

His devilish grin flashed white teeth, daring her to put the car in reverse and press the accelerator. *Checkmate, baby. You lose.* He shifted his stance and shrugged, willing to stand in place all damn day.

When a big dog loped down the sidewalk, it stole her attention and she glanced away. The flick of her eye wasn't much, but it was enough to lose the contest. He laughed as her gaze popped back to his. She grimaced, added a snarky eye roll, and spun in her seat for an over-the-shoulder glance. As Iris backed the Beetle, he read 'asshole' on her lips.

Lincoln pumped a fist in victory when her tires chirped the pavement. Head tipped back, he laughed long and hard, then followed the howl inside the city offices to finish his quest. Three annoyed females peered at him through separate service windows, each spot labeled with an official brass nameplate.

He grinned when he recognized the name in window number two—Ruth Stanhope. Bingo, he had a winner. She lifted a thinly sculpted eyebrow as he closed in.

"Can I help you?" Ruth asked. Instead of looking at his eyes, she inspected the dark ink that edged beyond the collar of his shirt. Similar designs obscured his forearms, and she surveyed those, too. Lincoln waited for her attention, then he waited a little longer. By the time she'd shifted her gaze from his arms to his face, he'd masked his irritation.

"I'd like the election paperwork for the city council seat," he said evenly.

Her mouth popped open, round as a hungry goldfish. "You live in Ashwood?" she gulped, and Lincoln stifled a laugh.

"Yes. For the required six months. Paperwork, please." His calloused hand lingered over the counter—wide open, palm up, waiting. Candy-apple-red fingernails searched the contents of her drawer and located a thick manila packet. Trapped in her fingers, the envelope hovered between them, but Ruth wouldn't let go. Lincoln grasped it, won the tug of war, and spun on his booted heel.

He trekked toward the door, but before Lincoln exited, he turned back and hollered, "Thank you, Ruth!"

The sound rocked her back, nearly toppling Ruth from her perch.

She didn't recognize him without a Lincoln's Pizza delivery T-shirt. No problem, he didn't expect her to. Most nights, a small team of teens handled the bulk of his deliveries, all competing for the chance to drive one of his beat-up Subarus.

Still, everyone at Lincoln's Pizza knew Ruth and her Thursday night delivery order—pepperoni and pineapple with extra cheese. When she was feeling wild, she'd live a little and add bacon. *Crazy fucking Ruth.*

***

"What an asshole!" Iris mashed the accelerator, chirping the tires. Angry momentum shot the manila envelope from the passenger seat and wedged it next to the door. As Lincoln's black Harley shrank in her rearview mirror, she pounded the steering wheel until her palm stung. "Why, why, why does that jerk get to me? Damn it, I hate that guy." Even as she said it, her skin filmed with sweat, because as much as she hated to admit, he intrigued her, too. Still the power he had over her body only pissed her off one hundred different ways.

They'd barely exchanged a word since March—since *that dance*. It must have been all the twinkling lights at Seth and Natalie's engagement party, or maybe it was the deep caramel tint of his mysterious eyes. He'd trapped her in his arms, held her close for a single slow song, and alerted every nerve in her body as he started his contemptuous tease.

Like an evil genius, he seemed destined to destroy her. His weapon of choice? Pizza with amazing crust and the most addictive sauce known to man. The entire town buzzed the moment he'd opened his restaurant, excited about the shiny new place right in the center of Ashwood.

And right away, Northside Grill's lunch sales took a hit. He followed that attack with a sniper strike when he hired a bunch of teens to make deliveries, plunging her pizza sales into a dark abyss.

Yet, even her own taste buds betrayed her, and she couldn't resist sneaking that addictive pizza every chance she got. Those rare slices took patience and a bit of luck. Sensing an opportunity, Iris drove a few blocks south. She signaled and circled back, casing Lincoln's Pizza while considering the risk. Maybe she had time. Possible capture heightened her appetite and her mouth watered, anticipating a thick, hot slice.

She parked around the corner, hiding her lime green bug from Lincoln. Slipping from her seat, swift feet covered the ground with intent. Her head cocked, listening for the rumble of his Harley. Just a few paces from the door, she sensed all was safe and pivoted inside.

Wallet in hand, her untraceable cash was ready, but no one was at the register. *Damn it.* On her toes, Iris tilted to her right and peered inside the kitchen.

"Hello?" She held her breath to listen for an answer or his bike. When a car drove past, her heart jumped and her gaze flicked toward the street, ready to run.

The girl behind the counter appeared from nowhere. "Hey, Iris, what can I get you this time?"

"A single slice of pepperoni." She tapped the glass case with her short fingernail.

"If you want to wait three minutes, I'll have a fresh pie coming out of the oven."

"Kara, this one's fine."

"Are you sure? Lincoln wouldn't like it, not when we have fresh pizza almost up."

"No worries. I won't tell him." How could she? She couldn't even speak to that man.

Kara worried her lip. "Are you really in that much of a hurry?"

"Yup. Gotta go." Her shoulders relaxed when Kara grabbed a flimsy paper plate and slid a triangular spatula under the largest slice. Crispy circles of pepperoni with burnt edges peeked through the gooey cheese. *Perfection.*

Iris offered her money, but found her cash blocked by an upheld hand. "I can't let you pay for it," Kara said with a shrug.

Iris frowned, her foot tapping against the floor. *I really don't have time for this . . .* "What? Why?" Three dollars hung between them, but the girl shook her head.

"Lincoln won't charge for these slices, not when another's ready to serve."

"But it's still warm."

"It's on the house." Kara stopped her protest with a sweet smile.

"Fine, thanks." Iris crammed the money inside the tip jar, shoving it in with irritated force—no wonder she couldn't sell pizza in this town, he was giving this deliciousness away. Before heading out, Iris stuffed a handful of napkins into her pocket. She'd need them to deal with the thick, delicious sauce.

Her hip pushed the glass door open, letting in a low rumble that echoed through the streets. The Harley's growl increased, and her skin went clammy as she sped for the refuge of her car. Panic scrambled her heart rate. It wasn't the man, but the unwelcome sound of his bike she desperately had to evade. The roar tightened her lungs, prickled her flesh, and triggered stomach-clenching fear.

Her fingers shook as she used both hands to yank open the driver's side door. Keys jangled as metal pecked at the ignition's slot. When she turned the key, the radio masked the terrifying growl. She cranked up the volume, just to make sure. Iris licked sweat from her lip and searched for her prize. "Where's my pizza?"

Her head tilted toward the car's ceiling. "No, no, no." If she had x-ray vision, she knew it would be right there, but to retrieve it, she'd have to open the door. A wave of nausea replaced her hunger. *Nope, not happening. Not with that thunderous sound outside.*

A defeated breath lifted her chest then exited her lungs on a sigh. Iris put the car in gear and pressed the accelerator slowly, hoping the slice of pizza would stick. It didn't. Slick with grease, the round paper plate left a glistening stripe on her rear window as the pizza slid to the ground.

One last glance in her rearview mirror spotted a familiar black and brown dog. She squinted, watching as the crafty animal looked both ways, loped to the slice, sniffed it, then gobbled it down. Iris sighed as wind tossed the thin paper plate against Lincoln's restaurant.

Tears filled her eyes. After all these years, how could something as simple as a Harley's pipes leave her so Goddamn weak?

FOUR

Even though she'd left The Grill early, Iris scaled the steps of City Hall ten minutes later than she intended, not that it mattered. The same aging few attended town meetings every month, and they usually spent the first half-hour rehashing gossip she'd already heard at the bar. She'd pledged her time in the past to festivals and clean-up committees, but now she needed to do more. If everything went as planned and she won the election in November, she'd have a shot to make some real changes.

As she scurried past the door of the small bare kitchen, Ruth waved Iris inside. Coffee sputtered in a tall metal pot next to a stack of pink bakery boxes. "Hey, sweetie, could you take in the napkins and cups?"

"Sure, no problem. I always loved being your right-hand gal." Iris fell into the role easily with her former boss and previous owner of her bar.

"How's the Grill? I bet you've had a steady stream of tourists right through summer," Ruth said, while arranging cookies on a large plastic platter.

"It's just like you remember." Iris brightened her shaky smile and painted a rosy picture, hoping the late-season hikers on Mount Adams would make up for the recent slump.

"Sometimes I miss that old place, but my knees and feet like my little window at City Hall so much better. The coffee's almost ready . . . you better hurry, we're running late." Ruth loaded Iris' arms with cups and napkins then turned back to her cookie arrangement. When she inhaled a whiff of chocolate infused air, her stomach rumbled loudly. She loitered near the refreshment table, but only

20

caffeine appeared. Sheriff Holden placed the tall metal coffee pot next to her tower of paper cups and stacked napkins.

"Let me plug the pot in," she offered and grabbed the cord. Squeezing around the table, she contorted like a paperclip to reach the outlet.

Jerrod cleared his throat as she straightened. "Thanks, Iris. If I tried that move, I'd be limping for weeks." Color lingered in Jerrod's cheeks as he awkwardly chuckled to himself and turned away.

She shrugged, happy that yoga was finally paying off. Iris peeled a cup off the stack, held it below the spigot, and filled it to the brim. Weak aroma wafted from the steam. *Decaf.* Damn it, she really needed caffeine. With her useless coffee in hand, Iris chose a spot three rows from the front. Her nervous legs bounced, chirping the folding chair until Daryl Nash shot her a bitter side glance. She shrugged. "Sorry."

A gavel slammed and her head jerked up as the meeting came to order. After reviewing the minutes from the previous month, the treasurer revealed the new *'Welcome to Ashwood'* sign. Applause hailed the much-needed improvement, but as usual, Daryl complained, accusing the local craftsman of dipping into the city's deep pockets. Iris gritted her teeth and wished there was something high-octane in her cup—anything to help her deal with that annoying turd.

Thirty minutes elapsed while the same people introduced the same complaints—climbing water rates, dog poop on sidewalks, and abandoned vehicles parked along the river. The litany slowed time, and Iris dozed until Ruth took the stage. "Tonight, I'm here to announce the candidates for the city council seat. Sheriff, would you kindly send up a deputy to pass these out?"

Jerrod jerked his eyes from his phone. "Oh, I got it, Ruth." He took the papers and ambled down the aisle, passing the list to outstretched hands. Iris smiled and thanked him when she grasped the sheet.

After he returned to his seat, Ruth lifted bedazzled reading glasses to her face, and cleared her throat before reading the list of candidates:

Dale Robert Anderson
Iris Camelia Greene
Julius Caesar Lincoln
Stanley Herbert Minor

Spotting her name, Iris smiled. Then her eyes hopped to the one just below it. *Julius Caesar?* She trapped a chuckle behind tight lips. What a name. *Wait . . .*

Julius Caesar Lincoln.

Lincoln. God, no. Not possible.

Time froze, and her eyes shifted from side to side. Where is he? A slight tilt of her head, a quick survey of the room. *Damn it,* she couldn't locate that evil man. Of course, he hadn't bothered to come. This was Lincoln's idea of a joke.

***

Lincoln glanced at her name and grinned. Iris had talked about her campaign for so long, half the town was ready to hand her the keys to the city. And he didn't give a flying fuck if she got it. Shit, he wanted her to win if it meant less work for him. It didn't matter who lifted the marijuana moratorium, he just wanted to open his shop.

Unfortunately, Iris had been too transparent, too trusting for her own good, and she'd talked to the wrong people. Over the past few months, a silent contingency had expanded against her. A few opposed marijuana in Ashwood, and he got that. Others didn't want another woman on the city council, and *that* pissed him off.

The old fools didn't give Iris the respect she deserved but exposing narrow-minded bigots wouldn't solve a damn thing. No, he planned to keep his mouth shut and win the election. He wasn't here to change the world, he just had to make money in it.

Iris might despise him, but at least the owner of Northside Grill shared his goals. He'd talked to Wade often enough to know where Iris stood on the cannabis issue. She was for it and for similar reasons—to keep local money in Ashwood.

The gorgeous woman might be an ally, but he didn't have the balls to wander into Northside Grill and beg for a truce. It simply wasn't worth the risk. He knew if he spent too much time in her radius, his obvious interest would humiliate him. Even as he sat in this boring as fuck meeting, he endured the pull of her sway.

She twitched and his body rebelled as Iris deciphered *his* illustrious name. A mother he didn't remember blessed him with a title he hated. By the time he was seven, he never answered to his full name at all. Lincoln was enough to live up to without Julius Caesar attached.

Iris smirked. Did she think his name on the list was a joke? Nope, not a joke—insurance. He needed this win. Lincoln had a kid to provide for, even if he lived in another state with his new and improved family. At nine, Russel's needs were manageable, but his teen years stretched ahead. Then there was whatever came next. College? Absolutely. His son deserved a shot, and on his dad's dime, not provided for by *the stepdad*, and not starting out life buried in debt.

A subtle tilt craned Iris' neck and he smirked. Now that she'd puzzled out his identity, she wanted eyes on him. Damn, the girl could move. With a swivel of her head she searched to her right—a slight lean and she peered to her left. *Watch out, Iris, the enemy's lurking two rows back.*

Her pen dropped to the floor and he choked on a chuckle. *Nice move.* The pen below her feet coaxed her down in one smooth glide. To spot the room behind her, Iris contorted into a strange, yet erotic position—ass in the air, head down, brown hair flowing like a chocolate veil. Lincoln held his breath when her flimsy blouse dipped to reveal the ample swell of her tit—full and lush trapped in a sexy-as-sin emerald green bra. *Shit.* His pants tightened and he savored the sensual pain.

Their eyes linked, and Iris froze upside-down. *Hello, angel. I'm right fucking here.*

Her plump, red lips formed an 'O', then she straightened and abandoned the pen on the floor. Embracing his evil side, Lincoln made a swift, calculated move. He stood, exited his row, and entered hers.

The sound of his boots stiffened her spine as he approached. He bent, picked up the ballpoint pen, and claimed the seat next to hers. Legs splayed as he slouched, he crowded her before he held out the pen flat on his palm. He waited, patiently.

Touch it. Take the pen.

The shiny object quivered like an angry scorpion in his hand. Quick fingertips grazed the center of his palm as she snatched the pen away. Her light touch rippled white lightning lust straight to his cock.

"Thank you," she whispered.

Lincoln croaked, "You're welcome."

***

Those ten excruciating minutes seated next to Lincoln put her on alert. Even after Iris got home from City Hall, her body hummed. Uncomfortable and agitated, she hadn't felt so off-balance since last March. How could one annoying man occupy so much headspace? She tried everything to drive him out—a new e-book, ice cream, a binge-worthy program. When nothing diverted her attention, Iris found her fingers tapping her phone's smudgy screen, adding hearts to her favorite lingerie. She checked again, hoping her favorite bras, panties, and baby-doll pajamas would appear on the website's daily-deal list. Iris sighed. *Not today.*

The clock ticked two a.m. and she shut off her electronics, ready to turn to a reliable sleep aid. Not the toys she kept in the top drawer of her nightstand—if she went there, only one man would star in her fantasy, and he was the reason she couldn't sleep in the first place.

Tonight, she needed a little help from her stash. Iris pulled out her jar of marijuana and her pipe, then let the process calm her mind. Breaking apart the oily bud, she evenly filled the concave bowl and tapped lightly. Lips on the mouthpiece, she held her thumb over the hole in the side of the pipe, flicked her lighter, and sucked. She inhaled deeply once the Indica flower ignited. The smoke burned her throat at first, but the heat dissipated as cool air entered the pipe's chamber. Her slow exhale clouded her view of the stars for a moment until the dank cloud drifted away. Smooth glass warmed her fingers as she took a second hit. She held this one a little longer, and relaxation spread throughout her limbs. Her senses shifted, night sounds magnified, and the stars softened in the inky sky. Iris tipped her head, resting it on the back of her lawn chair. Time stretched and she waited for it—sometimes, on nights like this, Ian would send her a shooting star.

"Are you there?" She listened for the sound of his voice, but her twin brother wasn't talking tonight. Calm weighted her limbs and she relaxed until the cool night air drove her inside.

Curled in her bed, warm and safe, she listened to the noisy silence. No wind. No lightning. No thunder. No one. Iris felt so alone.

***

Although her muscles trembled, ninety minutes of morning yoga didn't erased Lincoln from her mind. Last night, and now this morning, these rebellious thoughts were getting old. Iris tried to fight it, but her eyes drifted to her laptop. One little innocent splurge couldn't hurt. Besides, no one else was going to pamper her the way she deserved.

She brought up her favorites list and squealed. The price had dropped on a smoky-purple matching bra and panty set that was more lace than fabric. Plus, she'd save even more with the points she'd earned.

Her fingers flew, choosing the right size and least expensive shipping. Waiting five to seven days would only increase her anticipation. A euphoric wave washed over her body when she hit the *buy me now* button. "Happy Friday."

***

Her dreamy, post-purchase high crashed when Paige tipped her head into Northside's office.

"Boss, the jukebox jammed again."

"Did you try the screw-driver thingy?"

"Yeah, but the quarter's stuck."

"Probably another commemorative coin." Iris pictured the quarter with the big bison jammed in the slot as she fished through her drawer for the skinny tool that usually did the trick. Without music from the vintage machine, the silence in the bar echoed her footsteps and every customer in the place swiveled in their seats to watch the show. After five minutes of prying, she moaned, "It's completely stuck. Just switch the coin operator off."

"Do you want me to grab the fishbowl again?" Paige asked, already headed for the storage room.

"Might as well." In Ashwood, the honor system worked and her customers were generous, often tossing in a few extra dollar bills.

With music filling Northside Grill again, Iris looked for something to do. Even a pile of dirty plates and greasy pans were better than the bills waiting for her in her office. After she cleared the sink, she peeled off her yellow rubber gloves and winced. Two red, angry blisters stung the crook of both thumbs. She reached into her pocket for fresh band-aids and covered the wounds she'd earned earlier today pounding two dozen election signs into the rocky ground. But the blisters were worth it. Her signs were eye-catching—dark indigo with yellow writing. And even better, the friendly honks she got from passing cars let her know she had a shot in the election.

Surrounded by the noisy kitchen, Iris missed the storm-alert on her phone. The dishwasher masked a rumble, but she sensed a strange vibration through the floor. Her senses tingled, then a lightening flash brightened every window.

Thunder hit and the windows rattled. Iris pushed her line cook out of the way as she dove for the walk-in refrigerator. Her sweaty hands slipped on the chrome handle. She pulled harder, ducked inside, and yanked the door closed.

Once her nausea faded, she slid her back down the smooth metal door until her butt stopped on the cold concrete. White phantom lights sparkled at the corners of her vision and her fingers tingled. The swimming sensation in her head withered, and she blew out a long, slow breath. "I made it."

A knock thumped, resonating into her spine, then Paige yelled through the heavy door, "Are you okay? I brought your coat."

"I'm good."

"Can I come in?"

Hell no. "Not until it's over."

"I'll let you know."

Iris blinked back hot tears, knowing how much Paige cared. At least she wasn't alone. Eyes closed, she swallowed hard, and traveled to her happy place—the baseball diamond behind her high school. Her brother Ian covered shortstop, his best friend Cooper stood at first, and Danielle sat next to her on the grass, sipping sweet tea. She wrapped her arms around her knees, imagining the warmth of the sun on her shoulders. Ian adjusted his red ball cap, smiled her way, and smacked his glove with his fist. The sweet Kansas breeze picked up, blowing dust past his gleaming white cleats.

FIVE

"Push it forward, flop it over, repeat."

Iris did as Maggie instructed, trying to get the feel. "Like this?"

"Yup. Now add a bit more flour. Your dough looks too sticky."
Iris dipped her fingers into the flour, sprinkled it on her bread, kneaded, flopped, and pushed.

"Is that better?"

Maggie lifted her chin with an approving nod. "Mm hm."

"How can you tell, just by touch, when something is off?"

"Too many early mornings with my hands buried in dough. Maybe that's why my relationships never last . . . Men love wake-up sex, but I'm never in bed at that hour." They laughed, and Iris realized she had the opposite problem—often landing in bed after two a.m. Her teeth clenched as sexy thoughts navigated her brain toward Lincoln . . . again. She shoved with more muscle, taking her frustration out on the dough.

"Easy there," Maggie chuckled. "That beautiful dough hasn't done anything to you."

The soft elastic lump sprang back. "I'll try to be nice." Iris patted the mound and it bounced like a wiggly buttock. Her fantasies slithered deeper into the dark side, and she wondered if Lincoln had ink tattooed on his cheeks, though she knew his ass had to be taut and sculpted . . . *hot damn.*

A knock at the alley entrance to the bakery yanked Iris from her fantasy.

"Must be a delivery," Maggie said as she rounded the ovens on her way to the door.

Iris continued her task—push, fold, repeat—until the deep, sultry voice that had starred in too many of her dreams hit her ears.

"The new postman delivered this to the wrong spot."

"But that's not my package."

"Yeah, but I saw her car, so I thought I'd drop it by."

"Come on in, you can give it to Iris yourself," Maggie encouraged and the voice at the door didn't answer.

Shit. The dough took her abuse as his footsteps closed in. Iris flicked her eyes to the side. Her gaze stuck to the parcel in Lincoln's hands, immediately recognizing the logo on the small package. The box was discreet, but the swirly logo clearly branded her addiction to high-end lingerie. When he didn't speak, Iris slid her gaze from the box to his eyes. Lincoln stared at her hands, where dough suffered, protruding between her fingers' death grip.

A grin tipped his mouth at the corners. "Might want to ease up there, not everything can take that kind of abuse."

Iris gulped and extricated her grip from the dough one digit at a time. The sticky mess clung to her heated skin, spreading between her fingers in a gooey web. Lincoln chuckled and jerked his chin. "More flour,"

No shit, Sherlock. "Yeah, I know."

Nerves propelled Maggie's laughter "We're just trying some new recipes," she said. Iris shot her a look, but her naïve friend didn't get the message and kept blabbering, "You know, breadsticks, and bread bowls—I thought I might add soup to the menu for the winter months."

Lincoln glanced between them. "Looks and smells a lot like pizza dough to me. What do you think, Iris? You're elbows deep in the stuff. What's cookin'?"

"None of your concern." She picked bits of dough from between her fingers and tossed them into the trash.

Lincoln stepped closer. "Oh, don't worry about cleaning up. I can open this little box for you and let you peak inside. Did Santa come three months early?"

Her wide eyes locked on his, cheeks heating as he shook the contents. "Just give it to Maggie," she begged.

He shook it again, then tested the weight. "Couldn't be much in here. Let me guess . . ."

Iris took a step, ready to tackle him with doughy fingers if he didn't release the box.

"It's light and sounds soft. Do you have a thing for cute little stuffed animals, Iris?" he teased. "Or maybe it's yarn. I can just picture you at home with a glass of wine, knitting by the fire."

She gritted her teeth and moved forward, as he stepped back, tossing the package from hand to hand. "Ah, wait, Halloween's just around the corner. Did you order something sexy? Will a naughty pirate be tending bar at Northside Grill on All Hallow's Eve?"

Embarrassed heat flared at Lincoln's close guess. But it also reminded her of the profitable party Wade had captured from Northside Grill for the taproom. This year, instead of a live band and adult-only costume party, she'd be hosting a trunk-or-treat kiddie night that ended before bedtime. Mosquito Creek Taproom would probably have to push half the town out of their doors at two a.m.

"I don't think the PTA would appreciate that." She extended her hands for the package, even though dough dangled from her fingers like decaying zombie skin.

Lincoln seemed to know that he'd pressed the wrong button, but instead of giving Iris the box, he handed it to Maggie then coaxed Iris to the sink. "Wait right here." The steady power in his voice kept her feet in place and shot heat through her traitorous body.

He came back with a handful of flour, reached around her, and trapped her torso between his lean, muscled frame and the edge of the sink. Right hand over right and left over left, he worked the flour across her hands, between her fingers, and against her palms and like magic, the sticky dough fell away. Iris sighed, hating that the trick worked so fast.

She shifted against him, savoring his scent, sighing when he didn't let go. Lincoln leaned in and whispered, "I'd still like to know what's in the box."

Iris locked her knees as he stepped away. Her wet, dripping hands found the edge of the sink as his footsteps faded and the back door clicked shut.

Maggie giggled. "I know you hate that guy, but seeing him, wrapped all around you? Damn, that was hot. Next time, I'm kneading the pizza dough."

***

On Halloween night, Lincoln stopped his Subaru to let Ninja Turtles cross the street. Flashlights bobbed, and parents waved thank you while herding their little trick-or-treaters to the next house.

Turning into the parking lot, he noticed an entirely different crowd pouring into Mosquito Creek Brewing, and the female half displayed plenty of skin. He rounded the building, parked, and slid from the driver's seat. Drums, guitars, and vocals tripled in volume when the owner of the brewery opened the side door. Lincoln blinked before he recognized Wade in pasty makeup and slicked back hair.

Relief washed over Wade's undead face. "You made it!"

"Where do you want me to put the first pizza order?" Lincoln asked while lifting the Subaru's tailgate.

"Why don't we bring 'em into the breakroom? My staff can take it from there."

Inside the taproom, the band wrapped up their cover of *Mr. Brightside*. Moments later, a costume contest for best dressed witch erupted in catcalls and whistles. Lincoln and Wade each took an armload of boxes through the door. The heavy cape rippled, nearly skimming the ground, as Lincoln followed the brewer inside. "I gotta say, I admire your dedication."

A shrug lifted Wade's shoulders. "Oh, the vampire get-up? This was Ravenna's idea." He turned and lifted an eyebrow. "But seeing her in the other half of the couples' costume. Dude, totally worth it."

Couple costumes. Lincoln couldn't relate. In the past, women he'd hung with on Halloween never asked him to dress up. Maybe his tattoos erased a need for anything more.

"These pizzas smell great." Wade put down the boxes and lifted a lid. "They look terrific, too. Thanks for helping me out on such short notice."

"Not a problem. Do you still want three more orders?"

A quick nod confirmed the large delivery. "If you can handle it, yeah. I couldn't believe that ass from Portland bailed."

"I can handle it, no sweat." Even though he was already slammed, Lincoln would take an order this massive every damn day.

As Foundry started the next set, music pounded, and smoke-machines billowed fake fog around Lincoln's feet. There was a time when the pulsating superheroes and sexy cats might have lured him to the dance floor. Tonight, not so much. His eyes skated over the crowd on his way out. A group of women he recognized waved him over. Lincoln shook his head and waved back, relieved to be working rather than trying to blend.

Still, with the friends he'd made in Ashwood, he wondered if he had a shot in the election. Well, he'd find out in a couple of days.

"Thanks again." Wade tangled with his cape while digging to find his wallet.

Lincoln held up his hand. "Just stop by tomorrow. I'll have a discount figured."

"Appreciate it, man. And you gotta know, your pizza is better than what I'd lined up. Have you ever considered adding a food truck? Seth's builds are awesome, and I wouldn't mind seeing Lincoln's Pizza parked in front of Mosquito Creek Brewery."

"Huh. Never thought of that . . ." A food truck might be the answer to keep cash flowing when he transitioned his current space from Lincoln's Pizza to Cascade Cannabis. He mentally listed all the problems that would solve and was about to ask Seth's turnaround-time when glass shattered somewhere near the dance floor.

Wade spun. "What the hell?"

"You better get on that. Don't worry about meeting me for the next order, I'll find my way in." With the noise, the alcohol, and the crowd, Wade didn't need another distraction.

Backward steps took the men in opposite directions. "See you tomorrow, Lincoln. And good luck next week—you've got my vote."

"Thanks." His brows lifted, surprised. He'd assumed the entire Michaels' family would send their votes to Iris. With her signs plastered all over town, it was clear she wanted this win. And if Ashwood didn't support her, she'd be devastated.

As Lincoln's gaze slid over the mob again, he realized Iris was probably having a shit night. His stomach sank. With this throng packing the taproom, Northside Grill had to be a graveyard.

***

"Toss me another candy bar, farmer John." Paige's silver bracelets jingled when she snatched the fun size Snickers from the air.

"Nice catch." Iris bit off another chunk of black licorice and took off her straw hat. She wondered how many hours of yoga she'd need to put in to burn off the sugar she'd devoured today.

Alcohol was far less tempting than candy, because she'd never dream of drinking on the job. But downing whole packages of M&M's while she watched kids bob for apples, not a problem.

At least the Grill was finally quiet. The peaceful hum of the dishwasher reverberating from the kitchen actually soothed her senses. Iris hadn't recognized her headache until the last family herded their sugar-hyped children out the door. Even though the party ended at eight, and she hadn't sold anything harder than a light beer, Iris still considered the night a success. It tied her closer to a community that she loved as much as the small town in Kansas where she was born.

After popping the last bite of chocolate in her mouth, Paige tossed the wrapper in the trash. She glanced at her reflection in the mirror behind the bar, feathered her hand through the fringe on her leather vest, then smoothed her tie-dyed T-shirt into the waistband of her faded bell-bottom jeans.

"So, you're headed over to the party at the taproom?" Iris asked Paige. A flash of guilt tightened her employee's expression. She averted her eyes, hitched one shoulder, but didn't answer.

"Hey, it's fine. Seriously, I'd join you at Mosquito Creek's party *if* . . ."

Iris couldn't add *if she was seeing someone*, because God, that was so pathetic. But the last time she'd run into Wade and Ravenna, the pair looked so happy it made her stomach hurt. Squaring her shoulders, Iris grinned. "I can't risk that party. I'm way too irresistible in this sexy ensemble." She looped her thumbs under the straps of her oversized coveralls and gave them a tug. "Who knows, I might get a little crazy and throw the election."

When Iris pulled a sliver of hay from her front pocket and clamped it between her teeth, she finally got a chuckle out of Paige. "You are lookin' pretty hot, so you better play it safe and stick with candy tonight. But my ballots already cast, and I can't wait to celebrate your victory in a few days." As Paige headed for the door, the speed of her steps gave away that she was probably meeting someone. Before leaving, she turned and asked, "Do you want me to blow out the candles on the pumpkins before I take off?"

Iris stood, ready to finish the final chore and put Halloween behind her. "Nah, I got it. I'll pitch those jack-o'-lanterns in the dumpster myself. If I don't, I'll be scooping the remains off the parking lot tomorrow morning."

SIX

Light snow fell on Election day, soft flakes that warned of winter but would melt by the following afternoon in the predicted rain. Lincoln hadn't factored in the weather when he'd selected this town for his business, or how much he'd miss riding his Harley. This thin dusting of white wouldn't affect the votes one way or the other—in Ashwood, everyone cast ballots early.

Kara helped him load his Subaru with pizzas for the election night party.

"Do you think everyone's tired of seeing these boxes?" he worried aloud.

"No way." She laughed. "These pizzas are delish."

Lincoln quirked a brow. "Or just the easy choice when no one feels like cooking."

"There is that. Good thing Iris doesn't partner with Uber Eats," she teased.

"Don't even utter those words. I'm off, and you're in charge. Call if the place catches on fire." She rolled her eyes. "If you need anything, I can ditch the event and be here in ten minutes, tops."

"I'll be fine. Holden's around—and some of my friends are stopping in." She knocked the hood of his car with her knuckles as he slid into the driver's seat. "Good luck tonight."

Arms wrapped around her middle, Kara rushed back inside to escape the cold. One of her friends turned into his lot as Lincoln drove away. He liked that her crowd hung out at the restaurant, but it wasn't because they made him any money. Most of her friends only ate single slices, often waiting for the comped pizza. But that posse kept Kara content, happy, and safe.

He cranked the music on his drive across town, listening to the shit that reminded him of his Dad. What would that old Allman Brothers' fan think of his current run for public office? He'd probably laugh his ass off, at least until he started coughing in that way which should have forced him to cut back before it was too late.

Lincoln slowed to twenty when he reached the school zone, like he always did, even when the hours didn't demand it. Shit, he was getting old. The numbers at the high school surprised him. If everyone inside was hungry, he'd be calling in an order to have Holden bring more pies. Cars and trucks lined the lot, but he found a spot near the gym and backed in. At the same moment, Ruth chirped the lock on her Caddy.

Dressed for the festivities, she'd wrapped herself in a fitted winter coat. The fur lining the hood surrounded her face in a puffy white halo. High-heeled boots propelled her toward the gymnasium door, where she stepped up and held the entrance wide open.

"Why thank you, Miss Ruth," he said as he passed in front of her, arms laden with square boxes.

"It's the least I could do for your generous donation. Thank you." She'd accepted him, tattoos and all, after discovering he was the talent behind her favorite weekly treat.

"Happy to help when I can. And don't you look lovely tonight," he said as they walked in together.

"No need to flatter me," she teased. "I've already cast my vote."

"And here I thought pepperoni and pineapple might help my chances."

She blushed as he pointed out her tiny addiction.

Walking in, they found Jerrod Holden and his deputies at work, erecting tables along one wall. Lincoln left his pizzas on the table and went back for round two. On his return, he spotted Iris pacing the room. Her beautiful nerves were showing, patrolling polished floors in black high heels. *Damn.*

Once his arms were empty, he pulled the cuffs of his jacket, feeling a little inadequate in his faded jeans, black long-sleeved thermal, and leather. Yet, he was thankful for every fancy stitch she chose—the gods had designed that woman to wear a hip-hugging skirt.

The sheriff cut off his line of sight on a quick approach. "Thank God, provisions. I've been trapped here all day."

Lincoln got out of his way. "Your favorite combo is in the second box from the top, and there's plenty, Sheriff."

The feast started, but with nothing to do, Lincoln fought his growing nerves. He peeled away his leather coat, tossed it to the bleachers, and turned to find Iris watching. A slow grin spread across his face, as she stared. She blinked hard, shook her head, and gave him a small wave, then mouthed, "Good luck."

Startled by her grace, he blinked, too stunned to return the selfless sentiment. Iris inhaled deeply before she pivoted away and continued her trek across the gymnasium floor, leaving Lincoln free to resume his thorough inspection. Long and lean, her thighs flexed as she strolled. Overhead lights hit her just right, and Lincoln squinted at something intriguing. When she paused, the perfect angle revealed an outline of a circular clasp.

Lord have mercy. His heart galloped when he discovered a garter and stockings under her prim and proper skirt. Lightheaded, he sank to the bottom bleacher, still staring at the walking wet dream.

He thought he'd recovered until Iris extracted a pair of glasses from her purse. As she slipped them on her nose and read something on her phone, Lincoln broke into a sweat—he'd always had a thing for nice girls in dark rimmed glasses. Iris finished with her phone, put her glasses away, and he could breathe again. She licked her lips while making her way to the pizza table. After choosing a slice, she balanced her plate in one hand and diet soda in the other, then claimed a spot on the bottom bleacher, sitting alone. Lincoln longed to join her, if only to keep other men away, but the wall between them seemed too formidable.

Easing her feet from her shoes, Iris savored a bite while her burgundy painted toes wiggled in sheer black stockings. The nervous movement coaxed her skirt up a mouthwatering inch. Lincoln blinked. *Fuck yeah*. A bare sliver of skin peeped between her skirt and the top of her lace-rimmed stocking, all held in place by a delicate, sexy clasp. Lincoln committed the vision to memory, certain he would need to recall every detail tonight.

A loud commotion at the other end of the gymnasium peeled his eyes from those perfect legs. Ruth shuffled papers, and everyone's attention gravitated toward the sound, but Lincoln found Iris far more interesting. She finished her snack, folded her empty paper plate in half, slipped on her shoes, and resumed her nervous stroll. Lincoln could watch that gorgeous sway for hours.

Restless conversations hummed until Ruth stepped up to a podium. The stage wasn't tall enough to make her noticeable, but the screech from the microphone was. Ruth grimaced then leaned toward the mic for a second try.

"We have the results," she announced and looked up expecting applause. Smattered claps died away and she pressed on with a shrug. "I guess I'll just read them."

Lincoln shoved his hands against his thighs to stand. Lingering girth reminded him that Iris still loitered only a few feet away. They both faced the stage waiting for Ruth's results.

Counts for each candidate brought cheers from most, others grumbled and shook disappointed heads. The single city council seat was buried far down the list. When the time came, Ruth cleared her throat and announced the name, *Julius Caesar Lincoln,* with dramatic flourish. Those words, strung together, were damn fun to say, but not great to hear your entire life. Yet Lincoln was relieved to hear his name tonight, and more than a little surprised. *Shit, now what?*

Stunned, he backstepped into the shadows, shaking his head. Eventually, Sheriff Holden located him and offered a powerful handshake. "Congratulations. We'll be seeing more of each other."

"I guess we will. Thanks." Lincoln wondered how the sheriff would feel about his agenda. Marijuana was legal, but probably still created headaches for law enforcement. Daryl Nash limped past and stared him down but didn't offer to shake his hand. Finished with her announcements, Ruth left the stage and rushed across the room in a beeline to Iris. She trapped his main opponent in a tight hug. Iris shrugged off the loss and gave Ruth a watery smile.

Someone plugged music into the PA system. Cheers erupted and champagne corks popped in the high school gym. Lincoln laughed aloud, realizing that this small-town crowd definitely knew how to break a rule or two.

He grinned like a fool when Iris headed his way with two glasses of champagne.

"Congratulations Julius Caesar Lincoln." His name sounded like warm honey on her lips— smooth, soothing, and very sweet. She smiled as he accepted the effervescent drink from her fingers.

"Thanks." Their short plastic cups met for a toast. "I know you deserved this. You might not believe it, but I actually voted for you," Lincoln confessed right away.

Her eyebrows lifted, and she huffed. "I'm not sure that makes me feel any better." Though she forced a smile, hurt clouded her voice.

Leaning toward her, and surrounded by the buzz of conversation, his words traveled no farther than her ears—ears he wanted to nibble if he ever got the chance. "Here's the thing," he said, "I'm guessing we have the same goals for this town."

Her eyes widened. "We do?"

"You bet. That shop, Kush Mart, down on the Columbia River, keeps sucking customers out of Ashwood. Even if they won't admit it, everyone's losing money to the cannabis exodus."

A grin tipped the corner of her mouth as her shoulders relaxed. "I know."

Coaxed closer, he inhaled a scent he'd craved since the first time he held her on a dance floor. "I'm tired of money driving down the mountain and leaving Ashwood," he said against her ear.

Iris tipped her head and studied the truth in his eyes. "I'm just surprised to meet someone I don't have to convince." She nodded, nibbled her lip, then grinned.

Lincoln wanted to suck the bottom lip she worried with her teeth. "Do you want to help me change that?" he asked.

Her sexy heels brought her jade eyes close, glowing like ancient treasure. "Yes, Lincoln, I'd love to help."

Yes, Lincoln. Why did her words affect him so profoundly? His fingers twitched, itching for a touch. He downed his cheap champagne and watched her sweet lips part, so close he felt her warm breath brush against the hollow of his neck. She smiled, but a sudden flash transformed her sultry grin to shock.

All four side-doors of the gym opened at once, surrounding them in cold November wind. Lights flashed and a concussive bang thumped the air. Outside in the parking lot a band of men ignited short fuses on hundreds of firecrackers. A few M-80s stacked noise with celebratory whoops and rampant cheers.

When the detonation hit, her champagne spilled, her fingers clutched, and Iris shrank into him. Acute trembling drew Lincoln's arms tight around her, keeping her limbs intact. Iris clawed, seeming desperate enough to climb beneath his skin.

Clapping and cheering eventually faded to nervous giggles. Distracted by the celebration, no one had witnessed her panic, though Iris still clung tight.

"Come on," he said moving her with stiff steps.

"Thank you," she whispered as he caged her in his arms and whisked her to the nearest exit.

Lincoln hit the metal crash bar with his hip and hauled her into a dimly-lit corridor that ran between the gym and locker rooms. "Over here."

Iris did everything she could to increase human contact as he folded their linked bodies onto a wooden bench that ran the length of the wall. Her trembling fingers caressed a wet patch of spilled champagne on his shirt. Eventually, her staggered breaths broke free. "I'm so sorry . . ."

"It's okay. Were you in the military?" he asked, trying to source her panic.

"No." She shook her head. "I didn't do anything heroic to end up like this."

He held her slim shoulders and lean arms, so fragile in his embrace. Lincoln recalled the first moment he saw her last March. Shit, he hoped the rumble of his Harley hadn't messed with her head like this.

Once her trembling slowed to short bursts, Iris peeled her arms from his waist. She took three slow breaths and leaned against the masonry wall. Arching her neck, she tipped her head back and closed her eyes. Reaching out for him again, the fingers of her left hand knitted with his right. He couldn't recall the last time a woman had touched him that way, but the innocent laced handhold felt as intimate as sex.

Iris licked her lips, and her forehead furrowed. "No. I wasn't in the armed forces. I grew up on a wheat farm in Kansas. Storms were in the forecast, but that wasn't unusual in spring." Her words drifted down the empty corridor and bounced back like an echo from her past.

"I used to love thunderstorms." She sighed. "It was a Friday afternoon, so I didn't notice the lightning at first, but if I had, I probably would have gone outside to watch the storm." A deep breath lifted her breasts and Lincoln struggled to keep his attention on her face.

"I was alone at home when the tornado hit. Mom and Dad had traveled to Missouri for the weekend to watch my brother's baseball game." Iris smiled as pleasant memories mingled with the bad.

"I got home from work and turned up my music super loud, you know 'cuz I had the place to myself and all. We'd had lasagna the night before, so I put some in the microwave." She paused and added, "I think lasagna tastes better the second day, don't you?"

When he didn't answer her question, Iris tipped her head to the side. Lincoln gave her a nod and she blinked, but she didn't seem entirely present.

"You know what really makes me angry about *that day*?" she said. "The details won't fade. Everything—the sounds, the smells, the taste of dust in my mouth—it all stays crisp."

Lincoln ran his thumb over her hand. Looking down, she became aware of the small physical contact for the first time. She tried to tug her hand away, but when he wouldn't allow it, she hummed and gave his hand a squeeze.

"Some people say a tornado sounds like a train and others say it screams. When it hit, all I heard was my life being torn apart." Iris blinked slowly. "My ears popped, and shit, that really hurt, so I covered my ears. Through my palms, I heard the windows explode as my house groaned and the roof tore off. Debris and glass pelted my skin, and I dove for the pantry."

Iris dipped her chin to her chest. "The pantry tilted to one side, and I was trapped. Cans of corn, bags of flour, and broken jars lay scattered at my feet. Shattered glass sliced my legs, and white powder penetrated my clothes. The smell of vinegar overpowered everything.

You know, Lincoln, I haven't been able to stomach pickles since that day." Iris laughed and her eyes softened, pooling with tears.

"How long until they found you?" His hands twitched, wanting to haul Iris against his body to kiss her pain away. He'd do anything to erase her fear.

"I don't know for sure. There was so much debris, it must have been hours. Cooper came with guys from the fire department and got me out." She shuddered, then shook off the rest of the memory. "I was lucky . . . Seven people died that day."

"Iris, I'm sorry. Is there anything you need?" he asked, squeezing her hand.

She laughed. "You mean, now that I'm not trying to crawl under the bleachers?"

"Well, yeah, I guess."

"No, I think I'm fine." She eased their fingers apart and folded her arms around her torso. Iris bent forward until her forearms rested against her thighs. In moments, shivering began. "Damn it, this always happens after a bad episode."

Lincoln pulled Iris onto his lap. She accepted the comfort and snuggled against his chest. The heat from her body centered him, and he let himself imagine what it would be like to cherish this woman. Squelching the fantasy, he extracted his mind from a place he'd never belong.

He toyed with a tendril of her dark hair and her tremors eased but she didn't move. Lincoln held Iris while he memorized the design of her black lace garter hugging her supple thigh.

SEVEN

Tangled in her blankets, Iris woke at eight, too early for a bar owner. Sun streamed in her window, coaxing her from bed. She shuffled to her coffee maker, ate a banana, and began her morning routine. After grabbing her yoga mat, she turned on some instrumental music, and used both to find calm.

Sun salutation and measured breathing relaxed her. Inverting her body into a V, she planted her hands flat on the ground and flowed into a series of challenging poses. But this morning she needed more. Iris knelt, flattened her shins to the mat then curled backward, arching until her head rested on her feet. Her elbows grounded her, the rhythm of her heart slowed, and her mind went blank. *Peace.*

Moving again, a sequence of angled poses challenged her core and left her weightless. To finish her practice, she lay flat on her back, palms up, arms at her side. Iris breathed. Her body cooperated and sank deeper into relaxation. But her mind misbehaved and picked up every worry she'd just set aside.

A hot shower helped until she remembered the election signs dotting the roadsides, mocking her loss. She grabbed her gloves and a crowbar then spent the afternoon tearing her name from the cold, hard ground. Each sign reminded her that the town she loved didn't love her back—and it hurt. At least the cathartic destruction gave her a great upper body workout, but it also reopened blisters that had just healed.

After she trapped the last sign in her trunk, Iris headed to the dump to dispose of her foray into politics. She showered again, then marched into Northside Grill with wet hair and a pocket full of Band Aids.

Tending bar put Iris on an awkward stage, and the *Sorry for your loss* glances forced her to choose between standing her ground or driving customers out the door. Paige mixed drinks while Iris disappeared into her office, flicked on her computer, and dealt with year-end books. Each data entry transformed irritation to fear.

A few minutes after eleven, Paige appeared at the office door, her hip on the casing. "You have the place to yourself. I'll lock up on my way out."

"Thanks. I won't be too long."

"Yeah, right." Paige raised her eyebrows until Iris' cheerful façade fell away.

"Go home. I promise I won't work all night."

"It sucks what this town did to you. And I blame the Michaels'—every last one of those knuckle-dragging Neanderthals." Paige's disdain for the prominent family was predictable, but mostly undeserved. Her sister, Desiree, had her chance with Seth Michaels when she married him right out of high school. They'd started out too young and before long Desiree filed for divorce. But she wouldn't let him go without a scene which ended in spectacular fashion when Natalie came to Ashwood.

Iris grinned. She appreciated Paige's loyalty, even if it was for the wrong reasons. "I'm sure the loss was more complicated than that."

"You gonna be okay tonight? I could stick around and shoot a game of pool if you want."

"Nah, I'm working on payroll. Don't worry, it won't be long before the election's old news."

"I voted for you."

"I know you did. But Lincoln might be the better choice."

Paige's hands landed on her hips. "That's crap and you know it."

Iris shook her head. "I talked to him and discovered he wants the marijuana moratorium gone, just like I do. There's gonna be push back, and the person with a target on his back could lose customers."

A chuckle brightened Paige's eyes. "Hmm. I hadn't thought of that."

Iris didn't want to make money at Lincoln's expense, but right or not, opinions mattered more in a small town like Ashwood. "Go, enjoy what's left of your night."

"See you tomorrow." Her loyal employee and friend left the office door open and cranked the music on her way out.

Thank you, Paige.

The classic rock play list matched the bar—one of the oldest buildings in Ashwood. North of town, it marked a crossroads where the highway climbed toward Mount Adams. The Grill began as an all-in-one outpost—a bar and grocery, with three modest guestrooms in the back.

As Ashwood grew, the Stop-n-Shop went in, and the roads improved. The market portion disappeared in the early 60s and a kitchen and dining room replaced that space. The lodging closed about a decade later to make room for an office, breakroom, and a second set of bathrooms.

Iris endured flack when she bought the place from Ruth Stanhope and her husband, John. They'd owned two-thirds of Northside Grill, the other partner being Daryl Nash. Daryl never worked there, but he and his buddies occupied the stools at the bar like a private club.

When Iris took over, Ruth and her posse came in almost every night until the town noticed and extended their stamp of approval to an outsider—a gesture Iris would forever be grateful for.

Shutting off her computer, she left her office and found herself loitering under the lights behind the bar. A golden glow bounced from the polished wood and mirrors, enhancing the vintage vibe. She sighed when Aretha's voice filled the room.

Responding to the beat, she twirled to the dance floor until the lyrics made her feel like a natural woman. The rhythm washed over her and her hands followed, recalling how secure she'd felt in Lincoln's arms. Laughing, she stopped lying to herself—she was incredibly attracted to that tempting man.

Iris danced through four more tracks but was still too wired to go home. She searched for a time-consuming task and nothing took longer than cleaning the commercial ice machine.

She locked up Northside Grill hours later. The sky glowed purple and the crisp air prickled her senses. A diesel pickup rumbled past and she spotted an orange hard hat hanging from the gun rack in the rear window—a timber faller starting his day in the woods. Funny how night people and morning people crossed paths.

Was Lincoln a morning person? Her stalker urges took over and she drove into town but found his shop windows dark. Damn, even a glimpse of him would have been nice. Across the street, Goldfinch Bakery glowed. Iris parked, climbed from her Beetle, and readjusted her hairclip. She knocked on the door and a few moments later, her friend rounded the bakery counter holding a baseball bat by her side. Maggie laughed when she recognized Iris, propped her bat against a chair, and unlocked the door.

"Hurry, it's cold as ice out there," she urged.

"Not quite, I just cleaned an ice machine . . . so I know." Iris shivered.

"The ice machine? What an awful chore. Something must be bugging you. Oh, the election . . . I'm sorry I wasn't at the high school to cheer you on." The holidays were approaching—Maggie's busiest time of year—and Iris hadn't expected her friend to attend.

"Nothing to cheer." She tossed away her disappointment with a shrug. "At least not for me. Didn't you hear? I lost."

Maggie wrapped Iris in a hug. "Of course, I heard. I can offer consolation tea. Orange spice? Why don't you heat water while I finish folding this cream cheese Danish?"

Iris shuffled into the sweet-smelling kitchen, though the lack of sleep was slowing her steps. She watched Maggie layer butter and dough while the water heated. Trays of Danish landed in the refrigerator to chill while the water in the commercial teapot came to a boil. They heated croissants from the case, then sat across from each other while their tea steeped.

"I'm sorry, I know the election meant a lot to you." Maggie tilted her head to the side and stirred honey into her spicy tea.

"Yeah, but I'm not sure if that's why I'm out of sorts. I got a loud surprise."

"I heard those fireworks clear across town. Was it awful?" Maggie knew about the PTSD but had never witnessed Iris' full-blown panic attack up close.

"It wasn't as bad as it could have been. Lincoln helped."

"Lincoln?" Maggie's mouth dropped open.

Iris toyed with a tendril of hair. "I barely know him. But the moment I walked over to congratulate him those M-80s blasted, and I melted. The poor guy . . . he should have run in the other direction."

Maggie leaned in, ignoring her cooling tea. "But he didn't?"

"Not at all, and he helped without making a scene. Lincoln even waited out the aftershocks with me. While I centered myself, I told him *everything*." Iris stared into her tea while her fingers toyed with the rim of her cup.

Maggie sat back from the table. "Wow."

"Yeah. *Wow*." Iris sipped the cinnamon elixir, placed the cup on the saucer, then leaned in. "That doesn't mean I want to abandon our plan though."

"Should we give the dough another try this afternoon? Or maybe it's time to puzzle out his secret sauce." Maggie's blue eyes flickered with a competitive glint. "At least our efforts aren't wasted. We're both making money from our cheesy breadsticks."

Iris nodded, then lost her fight with an overpowering yawn. "I'll be back ready to work after a power nap."

EIGHT

The door chimed—a high pitch sound that tightened Lincoln's neck—and another body crammed into his restaurant, even though he'd selected small, hard chairs to keep people from loitering in the miniscule dining area. In time, the novelty of his recent win was bound to get old, but until that day, he'd paste on a grin and suffer. A portly man hustled to the counter and Lincoln's hands filmed with sweat. Grin in place, he waved, then turned to grab an apron. He just couldn't shake the hand of another stranger who thought they knew him.

Kara basked in the chaos, glowing while greeting the herd. He left her to it and used the kitchen as a shield. In a moment, his delivery driver, Holden, popped through the rear door, carrying three insulated bags under his arm. "Boss, you won't believe the tips I'm making tonight."

"That's great."

"Yeah, it's like I'm working for a celebrity or something."

"Or something," he mumbled and stared at the exit, tempted to take the next delivery.

Cackling laughter bounced from stainless steel counters and tiled floors. He winced. Damn it, couldn't these people tell he was an impostor? Kara popped her head around the corner. "Hey boss, the Wilson's are asking to meet the newest member of the city council."

"Keep them happy, and don't let anyone go hungry," he said as he washed his hands and stretched a crust for the next pizza—a Hawaiian with extra pineapple and bacon.

Kara smiled and pointed out the obvious. "The pizza case is full."

He gave her a look, and she nodded, sneaking him a sly thumbs up. At least his best employee could take a hint. A hiss escaped his tight lips while he took extra time stretching dough, then he spread on sauce, meaty toppings, pineapple, and a generous mound of cheese. The throngs in the dining area grew tired of loitering, bought slices, and went on their way. Another delivery rang in, and Holden was on it. When the bacon-topped Hawaiian came out of the oven, Lincoln added fresh sliced tomato and slid the pizza into a thermal bag. Zipping it shut, he told Kara she was in charge.

Outside, his breath puffed clouds as he stared at the car. With nowhere in mind, he climbed inside, turned the key, and pressed the gas. Instead of scraping the windshield, he watched as two half-moon patterns ate away the ice. Peering through the frosty portal, Lincoln pointed the Subaru north. Slick roads slowed his progress and gave him plenty of time to study the lights spilling from Northside Grill. Her green Beetle confirmed that Iris was inside, but Lincoln rolled away from Ashwood.

He drove in tracks etched into the snow by pickup trucks. The wide tread-marks pitched his four-wheel drive side to side as the road climbed in elevation and the snow deepened. Only a fool would go any farther, so he backed onto a wide turnout and cut the engine. Silence struck him immediately and cold leached around his feet. He popped open the lid of his pizza, grabbed a slice, and bit through the layers of crust, sauce, meat, and cheese. The predictable food left him wondering why he didn't have the balls to go into Northside Grill. At least there he'd be warm and have his eyes on Iris for a while. Election night had only intensified his obsession with the owner of Northside Grill.

Lincoln chewed on his second slice and turned the key to run the heater. Headlights in the distance closed in. The light bar on the top of the Ford would have increased his heartrate in the past, but he knew that rig and the man driving it. Jerrod Holden backed into the spot next to his, climbed out, and circled to the passenger side of the car.

To make room for his friend, Lincoln picked up the pizza box and shoved it onto the dash before the sheriff climbed in. The door slammed, and Jerrod asked, "You having car trouble or are you hiding from your adoring fans?"

"Car's fine. How did you know?"

"I haven't always run unopposed. Everyone cared for the first two election cycles, hovered too much. Now that I'm as broken in as an old shoe, they don't bother with fanfare. But you're a shiny *Lincoln penny*, and everyone wants to say they know you, voted for you."

"A penny. Please don't repeat that. Anywhere. Ever again. I'd hate for that nickname to stick."

Jerrod laughed. "Never thought of that." He muttered *Penny* again and reached for the pizza box on the dash. "You mind?" he asked.

"Help yourself."

"Thanks."

He never thought his closest friend in Ashwood would be the local law. But why not? Strange though, Jerrod seemed as solitary as he was, and he'd lived here all his life. Another thing he'd noticed, the guy always seemed grateful for a meal. He, on the other hand, would be thankful for anything besides pizza. Regret hit again—he should've stopped in at Northside Grill. The silence stretched, minus the chewing, quieter because of the snow.

Jerrod licked some sauce from his finger and asked, "You hiding from anything else? Maybe our local bar owner?"

Lincoln's surprised huff echoed. Was he really that fucking transparent? He shook his head. "Not hiding, no. Just don't know how to approach her after the way the votes landed."

Nodding while he hummed, Jerrod said while chewing, "I'm glad you were there for her on election night."

"You caught that?" Lincoln appreciated that no one had made a fuss. Iris had seemed edgy enough as it was.

"Yeah. Ruth filled me in a few years ago. Something about a tornado and getting trapped in her home. Iris is dealing with it better now than she had in the past."

Lincoln nodded. If that was better, he wondered what bad looked like.

***

After another long restless night, Lincoln was tempted to skip the December town council. The dull meeting risked putting him to sleep. His term didn't officially start until after the new year, but he had to figure this shit out.

A few minutes late, he pushed through the door and found a chair five rows back. The meeting went from dull to interesting in a glance. One aisle ahead and three spots over, Iris toyed with a tendril of hair near her neck that had escaped her loose braid. He tried to listen but recycling wasn't as fascinating as Iris Greene. His attention tilted her head, their eyes locked, and she flushed an alluring pink. A playful staring contest shifted Iris in her seat.

"And your thoughts on that, Lincoln?" His name spoken from the podium put their sexy game on pause.

"Ah—" With his mouth open, he struggled to remember the last crap he'd heard.

Ruth saved his ass when she added, "We wanted your opinion because of your location across from the Stop-n-Shop parking lot."

"Oh, that. Doesn't the city use that lot for summer events?"

He got a confirmation then offered his opinion. "Well, I guess it's only right for the city to kick in a percent of the paving costs." Morgan Pratt thanked Lincoln with a nod.

Unfortunately, the battle lines also etched deeper when Daryl Nash cursed, "That's bullshit," under his breath.

Votes tallied yay or nay, and the measure to repave the Stop-n-Shop lot passed.

The meeting ended with metal chairs screeching over linoleum floors. Conversations buzzed as everyone pitched in to clear the space. During the commotion, Lincoln got a backslap thank you from Morgan Pratt. He hoped the owner of the Stop-n-Shop would remember tonight when he needed a vote.

Lincoln planned to time his move against the marijuana moratorium perfectly. At least the fortification was crumbling. Just a few days ago, Pratt stopped in for lunch and bitched about another dip in his holiday grocery sales. He'd run the usual specials but couldn't figure out why so many of his loyal customers kept shopping out of town. That practical man wouldn't be hard to convince when the time was right.

Ruth brought out her usual decaf coffee and cookie bribe. Lincoln spotted Iris near the table but found himself trapped by a stream of veteran council members competing for his time. When he checked again, she had disappeared. The numbers thinned and he wandered toward the exit while pulling leather gloves from his pocket. Movement turned his head before he pushed out the door.

"Iris." She'd waited forty-five minutes. *Damn.*

"You were popular tonight." She laughed, blushed, looked at her feet, but she wasn't too timid to admit she wanted to see him. He liked that.

"I'd have cut out earlier if I'd known you were here."

A sweet smile parted her lush lips. Lincoln wanted to take her somewhere, anywhere, but every spot in Ashwood was someone's turf. The taproom belonged to her ex, and if they met at Northside Grill, a gossip storm would explode. Shit. He didn't even have a real spot to call home—just a cot in the storage room at the back of his restaurant.

It seemed Iris was a mind reader. "Could we sit in my car and talk for a sec?" Her eyes slid toward the good-old-boys still mulling around inside. Holding court at the center, Daryl talked a few decibels louder than the rest.

"That'd be great." His hand moved to the door, holding it open for Iris. Frigid wind rushed in and Lincoln used the crisp air to clear his senses. He followed her, she split to the right, taking the driver's seat, while he swerved left to fold in on the passenger side.

Iris had planned this. She'd come out to run the engine and turned on heated seats while waiting for him. Nice. The cozy interior, infused with her lavender scent, took his mind places it shouldn't go.

After turning the ignition, she cranked the heat and leaned her seat back, getting comfy. The car's intimate size swamped Lincoln with ideas of all the ways her limber body could wrap around him. She'd fit so nice on his lap between his torso and the dash. Or maybe he'd lay her across the back seat, trapping her beneath his weight. On warm summer days, he'd stretch her over the sloping hood, hair warmed by the sun.

A huff cleared the fantasy as Lincoln fought for space. With his spine flattened against the door, he searched her emerald eyes for clues. Did any of her thoughts linger on him?

Iris trapped her hands under one leg. "Lincoln, I want to make an offer," she said.

"I accept." Playful innuendo textured his words and she blushed.

Musical laughter coaxed a smile, and he watched her lips as she said, "Well, I know you have piles of paperwork to get through by the end of the year."

He groaned. "Don't remind me."

"I'd like to help, if you need it or want it."

He wanted so much more from Iris than help with paperwork. Stiff discomfort shifted Lincoln. Unaware of his girthy crisis, she tilted her head waiting for an answer. He cleared his throat. "Yeah, a second set of eyes would be great."

"Oh, I was hoping you'd say that. I have an eye for detail . . . not that you don't. Crap, I'm talking too much." Iris didn't look flustered often, yet sizzling nerves looked beautiful on her—more tempting if that was even possible.

"I've been juggling this stuff on my own for so long. It's nice to know someone gives a rat's ass." He laughed, but he meant it. It'd been a long time since anyone cared.

"I care." She'd managed to read his mind again, then reached across and squeezed his forearm. The quick touch left her heat signature on his intricate ink. "Why don't you come by Northside, you know, when you have time."

"I'll make time," he mumbled with intent.

In the next spot over a horn beeped, unlocking a truck as headlights flashed. That struck Lincoln as odd—no one locked their rigs in this town. Daryl spun back toward the front door of City Hall while sorting through his keys.

Iris whispered, "I wish we could do something about that old fart."

Gripping the handrail, Daryl took the steps with a stilted gait and pain contorted his upper lip. Lincoln remembered his dad moving like that—years spent under cars on the hard ground took a toll. "A part of me sort of likes the guy. Reminds me of my old man—pig-headed, honest, opinionated." He laughed. "Shit, I think I just described myself."

Iris didn't speak until Daryl climbed into his truck and left. "Is your dad still around?"

"Nah, he died when I was eighteen."

"I'm sorry. You were so young." She looked past him into the darkness. "I guess we have that in common."

Lincoln's hand traveled, resting on her thigh. "When did your dad pass?" he asked.

"Dad had a heart attack two weeks after that tornado . . . Mom found him right next to his tractor." He squeezed her leg and she covered his hand with hers, interlocking their fingers. "It's okay. At least he died on his land."

It wasn't okay. She'd been through so much—losing her home, losing a parent. He wondered what else she'd lost. "Damn, I'm sorry, angel." In silence, they shared mutual pain.

NINE

Iris spent three days staring at Northside Grill's entrance, willing him to walk in. When Friday rolled around, she caved and drove to Lincoln's restaurant. A hand-written note taped next to the closed sign coaxed her to his door. Snowflakes fell on her shoulders as she read, *Gone until Monday*.

Why now? He'd lose so much money when everyone was too busy with shopping for the holidays to cook. It made little sense. What had lured him away?

Before Iris left, she traced the cold glass with her fingertips and memorized the moment he'd return.

But Lincoln's Pizza didn't open on the day he'd predicted, and his continued absence needled Iris' senses. A thousand tasks kept her mind occupied—stringing Christmas lights, filling condiments, organizing spices, and sanitizing the walk-in refrigerator. Carrying a duster in her left hand and a stepladder in her right, she headed toward the bar ready to shine every bottle of hard alcohol until each one sparkled.

With both hands planted on her hips, Paige stepped into her path. "Are you planning to cut my hours?"

The blunt question knocked Iris back a step. "Cut your hours? No, why?"

"Because you're doing my job."

"Oh, okay." Iris blinked, recognizing the truth. She'd taken over the tasks of half her staff. *Damn it.* "I'm sorry, you're right . . . I'm just preoccupied."

Paige rolled her eyes. "Don't dance around it. Everyone knows Lincoln's been out of town and you're all bent out of shape. But he's back now, so—"

Relief washed over her, freeing her from a fixated cloud. "He's back?" Iris pivoted right and left, but indecision stalled her feet.

Steady hands landed on Iris' shoulders and Paige said, "Yes. He's back. Now go make your move."

"Make my move?" Her stomach tightened with queasy excitement.

Huffing and impatient, Paige leaned in. "Listen, Wade was okay, but damn, Lincoln is *fine*—sexy as shit with all those tats and that motorcycle . . . Mmm-hmmm. *An upgrade, for sure.*"

Iris nodded, but it took Paige spinning her toward the door before she finally got the message—apparently, her friend wanted her to find Lincoln *now*. Her mouth went dry and she nodded. "Okay, I'm going."

Her drive across town gave her too much time to think. He'd promised to drop by Northside Grill, but never did. Shit, he hadn't even bothered to say goodbye. She was tempted to turn her car around, or maybe go home and hide because stopping by, for no reason at all, might look as desperate as she felt.

***

A sharp knock rattled the employee entrance. Lincoln clicked save and pushed his laptop to the center of the card table. The metal folding chair squeaked as he stood. He grasped his chin, cracked his neck, then smashed his eyes shut, but nothing would erase the image etched onto his retina—tiny columns, tedious forms, and endless regulations. Somehow, the government had managed to take all the fun out of weed. *No surprise there.*

A second impatient knock struck the back door. Still closed for business, Lincoln figured someone in Ashwood needed treatment for acute pizza addiction. He moved to deal with the intruder.

Just as he crossed the threshold of the storage room, he saw her. The outside light hit Iris' hair and face just right. With snow falling, she looked angelic, standing in the cold, wearing an expectant smile.

She'd missed him—thank God—and he'd missed her, too. Too much for his own good.

"Just a sec!" he yelled while shutting the door to the square space which served as his sad excuse for an apartment. Hearing him, her grin widened, but he didn't want to let her in. Iris knew he bunked in his pizza place, but she didn't need to see the stark, windowless room. Lincoln grabbed his coat and turned off the inside light.

"Iris," he said as he opened the door.

Her eyes lifted. "Lincoln." In contrast to the falling snow, her smile warmed him.

"You're off tonight?" he asked when he couldn't think of anything else to say.

"I heard you were back. And your place is closed. So, I wondered if we—"

"Could take that night off together?"

"Yeah." Iris blushed. *So damn beautiful, so tempting.*

"I'd suggest a ride, you know, on my bike. But the snow . . ." Nerves floundered his thoughts and he searched for options.

"The snow." She bit her lower lip, jittery too.

A lean in hinted how much he wanted a kiss, how much he needed it. "How about a drive instead?" he asked. "I've got the Subaru. We could skip town, go get something to eat, maybe check out the competition?"

Disappointment clouded the sparkle in her eyes. "Right, the competition."

He'd turned her keen interest into business. *Shit.*

But then she nodded. "Sounds great. I'm in." Iris spun, wobbled, and slipped on the ice. His hands sprung forward and held her steady, fingers stretching across her ribcage. She laughed, and he felt the vibration. "It's so slick. Lincoln, are you sure you want to drive down to the river?"

His hands slid away from her body after he delivered her safely to the passenger side. "No problem. I put studs on this winter. Gotta keep my delivery drivers safe."

"It's nice how much you care about those kids." He opened her door. "I've watched so many of them grow up . . ." Her voice trailed off as she climbed in.

Lincoln circled the nose of his four-wheel drive Outback and pushed the key into the ignition. The frigid car coughed to a start. He gave it extra fuel until the sluggish engine warmed and purred, then adjusted the dials, sending heat to the windshield. Reaching across the car, he found the ice scraper in the glovebox and hopped out.

Iris unfolded from the passenger side and opened the back door. She found another ice scraper under the seat and muscled frost from her side.

"Thanks," he said as they worked together, clearing ice while the engine ran. They met at the rear window and each scraped half. Lincoln fought an overwhelming desire to trap her against the car, but it was far too cold for what he wanted to do to her against the cold metal.

Windows clear, they left town behind and headed toward the Columbia River Gorge. The glittering snow-scape made silence easy until Lincoln recalled what she'd said before she scraped ice from his car. "How old were my employees when you landed in Ashwood?"

"Oh." She seemed surprised when he disturbed the quiet. "I moved here about ten years ago. Your employees weren't in diapers, but I feel like I watched them grow up. They'd come into Northside Grill at the end of soccer season or to celebrate birthdays—marking happy milestones on the calendar."

"Nice."

"Yeah, it was. It still is."

Lincoln's hands tightened around the steering wheel—he wanted more, wanted it all, but wasn't ready to share his details. Waiting, he hoped Iris would expand her reveal. His fingers relaxed when she took a breath.

"I grew up in a small town, smaller than Ashwood. Sometimes I wonder if I missed out on a more exciting life by going from one close-knit place to another. But I like knowing everyone at the grocery store and my bar. Sure, the gossip can get thick, but at least we care enough to keep tabs. And when I hear a group of ladies at the Grill plan meals for a friend who had a baby, or spot the guys getting together to build a ramp for somebody who can't make it up their stairs, well, I smile. And I know that when my time comes, someone will be there to help me, too."

"I'm beginning to see that, the give and take." Lincoln's thumb tapped the steering wheel. "Coming from the Bay Area, I gotta tell you, Ashwood was a shock to the system."

"A good shock?"

"Eventually. It took a while before I learned to trust a handshake."

Iris laughed. "There's two sides to that trust. If you screw up and burn someone, you can't just scrape them off and move on."

"Mistakes leave a dent," he agreed.

"And people talk," Iris huffed, her thoughts took her places she wasn't ready to share, but Lincoln suspected it had something to do with Wade Michaels. He was a solid guy and Lincoln trusted him, had even become his friend. But he'd picked up the buzz last summer, and the buzz didn't make Wade look good.

Iris stared out the window for a while, watching the snow change to drizzle as they dropped in elevation. "Where are you taking us? she asked.

"Any preference?"

She hooked her finger on her lip. "Hmm. I'm craving something different."

Lincoln craved Iris but kept that to himself. "How about Pad Thai?"

"Perfect. Watch out, I like it hot." Her sexy smile went beyond casual flirting, and he swallowed a groan.

***

The snow on the return trip wasn't as forgiving as it was on the ride down. Nervous, Iris clutched the edge of her seat when his car drifted toward the ditch. She let the conversation stall as Lincoln gave his full attention to the road. Back in Ashwood, he offered to drive her home, but she declined when she spotted the flashing yellow snowplow lights.

"It's not too far, and they're clearing the roads," she said. "I'll be fine."

"Text me when you get there?" he asked.

"I could do that, if I had your number." Heat hit her cheeks, but she didn't think he noticed as they exchanged numbers.

Popping from her seat, she met him at the hood of his car. To halt the awkward goodbye, she flung both arms around Lincoln and gave him a quick hug. Wind-chill chased Iris to her Beetle, and she was thankful. The entire night had been perfect—easy conversation, and delicious food shared with a good-looking guy who paid for dinner. Then it got better. They wandered around Hood River and peeked through windows decorated for the holidays. The night finished at a cozy place that served amazing gelato. She picked up the tab for dessert, and they ate it at a small table while talking a little longer.

His number was in her phone, and a kiss goodnight would have shifted the night from nice to perfect. But she wasn't ready for perfect. Perfection left no room for better, and she wanted something to look forward to.

Slick roads kept her from obsessing. The evergreens hung heavy, draped in white cloaks like great wizards—magical and formidable at the same time.

Iris flicked on the radio and the twenty-four-hour Christmas station filled her car. All at once, she missed her mom and wished she'd used that ticket to visit her this year. It was her turn to travel, but late-season hurricanes were rolling across the gulf and Iris couldn't risk a flight to Corpus Christi, Texas without a heavy dose of meds—if she could get on the plane at all. Her mom said she understood, and Iris promised to Skype on Christmas Day.

***

Cooper, Danielle, and the kids crowded around the computer opening packages wrapped in silver paper Iris had sent for Christmas. She'd already opened theirs, a framed picture from their summer visit. They'd all traveled together to the coast and camped near the beach. On a perfect afternoon, everyone had huddled together for a shot near Haystack Rock.

"Awesome!" Jacob and Zach yelled while Lilly still struggled with the ribbon and wrapping paper. When she finally freed her remote-control car, she hollered. Iris made sure Lily's hotrod was just as cool as her brothers', but easier to navigate with simpler controls.

"Can we try 'em out now?" Zach yelled.

Cooper mussed his younger son's pale hair. "Probably need to charge the battery. Plug 'em in and we'll take the race cars out to the barn later."

"What do you say?" Dani said while trying to corral the kids' excitement.

"Thank you, Auntie Iris." Cooper and Danielle's kids weren't blood related, but she loved them just as much as if they were.

Smiles beamed over the computer connection, and Iris felt that squeeze as her heart filled her chest, making it impossible to breathe. She swallowed the sentiment and grinned. "You're welcome, kiddos."

Cooper and the kids dashed off to peel away packaging and plug in batteries, leaving Danielle and Iris alone for a few moments. "Did you get Ian's gift?" Iris asked.

"Yeah. Delivered it to your brother yesterday. It looks real nice. Your mom sent something, too."

"You know, I actually bought a ticket to visit Mom this year." She'd paid extra for refundable because she knew her plans were tentative. "At least Mom didn't get her hopes up. When the weather shifted, she called and let me off the hook."

"You wouldn't have been much fun, sleeping away the holidays, locked in a dark room." Danielle said, sympathy clear, even over the fuzzy video connection.

Iris had endured one awful year in Kansas after the storm. Right after Dad's death, her brother, Ian, left for bootcamp and her mom escaped to Texas to grieve. Iris tried to stay in her hometown, for Cooper, but the strong woman she once was faded in front of his eyes. More zombie than human, Iris had only snuck outdoors when the sky was calm. When she couldn't endure another storm, she'd left, but neither expected the move to be permanent. At the time, she had still worn his engagement ring.

A sly grin spread across Iris' face when she asked, "Have you opened the stocking stuffer?" She and Dani shared the same addiction for fancy lingerie—a habit they began together on trips to the mall in Wichita.

"I sure did, and Cooper loves it as much as I do." Danielle blushed and Iris giggled when she picked up the color shift over the stilted computer connection.

"I love mine, too." Iris pulled her blouse off her shoulder, revealing the fact that she had the lovely camisole on.

Cooper's head popped back into the screen. "What are your plans for the rest of the holidays? Anyone we should know about?"

Danielle elbowed her husband. "Stop digging."

Iris rolled her eyes. "Maggie and I are getting together. She's baking and I'm cooking while we watch *The Holiday* for the thousandth time."

"Oh, my God. I love that movie. Cameron Diaz and Jude Law are perfect together."

"I've always had a soft spot for Jack Black," Iris admitted, and her mind wandered to Lincoln. Maybe it was the beard. Those men definitely didn't have much else in common.

The girls sighed and Cooper laughed. "And I'm out. Merry Christmas, Iris." He blew her a kiss from lip she used to know so well, in another lifetime.

A tiny drone buzzed past the computer screen followed by the two younger kids. "I better let you go before something breaks."

"Too late for that." Dani laughed and tipped her head toward Cooper. "This guy's in for seven years of bad luck. He decided to play catch with Jake in the hall and shattered a mirror."

"Had to break in that new mitt," the guilty party yelled off camera.

"Love you guys," Iris said while reaching for the mouse.

"Love you, too." Dani blew a kiss, then disappeared with a computerized blip.

TEN

Iris swept confetti into a massive metal dustpan, knowing the glittery stuff would reappear for months. Still, she was satisfied—New Year's Eve had packed Northside Grill to capacity, maybe because Mosquito's taproom went silent over the busy holiday. She didn't know if Wade had planned to take a break in advance, or if he scrapped a party after his sister, Linnea, totaled her car.

A few days before Christmas, she'd taken a drive and gone missing, everyone in Ashwood searched, and fortunately found her before the night ran out. Her dive into a ditch brought the small community closer, as near tragedies often do.

Was that why she felt a little off? Maybe it was just her usual winter blues—a yearly disconnect that came with the Northwest's long, dark nights. Skyping with Danielle, Cooper, and their kids on Christmas Eve had cheered her. And dinner, dessert, and movies with Maggie was worth the few extra pounds. Christmas morning with Mom wasn't as easy. They'd both cried while tearing into presents in front of their laptop screens. Each gift was a sterile reminder that she didn't have enough courage to board a plane and fly East. Iris was determined that this year she would find a way to conquer this irrational, annoying as shit, life-numbing fear.

Iris picked up the dustpan, emptied it, and was headed for her mop when the man she'd wanted to kiss at the stroke of midnight walked through the door.

"Hope I didn't scare you," Lincoln said with a wave. "I saw the closed sign, but your car's still outside."

Loneliness evaporated, as she abandoned her broom. "Not closed to you."

He sauntered in, so loose-limbed and relaxed that she almost didn't notice the small package in his hand. Her heart jumped, and then she felt terrible. She hadn't bought him a gift. Had she missed some signal? Had their fragile connection progressed that far?

Lincoln lifted the package and shook it. "I meant to deliver this earlier. That new postman doesn't know his route."

Confusion tilted Iris' head, until she remembered the thong and bra set she'd bought for herself—the one on backorder—should have arrived the day before yesterday. She laughed and held both hands in the air. Lincoln launched the box in an underhand toss, an easy flick of the wrist that peeled the tension away.

"Nice catch." he said, "Hope Santa brought you something nice."

She blushed. "Oh, he did. I picked this out myself." Iris hid the parcel behind the bar and turned to find him inspecting the room. His eyes skidded across the pool tables, over the dining area, then returned to her again. "Haven't you been in before?" she asked.

"Not since last January, when I first scoped out Ashwood."

"What?" A flattened hand covered her heart with dramatic shock. "I'm hurt. It's been almost a year," her laugh masked a stab of real rejection, "and my bar couldn't lure you back?"

His shoulders lifted. "I was tempted, but once the battle lines were drawn . . ."

Their single dance, last March, had sparked a fiery competition. Would they still be at odds if the election night explosions hadn't thrust her into his arms? Possibly. No, probably. She had too much stubborn pride.

Lincoln still hadn't claimed a seat, so she waved him over to the bar. "Have you been delivering pizzas all night?"

"Yeah. My last drop off wasn't too far from here. I had that package in the car, and I spotted your lights."

She hoped more than convenience had lured him in. "Are you thirsty or hungry?" she asked. His gaze perused her, lingering, and she saw a different hunger in his eyes.

He nodded. "I'll drink whatever you're having." Iris selected two heavy glasses, then stood on tiptoes to reach for the whiskey only a few could afford.

"Damn, that's the good stuff," he said when she put a bottle emblazoned with a silver stag on the bar.

"It's the New Year. Don't you think we should celebrate something?" Aching sadness she couldn't hide leached through her smile, and Lincoln circled the counter which separated them, desire reeling them together on a string.

Steady hands cupped her cheeks. His thumb brushed across her lip. "Happy New Year," he murmured as he brought her mouth to his.

Lips parted, as his gentle caress tested her reaction. When she slid her arms around his waist, his tongue swept petal soft over her bottom lip. She opened to him, sighing when one hand twisted into her hair, angling her head to deepen his access. Her trembling fingers gripped the back of his shirt as his tongue mapped her response. Complete surrender had eased her longing but left her dizzy, off-balance, and a little confused.

The inch of space between their torsos heated until Lincoln backed away, separating their lips while keeping hold of her nape. Iris licked her lips, savoring his minty-tobacco flavor. Her shaking fingers loosened from the soft fabric of his shirt, then her arms fell limp at her sides.

His devilish grin stuttered her heartbeat. "Should have done that the first night we met," he said, stroking her jawline.

"I wish you had."

He chuckled, then both hands traced the length of her arm, holding her fingertips for a moment before he stepped away. "A kiss like that would have made my first summer in Ashwood much more interesting."

Intensity sharpened his fixed gaze. Was he questioning the kiss? Iris pivoted from his scrutiny and went back to the safety of her bar. She lifted the bottle with the silver stag label and poured. "So why Ashwood?" she asked as two fingers of amber liquid fell into the first glass. She slid it across the bar to him, stopping half-way before her hand drifted too close.

Lincoln picked up the heavy tumbler and raised it to the light. "The town fit my search criteria. No pizza delivery opposition and even better, no competition for pot."

"A calculated business move—nice and detached. I admire that, but still don't understand it. Emotions guide me, and it sometimes gets me into trouble." She'd gone with her gut when she signed the contract to buy Northside Grill from the Stanhopes and Daryl Nash. Every month, as she mailed two checks—one to Ruth and one to Daryl—she prayed she hadn't made an epic mistake.

He took a sip of his whiskey. "Smooth." Then licked his lips. His eyes targeted again, aimed with more purpose and he emphasized his words, most likely for her benefit. "I see no reason to complicate things that don't need to be complicated."

As she savored her first swallow of the expensive liquor, she committed that detail to memory. *Understood. Lincoln didn't do complicated.*

His cool nature forced her mind back to business. If she could strip away all emotion, would her decision to buy this place be the same? Probably not. Without its heartbeat, Northside Grill was merely a money pit.

"This old bar was a dive when I made the down payment." She chuckled. "I guess it's still a wreck, but it's my wreck now."

"Looks pretty damn perfect to me." An easy grin mingled with his compliment then he glanced across the room. "Do you play?"

She followed his line of sight and nodded. "I watch more than shoot, but I'm willing." Heat charged her words.

"Good God, I hope so." His flirty smirk slid her attention from his dark eyes to his tempting lips. She longed for another taste, but Lincoln headed toward the pool table before she could make a bold move.

To slake her disappointment, Iris admired the way his faded jeans clung to his ass and thighs as he selected a pool cue. His fingers slid down the length before making a choice. Her body craved that slithering caress. *Maybe someday.* After a glance over his shoulder, he selected a long, slender stick for her, too.

When she joined him near the pool tables, she didn't bother asking if he wanted more whiskey, instead, she poured another shot while he racked the balls. Fluid strength controlled his movement. but when he crouched over the table he winced and hissed.

"Long day?" she asked.

His eyes questioned her comment, and she slid her hand above her hip and added, "Your back. Are you hurting?"

"Oh. I earned that a few years ago when I had to lay my bike down. The muscles tighten when it's cold."

She moved around the table. "Let me help? I'm good with my hands."

"Angel, I never doubted that."

He reached for her hips, but she shook her head, intending to ease his pain. "Uh, uh. Turn around and lean against the pool table." She twirled her fingers in the air, directing his motion.

"You're serious?" He chuckled as he turned.

"Of course, I'm serious. I don't want to hear a lame excuse about your back when I kick your ass at pool." Her hands smoothed over his thin shirt, muscles bunching as he stretched.

"In that case, have at it." The swell of her hand circled near the hollow of his back, then her thumbs dug into a knot. When she applied extra pressure, he groaned, "Right there, shit that's good."

"This would be easier if you were lying down." She added pressure, leaning in to deepen the massage.

"Baby, everything's better if we're horizontal. I'll crawl onto that pool table, but only if you join me."

"Tempting, but not tonight." She laughed and dug into a muscle as he braced his boot on the wooden floor. His satisfied rumble transmitted heat to her core, but she ignored it and closed her eyes to cope with mounting need.

He was right—they could crawl onto that table, satisfy this craving, and move on. But that might quench the slow-burn smoldering between them, and that would be unfortunate. This flame hadn't burned quite long enough.

Easing the motion, she lightened her touch, caressed, then walked away. Lincoln stayed in place, braced against the pool table with his eyes closed.

"Thank you," he whispered and tilted his head to the side on a glance. Their eyes met, lingering. Hunger was there, but also something more . . . gratitude. Had no one cared for this man?

He straightened, stretched, did that neck-cracking thing that made her flinch, then moved to grab his cue. A challenging grin spread across his face as he crouched to cock the stick between his finger and thumb.

Taut as a cobra, his body snapped and broke the balls with an earsplitting crack. Solids and stripes scattered, and he sunk his first ball. Iris downed a gulp of whiskey and let the burn disperse her aching need. Hip propped, she watched his next shot and admired the way he'd used the angle when the ball clattered in.

He circled the table, sizing up his options. "How's Linnea? Is she out of the hospital?" he asked, his voice low and raspy, yet filled with intense concern.

She squeezed her glass, surprised by the abrupt question. "Oh, you haven't heard?"

"No. I didn't catch the details." Lincoln didn't bother to disguise a stab of irritation she recognized and shared. He might live in Ashwood, serve them food, even get invited to a party or two, but those who were born here had particular rights, favors often withheld from newcomers.

Stalking the table, he determined the best angle and bent. "I took some pizzas over to the ranger station," he said, pulling the stick back. "You know, for the volunteers. They found Linnea around the time I finished unloading the food. Everyone scattered. I haven't heard a word." He blew out a breath, then an easier slide sent the white ball into motion.

His shot sank, but Iris didn't see it fall. She was too busy catching another glimpse of the man who cared more deeply for his community than he liked to admit.

"Linnea's fine," she revealed. "Bruised ribs, broken nose . . . everything you might expect when a car dives into a ditch. It's a good thing they found her so soon." She shivered as her eyes wandered to the window, mesmerized by the snow swirling under the parking lot lights.

"It could have been so much worse." His words were closer than she expected. While she was distracted, he'd set down his cue on the table and moved. Warm and comforting, his hands smoothed over her shoulders and left a path of heat clear to her fingertips. She sank her back against his chest, shut her eyes, and absorbed strength from the rise and fall of his breathing. Strong arms wrapped around her waist. "Hey, are you okay?" he asked against her neck, before his lips pressed the tender skin.

"I'll get there. Sometimes the holidays are just too much." Iris sighed when he planted another warm touch at her temple with his lips. He squeezed gently before easing away. Lincoln's fierce tenderness enticed, but somehow that short embrace was enough. Talk diminished, except for compliments about well-aimed shots, yet the easy pace of the next three games seemed to tighten an invisible bond. Iris hoped the tether would last.

***

The memory of Iris' lithe body stretched over a pool table followed him home. She was undeniably gorgeous, and as he'd learned from past missteps, too good for him.

Tough on the surface with glittering perceptive eyes, her exterior hid a fragile woman. She'd never ridden a Harley, never smoked weed, and sure as hell didn't have ink anywhere on her smooth, delicious skin. A man like him might intrigue Iris for a time, but he refused to corrupt her.

Icy snow crunched beneath the tread of his tires, reminding him of a warmer place where he belonged. Not here. Not anywhere in Washington. Until this year, he'd spent holidays on his bike, achieving peaceful nirvana on palm-lined roads near the coast. How the fuck had he dropped onto the North Pole?

Once he got back, he paced beneath the overhang of his restaurant, pulled a pack of cigarettes from his pocket, and fished his lighter from his jeans. The flame lit, the cigarette flared, and a long inhale deployed a hit of nicotine.

On a contemplative drag he stared at his foreign surroundings. Snow blanketed everything. Maggie had strung icicle lights from the eves of Goldfinch Bakery, and at the Stop-n-Shop, Morgan Pratt stacked shiny toboggans under bright sodium lights. Shit, even the hardware store got into the spirit with fifty-percent-off inflatable Christmas crap out front. With their electric motors off, those puffy decorations looked like the entire cast of a holiday special lying dead on the snow. He used to feel just as dead inside, but this place and Iris had given an electrifying jolt to what was left of his shriveled heart.

ELEVEN

"Is this the last of the paperwork?" she asked from across her desk. Her nose wrinkled as Iris adjusted her glasses, squinting at her computer screen. The woman had no idea how fucking sexy those black rims looked perched on her face. Lincoln gripped the arms of his chair hard enough to dig wood into the pads of his fingers, punishing himself and his eager cock.

"Yeah. That's the last of it, unless the state finds another hurdle." Lust choked his words, and he shifted in his seat. "Now I'm on the hunt for a place to lease. After I close the restaurant, I'll start demo."

Wade still pressed the food truck option. The sensible plan would save him money, enhance cash flow, but stab Iris in the back. He wanted to find another way to keep his delivery drivers on the road, but his options were limited.

"Close the pizza shop?" Her fingers left the keyboard and toyed with the neckline of her blouse. The thin fabric, lighter now in the warmer weather, crumpled under her fingertips as she teased the delicate edge. Worry looked sexy on her, but he couldn't understand her interest. If he closed for a few months, his loss was her gain.

"Hopefully not for long. I need the cash flow." Lincoln opened his mouth, ready to spill that a food truck was likely the best option, but Iris cut him off.

"Let me know if I can do anything to help."

It was nice that she cared, but her concern was foolish. In a bigger market with nastier competition, this gorgeous, caring woman wouldn't last.

Flickering light illuminated her face as she clicked from screen to screen, zipping through the pages on the government website. She bit the end of her pen, as a fan kicked on, and circulated her lavender scent throughout the room.

Lincoln stood and stepped behind her, appearing to be interested in the documents on the screen. What he needed was another whiff. On his lean in, he grazed her shoulder and felt her body quake. It took everything to keep from nuzzling her neck. Instead, he hunched forward to point out a right-hand column of numbers.

"Could you check the math on that?" he asked, knowing it was one-hundred percent accurate.

"Sure." Her fingers trembled as she reached across her desk to recalculate his addition on a ten key. "We match. Our numbers, I mean . . ." Her neck flushed, tempting Lincoln again.

"Thanks for checking." Needing an escape, he straightened, took a step back, and crossed the room. He pressed his shoulders against the door, masked his desire with a casual stance, and observed the woman who had him trapped in her sensual snare.

Iris removed her glasses, brought her gaze to his, then perused the entire length of his frame. A bold grin spread across her face. She didn't care if he noticed her unhurried inspection. "So, we're solid," she said with a smirk.

Fuck. She's got eyes locked on my cock. The eager member pulsed while he waited for Iris to finish her thought.

She chuckled and pushed back from her desk. "I can't believe we did this. Our plan is in place." Excitement sped her words. "Will you bring the moratorium up at the next council meeting?"

Lincoln snapped his chin up and down. "I think we've got the numbers." He couldn't look away as her jade eyes sparkled.

"Fantastic." Iris giggled, pushed off with her toes and spun her chair, twirling around like a top. When the momentum slowed, happiness lifted Iris to her feet, and she erased the distance between them. Her arms snaked up, squeezed his neck, and she planted a kiss. His lips tingled, wanting more, but she let go too quickly.

"Thank you, Lincoln. If you hadn't taken this on, I might have lost Northside Grill." The unexpected honesty shocked them both. Lincoln laughed, pretending he hadn't believed the alarming truth.

***

Two days after the vote, a percussive knock rattled his employee entrance. Lincoln wiped his hands on a towel, left the heat of his ovens, and found a scowling man spying through the distorted glass.

He flung the door open but blocked the space with a wide stance. "Good evening, Daryl."

"Not good for you, Julius," Daryl seethed, baring yellow teeth and receding gums, blackened by years of chewing tobacco. Lincoln rethought the single cigarette he smoked each day, wondering if his lungs were just as nasty.

Leaning outside, Lincoln lifted his eyes to consider the sun as it burnished the horizon. "Looks like a pretty fine day to me—it's spring, and the sun is shining. Maybe I'll take the bike out for a ride." He added the last for the old mechanic's benefit.

Daryl's eyes narrowed. "Ride that death trap to another town and start looking for a different place to sell your drugs. It ain't happening here."

"Afraid it is. The state approved my application and the vote passed." Lincoln grinned, grasped the door, and tried to shut out the waste-of-time windbag.

"All that fancy paperwork don't matter." A gnarled finger with dirt under the nail pressed against Lincoln's muscled chest. "Listen to me, boy . . . You don't *live* in Ashwood, and outsiders don't get to make the rules."

Lincoln's eyes moved to that finger until Daryl took the hint and removed it. Jaw tight, he struggled to keep his respect for the mechanic intact. Stepping outside, he pulled the door closed behind him to protect Kara from the pointless rant.

"You know that's crap. I've lived right here for nearly a year," Lincoln said, wondering how he'd endured living in the miserable cell at the back of his shop for so long.

"Well, I've got news for you. This fucking excuse for a restaurant is *not* a residence—meaning you are a *squatter*. Sleeping on a cot in your shop does not count. And I've talked to my supporters on the town council, renting one of Seth's tiny shitholes won't cut it, either. Good luck finding a home at the start of whitewater season."

A clenched jaw slowed Lincoln's response. "We'll see about that."

Daryl turned and left in a cloud of obscenities, but Lincoln couldn't afford to waste any time. He paced the alley to restore his calm before ducking back inside. "Kara, I'll be back in an hour."

"No problem, but remember, I've got plans so you're closing tonight"

"Gotcha. I won't be gone too long." He grabbed his leather jacket and headed for his Harley. Ruth would let him know if Daryl had finally found a legit loophole.

***

Iris poured a little more wine and cranked her stereo, thankful that her nearest neighbors lived on the other side of a dense stand of trees. She'd tended bar until ten, come home and caught the weather on the news, and at almost midnight, she still didn't feel the least bit tired.

An unusually warm day in the forecast gave her the perfect moment for her favorite chore. She pulled out her massive drying rack, humming while she began the ritual that brought her joy.

Filling her sink with tepid water and gentle detergent, she watched the suds build like a fluffy cloud. One at a time, she submerged delicate bits of lace and silk, carefully washing each bra, panty, thong, stocking, and camisole. After draining the sink, she rinsed each in cool water twice, then draped her indulgence over the multi-layered contraption. Music and the process relaxed her as she washed and rinsed, danced and sang. Job complete, she stood back, admired her accomplishment, and yawned. "Sleep tight," she cooed to her pretty lingerie. "I'll rescue you in the morning."

Teeth brushed, face clean and moisturized, Iris slept better knowing her little lovelies dangled from the five-foot-tall accordion rack at the center of her kitchen. A faint *drip, drip, drip* onto a blanket of towels beneath it soothed her more than rain on her roof.

She woke refreshed and touched her guilty pleasures before making coffee. A few were still damp, and the display was too beautiful to take down. Iris settled with a bowl of cornflakes, coffee, and her phone to catch up on the latest posts. The blueberries topping her crunchy flakes tasted even sweeter while surrounded by the canopy of decadent lingerie.

Sipping her second cup, she couldn't decide if she should shower or put her unmentionables away first—No need to hurry, her shift at the Grill didn't begin until three. Legs shaved and moisturizer smoothed on, Iris wrapped herself in a freshly washed burgundy robe while she blew out her hair. She applied a dot of oil over her hair but still hadn't pampered herself quite enough. While wriggling her toes, she selected nail polish to match this morning's scanty silk.

A book kept her occupied while the second coat dried. She'd almost reached the climax of a smoldering sex scene when a knock hit her front door. Panic brought Iris to her feet. She spun and gawked at her surroundings.

"Crap, crap, crap. Please go away," she whispered, desperately hoping it was a delivery drop. The knock struck again. "Oh God, I can't open the door like this." If she did, she'd expose her darkest secret—a deep-seated addiction to naughty scraps of lace and silk.

"Just a second!" she shouted while her hands tightened the robe around her waist. "Why don't I love sensible cotton?" Because everything she bought was nothing short of fabulous, that's why. Bare feet scrambled for the rack in her kitchen as the knock hit a third time.

"It's just me, Iris!" Lincoln's voice boomed through the door. "We've got a problem."

Her problem just got bigger and sexier. "Wait a sec, I'll only be a minute!" she yelled as she grabbed another handful of lace.

***

Lincoln listened through the door. Like hell, he was going to wait—this was fucking important. "Iris, I hear you tearing around in there." His irritation climbed. Was she trying to hide a morning-after guest? Jealousy ignited. Damn it, they'd spent time together, and he'd tasted pure desire on her lips.

"Are you decent!" he yelled with his fingers on the knob.

"Of course, I'm decent."

That was good enough for him. He flung her door wide.

She froze in a spotlight of mid-day sun and yelped, "Oh, crap."

Decent? He'd never heard a bigger lie. In theory, sheer burgundy silk covered her. Yet when the sunlight hit that fabric, it only accentuated the gentle undulations of her mouthwatering curves. Lincoln shut the door, fought for air, and refused to look away, fearing that this dream might evaporate before he memorized each stunning detail.

His angel stared wide-eyed, surrounded by silky heaven, from her kitchen. In addition to what she had on, bras, panties, and a corset lay cradled over her arm. And, there was more. Fuck. How could there be more? Sexy decadence dangled from some sort of rack designed to torture his senses with every erotic shade imaginable.

Lincoln's heartbeat throttled and he widened his stance to keep from falling to his knees, though that wouldn't have mattered one bit. If he crumbled, he'd crawl across the floor and worship his queen—long may she reign over the altar of lust.

Iris inhaled a tight breath. "I asked you to wait outside."

"And miss this? Oh, hell no." Lincoln stumbled forward and planted his butt on a sturdy kitchen chair. "Carry on," he added with a wave of his hand.

An angry fist flew to her hip. "Carry on?" The swift move gaped her silk robe, revealing a triangle of lace below and nothing above. Lincoln's mouth went dry and his cock pushed against his zipper with unexpected force.

An alluring blush lit her cleavage. He tilted his head to peek past the fabric and grinned. Legs splayed in the chair, he slouched, getting a bit more comfortable. "I'm not going anywhere."

"Why are you here!" she yelled as he sprawled.

"We need to talk." His foot slung over his knee, settling in.

Shoulders back, Iris turned with a huff then took the first armload to her room. He stayed in place and listened while drawers opened and closed. She returned, this time with a basket, but damn it, she'd tied her burgundy negligee shut. Not a problem, the sheer fabric still clung to her curves.

Pretending she wasn't on stage, Iris folded each item and laid it in the basket with love. Lincoln enjoyed the visual perfection—even a soft bump and grind soundtrack wouldn't enhance this show. Her inner rhythm didn't need any embellishments.

"Were you a dancer?" he asked, not caring what kind—ballet, stripper, ballroom—he just had to know.

"Yes."

"Do you still dance, angel?"

That endearment earned him a huff, yet her lips tilted when she mumbled, "No."

"Iris?" The folding stopped long enough for his eyes to lock with hers and beg for an answer.

She inhaled deeply, then looked at her bare feet. "Ballet. I took my first class at four and quit when I was thirteen. When I hit my growth spurt, I was the tall, awkward, uncomfortable girl in class, so, I switched to volleyball." Her tone softened. "But I missed it. So much."

Those words jarred Lincoln with the weight of her regret. He wanted to fix that for her. Someday.

Basket full and contraption empty, she disappeared into her bedroom and Lincoln steadied himself with a breath. Using all his mental faculties, he sent her an urgent telepathic message, *Please, come back in that burgundy layer of lust.* Unfortunately, his mind-memo didn't work. Iris emerged calm, in jeans and a T-shirt, pretending the world hadn't just tipped on its axis. He blinked, still stunned, unable to rise from the wooden chair. Iris performed some sort of magic, folded the rack flat, and leaned it against the wall.

"What's so crucial that you needed to barge into my house?" she asked from the counter in front of her coffee pot. "Do you want a cup?"

"Coffee? Sure, black." Lincoln stood and wobbled toward the kitchen, still recovering from the most important ten minutes of his life. She'd altered him forever, a fucking epiphany, another line on his list of important firsts. First ride on a Harley, first tattoo, and the first time he pushed balls deep into a woman—all profound milestones, for sure.

But this was different ... transformational. He'd caught a glimpse of his angel's wicked side, and he liked what he saw.

Her hand trembled when he claimed his cup. Lincoln took a swallow before answering her original question, "Daryl's stirring up shit again, but this time he may have found something that'll stick."

"What did that old fart dig up?" she asked with a steady gaze.

"Some ancient rule about opening a business in Ashwood. If you're not a resident, you need prior approval from the city. And *that residence* has to be permanent."

"Aren't you staying in an apartment attached to your restaurant?"

"Not really . . . it's more of a storage room. And Ruth revealed a secret—the downtown blocks were recently zoned commercial. I think Daryl's behind it. I'm screwed."

"Damn, and the summer rentals are disappearing. What are the chances of finding something that will qualify?"

"I checked last night. Zero." His eyes settled on hers, reading disappointment. "It's a temporary setback. I'll find a place in September, once the vacation homes open back up."

He expected her body to slump, but Iris squared her shoulders and smacked her cup on the counter, sloshing coffee out.

"Oh, hell no." She paced the length of her living room then turned back to him with a stomp. "Not a chance. We're not buckling under that narrow-minded jerk."

Her reaction tipped the corners of his mouth.

Iris didn't return his grin; she only held his gaze and fisted her hands. "I've got a room right here. You'll just have to move in with me!"

***

The invitation flew from her lips, blasting holes in all her rules. Damn him. Those sexy tattoos had transformed her into a fool—a fool who just asked her obsession to be her roommate. Maybe he'd refuse and let her keep a scrap of her already shredded dignity.

He didn't respond. Another drink of his coffee moved his throat as he lifted an eyebrow, watching her over the rim. A grin tipped his lips when he pulled the cup away. "Bad idea."

Now that he'd said no, she wanted it even more. "Do you have a better one?"

"Not yet."

They discussed other options, and he left her place before giving an answer, seeming more shaken by her offer than seeing her half-naked.

Lincoln called that night at ten while she was at work and too busy to talk. Iris propped her phone against her ear with her shoulder as she pulled a tap. "What's that again?" she asked struggling to hear his words over the country music that was filling Northside Grill.

"I said yes." Beer topped the lip of the pint, overflowing onto her hand.

"That's great," she said, all sunny and high-pitched, revealing frayed nerves.

Lincoln chuckled. "Don't worry, Angel. This is short-term. Uncomplicated."

TWELVE

The next afternoon, Iris dug through her junk drawer searching beneath flashlights, gum, and scissors to locate an extra key. A deep breath settled her nerves as she drove into town, ready to make it official.

When she pushed through the door, Lincoln came around the corner, wiping flour from his hands, looking sexier than she remembered.

"Hey, roomie," he said, and she gave him a silly grin.

"Hi." She stumbled to the counter dangling a Smokey the Bear keychain from her finger. "I guess you need a way to get in."

"Thanks," he shrugged, "but that locked door didn't slow me down yesterday."

"Hidden talents?" she asked as she dropped the key into his palm.

"The hidden ones are the best kind." A sizzle surrounded them, but Iris knew they shouldn't act on the attraction. Living together came with certain unwritten rules.

"You know, Iris, I've never actually seen you in my shop before. Is this your first time?" His words caressed, thick with innuendo.

She looked at the floor and hid her embarrassment in a halo of dark hair. "Ah, no, not my first time. I often stopped in when you weren't around, and I always paid cash." Her eyes flicked up, and she found his grin, but couldn't stop her nervous chuckle.

"Cash?" He leaned forward, ropey biceps straining his T-shirt, palms flat on the counter. "What were you trying to hide?"

"My pizza addiction."

"But you have pizza at Northside Grill. I've had it. It's good," he admitted.

87

Iris nibbled her lip. "Yeah, it's good. But *your* pizza is *oh-my-god* delicious."

He laughed. "Oh-my-god delicious? I didn't know that was a thing."

"It's most certainly a thing, and I think it's your sauce." Her cheeks heated and she shook her head.

Lincoln's grin took on a sexier slant. "My sauce . . . good to know." Awkward silence expanded, and she pulled her lips between her teeth to reduce the smile that kept escaping.

They stared at each other until the door chimed and Lincoln's gaze slid to his next customer.

"Just a sec, Natalie. I've almost got Whitewater's lunch order ready." He disappeared into the kitchen leaving Iris alone with the woman who had recently married into the Michaels' clan. Her path didn't connect with Natalie as often—ever since the awkward breakup with Wade,

Iris found herself wrapped in a quick hug. "How are you?" After a squeeze, Natalie pulled away and her eyebrows lifted. "It's nice to see you, but sort of strange, too. I hardly ever run into you outside Northside Grill."

"I guess I work too much." Iris shrugged and smiled. "But that means I better get back where I belong. Nice to see you, say hi to everyone for me."

"Sure thing."

Lincoln returned with three boxes, bringing carnal energy with him. Iris shivered and decided it was time to escape the electric charge. After a small finger wave, she slipped out the door and crawled into her little green bug.

Pressure on the accelerator separated her from potential rumors but chatter wouldn't take long. And nothing buzzed faster than a new couple in Ashwood. To keep Daryl from digging for another reason to halt their progress, they planned to keep the platonic part of their living arrangement to themselves.

***

With a box balanced in one arm, Lincoln pushed through the side door off her kitchen, feeling like a trespasser. She wasn't home, yet her presence was warm and inviting. Everything reflected Iris—the matching canisters on her counter, her lavender scent in the air, and the throw blanket over a comfy chair. As he passed through her living room, he paused to stare at a modern painting hanging above the couch. Muted colors captured a pale blue sky over golden plains . . . a peaceful glimpse of her troubled past.

Unpacking took less than an hour, then Lincoln kicked off his shoes, grabbed a beer, and planted his butt in front of the TV. A search for the remote found it hidden under the lift-top leather footrest. Lincoln switched on the television and flipped channels. He liked lounging but realized he hadn't missed much without a TV.

A big place to hold a bunch of stuff wasn't a priority but sending money to his son was. Whether he lived in the same city with his boy or not, he'd always provided, just like his old man had done for him. Of course, he and his dad never needed more than a small two-bedroom apartment. Still, when Russ needed a little extra, which wasn't too often, he didn't question it, he just sent the funds.

He flicked off the set, stuck the remote in its place, and wandered outside to listen to the wind in the trees while enjoying his single smoke. Lincoln took a shower before he crawled under the crisp sheets Iris had put on his bed. A slow inhale pulled in a hint of her.

His alluring roommate didn't roll in until after two. But he woke and lay in the dark and listened to her soft music bleeding under the door. The floor creaked and he pictured her dancing, hips swaying as she made herbal tea. Imagining her lush curves, his hand drifted south, stroking until he found much needed relief.

***

Iris waited three days for a sliver of regret to set in, but it never came. A new roommate shouldn't be this easy. It definitely helped that the man in her kitchen was gorgeous. As she feasted on a visual banquet, her lips tested the heat of her coffee. With his back to her, wearing only a towel, Lincoln poured a steaming cup, and she damned the terrycloth that obscured his tattoos.

She searched his ink but found only shades of gray and black on his flawless skin. The perfect gradients adorned a man who moved with silent predatory grace. Iris hummed, satisfied, as he reached for the loaf of bread. His taut muscles bunched and flexed, improving her view.

The toaster took a while, and he stared out the window, watching the sun disperse a thin layer of fog. After buttering his bread, Lincoln glanced over his shoulder. She blushed. Grabbing his slice of warm toast, he spun while chewing, then leaned against the counter. His stance granted her a good, long look at his chest and abs, not to mention the bulge beneath the towel.

Eventually, her eyes slid to his. "I couldn't help admiring . . ." she said—an admission, not an apology.

"Be my guest." Lincoln devoured the rest of his breakfast, washed it down with coffee, and walked into his room. The door shut and Iris finally inhaled, exhaled, and stood. She warmed her cup, standing barefoot in the kitchen. The linoleum floor was a bit warmer in the spot where he'd lingered. She closed her eyes and painted a mental image of Lincoln without that towel. What ink was hidden? How far had he endured the pain?

***

The sun made a full-force appearance and a slow Monday went completely dead. Lincoln wandered outside, sunlight slanted, radiating heat from the sidewalk. Days like this had him missing Oakland. He loved the rush of a big city on a warm evening—the hum of traffic, streets filled with noisy people, sirens in the distance, even the oily, burnt tire smell that lingered in the smoggy air.

When a fresh breeze carried the aroma of burgers and brats past his nose, Lincoln wondered if the entire town of Ashwood had collectively fired up their grills.

With a few extra bucks to make up for missed tips, he sent Kara and his delivery driver home, then changed the message on the machine. Lincoln had one thing on his mind—his roommate. Their schedules overlapped in the morning, but rarely at night. Monday was her day away from Northside Grill, and Iris was home. He closed the pizza shop with her image occupying his mind.

Each mile on his Harley increased his anticipation. Rounding the last curve on their long gravel drive, the lights inside drew his eyes to the window as his engine rumbled to a stop. He closed in on the front porch, fingertips tingling. Restless desire sped his heart rate as he twisted the doorknob.

Something was off—the house was too silent. Iris sat at the kitchen table, stiff as a pillar, pale as salt. One hand gripped the table, the other lay splayed on the smooth wooden surface, and her arm shook with invisible strain.

His boots echoed as he crossed to her. Each noisy step tilted her head downward like an ungreased gear. Lincoln didn't speak until his fingers wrapped over her shoulder. "What's wrong?"

She shivered beneath his touch. "The noise . . . it surprised me."

"My bike?" he asked.

"Yeah."

"Shit. I'm sorry."

"Don't worry about it. I'll get used to it, eventually. You're early, and I forgot to turn on the TV. The sound of your motorcycle always bounces off the trees and rattles the windows."

Fuck. She'd been struggling with this since he moved in and hadn't said a word. "Iris, I didn't know. Tell me what I can do to fix this."

He settled behind her and massaged her shoulders. Stress released its vice-like hold, and she relaxed into his touch with a sigh.

"No need to fix me. Once I learn the sound, then it won't hit me so hard anymore." Iris tipped her head to the side, humming, and her cheek met the back of his fingers. Lincoln had never felt anything so soft. Her heartbeat drummed under his touch, and he knew if he bent and nibbled that spot on her neck, she'd taste sweet and clean.

"Do you trust me?" he asked.

"No." She chuckled, pivoting until their eyes met.

He huffed a laugh. "Smart girl. Let me try again . . . Are you willing to take a risk?"

"Yes?" she answered, heavy with hesitation.

"Let's take a ride. When you get the feel of the bike, it won't haunt you."

Her eyes widened and she kneaded her lip while considering his offer. Lincoln had never pleaded for a thing in his life, but he wanted this, wanted her on his bike. When she hesitated, he nearly dropped to his knees to beg.

Iris looked toward the front door and saved him from that humbling inclination with a nod. "I could do that." She gave him her hand and stood.

Buzzing like he'd won the lottery, Lincoln wanted to spin her around, but pulled her out of the kitchen instead. Now that she'd made up her mind, he needed to keep momentum on his side. "First time?" he asked.

"No. My dad bought my brother a dirt bike when we were twelve." She squeezed his hand before releasing it. "I pitched a fit until Dad got me one, too." The fire that had dimmed in her eyes flared.

"Competitive?"

"Hell yes," she said with a nod.

Lincoln tossed his head back and laughed. She'd grown up riding two-wheels. Iris had done it again—she reached into his soul and surprised him. *Damn*.

"Give me a second to change."

While she dressed, Lincoln dug through his closet to locate an extra helmet and worn leather jacket. She emerged wearing faded jeans, boots, and a sweatshirt layered under a denim coat. When she spotted his gear, she took off her coat and grabbed the safer choice, even if she'd swim in the soft leather.

"Is it still warm tonight?" she asked.

He nodded. "Yeah. You'll fry in that sweatshirt."

Iris pretzeled her arms to peel off the outer layer, but the sweatshirt refused to give way.

"Here, let me help." Lincoln teased her hoodie over her head, and the hem of her T-shirt lifted, giving him a glimpse of midnight blue lace. He grinned—today's puzzle was solved. Discovering the sexy details of her lingerie was better than solving the *New York Times* crossword.

"I thought I'd suffocate in there." Her green eyes flashed as she finger-combed her disheveled hair. Iris giggled and the nervous music scrambled his brain. Without thinking, he leaned in and claimed a quick taste of her sweet, tempting lips. She pressed into his kiss, but only for a moment, focused instead on the challenge ahead.

"Let's do this," she said, bouncing on her toes.

Lincoln led the way to the door, struggling to focus on the bike instead of her delicious mouth.

THIRTEEN

Oh God, that kiss . . . so quick and chaste. Iris savored the sizzle. His lips tempted her to abandon the motorcycle and ride the man instead. She held her breath as Lincoln mounted his bike with fluid athletic beauty. His muscles flexed, carved thighs trapped in faded jeans, taut in all the best locations.

He turned his head and held her gaze. "Your turn."

Impatience quaked her stomach, nerves prickling. Iris tugged the zipper up a few extra notches, securing Lincoln's jacket around her. The leather smelled like him—a delicious mix of spice, musk, and tobacco. Focused on the man, she gripped his shoulder as he braced the bike and she swung her leg over. Her heart sped when her feet found the pegs.

Lincoln quietly waited until she settled. He reached back and touched her thigh. "Ready?" he asked before he started the engine.

She rolled her head, trying to relax. "Ready."

His warmth transferred strength as the Harley roared to life—the rumble spread, loud and low, through her core and up her spine. Eyes closed, she absorbed the growl and let it soothe her nerves then her panic faded away. Laughing, she fastened her helmet and wiggled against him, grinning as she wrapped her arms around his waist. His stomach moved when he asked if she was good.

"I'm ready," she answered. "Let's go."

Tension eased as her thighs squeezed his lean hips. When the bike accelerated, Iris tightened her grip, but she didn't think he'd mind. Lincoln's body relaxed, trusting her instincts. Iris braced herself knowing he would push the throttle now that she was prepared. They sped east into the faint twilight as the sky faded to dark purple.

She hadn't been on a motorcycle since she lived in Kansas. But in her teens, she'd ridden often, solo on her dirt bike, tandem with her brother's best friend, Cooper. Saturated smells flooded her with teenage memories of long motorcycle rides in the country, make-out sessions in the tall grass, and skinny-dipping when her boyfriend's parents were out of town. She'd protected those memories—pleasant days and nights spent with Cooper—her first love, the man she'd planned to marry before the tornado rearranged her life.

The engine's vibration matched laughter she knew Lincoln felt. He leaned into a curve, and she went with him as one. He took the bike down a single-lane road following the edge of a wide valley. Somewhere far below, the Klickitat River snaked.

Miles passed and Lincoln slowed, pulling off at a paved overlook. As the engine stopped, silence hit her senses with a vacuous hum. Iris peeled her body away and missed the comfort of his heat. Legs tingling, she sprang toe to toe, lifted off her helmet, and shook out her hair. Nervous laughter bounced from the pavement, echoing her giddy joy.

Drunk on happiness, she felt foolish when Lincoln didn't share the same euphoric high. He tilted his head, his sly smile barely visible in the gray-scale light. The view of the valley offered her an easy escape. Iris turned toward the ravine to distance herself from a cool demeanor that had stripped her bare.

Standing at the edge, a floating sensation glittered her vision and her hands splayed over the stone abutment. She leaned into the wide wall which protected the overlook from the black chasm below. The smooth rock beneath her palms cut her post-ride-high to a manageable level.

Iris turned to find Lincoln only inches away. Arms folded over his chest, his leather coat creaked as he surveyed her with a devilish smile.

***

Nothing grabbed Lincoln's attention faster than a woman on his bike clinging like second skin. When he accelerated, she'd held his abs snug, but not too tight—just enough to press her soft tits through the layers of fabric and leather. Her intuitive movement gave him permission to do exactly what he wanted with the powerful machine. The way she went with him into a curve had him wondering if she'd grant that same trust in bed.

Curiosity teased. Lincoln tested Iris, braking hard to press her pussy against his ass. The heat of her center warmed his butt, and *fuck*, he felt her moan. Lightheaded with racing desire, he searched for a spot to pull over, ready to act on the erotic connection. He knew the perfect site, and it lay only a few miles ahead.

Twilight lingered at the familiar overlook; the shadows enhanced by a partial moon. But when he killed the engine, she created distance, and Lincoln hated himself for his stupid assumption. God, he wanted her, and hopeful arrogance had swelled his cock, but evidently, she didn't share the attraction he believed was crystal-clear.

The energy she gave off during the ride had nothing to do with him. Her excitement came from conquering a fear that had dogged her from Kansas to Washington. Of course, that triumph meant more to Iris than a connection he'd imagined—and fantasized about—for months.

Jitters took over, and she ran, turning from him to gaze into the dark river valley. This abrupt distance threw Lincoln, and he wanted to restore that part of Iris that was almost too easy to read. When she spun to face him again, her eyes glittering, he folded his arms over his chest to keep from reaching out.

"You liked it?" he asked.

"So much." She laughed and shoved her hands into her pockets. "I forgot about the buzz."

He nodded as his boots moved on their own, taking one hopeful step forward.

"From the ride," she finished, and shuffled her feet, erasing the remaining space.

He couldn't speak, afraid he'd spook her again. Carefully, he placed his index finger on her chin and lifted. Her mouth parted—so tempting. Her tongue flicked out, wetting her luscious lips.

"I loved it," she said.

"Angel, I know." His fingers left her jaw, spanned her neck, and slid into her hair. The other hand grasped her waist, pulled her body flush, and he devoured her gasp with a kiss.

***

Every sense Iris possessed lit up—pulse points throbbed, his musk mingled with the creosote from the pavement, her nerve endings tingled—heightening the tactile bliss of his touch. The breadth of his hand rasped against the back of her neck, angling her head to deepen the penetration. Lincoln seemed starved, desperate to devour what was left of her scattered wits.

The man tasted dangerous—of mint, tobacco, and spice. His trim goatee—much softer than she had expected—tickled her neck as he explored. The wind stilled and the rustling leaves went silent, leaving only the sound of a river's distant murmur and their shared satisfied moans.

Iris let her hands wander, and Lincoln rewarded her eager touch with a firm pivot of his hips. The shaft he pressed against her belly amplified her need and sent a surge of wet heat onto her lace and silk panties. Pressed tight against him, Iris wanted to claw away his leather and rip away his shirt. She gave into the impulse and freed him from his coat as he did the same.

With a dull thump, two leather jackets landed on the pavement at their feet. Pressed against his solid frame, her body softened. His hands explored while warm lips trailed kisses down her neck. When he lifted her shirt, the cool night air prickled her flesh. A sigh left her lungs when his hand cupped her heavy breast, and the silky bra enhanced the erotic glide of his thumb over her aching nipple. Iris hitched her leg over his hip, moaning when her heat pivoted against his shaft.

"Ah, shit yes," he groaned against her nape. Need flooded, and Iris wanted more. She didn't care what surface he chose—his motorcycle, the guardrail, or the warm pavement—so long as he quenched this consuming fire.

The calloused hand beneath her shirt moved to her back, and in one quick flick, set her breasts free, then he bared her upper half to the cool night air. She arched into the contact when he covered one peak with his mouth, crying out when he teased the tip with the gentle scrape of his teeth.

"Oh, God," Iris moaned, needing that attention everywhere. He sensed her desire and moved a hand to the button of her jeans. Zipper down, his fingers invaded her desperate flesh. Writhing, she gave him another inch to explore. Lincoln slid inside, curled his touch, and did wicked things to her clit with his thumb.

Desperate and fumbling, Iris yanked against his belt buckle. It jangled as she pulled it open, then she found the buttons on his jeans. Soft and worn, the closure gave easily, and his cock sprang free.

"Commando . . . Thank you," she whispered as her long fingers wrapped around the heavy girth. She couldn't span the circumference but did her best to stroke his entire velvet length.

Lincoln plunged his tongue in her mouth as his fingers dove into her heat. Iris stroked harder. Her breath sped, and her heart rate increased. As their bodies moved, the denim that covered them gradually slid away. She spread her legs, desperate for more.

"Fuck, Iris. Tell me we're doin' this," he growled.

"Please." She took a step back and coaxed Lincoln toward the wide rocky wall. The surface supported her hips at the perfect height, but the weather-smoothed stone still grated against her butt.

When she squirmed, Lincoln paused his kiss long enough to growl, "Hang on."

As she kicked away her shoes and pants, Lincoln found his T-shirt on the ground. He put the soft fabric between her ass and the stone, then kicked off his boots. Before losing his jeans, he located a condom in his wallet.

"Let me," Iris whispered.

Momentum slowed and Lincoln stared. "Wait . . . I gotta see you." His hands caressed her shoulders, breasts, and ribcage, mapping her body in the pale moonlight. "My God, you're beautiful."

Too enthralled by his caress to move, her head tipped back and she closed her eyes while Lincoln worshiped her curves with his touch.

"Now, Angel," he insisted. She opened her eyes to his and his naked need stared back. Iris bit her lip, tore open the condom, and smoothed protection over his considerable length. Then her touch drifted lower, caressing his balls.

"Need you." His hand clasped her wrist and halted her exploration. Iris nodded and wrapped her calves around his hips. Lincoln eased her forward, traced her seam with the smooth crown, then slowly breached her center.

Dark muted his visual senses and everything focused on tight heat. Warm, slick, and smooth, he bent at the knees to increase the penetration. Open and demanding, her mouth did crazy things to his tongue, sucking him in with the same insistence that her center took his shaft.

The sensory overload tingled his legs, his arms, his spine. When her kisses left his lips, she nibbled a path down his neck and let her teeth scrape against his collarbone, nipping the swell of his chest. "Fuck," he groaned.

She pulled away and the low light illuminated her features. Dark eyes studied him with wonder, giving him a glimpse of what could happen between them if he accepted her silent offer—she could be his.

Lincoln held his breath, completely stunned by her visual honesty. He'd lived too long, too hard, and too fast to believe there were many surprises left. Yet, this stunning woman revealed more to him every damn day. And each time Iris peeled away another layer, he couldn't help but accept the gift—a gift he didn't know how to repay.

Tangling his fingers in her hair, Lincoln tipped her head back and claimed her lips again. He pulsed his groin forward as Iris wrapped her arms around his shoulders and neck. Desperate for more, he grasped her ass, lifting her easily, elevating her from the stone abutment. She clung tight with her legs and arms as her center swallowed his cock.

Lincoln set a steady pace, lifting again, taking her balls deep. Each pass taunted her clit with his groin, and her moans mingled with his rapid pants.

Against his neck, she begged, "Harder." Her heels dug in, urging him on. Strong hands wrapped and lifted, driving deeper. "Yes. Right. There."

Peaked nipples teased his pecs and her body quaked. His mouth left hers to bury his face in her hair. Desperate fingers sank into her soft flesh and she moaned, wrapping her legs tighter. Her core pulsed, grasping his shaft, seeking and taking more.

"Holy shit," he groaned, nearly there, doing everything he could to bring her with him. Her cries became urgent, then Lincoln circled his hips, hitting her just right. Iris reared her head, and with a keening cry, flew apart. Her center convulsed, and he plunged again, meeting her bliss with burning need. Heat traveled the length of his spine and burst from his cock.

"Fuck, fuck, fuck," he grunted, his legs quaking, riding out his explosive release. Iris sighed, stealing kisses as another wave prolonged her ebbing orgasm.

Still connected, Lincoln found the stone rail to support her, then took her face in his palms. His kiss inhaled her breath, consumed her moan, and absorbed everything she gave. Eventually, her hands slid from his shoulders to his waist and she shivered.

"Damn it. Angel, you're cold." He held her tight against his bare chest, transferring some of his warmth.

"I'm good," Iris murmured against him, but the way she clung to him was more than need—his woman was freezing.

His woman.

A shift had occurred, a transformation that began long before sex. She'd trusted him with her darkest fears, and he'd found a way to meet her deepest need. Lincoln put that knowledge in a safe place to consider later. Now, her physical need for warmth came first.

Iris groaned in protest when he pulled from the welcome place between her thighs. Still hard, he sidestepped and dealt with the condom. Iris hopped off the stone abutment, her body jiggling in the most tempting way. She handed him his T-shirt and he used the soft fabric to clean up, then tossed the tee in the general direction of his motorcycle.

Lincoln helped her first, gathering her clothes. While she dressed, he didn't talk, only paused now and then to trap her in his arms and sample her tempting lips. Lingering in post-orgasm bliss, Iris let him taste and touch until she spotted headlights in the distance.

"Someone's coming," she said as he plied her neck.

Lincoln peeled his attention away and inspected the horizon. "Damn it."

"How long do we have?" she asked.

"Maybe five minutes."

"I guess we better go." Instead of pulling away, Iris wrapped her arms around his neck and rocked his world again, writhing against him while her tongue dove past his lips. When she came up for air, she asked, "Will you bring me back sometime?"

"Next time in daylight." Lincoln squeezed her waist, but the sound of the car echoed in the valley, getting closer.

"I'd like that," she said as he wrapped her in his jacket.

Leather on, he shoved his T-shirt into his pocket, and handed Iris her helmet.

Back on the bike, she squirmed behind him. Lincoln grinned, knowing that the engine vibrated all her sensitive places in a fucking good way.

FOURTEEN

The bike vibrated beneath her butt, prolonging her pleasure. As thrilling as the sensation was, it couldn't halt the emotional shrapnel ricocheting in her head. She held on tight to Lincoln's solid torso, grounded in his strength, yet the road, curves, and speed left her weightless and undone.

Questions sought answers. What had just happened? He'd offered help, and how did she thank him? With sex.

Her stomach turned. Good God, she'd trapped Lincoln into living with a messed-up roommate—a roommate he'd found clinging to the kitchen table—then she'd used her mess to snare him.

He could have left her to deal with her shit on her own, but he didn't. He fixed her, healed a gaping wound that years of therapy couldn't mend. After taking his gift—a gift she could never repay—she twisted a moment of celebration and pushed everything much too far.

On an open stretch, he reached down and placed a hand over hers—through two layers of leather, his glove and hers, she felt his warmth and soaked the comfort in. Iris clung, letting speed strip her thoughts away. The sound of his motorcycle didn't scare her anymore. In fact, it intrigued and captivated her nearly as much as the man. Wild, hot, and free, Lincoln unleashed a side of her that craved speed and passion and mind-altering sex.

Decorated with ink and wrapped in worn leather, he was an addictive concoction that stripped her self-control. Two miles from home and the clock was ticking. Did she need to apologize? Did she need to act casual? Where do you take your walk of shame when you live together?

In front of her house, he killed the engine. With his legs and arms taut, he steadied the bike and let Iris climb off. She scrambled a few steps away and removed the helmet, then held the object against her middle—a sturdy barrier between her and Lincoln. Her body longed for a touch and her lips ached for a kiss she shouldn't crave.

Lincoln's brows furrowed. "Are you okay? Did the bike get to you just now?" he asked, caring about her well-being again.

"I'm good. It's just, well . . . tonight got complicated."

"Complicated good or complicated bad?"

"I don't know. Do I need to apologize? Do I need to say I'm sorry?"

A puzzled expression shifted Lincoln's features, then he mouthed *Sorry.*

Damn, she'd chosen the wrong words. Hot tears pressed against the back of her eyes and muzzled her speech. Her trembling fingers clutched the helmet. She had to get away.

Extending her arms to their full length Iris silently begged, *Please, take it,* her voice trapped by embarrassed tears.

"Iris." Lincoln wrapped his hand around the helmet—their fingers touched. "What the f—"

She disappeared inside, wanting him to follow but praying he wouldn't. After shutting the door, she leaned against it, fearing he'd leave, that he'd climb back on the Harley to put distance between himself and his seriously fucked-up roommate.

But he didn't.

Outside, she heard Lincoln's boots pacing the sidewalk around the house. His steps echoed and Iris staggered to her room, chose a sleep set from her drawer, then padded to the bathroom. Locking the door, she let her nighttime ritual calm her nerves. After brushing her teeth, Iris washed her face and smoothed on creamy moisturizer. It usually soothed her skin, but tonight it stung the edges of her kiss-swollen lips.

In front of the mirror, tears rose again as her finger traced spots on her neck where Lincoln's attention had reddened her skin. She pulled off her T-shirt, then reached behind her back and unhooked her bra, letting the straps fall from her shoulders. Naked from the waist up, she stared at her torso, her eyes locking on each spot he'd bit and sucked. Her fingers traced sensitive nipples and her skin tightened. When Iris grasped the puckered flesh, the sensation shot to her center—an aching pulse thrummed between her thighs. Iris stripped her jeans away. A rush of cool air hit her wet folds and she let her fingers explore.

Need didn't coil and tension didn't build; she only wanted to touch each place where Lincoln had been. Widening her stance, Iris watched her green eyes darken as she pressed two fingers inside. Her lips parted, her breathing picked up, and all the chatter in her head began to fade.

Pleasure replaced worry when she slipped her touch from her silky center and circled. Each stroke erased shaky indecision, delivering mind-numbing bliss instead of pain. Her breast bounced as her attention sped, but she needed just a little bit more.

While her right hand circled, her left eased down, dipped in, and her hips pivoted. She bit her lip to keep from crying out. Bright lights over the mirror held her eyes, then her gaze dashed to her face. Lips parted, eyes wide, her hand pressed deeper, reaching for that spot where Lincoln had been. At last, satisfaction hissed out on a breath, and bliss-filled agony stared back from the mirror.

Her legs quaked, but she didn't stop until her hands milked every ounce of self-induced pleasure. As her breathing returned to normal, her breasts tingled with the cold. She used the washcloth to carefully wipe away the remnants of her release. The slow, careful act gave her some comfort. Then she lifted her spaghetti-strap pajama over her head, let the fabric slide into place, and wriggled into matching sleep shorts.

Before opening the bathroom door, she paused and listened for any sound that would point to Lincoln's presence in her house. Nothing. Though, she sensed he wasn't too far. Iris slipped into her bedroom, turned on her bedside lamp, and stood at the foot of her bed. She paced to her window, teased open her curtain, and peered outside. It took a moment for her eyes to adjust to the dark, to take in the outline of trees against the purple sky.

Where was he? Maybe he was avoiding her—keeping a safe distance, waiting until she slept before he dared to come inside. Sweeping her gaze across the breadth of her lawn, she spotted a faint red glow—the end of his cigarette. He turned and the pale moonlight hit him just right, accentuating his lean physique. With a bend of his arm, he put the cigarette to his lips. The tip flared as he inhaled

A thread of connection reached out from her to him. Iris sighed and left an open gap in her drapes—only a few inches, enough space to see the trees from the comfort of her bed. The night was warm, and she lay on top of her comforter, staring at the gap she'd left at her window. A turn to her side bunched her luxurious nightgown as she tried to settle. She'd never find comfort tonight.

***

Lincoln's eyes narrowed and he saw it again—movement at her window. He wanted to go to her but used the nicotine between his lips to keep his feet planted.

The lone daily cigarette settled his mind, but clarity was still out of reach, so he took another drag. After losing himself in the sweet spot between Iris's legs, he needed a hit of fucking enlightenment.

The night wasn't ending how he'd imagined, but for some reason he wasn't surprised. Shit, at least life in this small town wasn't dull. No, it wasn't the town, it was Iris. His gorgeous roommate had a way of grounding him while also turning everything on its head.

He inhaled another hit and absorbed the evening sounds. The surrounding forest pulsed with life, intensified by the unusual warmth of early spring. The season was leaning toward summer and nature was anxious. He was anxious, too.

Maybe Iris was right. Tonight had gone complicated. Fast.

From across the yard, he took another look at her window. Fuck, she'd forgotten to close the drapes. Was Iris watching? Did she need him as much as he needed her?

Hungry for a glance of his Angel, he couldn't stop his feet from moving toward her window. *Angel.* The label fit. Every time that endearment slipped naturally from his lips, she smiled. No, she glowed. The light it set off in her gorgeous eyes fed his dreams, made achieving what seemed impossible . . . possible. Would she ever be his?

Lincoln treaded across the uneven lawn. Her drapes didn't move as he drew closer, stopping inches from the glass. The bedside lamp was off, but light from the hall bled under her door. It bounced off her luminous, pale skin—slim arms, long legs, and a few inches of her stomach. The night was warm, and she was lying on top of dark blankets with silky lingerie draped over her luscious curves.

He swallowed hard when she shifted to her side, curling her body, making herself small. Her shoulder quaked as she inhaled a stilted breath. She lifted a hand and swiped her cheek. Lincoln dropped what was left of his cigarette in the dirt and ground it out with the toe of his boot.

***

His shadow appeared in her window. She wanted him there. His presence comforted her, and she let one final frustrated tear escape. A stream of unexplained tears dampened her pillow. Iris rarely cried—she never really had time for the indulgence—but tonight she couldn't seem to stop. A deep breath cleared her lungs, and she swept another tear from her cheek. Knowing he was there, that he cared enough to check on her, eased her mind.

She peeked at the gap in her drapes again and the glow from his cigarette flared then disappeared in a streak of red sparks. Gravel crunched as his boot snuffed out the embers. Damn, she'd messed up, and he was leaving. Throwing herself at Lincoln had cost her everything.

The kitchen door opened and shut again. She held her breath and listened. Two dull thumps vibrated the floorboards—his boots, probably damp from the overlong grass.

Without boots on, Lincoln moved as silent as a cat. She felt his presence drift through the house. Closing her eyes, Iris imagined him coming to her room instead of going to his. Imagined him stripping off his clothes. Imagined his warmth pressed against her while she drifted to sleep.

Her door opened, and she didn't have to imagine. The man had read her mind. Without a word, Lincoln shucked off his clothes, lowered to her bed, and pressed his body against hers. He slipped his cool hand beneath her silky negligee and pulled her against his solid chest. One leg tangled between hers. He pressed a gentle kiss against her neck and whispered, "Angel, sleep."

FIFTEEN

A deep inhale interrupted her erotic dream. *Bacon.* Iris stirred with two kinds of hunger. Overheated, she kicked away her blankets and groaned. He'd come to her last night, held her, and left before she woke. At least the pillow still trapped his scent. She rolled, closed her eyes, and sniffed the delicious scent of man.

But bacon lured her with its salty, morning-after perfection. Iris had a choice—she could hide in the safety of her bed or she could face Lincoln. When he added the bitter aroma of coffee, she had no choice—no one could resist that addictive combination.

Iris wrapped her body in her most demure silky robe and padded to the bathroom. Before she exited, she stared at the girl in the mirror. "Be good." With a tight knot secured at her waist and her shoulders squared, she drifted into the kitchen.

"Morning, Angel," Lincoln said without turning. He had his back to her, but his face shifted as he smiled.

"Good morning." Her path to the coffee pot gave her a chance to peek over his shoulder. Thank God, he was cooking enough for a small army.

"Help yourself." He tipped his head toward a plate stacked with meat trapped between layers of greasy paper towel. She chose a slice and moaned while she chewed. He'd bought the good stuff—thick, with pepper on the edges. *Yum.*

With her coffee cup full, and another slice in her hand, Iris sank to a spot at the kitchen table to watch the man move. His bare arms were poetry, and his shoulders flexed as he pivoted from the pan to the plate. So damn beautiful.

Lincoln peeked over his shoulder and grinned. Complicated began to look very, very good. He said nothing, but he didn't have to—in that one glance she knew he hadn't had enough of her. All her misery last night had been for nothing. She huffed, disgusted with her foolish self.

Iris shifted in her seat, easing the warm ache building between her legs. Lincoln added to her pleasant discomfort when he bent to dig through a lower cupboard for a bowl. Her interest piqued as he pulled milk, eggs, and butter from the refrigerator.

Her mouth watered for the man and the food he was making. "Want my help?"

"Nope. Just point me toward the vanilla." Lincoln spun from the counter and waited. Iris giggled when she realized how long she'd been staring at his expectant face.

"Oh . . . the vanilla. It's in the narrow cupboard next to the refrigerator." Lincoln grabbed it then turned to his task again, whisking eggs and milk in a bowl.

In no time at all, he had French bread sizzling, filling her kitchen with a cinnamon aroma which reminded her of Christmas. While the French toast cooked, he topped off her cup and pulled plates from the cupboard.

"You sure I can't do something?" Iris asked, hoping he'd say no. Watching him cook was heaven.

"Almost done." He placed maple syrup and butter on the table, put the plate of bacon within her reach, and raised his eyebrows, suggesting that she steal another slice. She thought he would go back and put a second round of bread in the pan, but he circled the table and stood behind her. Blunt fingers tipped her head to the side, she hoped to kiss her neck. Eventually, he kissed her, but not before he slid her silky robe from her shoulder.

"Hm. I thought I spotted this last night in the dark."

"My tattoo?" A deep purple iris with a pale-yellow throat adorned her shoulder blade. Slender green reeds surrounded the single flower, angled toward her spine. She hummed when his lips touched it.

"It's stunning," he said before sliding her negligee back into place. He huffed and moved away to add more bread to the pan. "You surprise me."

A slight shrug lifted her shoulder. "It's only one tattoo."

"Yes, but I think one may be more precious than many. Will you tell me the story behind it?"

She considered his request for a moment. "Someday."

He nodded and set the plate of French toast on the table. It was enough for a crowd, but smelled so good, Iris was glad she was the only one sharing the feast.

"Thank you, this looks delicious." She speared two pieces of French toast, laid them on her plate, and added a generous dollop of butter. It melted and dripped down the sides as she drizzled thick syrup on top.

Wasting no time, Lincoln sat and started with four slices of bacon, four slices of French toast, and a full cup of steaming coffee. He pressed the side of his fork through his toast, then stabbed the pieces with extra force. He ate almost half of his portion before taking a drink.

Lincoln eased back and set down his fork. Iris chewed slower when he locked eyes with hers. A wrinkle of worry narrowed his gaze. The once playful energy left the room, and Iris stopped eating. She tightened the ties of her silky robe, wishing she had on a more protective layer.

Clearing his throat, he measured his words. "I have a favor to ask . . ."

She'd assumed the bacon and eggs were his version of a morning-after breakfast, but the reality wasn't nearly so flattering—he wanted something.

Iris tried to keep the worry out of her voice. "I'll do what I can."

"I've told you I have a son," he blurted.

"A son? That's great, but I didn't know." Like a kaleidoscope, everything she'd assumed about Lincoln shifted and rearranged—spinning into a different, brighter pattern.

"Damn . . . I thought you knew." He pinched the bridge of his nose between his finger and thumb. Just the mention of his son unbalanced him, yet the wave of raw emotion looked good on Lincoln.

Her heart stuck in her throat. "What's his name?" she asked, picking up a slice of bacon while he gathered himself.

"Russ."

"Short for Russel?"

"Yeah, he's named after his grandfather on his mom's side."

Iris smiled. Lincoln had a family. Why did that seem strange?

"Russel Lincoln. I like it. It has a certain ring," Iris said with a grin. "Not as snazzy as Julius Caesar Lincoln, but—"

He shook his head and averted his eyes. "Uh. No, he doesn't have my last name. His mom and I . . . well, we were never that permanent."

"Oh, that's cool. He's still your boy."

"Yeah." It was Lincoln's turn to blush. "He is." Grinning wide, he didn't try to hide how much he loved his son.

"So, this favor?" Iris asked, ready to say yes, no matter what it was.

"Wendy, Russel's mom—she's got this rule. Russ can't visit me unless I'm living under a real roof. You know, in a house or an apartment."

"So, he's never seen Ashwood?"

"Nope. And I was wondering—"

"Of course, he can come to stay. This is your home, too. You didn't even need to ask." Iris laughed, hoping he would invite Russel soon.

Lincoln inhaled, huffed the breath out, then picked up his fork and used it to shift French toast around his plate. "Thanks," he said under his breath before digging back into his food.

"How old is he?" She wanted to know everything but that was impossible. The man sitting across from her had walls, but Iris would take what she could get.

"Nine."

"Wow. Right on the edge between a kid and a teen."

He chuckled and his eyes sparkled. "Angel, you have no idea."

SIXTEEN

The brass bell above Goldfinch Bakery's door flew off its hook, bounced twice, then rolled under a table when Iris rushed inside. Maggie flinched, and Ruth spun from her spot at the cookie case, flattening her hand over her heart. "Good God, Iris, you took ten years off my life!"

"Sorry." Iris scrambled to retrieve the bell, and it chimed as she hung it back in place. She slumped into a chair near the window, putting herself in time-out, impatient for a moment alone with her friend.

Maggie gave Iris a small knowing grin over Ruth's head and returned to complete the order. "I think two dozen will be plenty," she said while filling a second pink box with a delicious cookie assortment. The town council met the following night, and Ruth had stopped in a day early to select her sugary bribe.

Ruth leaned over the counter and lowered her voice. "I don't know if two dozen *is* enough. The numbers at the meetings have increased since Lincoln got elected." Her whisper carried as loud as a shout, and Iris rolled her eyes. Maggie tallied the bill, and Ruth's shoulders slumped as an opportunity for tantalizing gossip slipped away.

"Thank you for your business," Maggie added while passing both boxes over the counter.

High heels carried Ruth toward the exit. Turning her head slowly, her brows shot up as she passed Iris. "I know I'll be seeing *you* tomorrow night." A cloud of Chanel No. 5 lingered as Ruth sashayed toward her older model Cadillac. The cherry-red car stood out in Ashwood, but suited Ruth and her knot of close friends. They piled into the low-slung Caddy and drove to the nearest casino to feed the slots at least once a week.

Iris turned and found Maggie rounding the counter carrying a sweet bribe—tea and a plate of blondies, bulging with walnuts and butterscotch chips—an instant reminder of after-school snacks shared with her twin brother, Ian.

"I can't believe Ruth used to work the bar at Northside Grill in those heels."

Maggie huffed, "Don't try to change the subject."

"Change what subject?" Iris laughed. "We haven't even started talking."

"Girlfriend, you've been avoiding me." Her grin widened as she scooted a plate loaded with addictive goodness forward.

"Is this your way of charming the reason out of me?"

"Yes. Not that I need your confession. The buzz about you and Lincoln is all over town."

Iris waved heat from her face. "It's not what you think. Well, it wasn't . . . until last night." She sighed, then broke off a corner of the warm blondie and popped it into her mouth, moaning as the sweet, chewy perfection melted on her tongue.

"Last night? And I thought your new roommate situation was a counterattack against Daryl's latest roadblock." Maggie tapped the table with her index finger. "Details, now."

Iris chewed and nodded. "At first, it *was* Daryl. He found a loophole that would have closed the pot shop before it even had a chance to open."

"I heard about that." Maggie learned everything as quickly as she did. Tending a bar and running a bakery fed different vices, but both encouraged people to open up.

"Daryl's latest stunt really pissed me off. Without considering the consequences, I asked Lincoln to move in."

Maggie hummed. "Now *that* surprises me. You're not usually so—"

"Stupid?"

Her blue eyes danced as she laughed. "I was going to say spontaneous—a good quality if you ask me. I take it the roommate arrangements haven't gone as planned."

"Well, it was fine at first. He's actually easy to live with—clean, quiet, but very tempting."

"Tempting. Lincoln is that." Maggie's voice softened. "You could send him to my place, if he's not your type."

When a sly grin hitched the corners of her friend's mouth, undeserved jealousy flashed hot in her gut. Iris barely had a claim on the man—and only because she'd tossed her body directly in his path. Embarrassment flamed, and she swallowed hard.

Maggie wrapped a hand over Iris' wrist. "I was just kidding. I've never seen you like this. Tell me what happened." She tilted forward. "Did you do the deed? Are the two of you officially Ashwood's hot new couple?"

"No . . . Yes . . . Damn, it's so humiliating. We went for a ride on his motorcycle and I threw myself at him." Iris covered her eyes then peeped through her fingers. "We did *it* by the side of the road."

"Oh my God. That's so *naughty*."

Heat invaded again, but a wave of nausea followed. "I don't really know how it happened. Lincoln only wanted to take me out on his Harley. The rest of it? I guess that's all on me. He probably wasn't even interested."

"*Not interested*." Laughter burst from Maggie. "Not possible, Iris. He's completely obsessed with you."

Iris lowered her head and played with the crumbs on her plate. "I don't think so."

"I'm positive. Our windows line up." Maggie turned and stared across the street, right into Lincoln's wraparound windows. "That man is difficult to ignore."

Iris examined the pizza shop. The open sign was lit, but she didn't see his motorcycle parked nearby. Her nose scrunched and she shook her head, dismissing the man's interest, clearly remembering his warning about not doing *complicated*. "He's a friend, maybe with benefits, but nothing more."

With her teacup balanced in both hands, Maggie peeped at Iris over the rim. "Nope, not buying it. I don't know how he does it—it's very strange—but he seems to detect when you'll be in town. More than once I've seen him leaning against his building staring at the Stop-n-Shop. And every time he does, your little green car is parked in the lot. That man stays in place, stalking the street like a hungry lion until you drive away."

Iris bit the inside of her cheek. She'd noticed that too. The way he seemed to hover, sometimes out of sight, but always close enough for her to barely feel. Her eyes lingered on his shop again, and a flicker of hope replaced her nagging insecurity.

***

The distinct sound of Iris' Beetle lured Lincoln to the window. He watched, concerned, as his roommate ran inside Maggie's bakery. He grabbed a paper cup and filled it with ice and Mountain Dew. Cold, sweet bubbles tempered heat brought on by the knowledge that Iris was only a few dozen yards away. About five minutes later, Ruth tottered out carrying two pink boxes. She climbed into her big old Caddy, backed out slowly, then mashed the accelerator and used all eight cylinders to pick up speed.

Lincoln sauntered toward the kitchen, tossed his drink into the trash, and grabbed a knife. A mountain of tomatoes and green peppers grew as he chopped. Kara laughed at the pile. "Are we expecting a rush?"

His eyebrows rose, but Lincoln didn't answer her probing question. He cleaned his work area and glanced across the street again, but nothing had changed. The Beetle still hadn't moved. What had catapulted Iris into Goldfinch Bakery with her dark hair flying behind her in sexy disarray?

The corners of his mouth tilted. Maybe memories of last night had added that speed to her gait. He shook away the momentary ego-trip to debate other options. If Iris wasn't running to Maggie for relationship advice, perhaps they were at it again—trying to figure out his dough and secret sauce. They'd have zero luck, unless they included hemp flour and a dash of crushed hops. Those unusual ingredients added a subtle flavor which were impossible to recreate.

Lincoln kept his eye on Goldfinch Bakery. No one else came or went. With his distracting obsession so close, he couldn't get a damn thing done. "I'm taking a break," he said, tossing his flour-covered apron onto the counter.

"Go get her boss." Kara's laughter followed him out the door.

***

"Oh, my." Maggie's eyes went wide. "Here comes your man."

Iris sucked in a breath. "Damn." The hairs on the back of her neck stood up as Lincoln closed in. In seconds he pushed through the door, then stalled, looking out of place surrounded by so much sugary-sweet confection.

"Ladies," he said with a grin and Iris sighed.

When that sound escaped Iris's throat, Maggie choked on a laugh. "Um. I'm pretty sure I left a cake in the oven." Napkins flew from the table as the baker rushed out. A few moments later, a ridiculous clatter of pans in the kitchen turned Lincoln's head.

"You think she's okay?" he asked as he claimed the abandoned seat.

"The redhead who's spying on us from just around that corner? Yeah, I think she's fine."

"Not spying!" Maggie yelled from her hiding place.

Iris and Lincoln chuckled, and the laughter drained tension. When her giggle ended on a sigh, Iris blinked hard, not recognizing the woman she'd become around this man.

"Would you like a blondie?" she asked, inching the plate toward him with a trembling hand.

Lincoln coughed, then his head tilted, curious and suspicious at the same time. "What the hell is a blondie?"

"You know, like a brownie, but without the chocolate. They're great."

"Ah, glad we cleared that up." He shrugged and Iris blushed, realizing how strange her offer sounded. On a chuckle, Lincoln claimed a blondie and devoured half in a single bite. While chewing, he made a yummy humming sound. Without trying, the man had her panting again.

"So, Lincoln, have you ever been inside Goldfinch Bakery?" Her nerves spilled all over the awkward, pointless question.

He gave her a sympathetic smile. "Once or twice. I don't have much of a sweet tooth, but Russel will love it," he said. "I can't wait to show him around. Are you sure about having a nine-year-old boy sharing our place for a week?"

Our place. Iris liked the sound of that. "Of course. It'll be great. I love kids." With that admission, she blushed again. Until recently, she hadn't thought too much about her biological clock. If the right guy didn't come along, she'd eventually have a baby on her own, but at thirty-four, she figured she still had time.

Lincoln didn't notice her silent distress. "I think you'll dig Russel, and I know he'll dig you."

"Yeah? I hope he doesn't get bored."

"Not Russ. He's self-sufficient."

"That's nice."

"Just wait. You'll love him."

Like I'm already falling in love with his dad? Iris swallowed hard when the unexpected thought wormed in. Not possible. She could never fall this fast.

Awkward silence expanded again, and Maggie clattered a few more pans. Lincoln's grin smoothed the sharp planes in his features, granting Iris another glimpse of the caring man beneath the ink and goatee. He stood and grabbed another blondie from the plate. "I gotta get back. Any chance you'll be around our place tonight?" he asked.

Our place. Warmth spread through Iris as she decided to rearrange her work schedule. "Sure. Around eight?" She squirmed feeling like they were setting up a date.

"How about if I bring home your favorite pizza?" he asked.

She dared him with a look. "Are you sure you know my favorite?"

"Uh. Yeah. I'll prove it tonight." He bent in half and whispered against her ear, "And if I'm right, I win."

"What's the prize?" Her question came out low and sultry and way too warm.

"Angel. You are." With that, Lincoln straightened and turned toward the door. He sauntered away with the confidence of a man who'd just made her sigh, again.

SEVENTEEN

Lincoln left early—about a quarter to seven—figuring he'd beat Iris home. The little car in the drive proved him wrong. Shouldering through the back door, uncooked pizza in one hand, bottle of wine in the other, he paused and inhaled. Lavender. *Damn*.

"Are you home already?" she yelled. "I'm taking a bath!"

No shit. Should hot pizza or hot Iris come first? Lincoln toed off his boots, put the box on the counter, and turned on the oven. He'd brought her favorite—a deluxe with extra cheese, substituted kalamata olives for black, topped with sun-dried tomato and artichoke. Nothing weak about her preferences—in food, or sex. He planned to savor Iris tonight, especially after the high-speed roadside hook-up.

A splash diverted his attention, and he couldn't keep his thoughts on dinner. Mouth already watering, he crept through the house in sock-covered feet and sought an Iris-flavored appetizer. Wrapping his fingers around the bathroom doorknob, Lincoln cocked his head and waited for a splashy sound. When Iris turned on the hot water to heat her bath a few degrees, he licked his lips and twisted.

At that moment, the ancient land-line phone rang. Loud.

Shit.

He released his grip when she hollered, "Could you get that? It's probably my mom."

Her mom. Heat left his groin as he turned toward the annoying sound. "A land-line," he mumbled on his way. "Who has a fucking land-line?" He grabbed the archaic phone attached to the wall and held the receiver to his ear.

"Hello." The cord dangled near his feet. Lincoln stretched the tether as he paced and waited for an answer. Silence expanded on the other end, but he could hear breathing. "Hello?" he repeated.

A male voice drawled, "Uh, yeah. Is Iris around?" Must be someone from Kansas, maybe her brother.

"She's busy. Can I have her call you back?"

"No. Well, maybe. Sure."

Lincoln's eyes shot to the ceiling. "Just a sec." He pulled open the junk drawer. "Let me grab a pen and I'll get your number."

"No need. Just tell her Cooper called."

"Cooper." Metal and plastic clattered as he slammed the drawer and the line went dead.

Lincoln stared at the receiver then hung it back on the wall. *Cooper*. Why did that sound familiar? Didn't Iris say her brother's name was Ian?

His hand clasped his chin, tilted his head, cracking vertebra in cascading pops. But the physical release wasn't enough. His fingers tingled, itching for his single daily cigarette. He blew out a slow breath knowing that Iris had nothing to do with that ill-timed call.

Recalling the naked female in the tub, he shoved his jealousy aside, and followed her steamy lavender scent. Each step increased the snug fit of his jeans on his way back to the bathroom.

Patience gone, Lincoln grasped the handle and flung open the door. Iris screamed. Bubbles hit his socks as her body took rapid cover in scented froth. Slim hands covered her ample breasts, and her face flushed. With her glossy hair secured in a clip, she looked like a smokin' hot pin-up.

"Fuck, you're gorgeous." Grinning, Lincoln propped his shoulder against the door frame and surveyed the room. An e-reader sat on the edge of the tub next to her almost-empty glass of wine. Candles flickered on the counter, completing the fantasy.

"Angel . . . looks like you need more wine."

Her shock softened, and she tried not to smile. He took a step, and she stopped him with a look. "Wait." She lifted her chin. "I'm not sure if you've earned your prize just yet."

"Pretty damn sure I have."

"Deluxe with extra cheese?" she asked, making him prove that he got her favorite pizza right.

He grinned and stroked his beard. "Of course."

"Kalamata olives."

"Yeah, instead of black."

Iris removed her hands from her breasts and his reward began. He growled. *Hell yes*.

"Sun-dried tomatoes?"

He nodded and she slid up in the tub, giving him more eye-candy to enjoy. Gravity slithered white bubbles away from her perfect globes. When a few drops clung to the ruched tips, Lincoln moaned.

She shivered. "You're letting in the cold."

"Sorry about that. Let me find a way to heat you up." He shut the door, stepped forward, and leaned a hip against the counter while considering the view. Even with this gorgeous visual feast in front of him, he couldn't shake the question worming in his head.

"That call. It was a guy. Cooper. The name sounds familiar."

"Cooper," she repeated with a shrug.

Jealousy flared. "Who is he?" he demanded.

Iris narrowed her eyes, and he regretted his untamed reaction. She slithered back into the water, hiding his visual prize. "Cooper and I talk all the time. But before you get all Neanderthal again, I'll let you know that he's married to my best friend from high school. They have three kids and live over fifteen-hundred miles away." Ignoring him, she stretched out her right foot and twisted the faucet to add a dose of hot water to her bath.

The mix of angry woman and her sexy leg had him rock-hard in an instant. Lincoln tore his hand through his hair, then his fingers grasped the back of his neck and hung on. Jealousy and apologies were rare for him—both equally uncomfortable—and he took a long breath. "Sorry. I overreacted. I'm not used to feeling like this . . ."

The admission lifted her eyes and her features softened. Iris had him stripped to bare truth. For him, being *this guy,* was fucking difficult.

She smiled, reached for her empty glass, and held it up. "Could you pour me some more?"

He gave her a nod and took the glass and left the steamy bathroom. Water splashed and a few seconds later, the pipes gurgled as the tub began to drain. Damn it all to hell, he'd killed the moment, and now that moment was draining away. Glass of wine in hand, Lincoln located Iris, naked and damp in her bedroom. Bent at the waist, she squeezed creamy lotion onto her palm then spread it over her smooth, bare skin.

His cock throbbed—eager, hard, insistent.

As she rubbed in the lotion, she shared, "He's the guy I was engaged to when the tornado hit."

"Engaged. So you two have history."

Iris laughed and couldn't help the genuine smile. "History, yes. Cooper's mom was the nurse who delivered me and my brother."

"Wait. Are you a twin?"

Nodding, Iris shook the bottle. Before she could squeeze more into her palm, he moved to claim it. He gave her a hungry look and she crawled onto the bed. Lincoln managed, "Face down," on a groan.

He hovered inches from her body and ignored his urges, determined to coax information with his hands instead. "So, were the three of you a posse?" He spread a layer of lotion over her supple back.

She purred when he traced the length of her spine. "Not really. Ian and Cooper were best friends from day one. We were all in the same grade."

After applying more lotion, he let his thumbs trace her sexy lower back. "And you tore up the town together?"

"Not at first. The harder I ran to keep up with Ian, the faster they pulled away, leaving me in the dust. Dad felt sorry for me, I guess. He'd do what he could to and try to level things."

"Like the dirt bike?"

"Exactly. But Mom tried to keep us apart because she was the one who had to deal with our fights."

"You fought with your brother?"

She chuckled, and his fingertips absorbed the vibration. "You bet. Fists, fingernails, hair pulling. It didn't matter. I fought dirty, but Mom only punished Ian."

"Because hitting girls is against the rules. Sneaky little Iris Camelia Greene," Lincoln scolded.

Laughing harder, her body shook beneath his touch. "When did you learn my middle name?"

"Saw it on the election list, just like you saw mine."

He grabbed the bottle of lotion and put another dollop in the center of his hand. Crawling a little lower, he went to work on the rounded globes of her exquisite butt, caressing while his erection crowded his jeans. His fingers traced the crease of her ass and Iris sighed, trapped in pleasure, unable to speak. Desire doubled, but Lincoln's touch had brought her to an honest headspace, and he wanted to know everything she'd been trying to conceal. "When did Cooper switch to Team Iris?"

A long, relaxed breath expanded her lungs—she was under his spell. "Sophomore year, when an outfielder in the senior class asked me to prom."

"Was Cooper jealous?" he prodded.

"Not until I showed up on prom night in a strapless dress." A radiant blush bloomed across her gorgeous ass. Lincoln bent forward and kissed each cheek, biting the second globe when Iris lifted her hips. Her gasp begged for more, but he wasn't ready to give up his line of questions just yet. To escape temptation, he trailed his massage from her butt, down her legs, then to her feet. Her soft, disappointed sigh echoed in the room. That sigh shifted to a moan when his thumbs found the erogenous spot on the arch of her foot.

Lincoln grinned when her confession bubbled, unprodded this time. "I danced with Cooper once or twice at prom. He came over to the house the next day, like he always did, but paid less attention to Ian and more attention to me."

After kissing her left instep, he moved to her other foot. "When did he make his move?"

"It was gradual. Ian was a better ballplayer—the best our high school had ever seen. He was invited to an exclusive baseball camp that summer. While he was gone, Coop and I," her voice softened, "became a couple."

Lincoln tried to fend-off jealousy and failed. Instead of dealing with it, he sped time forward. "And he pulled you from the wreckage?"

Iris winced, and the muscles beneath Lincoln's hands tightened. He'd launched her from easy memories to painful recollections. "Sorry," he mumbled as he soothed the shock away. Lincoln bent to suck each tender spot at the back of her knees.

She relaxed, yet stress lingered in her voice. "He found me. But the physical rescue was only the beginning. The rest of the wreckage . . . I had to deal with on my own."

His touch kept her from drifting back to that painful place. From her calves, his hands smoothed over her thighs and hips. He planted a kiss at the center of her spine, between those sexy dimples just above her ass. A sheen of sweat bloomed, warm and inviting, over her lavender-scented skin.

"Enough talking," he said as his lips brought her back to the present.

The tip of his tongue teased the seam of her ass, and she held her breath. He traced his finger over the damp trail he'd left then moved forward to her core and slipped inside. "So wet."

Slick with her arousal, Lincoln's finger eased forward, found her clit, and circled. Iris lifted her hips, giving his hand room to dance. While she writhed, he sucked on her ass cheek, then left a stinging bite on her already sensitive flesh.

"Please. Again," she begged, her voice raw with need. He drew a lazy path to the other round globe, sucked it, then bit. In the same motion, two fingers plunged into her drenched center, pumping slowly, teasing, dipping deep.

"Turn over," he growled, while pulling from her tight cleft.

"Do I have to?" Disappointment clouded her sigh.

Spinning her, he settled again between her thighs. "Angel, I've got to take a taste." He dove in and she keened, her legs quaking when he flattened his tongue and possessed her pleasure with a long, luxurious lick.

Fingers tangled in his hair when he repeated that path again. Iris surrendered as he cupped her butt and brought her hips upward to deepen the feast. Her hands left his head, grasped the sheets in desperation, fisting the fabric while the rhythm at her center increased.

Tremors radiated from her core to her calves and thighs. The onset of her orgasm bowed her back. Lincoln sucked her clit and his fingers replaced his tongue, curling to give Iris the rapture she desperately needed. Her pleasure echoed from the ceiling, orchestrating the cadence of her descent. Each time she hummed, Lincoln drew her bliss out with one more intimate kiss.

Once she collapsed, Lincoln sat back on his heels but remained between her knees. Hands stretched above her head, Iris writhed and sighed. He loomed over her and kissed her belly button. Iris blinked then her nose scrunched. "You're still completely dressed."

"I didn't think stopping was an option," he teased.

"You made the right call." She laced her hands behind her head and raised her brows in silent request, eyes dark, begging him to strip. With a low chuckle, Lincoln climbed to his feet at the foot of her bed.

Propped on both elbows, Iris stared while he peeled away his shirt. An approving murmur resonated in the quiet room. Lincoln popped the top button of his jeans and watched as she bit her lip. Iris licked the spot where her tooth left a dent. Her jade green eyes were hooded, but instead of laying back as he'd expected, Iris wriggled to the foot of the bed. Two slim fingers covered his, working in tandem to ease his zipper down. The moment his cock sprung into view, her tongue danced out and licked the glistening tip.

Lincoln lifted his hands from hers, giving Iris freedom. She grasped a beltloop in each thumb and tugged away the soft denim. Right foot, then left, his jeans made it to the floor, revealing all the places ink had been laid into his skin, and the few places that it hadn't.

Curious fingers feathered over the Japanese dragon which dominated one leg. The scales danced as her touch triggered slight muscular movement. Iris repeated her finger's route with the tip of her wet tongue. The path led to his eager cock, but she didn't take him in—only traced the contours and veins. Exquisite torture disconnected his mind from his body. Every molecule seemed to align, reaching for her heat. He closed his eyes, laced his fingers in her hair, and surrendered the last shred of his control.

Her approving hum rewarded Lincoln for giving this trust, and her lips and fingers took that reward to the next level. One hand explored his balls while the other grasped him at the root. As slow as hot tar, and just as searing, her lips, tongue, and hands conquered the full length of his shaft. Exploring at first, Iris didn't bother to set a rhythm—she let his hips decide when he was ready for a measured pace. But when his primal instincts took over, she chased the tempo with a natural, slick cadence.

"I'm close," he warned. Iris moaned around his girth then tightened her lips. The slow climb sped his heart rate, and his limbs shook to contain desperate need. Pleasure scraped his senses, pushing against a threshold he couldn't control. All at once, bliss obliterated his body and she seemed to devour him whole. Shattered by Iris, Lincoln widened his stance to keep from falling, until the last wave diminished, and she released his softening length.

A smile tipped her swollen lips. She turned her face to his, pride dancing in her eyes, and he bent to kiss that full pouty mouth. "That was fun," she whispered as he pulled away.

***

He didn't know how long he'd slept—quite a while. His senses returned gradually, finding the scent of pungent artichoke and olives filling the bedroom. She must have cooked the pizza and brought a few slices to bed. When he heard her take a sip from her wine, he opened one eye and saw his angel—glasses on, reclined on a pile of pillows, holding a paperback with a bent-back-cover in her hand.

Her mouth twitched, but she didn't look away from the book. Iris sunk lower in the rumpled sheets and put one leg over his. He hummed when their bodies touched.

***

Iris didn't talk, hoping he'd fall asleep again so she could resume her quiet perusal. After his eyes closed and his breathing steadied, she let her gaze wander over his face—dark lashes, tanned skin, rich with olive undertones. The flecks of gray in his hair hadn't reached his beard, but when they did, she knew it would look sexy.

Iris lost interest in her book boyfriend, so tame compared to the man in her bed. Too bad. She'd paid full price for the new release, and the story was great, but not captivating enough to compete with Lincoln, even as he slept.

The glow from her bedside lamp hit Lincoln's sharp angles—strong nose, muscled neck, carved shoulder. His chiseled arm curled beneath his pillow. She loved the way his ink accentuated his muscular lines. He groaned and turned in his sleep, giving her a detailed view of the tattoos which crept up his spine and spread across his back. A gray jungle hid fierce-eyed animals in a tangle of vines and plants. Details sunk in—his scent, his taste, and the intricate patterns on his skin. Yet, there was so much more. All of it worked together to awaken a familiar pain. She was falling for him, taking a head-first dive over a cliff.

Love. That emotion—buckets of it—gushed from a deep, infinite well. It wiped out logic and left her defenseless every single time. Accepting the notion, she wrapped her soul around the warmth, let it fill her, because the weakened state had a pleasant side, a moment of pure magic.

EIGHTEEN

The sheets were warm, but Lincoln had already gone into work for the day. Iris padded to the coffeepot, poured a cup, thankful he'd made it strong. In the bathroom, humid air surrounded her, scented with his soap. She inhaled a deep satisfying hit of *him*.

Every nerve already longed for his touch again. *Tonight*, she promised the ache, counting the hours until the dull town meeting. She'd sit a few rows back with Lincoln in her sights. Oh, the anticipation. A tiny warning bell went off in her head—*you're falling too fast*.

After a long sweaty day at Northside Grill, she rushed home to shower, blow-dry her hair, and change out of clothes that smelled like greasy food. While in the bathroom, a low bass thump tingled the soles of her feet. Iris flicked off the hairdryer and smiled when she heard Tom Petty vibrating the house. While moving to the rhythm she smoothed her hair with a little macadamia oil. Wrapped in her towel, she bolted, shower-warm, to her room. Her closet displayed choices, but her decision was made by the decadence she wanted to wear under her clothes—stockings and a garter, paired with a smoke-gray demi-bra and matching thong.

She sighed as silk and lace disappeared beneath a skirt with a slit up the back and a simple A-line top. In her closet, she found peep-toe kitten-heels and carried the shoes and her necklace into the bathroom. She left the door open, to give Lincoln an opportunity to survey her curves.

He found her before she put the jewelry on. "Let me," he said, taking the thin gold chain in his hand. An amethyst pendant dangled while Lincoln waited for Iris to lift her hair. His lips tasted a spot at the bend of her neck, sucking until she gave him a breathy sigh. The noise seemed to satisfy him, and he backed away to fasten the clasp.

"Gorgeous. I guess we won't be taking the bike."

She hadn't thought of that. "I could change . . ."

"No. I'll be imagining what you have on under that skirt all night. And later, when I peel this away, I'll see if I guessed right."

A slow swallow caught in her throat. "Do you think it's too much? I just wanted to look confident, in case we have to deal with another round of Daryl's crap."

"Then it's perfect. Anyone with an ounce of testosterone won't be able to think about anything but that slit and the trace of lace at the top of your thigh."

She reached around, worried that she might be revealing a bit too much skin.

"Angel, don't change a thing."

Iris blushed and gave him a nod. Lincoln kissed her neck again before he left. Taking a washcloth from the stack by the sink, she ran it under cool water, and sighed as she dabbed relief on a few overheated places.

She should have brought an ice pack for the drive to City Hall. Her fingers trembled against the wheel while Lincoln played wicked games. He wasn't one of those guys that always claimed the driver's seat, but she'd offer it up for the ride home, instead of enduring more of this exquisite torture.

While she drove, his curious hands teased the hem of her skirt. Every time she pressed the accelerator, he revealed another inch of skin. The lace edge of her stocking appeared first, and he traced it. The clasp that held the stocking against the top of her thigh heated beneath his flicking thumb. Lincoln inched the fabric higher and spread his fingers wide.

"You're speeding," he said while flicking a finger across arousal dampened silk. His observation eased her foot from the gas pedal and Iris inhaled, knowing she only had herself to blame if she got a ticket.

***

Lincoln endured the meeting with his eyes on Iris. While the council discussed the farmer's market, she showcased the sleek arch of her foot by dangling her shoe from the end of her toe. A squint wrinkled her nose, but when she put on her glasses she went from cute to sexy.

After the meeting ended, her lush lips blowing heat from a cup of coffee distracted Lincoln enough to keep him from noticing Daryl barreling across the room. The old man nearly plowed into his chest, already yelling, "What a coward. Should a known you'd stoop to hiding behind a skirt."

"Not now, Daryl." Lincoln choked on the alcohol-infused cloud surrounding the gnarled mechanic.

The belligerent tirade rose in volume. "Looks to me like you're taking advantage of the weaker sex."

Lincoln pivoted, using his body as a shield, trying to minimize the number of people forced to endure the pointless rant. "No one takes advantage of Iris." Yet, he knew these accusations hovered near the truth.

Daryl raised his voice another decibel. "Everyone knows this is a charade. Tell me this, are you keeping your sugar mama happy?"

The room fell silent and Lincoln clenched his fists, though he knew he would never use them on this old husk.

Ruth stomped over with fire in her eyes. As her hands hit her hips, she asked, "Daryl, how much whiskey did you dump into your coffee tonight?" Lincoln ground his teeth. Shit, he'd rather fight his own battles.

"Back off, woman," Daryl barked.

"Not a chance. I didn't put up with your crap when I ran Northside Grill, and I'm not putting up with it now."

"You ran Northside Grill into the ground until you were forced to sell to an outsider. If it weren't for you, I'd still own that place."

Lincoln looked between Daryl and Ruth. He knew Iris wrote a check to both every month but hadn't picked up on this point of contention.

Before it went any further, Sheriff Holden made it across the room. "Daryl, why don't you let me give you a ride home."

That offer earned a vicious look. "I'd rather crawl home than accept a ride from you."

No one spoke as he lumbered out the door. Jerrod sighed then followed him out, shaking his head with each long step.

Lincoln's respect for the old mechanic evaporated faster than the strong scent of alcohol in the air, but he couldn't dismiss the ugly truth. He *had* used Iris' generosity to bypass the new laws. But until Daryl brought it up, he hadn't hated himself for it.

***

The crowd dispersed quickly. Iris reached for him, but Lincoln cut straight to the passenger side of her car when he exited City Hall. She didn't know which was worse—his anger or his wounded pride.

Driving in silence, he grunted when she passed the turn to their house. Iris inhaled a long slow breath and gave him answers he hadn't asked for. "When I first came to the Northwest, I was headed for the coast. We sold what was left of the farm to Cooper's family. After we paid off debts, Mom, Ian, and I split the profits from the sale. Mom went to live near her sister in Corpus Christi. And Ian, well, I'm not sure what he did with most of his share. My part wasn't a fortune, but I wasn't destitute either. It bought me time."

Lincoln shifted in his seat, turned towards her, seeming to want more. A little tension eased as she drove south of Ashwood.

"Before I left, I bought one of those big paper maps and laid it out, crossing out all the states that had tornadoes. Most of the west remained, and I'd only seen the ocean twice, so I looked for places with familiar names. It must have been that old *Goonies* movie that made me circle Astoria with a red sharpie. My mom forced me to take the minivan because it was safe. I loaded it with everything I owned and drove. It was just getting dark when I crossed the Oregon border. By the time I made it to Hood River, I couldn't keep my eyes open. Right off highway interstate 84, I spotted a Best Western sign and stopped for the night, picking that place because it reminded me of family vacations. Guess I was already homesick . . ."

While he listened, Lincoln's thumb fidgeted against the knuckle of his second finger. She could tell he wanted, maybe needed a smoke. "Go ahead," she offered. "Just crack the window."

"I'm fine," he grumbled.

"Well, I'm not. I need to talk and drive. And while I have you captive, you might as well get comfortable."

His low chuckle filled her car. He reached inside his leather jacket and fished out a pack. Flipping the top, he coaxed a cigarette, and hung it on his lip until he found his lighter.

The warn-smooth camel etched into the silver case fascinated Iris. "Is that old?" she asked.

"Yeah. It was my dad's." Keeping the flame away, he lit the tip. Without thinking, Iris synchronized her inhale with his. When he rolled down the window, it broke the spell his movements had cast over her, and she wondered how long it had been since she paid attention to the road. In through her nose, she inhaled long and slow, letting the tobacco scent soothe her senses, almost craving a cigarette even though she knew it would make her queasy.

"I woke early that first day in Hood River. You know, because of the time difference."

"Was your hotel room on the river side?" he asked.

"Yeah, but the curtains were drawn."

"And you'd arrived in the dark."

"Yup. I had no clue. I opened the curtains. It was windy and the sun was hitting the water, striking the edges of the whitecaps brighter than snow. The Columbia was alive with windsurfers and people racing over the water with huge bright kites. I'd never seen anything like it."

He nodded, smiled, and hummed, waiting a long moment before he asked, "Did you ever make it to Astoria?"

"Nope. I wanted to stay for another night in Hood River, but that place with the view was expensive. I drove around in search of a cheaper motel. The town was lovely, but not my speed—a bit too touristy for me. On a whim, I decided to cross over into Washington and add another state to my list. I took a random turn toward Mount Adams and ended up in Ashwood."

He reached behind her seat, found a paper coffee cup in the trash, and flicked in a bit of ash. "Why did you stay?"

"I was lonely, I guess. And this small town, with its single stop light, reminded me of home. I booked a cabin at that spot by the highway for a week and returned to Hood River to pick up my stuff. That night, I had dinner at Northside Grill, and sat alone. Ruth and John Stanhope were running the place at the time."

Lincoln hummed, grasping the chain of events—Ruth's husband was still alive.

"Ruth sort of hovered, made sure none of the guys at the bar bothered me while I ate."

"She must have had a cattle prod." They both laughed.

"Maybe she did. I was naïve. I came back for breakfast the next day and by the time I finished my hash browns, I had a job."

"Fate?"

"Probably not. I think she'd just found out that John had cancer and needed the help. When his cancer hit again a couple of years later, I was their manager. I ran the place for Ruth when John chose hospice. When he died, Ruth inherited her husband's share of the three-way partnership."

Lincoln took another drag, pivoted his head, and blew the smoke out the window. "Did Daryl have a say in the sale?"

"Not really. He didn't give a shit until he lost control." Anger fired her words, and he turned to study her carefully. She felt the weight of his inspection, but it didn't bother her anymore. His eyes on her felt nice, comforting. "They'd gone in together with dreams of Ashwood becoming the gateway to Mount Adams. But Northside Grill never made enough money to support all three. John and Ruth worked and paid him a reduced cut, and he'd come in on weekends, push his weight around, and brag about owning the place while he got drunk. There were a few nights when he took it too far, grabbing a girl's ass, or slipping behind the bar to pour shots for his friends."

"Always an asshole."

"Born that way I guess," Iris huffed.

"And when you bought Northside Grill?"

"He was pissed."

"Because you're a woman?"

Iris gave a sharp nod. "That, and an outsider."

Lincoln smashed the last of his cigarette in the bottom of the cup and shook his head. Now that he was relaxed, a wave of tired hit Iris. She wanted to get home, take off her snug skirt, and sink into Lincoln's arms.

"I made a down payment for Ruth and John's share of Northside Grill. Another chunk of money covered overdue improvements. Daryl didn't like the changes, or the fact that his free ride was over. After complaining to half the town, he finally took a lump of cash for part of his share, signed paperwork, and I slowly started buying him out."

"If you don't mind my asking, when will you own it outright?" he asked.

Iris swallowed hard, not wanting to admit how far she was in the hole. "If I keep sending checks, Northside Grill will be mine in twelve years. I could do it faster if I drained my savings, but I need the buffer."

With each improvement and repair her nest egg had shrunk—even smaller since Wade and Lincoln increased the competition. She knew from hard-earned experience, that it was only a matter of time before something else went wrong.

NINETEEN

Iris circled Russel's visit in bright red on her calendar and obsessed about everything she couldn't control. She planned meals, shopped, cleaned, bought new towels and sheets, but still didn't feel prepared. Craving advice, she called the people she knew with a son the same age as Russel.

"Hey, stranger," Cooper's voice echoed over the phone.

"Hey, Coop, is Danielle around?"

"Nope. Kids have some church thing. Can I help you out?"

"Yeah, I guess."

"Thanks for the vote of confidence. You sure took your time calling back. Was that Wade who answered your phone the other day? I thought that was over."

Iris regretted telling Cooper about that brief relationship. At the time, there seemed to be something there—something that could last. She wasn't going to make the same mistake again. "No. Not Wade. I've got a temporary roommate for a while, just until he finds his own place."

"Huh." His huff carried weight.

"What?"

"Nothing. I mean . . . Well, I just wish I was closer so I could watch out for you. Ian would—"

"Stop. You know I can take care of myself."

Leaving Kansas hadn't weakened the ties. He and Danielle both still cared, even with the history. After the storm, Iris hadn't intended to leave Kansas permanently, only until she found a way to deal with her fear. She'd left while still engaged to Cooper, and he'd given her plenty of time to figure everything out. But she couldn't go back to America's tornado belt, and he couldn't leave the farm. He visited Washington twice during the first six months, then begged her to come home and try a different cocktail of meds. She didn't want to live like that, and after a year, had express-mailed the engagement ring back to him with a long, tear-stained letter she hoped would help him understand.

When Cooper signed for the package, she got a text alert, but not a call. Iris knew she'd hurt him ending it that way. But he'd left her no choice, because he'd already talked her out of breaking things off twice.

One afternoon, maybe three months later, Cooper had surprised her with a call and an awkward question. He wanted to ask a girl out. She knew it was time, even though she hadn't accepted any invitations herself. The surprise turned to shock when he told Iris the woman's name—Danielle. He'd chosen Iris' best friend, the girl who would have held her bouquet if she'd ever walked down the aisle.

She had answered his question with a lie. "Danielle? Of course, ask her out, absolutely, that's great."

About a month passed and Danielle called to thank her, mending cracks in the fractured friendship. Six months later, Cooper asked Danielle to marry him.

They both begged Iris to come back and stand with them as the maid of honor. She wanted to, was thrilled for them, but the June wedding was in the middle of thunderstorm season, and Iris had to decline. It wouldn't have mattered if the wedding was in January—Iris still couldn't have boarded a plane headed East.

Each milestone Cooper and Danielle shared hurt a little less than the one before. They brought the kids for summer visits a couple of times, and the solid friendship strengthened, fitting comfortably between Iris' past and future—a tangible bridge to a place she hoped to visit again *someday*.

Cooper cleared his throat. "Hey, I know you can take care of yourself. That's obvious. But Dani and I . . . we worry about you."

"I know. I'm sorry if I snapped." She always did when her brother's name came up. "Coop, I've got a favor to ask—advice really."

"Fire away." She could hear his smile.

"It's about Lincoln."

"The new roommate?"

"Yeah. He has a son, about the same age as Jacob."

"Wow."

"Not a big deal."

"Right," he teased, and she ignored it.

"Anyway, his son, Russel, is coming for a visit, and I want to have stuff for him to do. But I'm at a loss."

Without hesitation he blurted, "Game system."

"He's bringing it. But I don't want my TV to be what he remembers about his stay in Ashwood."

"Oh, okay. Is this his first visit to your neck of the woods?"

"Yes, what am I gonna do?" A chuckle danced in her ear. "Come on, are you even taking me seriously?"

"Of course. I just can't believe you have to ask. You live in nature's playground. Take your pick—hiking, rafting, swimming, fishing. I'd kill to have all that at my front door."

"Yeah? Well, I hope it's not too much. You know how I can be." Cooper knew her and her tendency to leap ahead and take control. Iris didn't want to overstep and take on a girlfriend role. She knew things hadn't progressed that far, maybe they never would. Lincoln still hadn't let her very far beyond the surface stuff.

"Why the hesitation? If this guy is *just your roommate*, then what does it matter?" The teasing edge in Cooper's voice prickled the hair on the back of Iris's neck.

"Fine. We might be just a little bit more than roommates."

"That's what I thought." A wide grin she couldn't see propelled his chuckle. "Now that we have that settled, why don't you pick whatever's easiest. I'm guessing this Lincoln guy has a job. He won't have time to entertain his boy twenty-four-seven."

"You're right. Maybe a day of fishing. It's been a while, but I can still bait a hook."

"I bet you can," he said with exaggerated innuendo.

"Oh, shut up, Coop."

His laughter rang over the line, an infectious laugh she joined.

"You gotta know, when the kids hear that Auntie Iris is on Lake Osprey with another kid, they'll be jealous."

"There's a fix for that. Bring 'em out. I'd love to see y'all." Her drawl leaked through on a smile.

"I thought it was your turn to visit," he said, daring her to consider a trip.

Suddenly, a couple of thousand miles didn't seem quite so far. "Maybe it is."

Cooper hummed over the connection—she'd surprised them both with that. The ride on Lincoln's Harley had Iris considering all sorts of new things. "Give Dani and the kids a hug for me."

"Will do."

"I'll let you go. Thanks for the advice."

"Always here for you," he said before saying goodbye.

She ended the call, already planning a trip to the hardware store to replenish her fishing gear.

***

"Will I see a bear?" Russel asked three minutes into the drive from the airport.

"I don't think so. They're around, but skittish."

"Afraid of people?"

"Yeah. Nothing to worry about." Lincoln grinned at the disappointed sigh.

Russel was silent for less than a second before he asked, "What about cougars? Will I see a cougar in Ashwood?"

"Nope. Again, they're skittish."

"Well, what animals aren't skittish?" he asked from the back seat.

"Elk, deer, maybe a raccoon. Oh, and the neighbor's cat."

"Cats don't count, Dad."

The word *Dad* caught thick emotion in Lincoln's throat, loving that word from his son. He wanted this vacation to be memorable. If the animals on Russel's wish list didn't show, they'd be taking a trip to the zoo before Russ headed back to Utah. Traffic slowed. Until they cleared Portland, he'd be dealing with gridlock. He'd forgotten how much he hated the smell of exhaust.

"Mom says you have a girlfriend." The sudden subject change jerked Lincoln's eyes to the rearview mirror.

"Iris is my roommate," he answered evenly. Wendy knew better than to make that assumption, and he and Iris hadn't officially crossed that line. Probably shouldn't. One glance in his rearview mirror put everything in perspective—Russel came first.

"Do I get to sleep on the couch?" Russel asked. With that question, Lincoln figured out why his son was digging. He only wanted to work the sleeping arrangements to maximize gaming time.

"Not unless I keep the game system with me."

"Darn." His son dove back into questions about animals then moved on to explaining, in exhaustive detail, the nuances of his latest X-Box game. When Russ went quiet, Lincoln peeked back again and caught the sight of his son's chin dipping toward his chest. His eyes popped open, then he grabbed his jacket from the seat and smashed it against the window, creating a soft spot to lay his head for the rest of the drive.

Silence messed with Lincoln's head, leaving him too much time to think about Iris. No matter how he looked at it, he couldn't put what they had in a box. Friends, yes. Just friends, no. Business competitors and allies too. Then there was the phenomenal sex. His fingers squeezed the wheel hard. *Shit, when did this get so complicated?*

Iris wasn't like any woman he'd ever met. She never asked the hard questions that hung between them. Why? He stared at the horizon, wondering if he should be the one asking for more.

***

Iris planted herself on the front porch, sitting on a bench no one used, but jumpy nerves wouldn't let her stay in the peaceful spot very long.

Back inside and killing time, she inspected the guest room again. Technically, it was Lincoln's room, though he only used the dresser, not the bed, not even when she worked late. They both preferred sharing space and waking with their limbs tangled together.

Iris smoothed the new navy-blue comforter. She'd switched it out five minutes after Lincoln left for Portland, hoping he wouldn't mind the extra touch. He'd never changed it or anything else in the house. And that fact hurt. He still emphasized the temporary nature of the arrangement, and each time he repeated that he'd only be crashing at her place for a month or two, she closed her eyes against a wave of panic and bit the insides of her cheek to keep from asking him to stay. She wondered if any imprint of his existence would remain after he moved out.

Crunching gravel sped her heart rate, and the sound of a child's voice moved her toward the front door where she overheard, "Dad! This is so cool. The trees are awesome. Can we camp in the backyard tonight?"

Lincoln answered right away, "In a few days. I'll line up a tent."

Iris smiled recalling how much she used to love camping in her yard when she was a kid, with the comfortable glow from her house only a few hundred feet away.

Russel burst through the door with a backpack on his shoulder. He kicked off his shoes and spun, skidding to a halt when his eyes hit Iris. A blush covered his young face. He mirrored his father—dark hair, expressive lips, and brown eyes rimmed with long lashes.

"Say hello to Iris," Lincoln said with a palm at the center of his son's back for encouragement.

"Hi, Iris," he mumbled, barely loud enough for her to hear.

"This is my son, Russell."

"Glad to meet you." Iris took a seat on the leather ottoman hoping Russ would feel less intimidated if she was closer to his height.

"Thank you very much for having me." The few words sounded stiff and rehearsed.

Iris smiled. "You are most welcome. Why don't you follow your dad and put your bags away?"

He nodded, already on the move.

"Are you hungry?" she asked as he passed.

"Yeah. But Mom says I'm always hungry."

"Great. Meet me in the kitchen and we'll find something you like."

In less than fifteen minutes, Russel was settled with a bowl of mac and cheese, a cookie, and a glass of milk. He scarfed it down while Lincoln set up the game system. Iris grabbed a cookie and sat across from Russel at the kitchen table asking what he'd like to do this week.

When his exhaustive list turned to scouting the wilderness for animals, she knew the day she'd planned on the lake would be a hit, though bear and cougar wouldn't be around. When he mentioned deer, she promised to get up early and check for the doe and two fawns that wandered through her yard nearly every morning.

Russel finished his macaroni, rinsed his dishes, and joined Lincoln in the living room. As she rinsed the pans, Iris overheard their conversation over water tumbling down the drain.

"She's really pretty, Dad, and nice. I like Iris a lot."

"Yeah. I like her a lot, too."

The small compliment caught unexpected emotion in her throat, making it hard for her to breathe.

***

Russel challenged Iris to a video game after a chicken strip and mashed potato dinner. "I'll go easy on you," he promised, but over his son's head, Lincoln warned her with a lifted brow.

"I'll give it a try." Iris nestled her back between Lincoln's legs, her butt on the floor, her spine against the couch. He couldn't keep from touching her shoulder, her neck, or her silky hair, as she learned to navigate Fortnite. After dying a few times, she got the hang of the controls, and before long, was yelling at the screen as she followed Russel through abandoned buildings. Shells exploded around them, but she kept up and competed, guarding, as his son gathered treasure and took out enemy forces. Unfortunately, Lincoln hadn't remembered to warn his woman about the storm, forgetting how the shrinking darkness might make her feel.

"Keep shooting!" Russel yelled when her player froze. Lincoln looked down, then touched her rigid shoulder. She squeezed the controls, and the girl in the game dropped her grenade.

"The storm! It's coming, we've got to go!" Russel's runner hopped in a four-wheeler and sped away.

Iris shuddered when the cloud overwhelmed the character on the screen.

Leaning forward, Lincoln slipped the controller from her grip, and whispered, "Angel, close your eyes."

She obeyed and her shoulders curled as Lincoln pulled her from the floor to his lap.

"Dad? What's wrong?" He didn't like the fear in Russel's voice, but his son knew that sometimes, when bad things happened, not everything could be fixed.

"Iris needs to take a break."

"I'll turn off the game."

"Thanks, son."

In one movement, Lincoln pivoted Iris to his chest and stood. She wrapped both arms around his neck. "I'm sorry," she whispered, her voice trembling.

"Babe, it's okay." Broad footsteps covered the floor to her bedroom, with each step her breathing slowed a bit and she relaxed in his arms.

"Let me open it," Russel said, rushing ahead to get the door. Lincoln lay her on the bed and settled his hip next to hers, then rested his hand at her waist. His palm picked up the tremors that quaked through her body. Russ scrambled up. When he took her hand, Iris smiled.

"My game. Did it make you sick?" he asked.

She inhaled a deep breath. "I guess it did."

"I've got a friend who can't play video games at all. The flashing lights give him . . . what was it called, Dad?"

"Seizures."

"Yeah. That's it. So, we play board games or go outside instead."

Iris nodded at Russel. "That's a great idea. Maybe we can try that tomorrow night."

Lincoln stroked her cheek, and she tipped her face into his touch. "You want some tea?" he asked.

"I'll be okay. It's easing already. It just took me by surprise."

Russel gave her a hug. "I'm glad you're feeling better." Unfazed, he dashed away.

Iris followed his path with her eyes, then her gaze flicked to Lincoln. "He's wonderful."

"Yeah. He is."

Lincoln kissed her forehead, and she sighed. "Thank you. How do you always know exactly what to do?"

He never did, except with her. A hidden instinct kicked in, took over, and put his protective side on overdrive. Concerning because he knew he shouldn't care this much. Iris wasn't a woman who should settle for temporary—she was too good for that. Unfortunately, that was all he had to give.

TWENTY

Russel's heels sprayed gravel as he sprinted, fishing pole in hand. "Slow down!" Iris called to his back, laughing.

Five rapid-walk steps stalled him for a moment, then Russ yelled, "Hurry up, Iris!" Reserved speed and excitement took over as he bolted toward the dock.

Mary Fisher stepped out of the boathouse carrying sleek life vests. "Whoa, kiddo," she said blocking his path to the water.

Russ hadn't met the school principal yet, but after spending three days in Ashwood, his shyness had disappeared. He dropped his pole on the ground, rubbed his palms across his jeans, and stuck his hand forward to introduce himself. Mary shook the offered hand with a grin, and a new friend was added to his list.

A nod rocked his head as he listened to the rules, impatient feet shifting in the dirt. Lifejacket on, he *walked* toward the flat-bottom aluminum boat.

The dock tipped from side to side as Iris loaded the cooler. "Thanks for today."

Mary smiled and handed Iris a life vest. "You're welcome. I'm thrilled to get out on the boat during spring break, and on such a perfect day. Too bad Lincoln couldn't come along." The changeable March weather had granted a clear morning.

"Next time. He's using the day to get caught up."

"I'll bet. Russel's made quite an impression on our little town."

"Oh, you've heard?"

Russ tilted his head to Iris. "What's an impression? Are those the raspberry cookies I made with Maggie?"

Iris wrapped him in a hug. "No. It means I'll miss you a lot when you head home." She climbed into the boat first and held out a hand, but Russ scrambled in on his own. Once they settled, Mary cast off and fired up the small outboard. An oily cough from the two-cycle engine mingled with the damp, mossy scent in the air.

They crossed the lake toward a rough bank where shrubby willows clung to the shore. Mary killed the motor, leaving the sound of insects, birds, and the slap of water beating against the boat's aluminum side. Iris took up a fishing pole, ready to give Russ some pointers, but his attention turned.

"What's that?" he whispered as a heron skimmed the surface of the water.

"A Great Blue Heron." Iris kept her voice at a whisper, even though the bird had landed near the shore, which was quite a distance away.

"No. Not the bird. Up there. What's that other big thing under the trees?"

Iris strained her eyes and Mary gasped. "Good eye, Russel. I don't know how you spotted that black bear in the shadows."

"Awe-some. I just knew I'd see a bear."

Iris and Mary exchanged a look and mouthed a silent *Wow*, while the boat drifted a little closer. Without speaking, Iris pulled out her phone.

"Can I take the picture?" Russ whispered.

She handed it over and he took aim as two tiny cubs waddled from the forest. The heron lifted from the shore to escape the commotion, and Russel captured it all in a single, miraculous shot.

"Oh my," she said breathlessly.

Russ leaned forward to watch for several minutes as the cubs tumbled along the shore. Their mama lifted a heavy head to study the boat and the gawking people in it.

"She's watching us," he whispered.

"Mm-hm." Iris couldn't look away, afraid she'd break the spell.

The mother seemed to know they weren't a threat and flopped to her side on the ground while her cubs wrestled with a long stick. One crawled over a log and fell to the other side. When it waddled out of her view, she rolled to her feet, found the cub, and nudged her baby toward the shadows. The second cub squawked and chased her lumbering gait. Twigs snapped as dense underbrush swallowed the bears.

Russ turned wide-eyed held silent by the thrill, and Iris reached out to squeeze his hand. "You got your wish."

"I did."

Shared laughter bounced over the water like skipping stones. Mary readjusted her floppy hat and sighed. "Dale won't believe what he missed."

After catching a couple of trout and tossing them back, they ate a picnic lunch on board—bologna sandwiches, potato chips, and thin mint cookies.

A cold wind picked up and added chop to the water, and they headed back for the Fisher's place. Russel helped Mary clean the boat, and put everything away, learning that there was a lot more to boating than just floating on a lake.

On the way back to her car, Russel grabbed Iris' hand. She slowed her steps to savor the last of the magical afternoon.

"Thank you. I had the best time." He yawned and his hand fell.

"I did, too." Iris popped the trunk, loaded the poles, the empty cooler, and a nearly unused tackle box. Russ climbed into the backseat, yawning again. The warm car and unpaved road lulled him to sleep.

Driving in silence, Iris blinked hard to stay alert. Adrenaline smacked her awake when movement flashed to her right and she slammed the brakes, skidding over loose gravel to a sideways stop.

A startled voice from the back asked, "What happened?" She looked over her shoulder to make sure Russ was okay.

"I think it was a dog."

A big wet nose smeared the driver's side glass and Russel laughed. "Wow. He's ginormous."

Iris killed the engine and cracked open her door, wanting a closer look to make sure the dog was okay. A broad black and brown head with a lolling tongue pushed in. She scratched behind his ear and he tilted his head into the itch. "Hey, boy. Why do you look so familiar?" She glanced back at Russ. "Well, he's definitely friendly."

She didn't spot any driveways or homes nearby and hated to leave him by the side of the road.

"Can we take him home?" Russel asked.

Iris tried not to laugh. "Why don't we swing by the city offices? This big guy's wearing tags."

"Okay." Disappointment flattened his response, but his joy returned when she opened the door, the animal leaped in, and little boy laughter filled her car.

"Ask him to sit," Iris said. The dog obeyed when the word left her mouth.

"Wow. I bet he knows tons of tricks." As she drove, guessing the dog's name turned into a game. By the time she parked, Russel had settled on Tank.

Their noisy entrance into City Hall caused a commotion. Ruth waved them over to her window. "Is this Lincoln's son?" she asked right away.

After a glance at her nameplate, he extended his hand. "Hello, Miss Ruth, I'm Russel. Nice to make your acquaintance."

All the ladies in the windows sighed, and Iris held back a snorted laugh.

"Hello Russel. Nice to meet you." Ruth leaned out of her window to get a better look. "Tell me, what brings you here today?"

"We found this dog out by the lake, but I'm pretty sure he's lost and needs a home. So . . ."

Ruth's attention slid from the boy to the dog, and her smile faded. "Oh no. That's Daryl's dog."

"Daryl? You're kidding." Iris couldn't imagine this friendly pet attached to that gruff old turd.

"I wish I was. He usually keeps him tied up behind his garage. Do you want me to return Zippo?"

"Zippo?" Russel scratched the top of the dog's broad head. "That's a cool name."

Iris shook her head. "That's okay, I'll take him. We pass by the garage on our way home." Her shoulders sank as she thanked Ruth with a wave and turned toward the door.

Instead of loading the rottweiler mix right away, Iris led Zippo across the street to the park, giving him a few moments of joy before returning him to that awful man. He sniffed the path, peed on a tree, and picked up a big round rock, carrying it like a rubber ball.

"Do we really have to take him back? Zippo likes us already," Russel asked as they climbed into her car.

"We do. I'm sure Mr. Nash misses his dog." Iris tried to sound optimistic, but the lie burned her throat and her stomach twisted at the thought of facing the nasty man.

Iris stopped in front of the wide bay doors, breathed deeply, and stared at Daryl's Garage and Small Motor Repair while her palms sheened with sweat. Encouraging herself with a nod, she straightened from her seat, then bent at the waist to peer through the Volkswagen's open window. Her eyes landed on Russel. "Wait here until I find him."

As she approached the dark interior Daryl emerged, wiping his hands on a grimy towel. "Oh. It's you." His eyes landed on her chest and stayed while he asked, "Something wrong with your car?"

She gritted her teeth and waited for his attention to slide to her eyes. After a long, uncomfortable moment, she gave up and said, "No. I was out by the lake—"

"Don't tell me. It's that damned dog again."

Her shaky smile returned when Russel appeared, dragged by Zippo. The dog spotted its owner, tucked a stub of a tail over his butt, and clung to the boy's side.

Russel didn't note the dog's wary approach. Grin on his face, he trotted up to the mechanic with an extended hand.

"My hands are dirty, kid." Daryl glared at the dog. "Might as well cart that stupid animal to the pound. I'm tired of the way he runs off."

"The pound?" Russel's chin quivered. "You can't do that."

Daryl's features twisted into a grin, enjoying the shock in Russel's frantic voice. "That's where he's headed. Useless animal, craps everywhere and can't guard a thing." A gnarled hand reached for the collar and Zippo slumped away. "Get over here," Daryl growled and the dog whined, but obediently crawled ahead, dragging his belly across the greasy gravel in front of the old garage.

Russel cleared his throat, lifted his shoulders and asked, "Sir, may I have him, please?"

Iris' mouth popped open on a gasp. The noise turned Daryl's head and he grunted—his version of a laugh. The asshole was enjoying this. Faced with an urgent decision, she blurted, "We'll take Zippo off your hands."

"Good. I never thought I'd get rid of that miserable mutt." A small victory lifted Daryl's eyebrows as he stuffed his rag into his back pocket and turned away.

"Yippee!" Russel bounded to her car. "Come on, Zippo!" The big black and tan dog leaped from the dirt and followed.

Iris stood in place, stunned, until she heard Daryl mutter, "All that stupid woman does is collect strays."

Anger boiled. She secured Russ and his dog in her car then returned to the dirty garage.

Nash seemed to be waiting for her in the shadows. "Change your mind already?" His smirk bared yellowed teeth.

"No. I just want it in writing that you're giving Zippo to me."

His pale blue eyes narrowed. "In writing?"

"Sorry, but I've been in business too long to trust with only a word." Iris bent the truth—her caution was reserved for only this man.

Daryl snorted. "First smart thing I've ever heard you say."

She clenched her teeth as he pulled a yellow pad from under the counter and scratched out a note. *Daryl Nash gives Iris Greene one worthless dog.* He signed his name, tearing a small gash into the paper with the point of his pen.

"Thank you." She folded the meager contract and waited for his full attention. "Lincoln, Russel, and I will welcome that wonderful dog into *our* home."

He glared past her, out his wide shop doors. "That's Lincoln's kid?"

"Yes."

"Taking *my* dog."

"Not your dog. Like you said, it's just a stray." He went to move around the counter, and Iris blocked his path. "Don't do it, Daryl. The dog's mine and is welcome in my home. Not a stray. Or is that how you see all of us? *Strays.* Me, Lincoln, his son. We weren't born in Ashwood, and if you had your way, we wouldn't be welcome here, either."

A sneer contorted Daryl's features. "Get the fuck out of my garage."

She backed a step, then planted her feet. "I'll leave. But know this," her voice shook and she clenched her fists, "you're Ashwood's past, and we're the future. Get over it or get the fuck out."

Daryl sputtered as Iris spun and rushed back to her car. Her hands shook when she tried to open the driver's side door. A deep breath calmed her tremors, but she didn't want Russel to see her like this. She counted to ten and blew a breath through thinned lips before getting into her car.

***

Iris tossed food, a bed, and tuggy toys into her trunk. The parade with a boy and a dog through the hardware store drew more attention than a streaker at a football game. Lincoln opened the front door when she pulled up at home with her windows rolled down, a dog hanging half-way out one window.

Her man looked pissed. "It's not what you think . . ." she said as he closed in.

Russel hollered from the back seat, "Zippo would have gone to the pound."

Lincoln muttered, "Zippo," and pinched the spot between his eyes. "You've got to be kidding me."

Arms, legs, and paws tumbled from the car. Russ ran after the dog yelling, "Look Dad! He loves it here!"

Iris shook with laughter until she found herself trapped between Lincoln and a warm fender. Her insides melted when his fingers tipped her chin. "Did Russel talk you into this?" he asked, intoxicating her with a blend of pissed, concerned, and sexy.

She blinked slowly, trying to think. "Russel didn't talk me into bringing home this dog, Daryl Nash did." That name dampened the sizzling chemistry.

Lincoln's eyes narrowed. "Come again?"

A furry streak ran past, followed by a boy. Russel stopped long enough to say, "Dad, Dad, Dad. This old guy didn't want his dog anymore. And . . . and he was gonna get rid of him. We had to save Zippo. He's a real good dog. I'll show you. I already taught Zippo how to speak."

A low woof burst from the lumbering rottweiler, and Russ sucked a huge inhale. Both sounds tipped Lincoln's firm lips into the slightest grin.

"Look, we already bought him toys, and a dish, and a bed. Can he sleep in my room?"

Iris's giggle mingled with barking, and Lincoln suppressed a laugh. "Why don't you take that beast inside and get him some water."

Russel scrambled into the car, grabbed a metal bowl, and sprinted for the house, followed by Zippo. "How much do I owe you for that mutt?" Lincoln asked.

"Hmm." She bit her lip. "Why don't we settle up your debt tonight on the couch?" She wrapped her hands around his middle and stole a chaste kiss. Lincoln growled. She put a little extra swing in her step as she went to the car to grab a box holding a dozen cans of wet dog food and a big red ball.

She left the trunk open for Lincoln. He grunted, hefting the giant bag of kibble. "Was this the biggest bag of dogfood they had at the Stop-n-Shop?" he asked.

"Yup." Iris called over her shoulder, "I'm one hundred percent committed to this dog."

***

Zippo crawled under the kitchen table, flopped to the floor, and snored while Russel detailed his day on the lake. Lincoln listened as he spread peanut butter on bread and whistled when Russ got to the part about the mama bear and cubs. The whistle lifted Zippo's head, but when he wasn't asked to move, he settled his jowls onto his paws, closed his eyes, and heaved a contented sigh.

"How did that dog find you again?" Lincoln asked Iris when Russ had to stop talking to take a bite of his snack.

She paused on her way toward the door. Running late, she already had her keys in hand and would be working past midnight at Northside Grill, maybe later if spring break crowds stuck around. Lincoln wanted to ask her to stay home tonight, but she'd already sacrificed her entire day for his son.

His question slowed her progress toward the door. "We found him trotting along the gravel road that circles Lake Osprey."

"How'd he get out there? Doesn't Daryl live next to his garage?"

"That rottweiler was probably headed for the Canadian border to escape that awful old man. I think he'll stick around, unless he tries to follow Russel home."

"Shit. I never thought about that."

Listening to every word, Russel chimed in, "Not supposed to say bad words around me, Dad. But don't worry, I won't tell Mom. And don't worry about Zippo, either. I already talked to Mom about that, too. She said if I could find a way to get him home, I could keep him."

"When did you talk to your mom?"

Russel held up a phone, and Lincoln felt for the device in his right front pocket. It wasn't there. He gave his son a lifted brow and got a hopeful shrug. "Maybe I'm old enough?"

Lincoln shook his head. His boy was growing up too fast, and he'd already missed so much. "No phone, not yet."

Slim shoulders sank, but his disappointment didn't keep him from taking another bite of his sandwich. Lincoln's eyes fell from his son to the animal snoring below his chair. When Wendy made that offer, she couldn't have imagined a beast this size or how much this dog would poop.

Iris kissed Lincoln on the cheek on her way to Russ. "I'll see you both in the morning." She planted a kiss on the boy's head before she headed for the door. While she was bent, Russ lifted an arm up and squeezed her neck.

"Today was awesome." As his son let her go, Lincoln spotted a shimmer in her eyes.

He followed Iris to the door and took her hand before she could escape. "Thanks for today—for the boat ride, the fishing, the bears . . ."

A watery smile tipped up for a kiss. Need took over and he pulled her in, kissing her thoroughly before she headed out the door. As his arms released her, Lincoln worried about how much it would hurt when he had to move on. Wade had stopped by the shop while Iris and Russel were on the lake and dropped off schematics for food truck options. The build made sense financially, but at gut level, it sucked. Yet, for his son's future, it was the best choice he had.

The rest of Russel's week in Ashwood sped by in a blur of hikes, pizzas, video games, and goodbye visits. The night before he left, Iris helped Lincoln tuck his son in. When they closed his bedroom door, they both stared for a moment at the pile of luggage, ready for the drive to the airport in the morning.

She leaned into Lincoln's side. "I'm gonna miss him."

"Me too." Lincoln pulled her warmth against his chest, needing her there to hold him together.

"Are you going to let him get on that plane?" she asked as his arm encased her.

"Only if you come with me to the airport. Do you have time?"

"Of course."

He bent to claim her lips and she plastered her body to his. Tonight would be Lincoln's last evening camped on the couch. As much as he'd miss his son, he looked forward to holding Iris as she slept tucked against his body. But when Russ left, the changes to Cascade Cannabis and Lincoln's Pizza would ramp into a higher gear. He closed his eyes and counted down the nights he had left in her bed.

TWENTY-ONE

Russel arrived and left at the perfect time. He'd been there long enough to pepper Iris with a thousand prying questions, gathering answers Lincoln was too gutless to ask.

He discovered Iris was all in—not a surprise. This was a woman who bought a seventy-five-pound bag of kibble after spending ten minutes with a dog. She gave too much, too easily, and that trust left her exposed. What began as a living arrangement had morphed into a relationship—one with cracks, and he was the broken half. Lincoln needed to figure out how to protect her from the fallout that would soon descend. In a town this size, that was nearly impossible.

A meeting with Seth to discuss food truck options was long overdue, and the short drive to Whitewater Homes tied his gut in knots. He'd made a last-ditch effort to find another spot for his restaurant, but that came up dry, and he committed to the mobile pizza place. That option guaranteed a steady cash flow while he opened Cascade Cannabis. And with the paperwork approved, he'd already started lining up suppliers of edibles, functional glass, and weed.

Seth's wife, Natalie, glanced from her computer to the window when he crossed in front of Whitewater's office. She waved him in with a sunny smile. "Hi, Lincoln. Give me a minute and I'll find Seth. He's somewhere in the shop, working on a tiny home. And you're in luck, Wade and Ravenna are in Ashwood this week. You can nail down plans for your grand opening at Mosquito Creek Taproom."

"Great. Two birds." He nodded and took a seat in the office. Natalie's enthusiasm didn't cure how fucked up this felt.

"Help yourself to water or a soda. I'll be right back," she said on her way out. Seth's wife, also a relative newcomer to the small town, blended into Ashwood easily. It helped that she was married to one of the Michaels, and that her amazing landscape photography hung in half the homes in town.

Seth, Natalie, Wade, and Ravenna piled into the office, shrinking the space, and raising Lincoln's heartrate. The first part of the meeting covered details for the food truck. After he signed off on the final plans, Seth lifted from his seat, opened the top desk drawer, and tossed Lincoln's check inside. Air hammers rung from the shop and he glanced toward the door.

"Gotta get back to it, so I'll leave you to your details. Stop by anytime to check on the progress. And let me know when you want to start demo." Excitement glinted Seth's eyes.

Lincoln nodded, but didn't share the same zeal for tearing out the walls at his pizza place. The first whack of his sledgehammer would launch talk all over Ashwood, and his time with Iris was bound to come to a swift, painful end.

"Will do, thanks." He exchanged a quick nod with Seth as he left. As if attached by an invisible string, Natalie rose and followed. "I've got hours of work in my darkroom," she added on her way out.

The door swung shut, cutting off the whine of a table saw. "Alright!" Wade clapped his hands and pivoted. Ravenna turned her chair, huddling up, knees close, like a team. Lincoln bristled, thrown by the comradery.

His unwritten partnership with Iris had come easy, but this thing with Mosquito Creek pinched like a pair of dress shoes. He'd worn something just as uncomfortable to his father's funeral, and still remembered tossing the stiff leather footwear into a dumpster ten minutes after he left the cemetery.

Wade leaned forward, elbows to his knees. "I've got a date in mind for the grand opening."

"A date. Is there a reason behind it?" With a single question, Lincoln dove in.

"Yeah, but here's where it gets complicated. Every year, Ashwood hosts an annual Whitewater festival. This time it's gonna be big." He rubbed his palms together. "And it will make both of us a pile of cash."

On a nod, Lincoln warmed to the idea. "Okay. I'd like to get in on that."

"I thought you might. There's this famous photographer, Parker Knight. She's filming a high-profile kayak event here this summer. I just got a call from my cousin, Amanda, who happens to be Knight's intern. They want to line up the taproom for some evening events. I'm sure Iris has told you about it. Northside Grill's hosting the kick-off dinner."

Lincoln nodded, playing along, but he didn't know if she'd heard about this yet. Still, he was relieved—Iris deserved a break. "And the date?"

"The last weekend in May," Ravenna added, a lilt of apology in her tone.

"Memorial Day. Damn, that's barely two months."

"I know, but it's gonna be big. Kelsey Fisher's company is handling logistics. Pretty soon you'll start seeing Venture vans everywhere. I've gotta bring in a couple more food vendors to handle the volume. Are you okay with that?"

"Competition? Not a problem." Flexibility suited him just fine.

"With the attention on the Whitewater festival, you might lose out on some publicity," Ravenna said, then bit her thumbnail, troubled for him. Lincoln began to see why Wade had been drawn to this woman. Her beauty was undeniable, but it was more than physical—she clearly wanted what was best for all concerned.

Lincoln shrugged. "I don't need publicity—I just do my thing."

"Fair enough. We'll keep you in the loop as details come in. But I'm assuming Iris will have the same info coming her way."

Lincoln wondered why Iris hadn't mentioned this event, but she'd been distracted while Russ was around. He gave Wade and Ravenna a nod, hoping to wrap up this meeting. "So long as the timeline syncs with Seth, this should be fine."

"I already ran it by him, and it's not a problem." Wade's comment coursed irritation through Lincoln's veins, but he tamped it down, shrugging it away. Seth and Wade were cousins, and they worked together all the time, but he still didn't appreciate someone meddling in his future.

He cleared his throat. "Anything else?"

"Not today."

"Okay, I gotta get back to it. I'll keep in touch." Lincoln stood, ready to end the meeting.

Wade pulled him from a handshake into a back-slapping hug. "This is gonna be great."

"Looking forward to it," he said, but dread overshadowed all other emotions. After stepping out the door, he pulled out his phone and looked at the calendar he'd just committed to. Instead of excitement he felt like he was staring at the date of his execution.

***

Seth held the sledgehammer by the heavy end and offered the handle to Lincoln. "Want to do the honors?"

One hand pushed on his safety goggles and he accepted the sledgehammer with the other, ready to take out his frustration on this fucking wall. "Sure."

Everything seemed to be coming apart all at once. Russel was gone. He'd laid off his workers, disappointing every single one. So far, he'd managed to keep the food truck plans quiet, not that the secret would last. Shit, he had the coward thing down, but it was safer than sharing the truth with Iris.

"Ready?" Lincoln asked before he pulled the sledgehammer back.

"Go for it." When Seth's words met Lincoln's ears, he aimed the hammer and threw his anger into the swing. Gypsum burst and a massive hole gaped. Knees bent, he cocked his arms for a second wicked strike. The hammer shook the building and a chunk of wall tumbled to the floor.

"Damn!" Seth laughed. "Daryl wouldn't flip you so much shit if he knew you had that in you."

Lincoln grinned. "Are you kidding? That old mechanic could probably kick my ass."

"I heard about the way he conned you and Iris into taking that dog."

"Zippo's great. I guess it turned out okay in the end." Damn, he was already getting attached to that dog. But who would get the mutt when he had to move out? A shrug and another swing of the sledgehammer kept Lincoln from revealing too much about his uncertain future.

Guilt kept him in town late, scooping smashed drywall, splintered wood, and broken glass. His life felt just as shattered as the remnants of the building. Iris needed to know the truth, but he didn't want to lose her sweet friendship or her addictive warmth in bed.

TWENTY-TWO

Iris peeled away her glasses, tossed them next to her keyboard, and rolled her chair with her heels to get a better look at Northside's employee entrance. She launched to her feet when she spotted Maggie behind a cart laden with rolls, breads, and decadent desserts. "Let me help you with that."

"Thanks."

In one glance, Iris knew there was something on her friend's mind.

"Do you have time to hang out after we're done with this little chore?" Maggie asked.

"Sure, but I have a better idea . . . I'll hand this off to Paige, then meet you at the bar."

Iris whipped up her latest concoction—cucumber-mint iced tea. "Are you hungry?" she asked before they found a quiet spot to sit.

"No, just thirsty. Thanks for the tea, it's so refreshing. I've missed you. Maybe I'll take over all the deliveries now that Lincoln has you so preoccupied," Maggie said with a laugh.

"I'm sorry. Having Russel here was awesome but crazy. And I took so much time off that I got behind on everything."

"Don't apologize for escaping single status." Maggie leaned in. "You could make it up to me by spilling the details about all his tats."

"If we're gonna talk about Lincoln, I'll dump these drinks and whip up Long Island iced teas instead." Iris covered her blushing face with both hands.

"Damn. That sounds so bad it's got to be good." Maggie scooted her chair forward, leaning in to hear the dirt.

"It is, but Lincoln's been a little off since Russel left." She lowered her voice. "I've done what I can to make him feel *better*."

"Better?" Maggie lifted her eyebrows and whispered, "Can we even talk about it here?"

"Not a chance. I'm pretty sure we've violated a law or two in the last few days." Iris waved heat from her face and squirmed.

"I'm so jealous. Every woman in town wants to trade places with you—from the ladies at City Hall right down to his employee."

Iris rolled her eyes. "Are we talking about Kara? She's barely out of high school and he's thirty-five."

"I'm not kidding. She comes into the bakery and gushes about Lincoln with her friends. Don't worry, she worships Julius Caesar Lincoln from afar."

"Oh, Lord, he hates that name. I don't know what his mother was thinking. But I probably never will—he rarely talks about his family."

"Clearly, talking isn't a high priority." Maggie leveled a look. "Have you even noticed that he's closed the restaurant?"

"W-What?"

"It's true. Kara said he gave two weeks' pay with a promise to hire everyone back as soon as he could."

"Damn it, that doesn't make sense." A growl passed through her clenched teeth. She'd offered her help during the transition and knew he needed the cash flow. If he was too proud to accept her support, she'd just have to find a way around it. It might irritate him at first, but he'd thank her for her help, eventually.

"His skills must be mind-blowing for you to miss something that big," Maggie teased, swirling her straw, mixing mint and cucumber into her tea.

"Well, some blowing has been going on . . ." Hot details from the past few nights deepened the blush on Iris' cheeks.

Maggie looked at her drink and smirked. "Maybe you should make those Long Island iced teas after all."

***

Kara burst through the back door, leaped over a stack of two-by-fours, and tossed her arms around Lincoln's neck. "Thank you, thank you, thank you!" She jumped away with an embarrassed blush but still bounced with unrestrained joy.

"Whoa, watch it, you're in a construction zone. What's going on?" he asked, knowing he'd done nothing worth celebrating since the layoffs.

"Sorry, boss. I'm just so excited." Kara stalled long enough to take in what she'd hugged and grimaced. Sticky sweat and sawdust clung to every inch of his skin and he stank, but he'd worked for every drop of perspiration. Lincoln's Pizza was gone, and Cascade Cannabis was beginning to take shape. "We can't believe you didn't tell us," she said, still dancing.

"Tell you what?"

"That you're moving Lincoln's pizza to Northside Grill!"

Excitement bounced Kara's feet as Lincoln's stomach took a dive. "Northside Grill?" *What has Iris done?*

"Totally makes sense," Kara said. "I mean obviously . . . You and Iris have *a thing*."

Lincoln's mouth went dry, stealing his speech.

"It'll be awesome. I'll get all my friends to come hang out at the Grill. And Iris always has the best music on that retro jukebox."

He nodded and connected invisible dots. Silent, gripping the nail gun tighter in his shaking hand, he left Kara's assumptions intact.

"Do we get to keep driving the Subarus?" she asked, backing toward the door.

Lincoln swallowed hard. "Let me get back to you on that. Iris and I still have a few things to sort out."

"No problem. I guess I'll see you later at Northside Grill." Kara leaped through the exit, talking to herself, "That place is super awesome—there's music, and dancing, and the guys working there are totally hot . . ."

Minus the hot guys, he agreed, but Lincoln didn't need this entanglement. Every tether Iris fastened would only have to be unwound—and each one would leave a painful mark.

Why hadn't Iris run this reckless idea by him first? Probably because he hadn't given her a chance. She might have been under him moaning, or tied up and screaming, or couldn't talk with her mouth wrapped around his cock.

***

Iris jumped when Lincoln pushed into Northside Grill, sloshing margarita mix onto her shoes and feet. She'd underestimated his reaction—the man was hot, hot-headed, hot-blooded, and just crazy-hot.

Without a word, he tipped his head toward her office before he disappeared into the back. She wadded a handful of paper towels and wiped the mixer from her little silver flats—her favorites, the ones that revealed a bit of toe cleavage. Damn it, her shoes would be sticky for the rest of the night.

Crossing her office threshold, she found him in *her* chair, behind *her* desk. Advantage lost, Iris huffed and dropped into a lesser seat, feeling small. Her hands gripped her knees, and Lincoln's scowl softened, barely.

"I got blindsided today by a nineteen-year-old." Irritation punctuated his words.

"Kara just had a birthday. She's twenty," Iris corrected, instantly annoyed.

"And you know this because you filled out her employee paperwork."

"Yup. She starts next week. I haven't had time to get hold of the rest of your staff yet."

"Iris, you shouldn't have done this."

"I'm only trying to help." Iris leaned forward, gaping her low-cut blouse. Heat flared in his gaze as the sheer top dipped. His eyes lingered then traveled to her skirt. Was it wrong that she'd selected this outfit to unhinge him? Yes. Did she care? Maybe just a little. But the lines between friendship, business, and sex had already been destroyed.

She rose from her chair, circled the desk, and leaned her ass against the smooth wooden surface. Her stockinged legs stretched forward in a long sleek line, not touching the irritated man, merely blocking his escape.

Lincoln's jaw clenched and his gaze skated over her body, pausing as he tried to solve his favorite daily riddle—the color of her lingerie.

She folded her arms across her chest. "Lincoln, I had to hear about your demo-work from Maggie. You need the cash flow until the pot shop makes a profit. Please, let me help."

"I'll manage. You've done too much already."

"Not true. You're paying rent, fixing faucets, you've even started mowing the lawn. I've gained more than I've lost, and I'm not talking about the extra pounds that have settled on my hips now that you've made yourself at home in my kitchen."

"Such gorgeous hips . . ." He leaned in and stroked her curves, threatening to take the conversation in a different direction. "Angel, tangling our businesses complicates everything. It's too long-term."

Apparently, the past few weeks had only shifted the rules of the game *for her*. Iris swallowed, trying to read the man who'd been so guarded since his son left. "I don't see why that has to be a problem. The pizza business is still yours. I'll just host it for a while."

He blinked, long and slow. Was he finally being reasonable and considering her offer? When he didn't object, she pressed on. "I've thought it over. Instead of rent, I'll take some of the profit from the inside pizza sales, and you can keep the take from delivery. I'll cover employee costs in house, and you cover delivery expenses."

His eyes dropped to the spot where her legs crossed his. "Iris. You're giving too much."

"I'm not. You've forgotten about connected alcohol sales. I may even pull some business from Wade now that his customers can't grab a slice of pizza at your shop and wander over to the taproom."

He shook his head and blew out a ragged breath. "Babe, no. It's too late."

She waited, but he wouldn't move, wouldn't meet her gaze. "Lincoln. What did you do?"

Eyes on the floor, he tangled both hands in his dark hair. "A while ago, before things got complicated between us, Wade approached me. He offered me a spot at the taproom for my food truck. I took Wade's offer."

The news rocked her to the side. Lincoln shot to his feet, grasped her waist, and pulled her against him. She stiffened. He bent his neck and whispered, "I'm sorry," against the nape of her neck.

She went still, hating how much her body craved this traitorous man. "Apology not accepted." Her arms moved and open palms pushed his pecs, but he refused to give any space.

His words ruffled the hair at her temple. "This is for the best. Anything else is too . . ."

"Don't you dare say *complicated*," she hissed.

"Angel, please."

The endearment twisted her stomach. Did she mean anything to his man? She'd shared his bed, his plans, his hopes for the future. They'd even marked dates on the calendar to visit his son together. Was it all a lie?

Her head fell forward until it hit his chest, and her loose hair covered her face. "Why Wade?"

Lincoln's arms coiled tighter, coaxing her soft places against his hard. His hand followed her spine then gripped her neck. "Wade's got nothing to do with this. It's just business."

He tilted her face to his, waiting for her eyes—eyes that burned with tears. Lincoln claimed a demanding kiss, pressing his tongue against the seam until her lips surrendered. Iris opened to him. The sting of his betrayal was laced with desperate need.

The rasp of his beard and smoky spice on his tongue obliterated her defenses. She accepted his sorrow, his fear, and his lies, knowing this taste of Lincoln's lips would be her last.

Her gentle kiss went hard. A nip of his lip widened Lincoln's eyes. She licked the sting until he trusted her with his tongue, then her teeth pinched that flesh too.

Shaking fingers twisted into her hair, pulling the strands. "Punish me," he growled, "I deserve it."

Heat rolled from his anger and Iris shivered—chilled and aroused by his reaction. His eyes blazed with passion, but she turned her gaze away, rolling her hips, tempting him, while freezing her heart against the pain. Sharp fingernails dug into his bicep, igniting his aggression with explosive fuel. Each punishing kiss he delivered defined a border, carved it deep, tattooing a permanent line she would never cross again.

He tore her shirt away, tossed it aside and snared her bra with his hands. When Iris closed her eyes—shutting him out—Lincoln spun her to face the desk. His touch went soft and traced her spine, then he gently pressed his palm between her shoulder blades and coaxed her forward, flattening her breasts against the desk's cool wood. Her surrender bled hot tears from her eyes. As trembling fingers traced the indigo ink of her single tattoo, her silent tears flowed freely. He bent, kissed it, then rose, lifting her skirt as he stood.

Iris moaned as his belt clattered, zipper opened, and denim fell to the floor. A breath filled her lungs when he used his feet to spread her wide. She gasped when he tore her thong then sighed as his smooth crown stroked the seam of her ass.

Greedy for his length, she arched, inching up on tiptoe to align his shaft with her wet heat. Hands kneaded her hips, forcing her to wait for the inevitable invasion.

"Please," she begged.

"Tell me you want me," he growled.

She swallowed. "You know I do."

His cock and hands drifted away. "Say it," he insisted.

"Lincoln, please. I want you. Fuck me now"

Fingers pressed, hips lunged, and his cock penetrated her cleft. She savored the bite of her garter trapped between her thigh and the desk. Lincoln inched out, plunged again, branding her senses.

"Don't shut me out," he growled while extracting his cock from her pussy, then spun Iris to face him. She could have denied him this, but she needed him to see her, too.

Slick with sweat and sex and tears, Iris wrapped her legs around his waist, using physical pleasure to delay the pain. Skilled fingers strummed her center. Iris widened her eyes and moaned. Thrusts paired with pressure from his thumb. Her thighs quaked, breasts tingled, and nipples tightened to eager points.

"Come for me," he commanded, and she obeyed. White lightening dashed through her vision, as she cried out. Lincoln's hips pushed her across the desk. He grasped her waist and held, increasing his pace. Vicious grunts filled her office, but he didn't care who heard his lusty claim. After one final thrust, he collapsed, his weight pressing her to the desk. Every pant added pressure and stole her oxygen.

Iris gasped when his cock left her body. He yanked up his jeans and stared into her tear-swollen eyes. "Did I hurt you?" he asked, far too gently.

Please, don't pretend you care. She blinked and shook her head, mouthed a soundless, *No.* A truth, and a lie. Physically she was satisfied, emotionally she was shattered.

Fear clouded his gaze when she stood and pushed her skirt back into place. He backed away, found her blouse, and worried the fabric with his calloused hands.

His distance gave her the moment she needed to find her voice. "Lincoln . . . This was the last time we mix business with pleasure."

He didn't protest, only looked at the clothes he'd mangled with his hands and said, "I'm sorry."

After she put the blouse on, he slipped through the door and snicked it shut behind him. The air conditioner whirred and she shivered. Music from Northside Grill rumbled the floor, transmitting its pulsing vibration through the soles of Iris' bare, sticky feet.

TWENTY-THREE

Iris tripped over a cardboard box Lincoln had abandoned near her front door. Exhausted, she kicked off her sticky shoes, left them next to his beat-up backpack, and turned to deal with the fallout she created when she tried to micro-manage Lincoln's life.

Still, she was pissed. He refused to accept her help. *Damn it all to hell, why did he have to accept it from Wade?*

After grabbing a beer, she planted her hip on the doorframe of the guest room. The closet was open, as were two dresser drawers. At the base of a bed where Lincoln never slept, Zippo snored. The man ignored her presence as he gathered the last of his belongings.

"What the hell are you doing?" she asked. His shoulders tightened, but he kept packing. She hadn't pegged him as passive aggressive. Irritated with this new side of him, she waited, silent, until he answered her question.

"Moving out," he said while stuffing socks into a brown paper bag.

"Why?"

A shrug hitched his shoulders, confirming what she suspected—passive aggressive. And just because he'd lost a round, he was quitting the game. When Iris stepped into his room, Zippo stood begging for a head scratch. She bent, gave her big puppy some love, wishing love was always this easy.

"Answer this for me," she said. "Have you ever lived with a roommate you didn't fuck?" She winced, fearing she'd pushed too hard.

Lincoln choked on a grunt. He straightened and faced her, his eyes an obsidian storm. "Yes. I've had roommates I didn't *fuck*."

"A woman?" she clarified, baiting the hook.

His inked, muscled arms folded over his chest. "Yes."

"Good. Then put your shit away." To ensure that he stayed, Iris added as she turned to leave, "Unless you think you can't handle it." She didn't know why keeping him here meant so much to her, but it became essential the moment she'd stumbled over his stuff piled by the door.

Anger he'd buried found an escape valve. "Can't handle it?" he yelled and the dog whined.

"Yeah. Maybe you can't," Iris snapped. A quick glance over her shoulder caught his eyes on her ass. She smirked, satisfied, knowing he'd take her challenge.

Shoulders squared, he said evenly, "You think I can't handle living here—in this house—without banging you?"

Iris faced him, nodded, and mirrored his arm-crossed stance. "We began this arrangement to guarantee the success of Cascade Cannabis. I don't give a shit what you do with your pizza business—close it, move it to the taproom, open a fucking franchise—not my concern." She swallowed hard, trying to restore her cool.

"Are you sure about that?"

"Yes, I'm sure. I tried to help your employees and *you*. Clearly, I overstepped." She blew out a breath. "I was wrong."

Lincoln relaxed, took a step toward her, his hands dropping to his side. She wanted those hands on her again, but they both knew sex was making this living situation too intense.

"Here's the deal." Iris used her last ounce of self-control to keep her voice from shaking. "The sex has been great, but it clouds things . . . Now, it's done. Business is business. Pleasure is pleasure. Let's not mingle the two."

His eyes narrowed and he nodded. "Fine."

"So, you're staying?"

"For now, yes. No sex, no problem."

"Glad we cleared that up." Iris heaved a relieved breath. Lincoln staying shouldn't matter so much—shouldn't matter at all—yet it did.

Still pissed, adrenaline surged. Since sex was out, she only had three other options to take the edge away—a bowl of weed, alcohol, or a bath. In the kitchen, she found a half empty bottle of wine and twisted the cork.

Lincoln came in, paused, and grabbed a beer, then went to the pile he'd left by the front door. He lived light and in minutes, the pile would be gone.

"Are you done in the bathroom?" she asked, while grabbing a glass.

"Yeah." His eyes skated past her without a pause. Her presence in the room mattered less than the dining room chair.

With a nod, she left to take over the bathroom—silk robe ready on a peg, glass of wine on the wide edge of the tub, the rest of the bottle within reach. She spun the handle, tested the temp, and added lavender bubble bath. Soon, the room filled with her favorite clean scent. Iris slipped into the water, closed her eyes, and listened to the comforting sound of the man unpacking on the other side of the bathroom wall.

***

Iris woke early, showered, fed Zippo, made coffee, drained most of it into a travel cup, then turned off the pot before she headed out the door. She did this while Lincoln watched from across the room, just like she'd done every morning for the past four days.

After she'd gone, the dog trailed him around the house, at times only inches from his feet. This annoyed Lincoln at first, but after a few days, he didn't mind his fur-covered shadow. At least the dog's footfalls confirmed that he wasn't invisible. If he'd counted on Iris to provide the clues, he'd swear he was a ghost.

He seemed to live alone as her hours at Northside Grill increased. Yet, somehow Iris surrounded him. The dent in the couch where she sat, her lipstick stain on a glass, the scent of her soap, her shoes by the door—each detail reminded him of everything he'd lost.

Without the restaurant to eat up his nights, Lincoln searched for ways to kill time. He bought an X-Box and gamed with Russel. He downloaded a dog book and started teaching Zippo tricks, but the dog was smart and caught on to playing dead way too quick. Walls were up in the pot shop, so he textured, painted, then waited for fixtures to arrive. He posted jobs, studied résumés, and scheduled interviews. At night, alone, he'd try out different bubblers and sample different varieties of dank weed, then fall into a dead-to-the-world sleep.

It was Saturday, his Harley beckoned, but Zippo wasn't doing much better than he was, and Lincoln didn't want to leave the big dog alone.

When Lincoln slammed the screen of his laptop shut, his furry companion lifted his head and whined. "Need to go outside?" he asked as he stood. The dog dropped his jowls back to his paws, uninterested, and heaved a sigh. "Forget this bullshit," he said, heading for his boots. "You wanna go?" Zippo jumped and stomped the floor with elephant-feet. A rare chuckle shook him. "I guess that's a yes."

His hand dragged over the seat as he passed his Harley on the way to his car. Fuck, he needed that escape. Chasing that inclination, Lincoln decided to waste an afternoon at the taproom researching motorcycle sidecars.

***

His beat-up Subaru stopped in the spot next to Wade's fifty-thousand-dollar truck—slick, with a mosquito logo on the side.

Maybe in another life. Zippo barked, eager. The rottie-mix knew there were friends to be made and he wanted out of the car.

Outside Mosquito Creek's taproom, he tied Zippo's leash to a table leg. Not that he needed to, the dog already had a halo of young women fawning over him. They'd never let the slobbery beast escape. Lincoln jogged to the door and pushed it open. The scent of fermented grain and spicy hops hit him like a living wall. He made his way to the long counter, tipped his head to the chalkboard, ready to select a beer.

"Hey, Lincoln. Nice to see you."

"Hi, Linnea." Her smile greeted him with genuine warmth. Rick was a lucky man. Until he'd wrecked everything with Iris, he'd been one of the lucky ones, too.

"What can I get you?" she asked.

"Give me a sec." He perused the list. With the evening chill coming on, he chose something dark. "How about Buzz at Dusk?"

"Great choice." Linnea poured the pint while Lincoln spun to scan the room. Wade's sister wasn't the only face he recognized. Dillon, Mosquito's friendly master brewer was easy to spot, and shot him a wave. Lincoln nodded then noticed Ravenna on a ladder in the depths of the brewery, near the tanks. Annie worked behind the bar, picking up empties.

A friendly vibe charged the atmosphere and he immediately understood Iris's concern. The younger crowd favored this lofted industrial place. Still, Northside Grill had a pulse that pounded to the beat of Ashwood, a rhythm rich with history. Once the new shine wore off Wade's attraction, the numbers at Northside would rebound and continue to climb as soon as cannabis kept the locals and tourists in town.

Wade approached Lincoln as he accepted his pint from Linnea. "Hey, do you want to come on back, maybe check out the brewery?"

"Another time. My dog's tied to one of your tables, licking everyone who gets too close."

"Then I'll follow you. A dog? Sounds serious. When did you and Iris take that plunge?"

Lincoln bristled at first, but Wade's question didn't seem to be prying. Evidently news about their breakup wasn't circulating quite yet. He wasn't surprised. He appreciated that Iris didn't gossip, but still, it would almost be easier if she trashed his name around town.

Ravenna caught up before they headed through the large bay doors. Wade reached an arm around and tucked his woman to his side. "Hey, babe, come take a look, Lincoln brought along his dog."

Ravenna craned her neck, giving her full attention. "When did you and Iris get a dog?"

"It's a long story, but he's sort of a rescue. We inherited him from Daryl Nash."

Outside, Ravenna broke away and crouched. "Just look at this face. What's his name?" Her small hands squished the dog's jowls before she kissed the top of his head.

"Zippo."

"Aren't you sweet?"

Wade grinned while watching his girl lavish attention. "I'm in trouble now." The big beast rolled to his back and accepted her love.

She cooed, never taking her eyes off the dog. "You know, I've heard about Daryl's nasty side," she said as the dog's leg scratched the air when she found the perfect spot. "I bet he thought he put one over on you and Iris."

Wade added, "Looks like you made out just fine."

Lincoln wished life was that simple. "Yeah . . . he's a great dog."

He took a seat, and Wade settled on the other bench as Ravenna asked, "Do you mind if I take Zippo next door? Natalie would love to see this big lovable puppy."

"No problem." Lincoln untied the leash and chuckled as Zippo tugged Ravenna toward Whitewater Homes.

"Let me know if you need help," Wade hollered at her back.

Over her shoulder and attached to the dog, she shot him a look. "I might be small—"

"But you're mighty. Yup, gotcha, babe." Wade's eyebrows lifted. "Never underestimate a petite Italian woman."

Lincoln endured the bliss bubbling from these two and gulped his beer. After cooling his envy, he turned the conversation to easier topics. "Are you still okay with my underage staff working the food trucks?"

"Not a problem. Taprooms don't fall under the same rules as bars. Shoot, people bring their kids in here. I even serve root beer and apple juice in kiddie cups."

"Great. Running both businesses will be new to me, and I want to keep Kara on to manage the pizza truck."

"Yeah. This arrangement's new for me, too. I'm sure Iris told you, bringing food to Mosquito breaks a promise." A hard swallow didn't clear guilt from Wade's face

Lincoln clenched his jaw. "What promise?"

"I never intended to serve food at the taproom—at least not full-time. Iris used to help me out, cater events, and keep the costs manageable. But now, well . . ."

It didn't take a genius to decode the message. The guy had made a bedroom promise. After the relationship fell apart, the deal was off. Lincoln understood, but it didn't mean he liked it. Fuck, he'd pulled the same exact shit.

Wade blurted, "But obviously she's cool with it now—"

"Obviously?"

"Yeah, you and Iris. Everyone can see what you have with her is solid. It floored me when you two moved in together. Hey, don't get me wrong, I think it's great, but I know how cautious she is."

Cautious? Lincoln would never use that word to describe Iris.

Wade shrugged. "She's got to be good with this or you wouldn't be sitting here. Am I right?" With that, the brewer shifted the blame to Lincoln, and he endured the weight.

"Yeah, she's good with it." A swallow of beer helped him choke down the lie.

Wade filled the silence. "I felt bad about the way things ended. I was an ass. Seems like someone always gets hurt." He squirmed. "We all have a history, and I guess some things aren't meant to be."

"Are you talking about Cooper?" Lincoln asked, mentally listing all the men who took a number and got in line ready to hurt Iris. He'd moved to number one on that list.

Wade's pale brows lowered, assessing, confused. "No, I meant the timing of things. Iris and I . . . we were friends before I met Ravenna. Wait, who's Cooper?"

"Doesn't matter," Lincoln blurted, wondering if this whole mess narrowed down to bad timing. Shit, could everything be that simple? He glanced across the gravel lot and time rewound to last March. He'd stood near those trees a witness to her fear, then gone inside, danced with her, held her close, and fought the undeniable pull. After that single dance, he'd watched, disappointed, while Iris fled his arms and dove into Wade's. From the moment they'd met, Iris felt so right, but he'd toyed with her and turned the instant connection into a game. Fuck, had he been the catalyst of all her pain?

Nausea stewed. Lincoln couldn't deal with any more of this shit. He stood, leaving most of his beer in the glass. "I better find Zippo, then I gotta take off."

Wade glanced at the half-full beer. "Catch you later." The quick nod that released Lincoln was packed with questions.

After locating his dog and saying goodbye to Natalie and Ravenna, Lincoln escaped Mosquito Creek Brewing. Curled in the back, Zippo snored while he drove. Lincoln used the miles to grapple with everything he'd discovered about his roommate.

Iris was far more guarded than he'd ever realized, and as far as he could tell, she'd chosen to reveal herself to only one person in Ashwood. Unfortunately, that beautiful, vulnerable, amazing woman made the mistake of choosing him.

TWENTY-FOUR

When her house ceased to be a sanctuary, she shifted yoga practice to her office at Northside Grill, but peace wouldn't come. While scanning the internet for things to do, Iris discovered an answer to another lonely day off. Pulling out her credit card, she signed up for a course to renew her motorcycle endorsement. That led to a few hours of tempting research, and before she knew it, she found herself in the showroom at the Harley dealership. Yes, money was tight, but she missed the rides on the back of Lincoln's motorcycle and wanted to feel that freedom on her own. She deserved this, and his rent checks easily covered the down-payment on a bike.

Iris put Paige in charge of Northside Grill, then begged Maggie for a ride into Portland, but only if she promised to keep the trip a secret. The first moments of the class brought everything back. A few hours later, she was signing the last of the paperwork with a wide grin on her face.

"I passed!" Iris said when Maggie picked up the call.

"Congrats. I'm just around the corner reading a book, give me a sec."

A minivan with the Goldfinch logo on the side pulled to the curb. Iris opened the passenger side door and inhaled the delicious scent that always lingered. She hopped in and waved her paperwork in her hand like a checkered flag. "I did it! Now to pick up my bike."

"I've never seen you so excited," Maggie said as she headed across town.

"Better than Christmas." Iris knew that wasn't a very difficult benchmark to surpass, but she'd take it. "Thanks for this—for the ride, for spending the day in Portland, for keeping my adventure quiet."

Maggie studied her at a long stop light. "I can't believe you hid this from your man."

Iris hadn't revealed the latest relationship developments to anyone and wouldn't until Lincoln moved out. The truth—that she'd botched another relationship—was too embarrassing. She'd pushed for more, hoped for too much, and asked for things Lincoln made clear he'd never give. She wanted more, maybe something permanent, and Lincoln didn't do permanent. Iris knew that from the start, but if he'd been willing to go there, she'd have taken that risk with him.

With an exaggerated wave, Iris tossed her errant thoughts away. "Oh, he's been so busy, I doubt he'll notice the bike for days."

"Really? Seems like Lincoln would want in on this."

Turning to face her friend, Iris said, "No. He's always kept some distance."

"That's not what I see from my bakery's window. Most nights that bad-ass man leaves his construction zone at five, drops by the Stop-n-Shop, then heads home to make you dinner. Don't get me wrong, I think the domesticated version of Lincoln is sweet." Maggie laughed. "I wish I had a man running home to have his wicked way with me."

Iris pulled her lips between her teeth. With her later hours at Northside Grill, she hadn't been around to learn anything, let alone to figure out how Lincoln felt. Had something changed?

Her obsession lingered until Maggie's van stopped at the East End Dealership.

Iris lifted a hand and shaded her face from the glare bouncing off the row of bikes angled toward the entrance. Her heart raced when her eyes landed on one particularly stunning motorcycle. The sales guy knew she was on her way, and he'd positioned her machine front and center—gorgeous chrome, pearl paint, all wrapped around an air-cooled engine, eager to release its power.

"Is that it?" Maggie asked.

"Yeah."

"Girl, that's so damn hot."

She giggled. "I feel like a fraud just looking at it."

Maggie smacked her arm. "Shut up. You're the coolest person I know." When Iris rolled her eyes and smirked, her friend shrugged. "Okay, I'll admit, the inked boyfriend and your new leather jacket—that totally helped."

They laughed, then Iris grabbed her gear. "Why don't you head back to Ashwood? The paperwork might take a while."

"Are you sure?" Concern clouded Maggie's expression. "I could follow you back."

"Yeah, I'm sure. How about if I send you a text when I get home?" she offered.

"Okay. But don't forget, or I'll come over and disturb whatever you and Lincoln have going on tonight."

Iris blushed, wishing any part of that was true. "I promise," she said softly.

"And let me know what your man says when he spots his bad-ass chick on her own ride."

"Will do." Iris had no idea how he'd react, and she didn't mind when the paperwork took longer than expected.

The sun hung low on the horizon when she approached her Harley. She slid her fingertips across the handlebars and grazed the seat with her palm. A breeze, warmed by the promise of summer, ruffled her hair. Time to ride. Iris took a tie from her wrist, secured a low ponytail at her nape, then pulled her helmet on.

Anonymous, and hidden by her visor, she felt different, more alive. Leg over, she settled on the seat. It creaked beneath her butt when she leaned to press the starter. The low growl rumbled through her. Iris waited for it, but the fear wasn't there. She revved the throttle, enjoying the vibration, then glanced around, embarrassed by the amateur move. *Damn*, she'd been caught by a guy walking across the lot. He stopped. Hell no.

Lincoln. Why was he here?

As he chuckled, she realized he didn't recognize her in the helmet and new leathers. The casual smile he sent her way warmed her senses—friendly, comfortable, nice. He hadn't cranked up his usual heat since the night he tried to move out. God, she missed that sizzle, but his pleasant smile was good, too. Could they be friends? They'd skipped over that part on their trip from competitors to lovers.

Iris returned his nod and hesitated. Her fingers tingled, tempted to shut off the bike. Maybe they could ride home together, take extra time on their way into Ashwood. While that notion had a certain appeal, she dismissed it, eager to begin this journey on her own.

Thighs hugging her motorcycle, she gave it fuel, lifted her feet from the pavement, and laughed as momentum carried her away. Nerves faded when she left freeway traffic and took the two-lane road on the Washington side of the Columbia River. Every element hit her with greater intensity—the cool patches beneath the trees and the earthy smell. Visual details came easily too—potholes, cars, even a deer loitering by the side of the road in tall grass. The bike unmasked an incredibly vivid world.

Her return trip was far too short, but dark approached and she didn't want to risk dodging animals that might be lurking in the shadows. Safely home, she parked her bike and grinned as she stole Lincoln's vacant spot. Iris sent Maggie a text saying she'd made it and received a smiley face with hearts for eyes from her friend. The message ended her ride home perfectly—she grinned and went inside.

Zippo nearly knocked her over at the threshold. "Hey, boy. I've missed you. Come on, let's go play." After grabbing a beer and Zippo's big rubber ball, she took him outside for a game of fetch. Wind bent the branches of the tall evergreens, rushing overhead with an ocean-like sound. Breathing came easier as her home surrounded her with familiar warmth. Like a fool, she'd avoided this place, hiding from a conflict that she needed to face. When she'd asked Lincoln to stay, she'd hoped to find a path to friendship, but now, she wasn't sure either of them knew how to get there.

***

He'd almost made it inside the dealership when the growl of a Harley turned Lincoln's head, and he found a woman straddling a shiny new ride who looked hot and felt strangely familiar. Afternoon sun flashed from her visor as she dipped her chin then cocked her helmet to the side. That familiar sensation expanded. *Who is she?*

Not knowing would bug the shit out of him for days. Desire heated his gut, a pleasant awareness—he hadn't wanted anyone except Iris for months. The surge to his groin gave him hope—maybe someday what he felt for his roommate would fade.

He lingered long after the girl gave her Harley fuel and rode on. When the sound of her engine died out, he stepped inside and let the scent of oil and leather peel away the last hint of longing.

The kid working the counter had the balls to laugh when he asked about a side car for his dog. Eventually, the manager dug up the name of a place in Seattle that did custom work, something that would suit his one-hundred-fifteen-pound mutt.

With the sidecar shop's number in his pocket, and a leather-clad mystery-woman on his mind, Lincoln mounted his bike. Another night alone stretched ahead, and he chose a longer route to Ashwood—a road that angled toward Mount Saint Helens before heading home.

***

The rumble from his motorcycle eased Iris from a pleasant dream, riding in the sun on a winding road. She smiled, yawned, opened her eyes slowly. *No fear. Halleluiah.*

She laughed to herself—that low engine growl didn't mess with her head anymore. Zippo leapt up and danced at the front door, feet pounding, butt wagging. Iris rubbed sleep from her eyes and stretched. Three episodes of her latest binge had elapsed while she was out on the couch.

The motorcycle went quiet. Gravel crunched under heavy boots. Lincoln growled, "What the fuck?" He'd spotted her bike. She grabbed the half-full glass of wine she'd been drinking, then swallowed another taste.

Lincoln burst in, his eyes skated, searching with a predatory gaze. Anger tightened his angular face. "Who the hell is crashing here tonight?" He slammed the door and tossed his leather jacket aside.

"What are you talking about?"

Boots echoed as angry steps carried him on a search of every room in the house. "I'm talking about that fucking bike. Who did you bring home?"

Lincoln was jealous. Iris nibbled her lip and enjoyed that fact a little too much. "Oh. You mean that hot-as-hell motorcycle parked out front?" She grinned and he scowled.

"Yeah. The one parked in my fucking spot."

"Your fucking spot?"

"Yes, damn it. Mine." His declaration reached out and wrapped around her, invisible tentacles squeezing her heart—a blend of pleasure and pain. His eyes darkened with need. Lincoln took a step forward and Iris squirmed. Her body longed for what had always happened next—before everything went to shit.

"That bike," she said, "is mine."

He rocked back, absorbing what she'd just said. "Yours?"

"Yes. Mine."

One side of his mouth twitched. His chest puffed and he gave her a delicious look, a precursor of the ravishing onslaught to come. She could almost reach out and touch the energy, but before he moved, Lincoln blinked hard and reeled his desire back in. Damn, she missed that inevitable frenzy.

"When and where did you pick that up?" he asked.

"Today. In Portland. At the East End Dealership."

He tossed his head back and laughed. "That was you? The smokin' hot woman wearing leathers on her new ride."

Joy lifted Iris to her feet. "Yup. You're looking at the proud owner of that amazing bike." Admitting it uncorked her excitement, and Iris couldn't stop her forward momentum. He closed the remaining distance and wrapped her in his arms. With their mouths only inches apart, she whispered, "Thank you for giving me freedom." Her vision blurred.

"I've missed this," he admitted.

Warm, wet tears trickled down her cheek. "I've missed you, too."

"Angel . . ." He swiped her cheek with his thumb.

Scorching need made her reckless. "Would it be too much, too dangerous, if we put everything aside for just one night."

"Dangerous? Angel, I'd endure the fires of hell for one more night with you."

TWENTY-FIVE

Lincoln clung to the woman who possessed everything he needed to feel whole. But if he took the love Iris offered, he'd destroy her in the taking. For just one night, he'd pretend he was the man she needed. Pouring himself out, he gave Iris all he had, knowing that tomorrow, he'd leave.

Rough fingertips traced the smooth contours of her jaw. Eyes closed, Iris leaned into his touch as his palm cupped her face. Her heavy sigh brushed his neck with warmth, and he inhaled her breath, taking her sweet essence into his lungs. Green eyes opened, half-mast and dreamy. Wisps of dark hair—windblown from her ride—caressed her shoulders. Lincoln smoothed the strands and cherished his imperfectly perfect Angel with a tentative touch.

"Kiss me," she whispered. Temptation melted into his fingertips, and he snapped the tripwire with a tilt of his head.

His lips covered hers, then he swept his tongue inside. Heat roused a unison moan and synchronized their intent. Lincoln bent, scooped her legs, and lifted Iris to his chest. She clung to him and her head tucked into the hollow between his neck and shoulder. The rapid pace of her breathing brushed his skin. Using his boot, he kicked her bedroom door open and moved to the foot of her bed. Taut arms slowly released her warm pliant body, and he let her legs slide down until her bare feet met the floor.

Taking her lips again, Lincoln tried to be gentle, tried to slow his pace, but her warm, wet tongue thrust against his. She shattered his control when she sucked the tip of his tongue into her mouth. Threads snapped as Lincoln rapidly pulled her baggy T-shirt from her body. After he tossed the cotton away, he paused to enjoy the unexpected view. No lingerie. Iris was entirely bare on top, pale skin,

190

nothing but thin shorts hung from her hips. After her ride, she must have peeled off her leather and jeans, and slipped into almost nothing.

Iris stood before him, perfectly still. "I waited for you . . ." Her voice trembled. "I hoped . . ."

"Angel, I've been right here. Waiting every damn night," Lincoln confessed and committed himself to her with another kiss.

Warm, wet, and pliant, she melted into his secure embrace. He deepened the exchange until her fingers began to grasp at his clothes. Lincoln bent at the waist, then lifted her tender breast to his lips for a spicy taste. She arched when his mouth made contact, keening as he sucked hard on the peak. Her small hand gripped the back of his head, pulling his hair until he bit the tip.

"God, yes," Iris cried as frantic hands tore his shirt from the waistband of his jeans.

"First time's gonna be fast, Angel," he warned.

"Mm-kay, please promise that the second and third will be slow."

Her request spread a smile across his face. "I'll see what I can do." He toed off his boots, stripped away his clothes, and kicked the denim across the floor. Iris giggled and the musical sound lit shadowy places in his soul. Tonight, he'd memorize her contours, her sounds, her scent, and store enough of her radiance to last.

Once he was bare, Iris pulled him to the bed, curling her body into his. Potent desire rushed through him like an uncontrolled blaze. He trapped both of her wrists in one hand over her head. She purred and arched her back, gliding her soft curves against his muscular planes. With his free hand, Lincoln hooked her knee and spread her open.

"Yes." Iris bucked as his fingers gripped her thigh. She panted against his neck and her heartbeat thundered, demanding more. Instinctively, he mapped a path to her core and found drenched, needy flesh. Two fingers plunged inside and pumped, then traced slick heat over her taut nerves. The steady circles he drew on her clit levitated her hips from the mattress.

"Please," she begged.

"Angel, do you need my cock?" he teased, strumming her pleasure.

"Now, yes," she keened almost incoherently.

Lincoln pivoted over her, gripped her wrists tighter, then penetrated her mouth with his tongue. He swallowed her moan and settled his torso. Soft full breasts flattened against his hard chest and her stomach heaved beneath his abs. She wrapped her calves over his butt, lifting until her slick entrance teased the tip of his cock.

One smooth thrust impaled, and her breathy cry hissed out. Lincoln quaked as he sank in, eased back a fraction, then pressed in fully. Her center clenched, binding his body to hers—adhering Iris to his soul.

Slowly their hips eased apart, releasing inches which would only enhance their pleasure with the next hot, tactile glide. He plunged again, harder this time, and she arched away from his kiss. Lincoln bent to taste her sweat-slick neck, then drove in with another mind-searing plunge. The tempo increased and tension coiled, straining toward a shared release. Her hands clutched his back, grasping and clawing as her body quaked beneath his.

Tight and wet, she coaxed white-hot tendrils across his spine. All at once, his senses sharpened to one point and liquid fire burst into her sheath. Iris cried out as her arms and legs tethered their bodies in shackled bliss. Each thrust stretched his pleasure and drew another gasp from Iris' lungs.

A satisfied hum vibrated between them and she slowly released her grip. Her tongue licked a path up his neck. He met that tongue with his lips to claim another taste of her sweet mouth. Still connected, Lincoln rolled them both across the mattress, bringing her to the top. Iris kept her attention on his mouth, writhing over him, never letting his girth fade.

***

Laying side by side, her fingers traced places on his body she'd come to know so well, but never well enough. It was too late to learn the meaning of the designs etched into his abs, arms, and back. So many things she'd wanted to know; now, she'd never understand. Her fingers began to tremble, and Lincoln took her hand, turned it, and kissed her palm.

Perhaps they were even. He'd never learn the significance behind the delicate flower tattooed on her back. But that was okay, she wasn't sure she understood all the nuances of the message herself.

Twilight tinted the light in her room a pale gray. Lincoln brought her lips to his and cut off the inevitable goodbye. Instead, he gave her marvelous perfection again. She'd never felt so treasured, so completely understood. Trapped in his arms, listening to the rhythm of his heart, she let herself pretend for another hour that she belonged to this man.

***

Morning light slanted through her window. Iris stretched, reaching. The bed was cool, but the scent of fresh tobacco drifted from her rumpled blankets. She lay there and listen for the shower, or the coffee maker, or the tick-tick-tick of Zippo's nails against the kitchen floor. Silence. He'd done the last thing she'd expected . . . Lincoln took the dog.

She inched one arm and one leg to his side of the bed, searching for a trace of his heat, using the unscientific measurement to determine what time he slipped from her sheets. Had he been there? Maybe not. Perhaps all those orgasms were just a dream.

Iris curled into a ball, taking inventory of the places she ached. Each pleasant twinge confirmed the reality—he had imprinted her body with the memory of him. Eyes closed, she recalled each detail—bouts of sleep cut short by a man doing wicked things with his lips, hands, and tongue, bestowing bliss with expert ease.

Painful sobs filled her room. She rolled to her back, grasped a pillow, and smothered the heartrending sound with the feathered weight. Muffled cries bled into the goose down and fabric. Both hands pulled the pillow tight and hot carbon dioxide replaced oxygen in her lungs.

It would take hours to die this way, and no man was worth that. She screamed, then cried, finally laughed through her tears at her drama-filled moment, then tossed Lincoln's pillow to the floor. All at once, she felt empty, hollow, carved out by his love.

Love.

Ah, fuck. Love.

That reckless emotion had conquered again, beginning with small things—his perfect French toast, the way he held her hand when they walked, how much he loved playing video games with Russ.

A good man, a terrific dad, a thorough lover. He was flawed perfection in flesh, a soul who dovetailed with her weaknesses and made her strong. As much as it hurt, she couldn't regret loving him—he'd given her so much.

Blankets kicked to a mountain at the foot of her bed, she located her phone and asked Paige if she'd keep an eye on Northside Grill for the afternoon. Her work and restaurant would be there for her tonight. While the sun was out, she intended to climb on the bike and find a new road. Her broken heart was out there somewhere, waiting to be found.

The sight of Lincoln's Harley next to hers gave Iris a moment of false hope. She laughed at herself for wishing. He'd taken his car, his crap, and Zippo when he'd gone.

Washington's arid desert appealed to Iris today—unfamiliar roads over flat terrain she'd avoided because the heat spawned thunderstorms. That menace didn't seem so dangerous anymore. She checked her weather app—more habit than caution—and found a promising route.

Miles stretched, hours of perfect escape. Hunger eventually paused her journey at a place that reminded her of Northside Grill—a little smaller, but just as broken in. The full parking lot was a very good sign. Taking a seat at the bar, she ordered a beer and a burger, soothed by the familiar sight of a television surrounded by liquor bottles.

Iris politely cooled the conversation with a guy who took the seat next to hers. And the attention he gave, while not wanted, smoothed the edges of her battered ego. He wasn't bothered by the fact that he didn't have a shot and talked for a while about ordinary things, which was nice.

Ryker left, knowing where to find her in the future—only a few hours to the west, in a town he'd never visited. Leaving her with a promise to stop by Northside Grill sometime, Ryker joined his usual crowd at the pool table.

Iris switched to iced tea, added sugar, and picked at a few cold fries. She was about to head home when the scent of wet pavement blew in on a stiff breeze. Another gust threw open the entrance and tossed thin paper napkins from the bar into the air, scattering and settling the scraps of paper like doves.

Startled and alert, her feet found the floor.

"Are you ready to settle up?" the waitress asked, strangely calm.

"Yeah. I guess." Iris looked past the young woman, tilting her head, trying to find the heavy door of a walk-in refrigerator.

"Give me a sec to get your change. Hey, you might want to wait out this storm. It'll pass in no time at all." The girl's easy shrug put Iris at ease. Her eyes flicked to each face in the dimly lit bar, searching for any sign of alarm, but no one seemed to notice the rain hitting the windows or the flag whipping outside. A few people dashed in from the parking lot, laughing and wet, escaping the heavy downpour. She sighed, rolled her shoulders, and sipped the last of her tea. A tornado wasn't a threat. Not here, not today.

Iris paid the bill, then challenged her fear. Outside, under a lean-to-awning, she spotted two guys having a smoke, their butts on the picnic table, their boots on the bench. Drawn to the shelter, she took a spot at the far end of the weathered seat. The scent of fresh tobacco brought her comfort while she stared at the tormented sky.

Glorious. Stunning. It was almost like she'd never seen a storm. Clouds—powerful and dark—boiled with glorious beauty. A gust pushed dust across the lot, then into a grassy field across the street. At the same moment a bolt of blue light severed the sky. Iris held her breath and waited for the terrifying sound. The rumble hit and she absorbed it, her heart slapping against her chest. Her palms went clammy, but she endured the fear, inhaling damp air while the thunder faded. The two strangers, unaffected by the storm, kept on talking about a fishing trip to Alaska.

They paused for a moment and Iris turned her head. "Do you want a smoke?" one offered.

"No thanks. I'm just enjoying the storm."

She got a nod as the sky lit again. "This is just a squall, but the weather's heating up. We'll get some decent shows soon."

"Can't wait." Iris chuckled, letting her nerves fade into another roll of thunder. The air cooled, the clouds peeled north, and the horizon brightened into a more intense shade of cerulean blue.

After they finished their smokes, the guys took their conversation inside. The sun hit the pavement, heating shallow puddles into steamy furls. Iris got up, pulled a small towel from a cubby on her Harley, and wiped rain from her seat.

Back on her bike, the road was drying, but she still took the first few miles toward Ashwood slowly. Only one person would understand the magnitude of this small achievement, but as much as she wanted to share it with Lincoln, she knew she couldn't. She needed to reinforce her defenses before speaking with him again. Time—and maybe an early birthday present—would help. Tonight, she'd get online and order a lace and silk band-aid for her battered heart.

TWENTY-SIX

Zippo turned three circles, grunted, settled on his bed in the corner, then stared at Lincoln. Even with a big pillow, the concrete floors weren't as comfy as his spot near the heat register in Iris's living room.

The dog sighed and Lincoln echoed the sound. "Yeah, boy, I know. I'm a fucking fool."

With a grunt, he pushed himself from the twin-sized cot—the only spot to sit in the storage room. He stepped over a stack of trim and hoped Zippo could ignore the buzz of the saw and the shot of air hammers while he and Seth installed shelves. The store was coming together. Before he opened the doors at Cascade Cannabis, he'd have to find a place to live. Until then, he'd avoid Daryl as best he could.

He wanted a place with a couple of bedrooms, away from town, and a yard. Something homey with a room for Russ when he came to visit. Shit, he'd just described Iris' place . . . That fact hit him with a fresh wave of regret.

Until he found a spot, he and Zippo would have to squeeze in with inventory—bongs and pipes, edibles and oils, and after the marijuana arrived, racks upon racks of dank, high-quality weed. As much as he enjoyed a pipe filled with flower, he didn't want to wake up smelling skunky.

***

"Coffee, coffee, coffee."

Her mumbled prayer stopped when a snuffle came through the plastic cover that secured the unused doggy-door. Iris eased the trapdoor away and a wet nose pushed inside. Zippo's lolling tongue hung from his big head as over one hundred pounds of muscle and fur danced, replacing the silence in her house. Iris laughed, joyful, to see her puppy for the first time in days.

She bent and grabbed his muzzle, slowing him enough to lay a kiss on top of his broad head. "Zippo! Ooh, I've missed this squishy face." She kneeled, snuggled the happy giant, and squeezed him to her chest. "Does my good boy want a treat? I don't know if you deserve a reward. Does Lincoln even know where you are?" Zippo's ears perked when he heard the familiar name. "I hope your naughty, wandering habits haven't returned."

His butt plopped to the ground and his brown eyes stared, filled with hope. "Looks like you want some *food*." Zippo recognized the word and barked enthusiastically. She filled a serving bowl with water, put it in the usual spot and took out a carton of eggs. While their brunch scrambled, Iris sent a text, which Lincoln responded to immediately.

Thank God, you found him. Be there soon.

Crap, she'd have to face him after only four days. Her hands shook while she scooped the eggs from the pan to her plate and to another serving bowl. Iris added pepper to hers and let Zippo's cool on the counter. Still eating when the front door opened, the pup scarfed the rest in one big bite. He flew across the room, hurling toward Lincoln with reckless speed. Braced for the onslaught, Lincoln calmed the dog with a firm, "Sit." Zippo sat long enough to have his ear scratched. "You had me worried, big guy."

Iris watched the exchange, feeling like an intruder in her own home. Lincoln took a breath then finally looked from the dog to her. She'd prepared herself but couldn't absorb the heat in his eyes without blushing. "Sorry about Zippo, but thanks," he said.

"It's okay. I wouldn't mind having him around. I-I miss him." A small smile tipped the corners of her mouth and she licked her lips, wanting so much to tell him she'd missed him, too.

He nodded. "You been okay?"

"Mm hm. I'm on the bike a lot."

Dark eyes studied her. "Even with the stormy weather?"

Iris lifted her shoulders. "That thunder didn't slow me down."

A slow grin mellowed Lincoln's expression. He stepped into her living room but not too far from the front door. "Hey, that's great. Maybe we can take a ride sometime?"

"Yeah. Maybe. But even if we don't, the offer stands—I'd be happy to keep an eye on Zippo. He's used to my place."

"You're right. And I'm sorry. I shouldn't have taken him without talking to you first."

"I get it. He's Russel's dog, so it's right that he's with you."

Lincoln hesitated. "Are you sure you don't mind? You know . . . shared custody?" He laughed, but the words hurt them both. What they had was over, and they were ironing out the arrangements—making it official, moving on.

"I don't mind at all. And it doesn't have to be a formal thing—I'll leave the doggy door open and you can just hang onto that key."

Lincoln huffed, "Never needed the key, Angel."

Angel. The word trapped a painful exhale in her chest, and Iris couldn't do anything but give Lincoln a quick nod.

"I guess I'll leave him then, if you'll be around today."

Iris looked down at the T-shirt she'd thrown on over her yoga pants. "I'll be around. I was about to get in a workout." Her fingers drifted to the bun she'd tossed at the back of her head. She shrugged, knowing she looked a mess. The dog loped across the room, circled three times, and curled in a square of sun which streamed in through the window.

"Guess he's staying." Lincoln chuckled and turned to leave. She fought the urge to stop him from walking out. He twisted the knob, opened the door, and pivoted to face her before crossing the threshold. "One more thing I forgot to do . . ."

Her chin lifted, eyes meeting his intense gaze.

"I should have said goodbye," Lincoln said too easily.

Iris couldn't speak, just gave Lincoln a fragile wave. He smiled at the small gesture and walked out the door. His bike growled. Relief washed through her as he rode that high-powered memory away. Later that afternoon, she sent Lincoln a text.

I'm going for a ride. Zippo's fine at my place but you might want to stop by and feed him dinner.

She got a thumbs up—quick and impersonal. She blinked and stuffed her phone into her pocket. Iris climbed on her bike and rode.

***

When Paige knocked on her office door, Iris tilted her eyes from her computer, hoping her latest bout of tears didn't show. "Sorry to bug you, but that old fart is at the bar, and he's asking for you."

"Daryl? Crap. His check probably got lost in the mail."

"Do you want to meet him there or should I send him back?"

"Ask him to come to my office. It'll do him good to see a woman behind a desk."

Paige laughed. "You got that right."

After smoothing her hair, she secured an extra button on her blouse, effectively blocking that man's eyes from places they always wandered. He limped through her door without pausing for an invitation. Surveying her office, Daryl huffed, grunting as he dropped into a seat.

"What can I do for you?" Iris asked, trying to speed the meeting along.

"You can pay the money you owe me."

Crap, that confirmed her fear—the check got lost in the mail. The fifty-dollar late fee irritated her, but she could afford it. Kayakers paddling The Little White, and a closed sign at Lincoln's Pizza had filled her till.

She pulled her checkbook from her top desk drawer. "I want you to know, I mailed it on time."

The pen made it to the paper when Daryl blurted, "Oh, I got the check."

Her head pivoted. "Then why are you here?"

"Like I said, I want the money you owe me. All of it."

Her pen clattered to the desk and his sneer widened. "You can't d-do that," she stammered.

"Are you sure?" Daryl's evil whisper prickled the hair at the back of her neck. Blood whooshed in her ears, and she barely heard when he added, "Did you ever bother to read the fine print?"

Iris reached into her bottom drawer searching for the buried red file, the spot where she kept important documents. While bending to retrieve it, she gagged on the grilled cheese she'd had for lunch.

A loud smack brought her head up with a snap. Daryl's slap covered a copy of the contract on the surface of her desk. "It's all right here. And I've highlighted the best parts. I can call the loan if you're ever late on a payment. And last year—when the roof needed fixing—you were late."

"What? We talked about that!"

"Do you have that in writing? Because, *sweetheart*, all I've got is your check dated two weeks late."

Iris grabbed the contract. It was there, words stained in yellow highlighter—the same color as his nasty teeth. He was right. But the next line gave her hope, and she squared her shoulders. "I have thirty days." Even as she said it, she knew her false confidence didn't matter—a month wouldn't be enough time to fix this.

Daryl stood, leaned over her desk, and sputtered, "Th-thirty days?" Flecks of his spit peppered the contract.

Her finger ran across the letters, smearing spittle and ink. "It's right here. Thirty days from the time requested. I have thirty days!"

Her voice rose, loud enough for staff in the kitchen to hear every word.

"Fine. I want it all. Thirty days from today." He flipped over the contract and scrawled a formal request then shoved it under her nose. "Sign it, you miserable bitch."

Pen to paper, her hand trembled, distorting her signature.

Daryl took a picture of the document with his phone. "You owe me $48,712." He surveyed her office and sneered. "Good luck."

He turned and rushed out the door, yet his odor lingered. Iris didn't know if it was his foul stench or shock that threatened to bring back her lunch. The garbage can was close, and she gagged. Her stomach emptied in three painful heaves. After wiping her mouth with a napkin, she took the can to the dumpster and tossed the entire thing, then threw two cardboard boxes on top, keeping the evidence from her employees as best she could. But she couldn't hide this, and the clock ticked. She took a breath of clean air, infused by the crisp scent from the big cedar behind Northside Grill. While she stared at the employee entrance, an overwhelming need to protect her place from that asshole filled her chest with fire. But shit, she only had thirty days. Her only option was to find a buyer for Northside Grill, or Daryl would get his nasty hands on her place . . . again.

When Iris wandered back inside, she found Paige and Ruth sitting in her office.

Her friend bit her lip and apologized, "I tried not to listen in, but . . ."

"And Paige came out and found me in the bar."

"My fault. I left the door open." Iris staggered inside and shut the office door a half-hour too late. "Who else knows?"

"Just us, sweetheart." Ruth stood and took her hand. "Come, sit, fill in the details." She placed Iris in her spot then pulled the rolling chair around the desk, forming a huddle.

"You must have heard; Nash wants his money." Iris swallowed hard and stared at the spot of dirty carpet between their feet. "Not to be rude, but Ruth, do you want the rest of your loan settled up in thirty days, too?"

"Did he really threaten that?" Paige asked.

A hollow laugh shook her shoulders. "It's not a threat, it's a countdown." A gentle hand reached out and touched her knee. Too numb to cry, she tilted her head up and found Ruth's encouraging smile. God, she hoped her dear friend had an easy answer.

Sympathy softened Ruth's voice. "I knew that man was a bully, but I didn't know he was capable of this. And no, I don't want you to change your payments."

Hysterical laughter burst from Iris until she bit her lip to stifle the sound. "Well then, can I interest you in a bar? No wait, I'll offer it to Wade. Or even better . . . Lincoln!"

A snort contorted her choked cries. Hopeless reality crushed, and her torso fell to her knees. She covered her head with both hands to protect herself from a second devastating tornado. It didn't matter if this cyclone was financial—it still had the power to strip her home, her town, and the people she loved away. Suffocating sobs wracked her body. Soothing hands lay on her back and her friends let her weep. She was thankful for those hands. These women wouldn't tell her lies or try to solve a problem no one could fix.

Her sobs slowed, then Iris straightened and accepted a box of tissues. While she dried her eyes, Ruth left for a moment and came back into the office with a bottle and three glasses. "I know you need this, and a lady should never drink alone." Ruth poured three shots of the best bourbon in the bar. "Iris, honey, we'll figure something out."

A nod moved her head, but she'd been on her own for so long, she didn't know how to function any other way.

Paige passed the short, heavy tumbler to Iris then raised her glass. "No one in Ashwood wants to see anyone but you behind the bar."

Iris gave another robotic nod, filled with doubt. This town hadn't supported her in the election . . . why would they rally now? Ruth lifted her glass, and Iris went along with the charade.

"Here's to kicking Daryl's ass," Paige said with confidence. Iris brought the glass to her lips, drained it in one gulp, and lost her breath. The other ladies took tentative sips.

Ruth licked her lips, savoring the taste.

Paige swallowed and cringed. "I think I'm more of a lime and tequila shots girl."

The heat from the liquor cleared Iris' mind. "I need a day to wrap my head around this."

"Of course, you do," Ruth agreed. "Let's meet again tomorrow night."

"Not here." Keeping this quiet for as long as she could was all Iris had left. "I'll talk to Maggie. Let's meet at Goldfinch Bakery after she closes tomorrow. And please . . ."

Ruth patted her knee. "We know, honey."

Then Paige leaned in. "This is just between the girls."

TWENTY-SEVEN

Maggie brought out cookies and a pot of Earl Grey tea. As good as those cookies looked, Iris skipped the sugar, preferring a hit of caffeine instead. When she left Northside Grill last night, she took the bottle of excellent bourbon with her and woke with a pounding headache that cut her morning yoga session in half.

"Who's in charge at The Grill?" Maggie asked.

"Believe it or not, Kara. I've kept her on until Lincoln wants her back. That girl is amazing."

"She'll learn a lot from you." Her friend conveyed support with a squeeze of her hand. Last night Maggie had come over, listened and shared a good cry. Iris waited until Maggie left to get drunk, and maybe a little high. It helped her forget, but no matter how much caffeine she consumed today, she still couldn't open her eyes.

A Cadillac rolled to a stop in front of the Goldfinch Bakery window. Ruth tottered out on high heels. "I don't know how she does it," Maggie said with admiration.

"I stopped comparing myself to her years ago," Iris admitted. "One thing I know, she loved her husband and took care of John until the end." Maybe finding love like that someday would put this all into perspective. If she ever found real success, she'd rather share it with someone. For a while, she'd hoped that someone would be Lincoln.

Ruth pushed through the door with an over-optimistic, "Hello, darlings!" Paige pulled up and Ruth waited, holding the door open for the last member of their posse.

The after-hours activity at Goldfinch Bakery didn't go unnoticed. Lincoln emerged from his under-construction shop where paper covered the windows and a Lincoln's Pizza sign still hung over the door. Iris considered the man as he leaned against the building and pulled out a pack of cigarettes—his single smoke of the day a few hours early.

Their eyes linked through the portal of the wide-open door. His gaze asked, *Angel, what's going on?*

Iris gave him a nod, but the gesture was cut short when Ruth let the door swing closed. Glare reflected and frustration clenched his jaw. The urge to tell him everything tightened her stomach, but Iris wouldn't bother him with the details. Even if he still cared, there wasn't a damn thing he could do to help her get out of this mess.

Paige and Ruth took spots at the small round table. "If anyone asks, we're starting a book club," Iris said, wanting to keep her predicament quiet for as long as she could.

Ruth laughed. "Well, I only read erotic romance . . ." When all eyes landed on her, she added with a grin, "Why don't I pick the first book?"

Sweet, innocent Maggie shocked everyone when she blurted, "I'm in." Unrestrained laughter filled the bakery, a pleasant distraction. Gradually, the room went quiet as tension replaced their momentary joy.

Iris annihilated the silence. "I've decided to take a trip."

"What?" Three surprised women gaped at her, their eyes widened with worry.

"I'm sunk, unless one of you has a big-ass bucket of money you'd like to donate to a lost cause." Shaking heads gave her an answer, and Iris shrugged. "Then Northside Grill has to go on the market. Fortunately, the economy has improved. I'm confident I'll get enough to pay off both loans," her eyes paused on Ruth, "and I'll still have something left over to do whatever comes next."

Ruth shook her head. "This decision is too rash. I don't like it one bit."

"Do you want to take over The Grill?" Iris asked. That was an option, but Ruth would need to pay off Daryl's loan to do it.

"No. I couldn't handle the hours anymore. And I'll be honest, I'm still whittling away at John's medical bills."

Iris slid her eyes from Ruth to her top employee. "And I'm guessing you don't want to work for Daryl."

Paige swallowed her bite of double chocolate cookie. "Not a chance. I'd like to keep my job, but I'd rather work for you."

"Impossible, but I'll do my best to find a buyer who will love Northside Grill as much as I do." Unlikely, especially because she loved that wreck like a best friend. She'd accepted its weaknesses and celebrated its strengths, but it was time to let her baby go.

Iris flattened her hands against the table. "Back to my travel plans . . . I know it seems like bad timing, but I haven't had a real vacation in almost ten years."

Maggie gasped. "Oh, that's just sad."

"Look who's talking," Iris teased, and got a shrug. They both knew the glamour of owning a business was a farce.

"I've called a commercial realtor based out of Hood River, and he's coming to look at The Grill tomorrow."

Ruth held up her hands. "Wait, wait, wait. I thought we were here to find a solution that would help you keep The Grill."

Iris blinked hard and her voice went quiet. "We all know that's not going to happen, Ruth." Silence hung, a new bout of tears clogged her throat, but she coughed and pressed on. "I need this vacation. When I get back, I'll be stuck in a nine to five, probably in Portland. I'd like to leave the day after tomorrow, but to pull it off, I'll need your help."

"Anything for you," Ruth promised.

"Name it," Paige added, and Maggie gave Iris' hand a squeeze.

"Paige, can you and Kara run The Grill? I promise to call twice a day."

Her suggestion earned her a look. "I've got a better idea. Enjoy your vacation, and I'll call if something comes up that Kara and I can't handle."

"That sounds great. And Ruth, I know this is asking a lot, but can I give the realtor your number?"

"Of course. I'll tell every potential buyer what a gem you've created in our town."

"Perfect. Thank you so much. Maggie, would you mind staying at my place while I'm gone?"

"Sure, but why?"

"Zippo's already confused with all the changes, and he sort of comes and goes as he pleases. I'd worry about that dog if I had to lock him out."

"Do I just need to keep his water and food bowl full?" she asked.

"Yeah, and maybe toss a ball for him once in a while."

"Oh, I can do that."

"Thanks." Iris pulled a folded piece of paper from her pocket. "Here's my itinerary."

"Whoa." Paige flattened the paper. "You're planning to take the bike."

Iris couldn't stop her grin. "I'm so excited. I plan to ride about two-hundred miles each day, that is, if my butt can handle it."

Maggie exhaled a breath she'd been holding. "Oh, my God. Iris, you're going back to Kansas!"

A few tears escaped the corner of her eye, and when Iris looked up, she found her friend's eyes swimming, too. Maggie knew how impossible this had been for her.

"Do Dani and Cooper know you're coming?"

Eyes bored into Iris, filled with questions from the other two ladies. She blew out a breath. "Cooper's an old boyfriend, and Dani's his wife. They bought the place where I grew up and built a new house on it."

Ruth's eyebrows lifted. "Why do I get the feeling there's more to this than you're letting on."

Iris shrugged. "Fine, Cooper and I used to be engaged, but it's not what you think. We've only kept in touch because he married my best friend from high school."

Ruth nodded and seemed relieved. Clearly, she was still holding out hope for Lincoln.

"I called Cooper and Danielle this morning. I'll be staying with them when I get there. I gave him your number, Maggie. I hope that's okay."

"Totally fine. I just wish you weren't taking this trip alone. Could Lincoln go with you?"

"I like that idea," Ruth agreed, and they all glanced toward his shop but the sidewalk was empty.

"You all know Lincoln and I took a step back. I don't plan to tell him about this trip."

"Is all this a secret?" Paige asked.

"I guess . . . but we all know that won't last once a massive *for sale* sign goes up on Northside Grill."

"Oh, my God. I never thought about that." Paige sniffled, and the others followed, fighting tears.

"Everyone, stop." Iris waved both hands, fanning away hot emotion and Maggie pushed the plate of cookies closer. Iris caved and grabbed a double chocolate, biting into the cookie like it solved everything.

Ruth nodded. "We'll stop fussing, but I still think you should tell Lincoln what's going on."

"Why? He can't fix this. It's too big. Damn, it's too big for anyone in Ashwood."

She sighed, somehow ready to let go. Everything in her future—except this trip—was a big unknown. Eventually, she'd thank Lincoln for the gift he'd given her. That first ride on his Harley had started her recovery, but she needed to leap this final hurdle alone. And the timing was perfect. With her thirty-fourth birthday less than two weeks away, she'd finally be able to spend that day with her twin brother. "I'll be fine. I just . . . need this."

"I get it." Maggie took another look at Iris' notes. "You're amazing, you know that, right?"

"I'll need to be amazing to pull this off." She chuckled but wondered if she was crazy to take such a long solo ride. Too excited to keep still, Iris sprung to her feet. She went to the window and looked east. "Paige, I promise to be back before Memorial Day. If anything comes up for that big whitewater event, just give me a call."

"Will do."

Iris tried to put on a positive spin. "Who knows, maybe the new owner will use that event as a grand opening."

Instead of a cheer, her suggestion earned a round of moans.

TWENTY-EIGHT

"Are you on the road?" Cooper blurted when he picked up her call.

"Hello, Coop. How you doin? I'm great by the way, thanks for asking." Iris grinned as she stretched, working off miles on the bike.

"Stop being such a smart ass. When you didn't call, I thought you'd changed your mind and turned around."

"Nope, I'm committed. The weather's perfect and I'm making great time. I'm somewhere near Boise, but my butt really hurts, so I'll find a place soon and stop for the night." Her brisk walk circumnavigated the pet area at the rest stop. An older couple strolled nearby, waiting for their little dog to do his business. The short black and brown furry coat reminded her of Zippo and her heart clenched, missing that big mutt.

"You gonna make it by your birthday?" he asked.

"Shouldn't be a problem. I want to spend it with Ian."

"I could go with . . ." Cooper offered.

"That's okay. He's probably sick of you anyway."

He laughed and she absorbed the encouraging sound. Soon, she'd see the face that went with it and the land he lived on. She didn't know which pulled at her more—her old friends or her old home. "Well, I've done my duty by checking in, and you're not the only one expecting a call."

"Lincoln?" he teased because she hadn't revealed the details of her latest failed relationship.

"No. I've gotta check in with Maggie and my mom."

His *uh-huh* had a question behind it, but she wouldn't give him any answers today. "Don't forget to text tonight or I'll send out a search party," he reminded.

"Such a boy scout." They both chuckled at the well-targeted description. "Will do."

Her call to Maggie went to voicemail, but she told her friend her exact location, keeping her promise to check in.

Mom worried about the motorcycle, told her to be careful, and offered to drive up from Texas and meet her for her birthday. Iris appreciated the offer but asked Mom if she could take this first trip home on her own.

Her call to Ruth answered a few questions from the realtor. Keen interest in Northside Grill accelerated her heart rate, and it should have made her happy, but the attention from potential buyers was coming too soon. At first, she worried about selling the restaurant in only thirty days, now she hoped a month was enough time to let it go.

Paige picked up after one ring. "Everything's fine. You need to stop calling and just have fun."

"I know. It's just that I forgot to ask you to empty the jukebox fishbowl."

"Already on it. Daryl's hanging around, and I've seen his quick hand before. I'll keep it empty or he'll dive in and pay his tab from that collection jar." Paige laughed, then cut the conversation short. "Order's up. I gotta go."

With her obligations met, Iris forced Ashwood from her mind. The short stop, and a snack from her backpack gave her a burst of energy to push a little farther. She checked in at a Best Western right after dusk, got some takeout from the diner next door, then spent an hour in a bath soaking away the miles.

***

It was too quiet, and Lincoln hadn't seen Zippo all day. He armed the security system before he escaped the shop. There still wasn't any marijuana stocked, but the bongs and pipes lining the shelves cost a ton. Needing a break, his dog's absence was the perfect excuse to visit Northside Grill.

And he knew something was up. He'd already tried to charm information from Maggie. When he asked her about the gathering at her shop, Maggie only blushed and gave him some bullshit story about a book club. He didn't buy her lie, and the strange response only baited a hook he couldn't leave alone.

The sun warmed his back and Lincoln gave his Harley fuel then let the powerful engine carry him to Northside Grill. Even from a distance, he noted distinct changes. The windows were too shiny, the shrubs evenly trimmed, and big wine barrel planters flanked the front door, brimming with bright orange flowers. All that was enough, but when he spotted the River Realty sign, he nearly lost control of his bike. "What the fuck."

After parking he rushed across the lot, and his straight right arm flung the door open wide. Every eye in Northside Grill snapped to his face. His gaze swept over the room, twice. Not finding Iris, he headed toward her office, but Paige blocked his path to the back.

One stern look told him to control his shit. "She's not here."

He sucked a slow breath through gritted teeth. "Outside." As he passed through Northside Grill, he absorbed more disturbing alterations—small vases filled with fresh flowers topped the tables, the dartboards near the pool tables were gone, and the bulletin board—usually crammed with layers of local fliers—was almost bare. Only licenses required by the state remained. *Shit, shit, shit. Something big must have gone down.*

Lincoln pushed through the back door, blinked away the blinding sunlight, and spun. "Where is she?"

"On vacation," Paige blurted.

His eyebrows lowered. "You didn't answer my question. Where the fuck is Iris?"

"If she wanted you to know, she would have told you herself."

His fingers tingled.

Her eyes narrowed.

Lincoln wanted to grab her shoulders and shake the information out of the girl, but instead, he took a step back. "Look, Paige, I know I fucked up."

She folded her arms over her chest. "No shit."

"I'd like to help. But to help, I need to talk to Iris."

"Then give her a call."

His fingers scored his hair. "Fine. Can you at least tell me why Northside Grill is up for sale? Is she . . ." his voice caught, "is Iris sick?"

She shook her head. "No. Not sick." As she blinked, her eyes lost a little of the glittering rage.

Relief huffed out and he could breathe again. "Okay. Did something happen with her brother or her mom?"

Paige looked past him, rolled her eyes, then shrugged. "Fine. I can't believe you haven't heard, the talk's all over town. It was Daryl. He called the loan."

Lincoln's brows furrowed. "And she's not fighting it?"

Her feet shifted, and then she sighed. "It's a mess. It's too big to fix, and Iris doesn't need another headache. She asked me to keep Northside Grill going while she takes some time, and that's what I'm doing for my friend."

Lincoln smiled at the girl who had Iris' back. "Okay. Can I count on your help if I come up with a solution?"

A grin tipped the corners of her mouth and she gave him a slow nod. "Absolutely."

"Can you get away tonight, meet me at Goldfinch after it closes?"

"I can do that."

A nod dipped his chin. "Later, Paige."

She lifted one hand, sending him off with a small wave. "Later, Lincoln . . . and good luck."

He jogged around Northside Grill, mumbling to himself, using every second of the next four hours to come up with a plan.

***

Ruth opened her front door as he lowered the kickstand on his bike.

"It's about time you got here," she said from her porch.

The light in her eyes told Lincoln he'd found an ally. "I just left Northside Grill. Paige wouldn't tell me much."

"I'm not surprised."

"Ruth, what's going on?"

She filled him in on everything she knew and a few things she'd guessed, but neither knew why Iris wasn't fighting for her future in Ashwood.

Ruth paced her front porch. "I've known Iris for over ten years. When she got here, that storm in Kansas had her so jumpy she'd hide every time a stiff breeze came up. But she fought through it. I just can't figure out why she's running away from this."

Lincoln hesitated. "Maybe she misses her life in Kansas. Now that she's over this fear of storms . . . maybe she wants to go back."

"Back to what?"

Jealousy caught the name on his tongue. "Cooper."

"No way. He's married with kids. Even if something lingered between them, Iris would never act on it."

"Her brother?" Lincoln asked.

"Is a brother who's never bothered to visit a good reason to go back?"

Lincoln looked over Ruth's neighborhood—compact houses, green lawns lined with rhododendrons, most with pickups parked out front. "I remember Iris saying she'd settled in this small town because she liked the way it was knit together. That everyone looked out for each other, that someday—when hard times hit—the town would be there for her."

Ruth's eyes widened, seeing what Lincoln was getting at. "I wonder if she felt let down when her town, her friends, didn't elect her to the council?"

"It had to hurt. But it's still not a solution."

"Lincoln, we don't have a lot of time. I'm already stalling potential buyers."

"Already? I can't believe the commercial real estate market changed that much." He'd bought his building for next to nothing a little over a year ago.

Ruth nodded. "I guess some whitewater rafting event is drawing more attention."

"Oh, that." His focus on Cascade Cannabis had blinded him to almost everything else. Even the Pizza truck hadn't crossed his mind in days. Now that it had, he wondered if his mobile business could help Iris out. "Listen, I've got to stop by Goldfinch Bakery and talk to Maggie. Paige promised to meet us there tonight for—"

"Another book club meeting?" Ruth laughed and Lincoln smiled, knowing he'd missed an inside joke. She waved a manicured hand in front of her face, still laughing. "Never mind. You had to be there."

"So, are you in?" he asked when she could breathe again.

"Absolutely."

He clapped his hands, rubbing them together. "Good. We'll do this. I haven't got a clue what *this* is, but Iris will not lose Northside Grill."

TWENTY-NINE

Lincoln's mouth watered when Maggie brought out a fresh batch of cheesy bread sticks. He'd forgotten to eat and grabbed one right away. Chewing the familiar flavor, he found her watching.

"How close am I?" she asked. "You know, to your recipe?"

Index finger held in mid-air, he made her wait until he swallowed the bite. "You've almost got it, there's just one ingredient missing." His grin expanded, knowing she'd never get it exactly right.

Maggie slapped the table's surface. "Darn it! That nutty flavor, I can't figure it out. I've tried a touch of hazelnut flour, but the texture's just not right."

Lincoln chuckled. He wouldn't give his secret ingredient away, not just yet. Maggie would never guess that a touch of hemp flour gave his pizza crust that special taste. When Paige came in, she grabbed a breadstick and sat, eyes narrowed, unflinching, making it impossible for Lincoln to relax.

Dust flew as a car skidded to a stop outside. Ruth climbed from her Cadillac and everyone had to laugh. Clad in a pink and green camo jacket and matching pants, she'd dressed for combat. The high-heel boots weren't built for rough terrain but were perfect for marching across the casino floor with authority. She paused in the doorway for dramatic effect. "I haven't had a reason to wear my fighting gear in quite a while." Ruth didn't crack a smile as she came in, pulled a spiral notebook from her purse as she sat, flipped to a blank page, and pulled out a pen.

"Hit me with your ideas and I'll write them down." Her pen hovered over the paper, but silence filled the room. "Come on, don't be shy! This is the brainstorming part. There are no wrong answers."

After taking a breath, Paige leaned in. "I thought of something . . ." Her slight hesitation revealed rare nerves. "When I talked to Iris yesterday, she asked me to empty that fishbowl—the big one where

218

everyone's been tossing cash since the jukebox broke down. Instead of keeping it by the jukebox, we could put it on the bar and get the word out. Like a donation." Her shoulders sank. "I know it's not much, but it's a start."

Maggie nodded. "I like it. Why don't we put fishbowls all around town? I'll put one here and attach a sign."

Ruth stopped taking notes. "I can't put a collection bowl at City Hall, but I'll talk to Morgan Pratt. I'm pretty sure he'd be happy to leave them at every checkout at the Stop-n-Shop."

Lincoln didn't know if it would be enough. "Is there any way to take this beyond Ashwood?"

Paige's face brightened. "Yes! The food truck! How fast can you get it ready?"

Three women waited for his answer, and Lincoln started to sweat. "A couple of days, but only if I can get Kara's help. And where would I take it on such short notice?"

Maggie held up her hand. "Maybe you could ask Wade. Dillon stopped by the other day, and he was talking about their festival schedule. Since you're already working with Mosquito Creek Brewing, it might be an in."

"I'll talk to him, but I'm not sure how Iris would feel about it . . ."

"Don't worry, she's so over him," Paige blurted then shrank, knowing she'd overshared.

The revelation hit Lincoln. What did that mean for him? The moment he'd found out that she left, he realized what a fucking fool he'd been. He certainly wasn't over Iris. She wasn't a woman he *could* get over. No, if he couldn't find a way to fix this mess, she'd be the one who got away. He grasped a slim strand of hope, and was prepared to drop to his knees, grovel if he had to, and beg her to come back.

Lincoln set the thought aside as they divvied up the work. Ruth agreed to buy fishbowls and put them in every business in town.

Maggie planned to design labels and took a sheet of paper from the notebook to sketch a few ideas. Taking out her phone, Paige went to work on social media, then paused, looking between them, "Wait . . . we need a tag line, a slogan that'll draw attention."

The room went silent. Maggie jotted a few ideas, scribbled, then tried again.

"I think I may have something." Lincoln said and scratched his head. "How about *Keep Northside Grill Greene*?"

Maggie nodded and Paige gave him a rare smile. Ruth wrote the slogan at the top of her page and underlined it twice. "Perfect."

They took their assignments and went separate ways. Lincoln left Goldfinch Bakery and headed directly to the taproom. He found Wade behind the bar with his sister, Linnea. When they heard the reason Northside Grill was on the market, they both pulled out their phones. In moments, the entire Michaels' family had pledged their support.

Lincoln shifted his focus from the cannabis shop to his mobile business. Before he knew it, he found himself towing a mobile restaurant behind a Mosquito Creek Brewing truck to a festival in Bend, Oregon. On the passenger seat, an open-top box held two round fishbowls with Keep Northside Grill Greene printed on the side.

***

"How was it? Did my dough turn out? Did I make enough for the event in Bend?" Maggie's excitement almost made up for Lincoln's complete exhaustion. After he stopped serving pizza on Sunday, he'd helped with cleanup then headed back to Ashwood, instead of staying an extra night with the rest of the Mosquito crew.

"It was perfect," he mumbled, trying not to yawn as she took the pans he'd borrowed for the festival. Aluminum clattered as she hopped, thrilled with her success.

Lincoln had given Maggie his recipe, and she prepped all the dough he needed ahead of the food and brew event. He threw them on site, offered three different combos, and found a whole new set of fans.

"I ran out early on the last day, but the customers drinking Wade's beer kept filling those fishbowls. How are the efforts going here?"

"Before your weekend's earnings we were over eight grand. That's the take so far from the taproom, the beauty parlor, and The Stop-n-Shop."

"Damn, this might actually work."

The bell over the entrance brought Lincoln and Maggie from the kitchen to the front of Goldfinch Bakery. They found Ruth flopped in a seat. "Good, you're both here. Julius Caesar Lincoln, we have a problem."

He winced, wishing Ruth didn't enjoy his entire name so much. "Is it Daryl again?"

"No. A fantastic offer came in on the Grill. It's so good, Iris would be foolish to pass it up."

"Shit."

"Does Iris know?" Maggie asked.

"Not yet. With this offer, she might take it without knowing about our project. But if I tell her and we don't succeed, she'll be crushed."

Lincoln hesitated. "Where is she?"

Maggie counted the days on her hand. "Wyoming or Nebraska. She took extra time in Yellowstone."

"Kansas tomorrow?" he asked.

"Yeah. And only a day to spare before her birthday."

Lincoln nodded. Of course, she'd want to spend that day with her twin brother, Ian. "We can't tell her about this over the phone." A long moment stretched as he stared out the window and swallowed hard. "I'll go."

Ruth's hand smacked the tabletop. "He's gonna go get his girl!"

Maggie sighed. "Thank God."

He looked between them. "You knew?"

"Everyone knows." Ruth rolled her eyes. "She loves you. I hope you love her." Ruth's eye's held, waiting for his answer.

His stomach tightened and he couldn't lie to himself or anyone else anymore. "Don't you think I should tell her first?" he asked.

"Great idea." Maggie nodded. "But to do that, you'll have to get on a plane."

***

A truck rumbling down the alley lifted Lincoln's eyelids thirty minutes ahead of his three forty-five alarm. Thoughts of Iris, more vivid than usual, lingered from a vivid dream. He stared at the ceiling, still tasting the memory of her on his lips. It was quiet, except for the truck—the comforting rumble of Zippo's snore wasn't there to soothe him. Maggie had kept the dog due to his flight to Kansas.

Feet on the floor, Lincoln stood, stretched, scratched his stomach, and was headed to the bathroom when the Cascade Cannabis front window disintegrated with a crash. The alarm system deployed, rattling his senses with bright lights and a deafening siren. Naked, he punched numbers into the keypad, fingers scrambling, getting the code right on the second try.

Silence created a vacuum, and Lincoln opened his jaw wide, popping his ears to drive out the ringing. After a glance at his bare feet, he ducked into his room and pulled on jeans and boots. Glass crunched as he made his way back into Cascade's showroom.

This wasn't a prank. Even from a distance, he could make out something on the softball-sized rock that lay on the floor, surrounded by a halo of glass. The rustic missile had a *Keep Northside Grill Greene* flyer trapped beneath a layer of clear mailing tape.

Flashing lights illuminated the street—pulsing red, blue, and fiery pink. Lincoln picked his way over the glass to open the front door, though he could have passed through the window since most of the glass was gone. The sheriff turned off the strobes when he spotted Lincoln at the door.

"Thanks for coming so fast," he said as Jerrod unfolded from his Ford.

"No problem. At least we know your expensive alarm system works." He readjusted his hat and stared at the gaping hole. "Damn." Inside, the sheriff took in the details from the perimeter of the room. "Did you touch the rock?" he asked.

"No. I was about to grab a flashlight to check the outside for damage."

"After I take a look around, I'll bag that rock for evidence and try to get some prints. Did you see anything?"

"No, but I bet my security cameras did." They exchanged smiles.

"Do you need help cleaning this up?" Jerrod asked.

"Actually, yes. I've got to leave for the airport. There's a sheet of plywood left over from the construction propped in the back. It should just cover that shattered window."

"How long will you be gone?"

"Don't know for sure . . ." Lincoln hesitated. "I'm going to see Iris, maybe patch things up." He knew it wouldn't be as easy as fixing this window—he'd done more damage to their relationship than the rock had done to the glass.

Jerrod gave him a nod, then they worked together, slapping plywood over the hole. Lincoln was handing over a jump drive with footage from his security system when Maggie popped by, curious.

She began her days early to serve warm baked goods by six a.m. Seeing her reminded him that he was already running late. After hearing what had happened, Maggie pulled him into a hug and wished him a safe trip. As Lincoln pulled away, he spotted Jerrod following the friendly redhead into Goldfinch Bakery.

***

Iris spotted the water tower ten miles from home. This one was different, modern. The tower she remembered—bulbous and perched on metal legs—had been swept away by the storm. Her favorite burger place was still there, with a brighter coat of paint and round tables outside. Of course, the video store was gone, and so was the florist, where her mom had worked part time until the storm swept both away.

Taking the turn off Main, she rolled past the First Baptist Church. The simple white steeple had towered over so many of her Sundays. A particular Friday would never leave her memory—the afternoon Cooper held her hand as she stared at her father's lifeless face one last time.

After that day, she and Cooper decided to relocate their wedding to the county park, under the big gazebo rather than hold the ceremony at the church. His mother had protested the change of plans until Iris broke down and cried. In the end, it hadn't mattered. Eventually, Cooper's mom got that church wedding for her son, when he walked down the aisle with Danielle.

She'd expected everything to look smaller, as childhood places withered with time, but the fields leading up to the farm where she grew up looked just as vast and completely unchanged. The land was the same, and so was the old barn. But the house was not. Cooper and Danielle had built a single-story ranch rather than a tall, gabled farmhouse. Painted a sandy gray, it blended with the land, hunkered low as if it was hiding from another tornado.

Iris came to a stop and Danielle ran out the front door. She'd just cleared the bike when her closest friend from high school trapped Iris in a hug. "You made it!"

"I did."

Danielle pulled away, gripped Iris' shoulders, and burst into tears. The sudden waterworks weren't a surprise—happy or sad, Dani always cried. As Iris realized how much she'd needed this, her tears fell, too—the trip, the hug, the journey, set everything right.

In the distance a plume of dust signaled Cooper's truck. Iris pulled away from Dani. "Does he already know I'm here?"

"I sent him a text as soon as you pulled up."

"Could we go inside? I'd like to take a moment. I've been on the road for a while."

"Of course, what was I thinking? Let's get you settled."

Iris followed her friend into a house she'd only seen in pictures. The place was homey and dotted with evidence of a full life. Kid's shoes by the front door, a science project spread out on the dining room table, and pictures of two boys and a little girl on the wall. She used the bathroom, washed dust from her face, and came out to find Cooper and Danielle in the kitchen.

He scooped her into a swinging hug and laughed. "I wondered if I'd ever see this day."

"So did I," she admitted.

All at once Iris longed for Lincoln, the man who'd given her this moment. Guilt stopped her fingers from reaching for her phone. She'd cut him out of her life, hidden this trip from him, and then expected him to reach out.

How many miles had she spent hoping to see his name on her missed call screen? Curious as hell, she let her stubborn side keep her from asking Maggie, Ruth, or Paige if Lincoln knew about her trip. One afternoon a storm rose ahead of her on the road. She'd stopped to watch it build, then wisely chose a different highway to avoid the deluge on her bike. But the reroute had nothing to do with fear and that fact needed to be celebrated. She had toasted the moment with a beer at her next stop, alone. The beer had gone flat while she battled with her pride, but she never found the strength to call Lincoln.

Then another day came and went, and she figured he had to know about her trip by now. Yet, why didn't he bother to call? Was he angry because she hadn't said goodbye? Maybe he'd already moved on. Understandable, even if it hurt. The miles on her bike gave her time to think. Time to discover her role in what had gone wrong.

He'd hurt her, yes. But had he really betrayed her? No. The food truck deal with Wade started when she and Lincoln were competitors and had little to do with her. His priorities had never wavered. Every choice he made put Russel first, and she admired that. No, what she felt went much deeper than admiration.

His flaw—he had too much pride to ask for her help. Pride. Iris struggled with that affliction. And even though she expected honesty, she never told him the truth—that she'd fallen deeply in love with him.

THIRTY

Lincoln's airplane bumped through a layer of clouds on its descent into Wichita. Because the only seats left on the plane were at the back, it took thirty minutes to disembark. He was tempted to hurdle over the seats just to get to Iris faster.

Shouldering his backpack, he followed rental car signs at a jog, gathering long glances from security as he passed. A short line drew him to a random counter where they assigned him a daily deal. He was out of the airport parking lot with Iris on his mind before he noticed the gutless engine in his stripped-down car.

Merging onto the freeway, the tin-can balked then limped to sixty. He didn't care how much the vehicle whined so long as it didn't give out before he made it to her hometown. He'd already programmed her childhood address into his phone—a precise location he'd researched and memorized following her disturbing reaction to the fireworks on election night.

Wichita looked nothing like cities in the west. Without the mountains to direct him, the empty horizon messed with Lincoln's internal compass. Headed south, he depended on the thin highway for his mental map.

He left the interstate forty-five miles outside of Wichita and discovered a vast space that reminded him of Iris. Lincoln found her expansive love as disorienting as this big sky—often bewildering, sometimes terrifying, but always wonderful.

Consumed by her mystery, he nearly missed the twenty-five mile per hour sign on the edge of her hometown. Another marker posted statistics—Oxdale, Kansas; Population: 1,013. His fingers drummed the steering wheel as he estimated the numbers—maybe three-hundred homes. Small enough for a tornado to lift from the map completely. But when that day came for this community, they didn't give up—they rebuilt.

The phone on the passenger seat told Lincoln to take the next right. His heart thumped against his ribs. *Not yet, not yet.* Reaching across, he silenced the electronic voice and drove farther into Iris' childhood streets. A four-way stop halted him at the town's center—a collection of flat-roofed buildings of brick and stone. Two banks, a barber shop, and a pharmacy occupied each corner. Alone at the intersection, Lincoln glanced both ways before he turned right, heading down a street lined with large magnolias.

His choice put him behind a yellow school bus. Each time it stopped, the lights flashed and a red sign extended from a long metal arm. Children leaped from the bottom step wearing bright backpacks, the youngest met by adults, who got a hug and held out a hand. Eager faces tipped up relaying details about their day at school. Lincoln envied those moments, missing them with his son, considering the possibility that he could have a shot at that joy again.

When the bus turned, he continued straight, until the road terminated at a wide field. Decision time. Right or left. He picked up his phone and located himself on the map. Iris was near and he was ready. Lincoln chose left.

The car jolted when the pavement ended, and the road's washboard texture forced him to a crawl. He bumped along until the road flattened over a slight rise in the grade. In the distance, Lincoln spotted a groomed clump of trees—an island of dense green in a predictable pattern of open fields.

About a hundred yards out he realized the wide branches shaded rows and rows of tombstones—some tall and narrow, others low and wide. The massive cemetery bore witness to how long this small Kansas town had survived.

A flash of metal turned Lincoln's head. Between pillars of granite, he spotted her Harley, the pearl tank and polished chrome.

Iris stood nearby. Her hair whipped in the breeze as she bent toward one of the larger stones. Such beautiful sorrow. He couldn't breathe.

His foot pressed the brake, then he glanced behind before sliding into reverse, backing the car until he met the cemetery gate. After pulling through the metal partition, he parked in a wide spot and killed the engine. Unfolding from the seat, the prairie air hit him—humid and thick, scented by moist earth and crisp sage. One hand pushed the door quietly shut, then he made his way to Iris.

He walked slow and quiet, measuring his steps, absorbing her details. Other than her hair in the breeze, she was perfectly still. As he closed in, she lifted her hand to brush a tear from her cheek. Then she bent to trace letters carved into stone.

Lincoln moved closer, looked past her shoulder, and stared. He expected to learn her father's name and read Ian Fraser Greene. The dates stood out, unexpected, far too young to belong to her dad.

This was her twin.

Ian and Iris shared a birthday. Seeing May 9, 1985 on a tombstone stuttered Lincoln's heart. He looked at the next set of numbers and learned that Ian had died at twenty-three.

"Lincoln." It took him a moment to lift his gaze from the smooth granite. He blinked, staring into emerald eyes glistened by tears. Without a word, he gave her his hand. She intertwined their fingers, lacing, so sweet.

Her inhale staggered. "I'd like you to meet my brother. Ian, this is Lincoln. He's . . . he's . . ." She tilted her head and let him define the breadth and width of their complicated relationship.

"I'm the man who's completely lost without your sister," he confessed.

Her hand trembled. Lincoln turned to Iris and encased her in his arms. Making herself small, she folded against his chest and dissolved into his solid strength. As he held her, he memorized the vivid details of her brother's grave. A band of ivy and five deep indigo flowers surrounded Ian's name. A pattern he'd seen before—inked permanently, marked into her skin.

Lincoln kissed her temple. "I'm sorry I took so long to get here."

"Somehow, I knew you'd come." Her arms wrapped around his waist, he kissed her head again and then eased away.

Her face tipped to his, brightened by the slightest smile. "If you're okay with this, there's one more person I'd like for you to meet."

"I'd be honored."

She led him past other markers, dates reaching back, all bearing the name Greene. Her history. Iris paused, released a slow breath then accepted his arm around her. "This is my dad."

"Hello, sir," Lincoln whispered.

Iris shrugged in his embrace. "I know they aren't really here . . . But until today, I'd never taken the time to say goodbye. I was here when we laid Dad to rest, but it was such a blur, I don't remember the details of that day. And when Ian passed, I bought a ticket, went to the airport, and tried to board the plane . . ." A sob shook her body. "But I couldn't do it. Mom had to bury him alone."

Lincoln held her tight. "Angel, I'm sorry."

Iris tilted her head until her forehead tapped his chest. "I don't think I'll ever forgive myself for failing her."

***

Iris lifted her eyes, blinking until she felt Lincoln's gaze. He smiled and she eased from his embrace, took his hand, and led him back to her bike. Inside the leather saddlebags she'd stowed two small flower arrangements, each wrapped in tissue paper. She peeled away the paper and cellophane, stuffed it in the saddlebag, then gave one arrangement to Lincoln. He cradled the yellow and orange flowers in the crook of his arm with care. Taking the other bouquet, she led him to her father's grave.

"Do you need time alone?" he asked as she knelt.

"No. This feels right. I wouldn't be here today if I hadn't met you."

With that, he knelt beside her, wet earth soaking the knees of his jeans. Iris closed her eyes then took Lincoln's hand. "Daddy. I'm sorry it took me so long to visit, but I knew you'd understand. I already talked to Ian. But just in case he's being his same stubborn self, tell him that I love him. Tell him that I don't blame him for leaving so suddenly the way he did. I had to leave, too. I guess the farm wasn't the same without you." Iris laid the flowers at the base of the stone. A light wind blew a few petals across the grass.

"Dad, I want you to know I'm happy." When she took Lincoln's hand, he made a low satisfied noise and she smiled. "I moved to this great little town. I bought a restaurant. Well, it's really a bar. Mom didn't like the idea at first, but once she saw it, she said it was nice. That restaurant has hit a rough patch and I'm going to sell it. But that's okay because I've got people in my life I can lean on. And I love it when they lean on me." Iris gave Lincoln a shoulder bump and he squeezed her hand.

She turned to find him watching. His steady gaze made her bold.

"I think I've found someone," she said as Lincoln held her eyes. "His name is Julius Caesar Lincoln." Saying his name spread mirrored smiles. "He's solid. A good man who cares about his friends. And he loves his son."

She found Lincoln's eyes, tears spilled, a rare moment she paused to take in. "Dad, I'll let you know how it goes. Give Ian a hug from me for his birthday. Love you, Dad. I miss you so much."

Iris listened to the breeze and the birds, trying to hear her father's voice, but he didn't answer. As the years passed, he murmured less and less, the rich baritone fading. Lincoln stood first and gave Iris his hand, pulling her up. Before she moved on, she bent to trace her father's name.

She'd already confessed everything to Ian—how sorry she was and how much this hurt. Iris bent at his grave, laid the flowers on the manicured grass, and let her fingers glide over the blue iris and green reeds which matched her tattoo. "I'll talk to you soon."

Ian always seemed to be with her. At times, she heard his voice like an echo. It resonated a little louder here, magnified by the people and the place. A low murmur approved of the man holding her as she strolled back to her motorcycle.

Iris scanned the cemetery but didn't find Lincoln's bike. "How did you get here?" She couldn't imagine missing the sound of the pipes.

"I flew into Wichita and grabbed a gutless rental." He tipped his head in the general direction of the front gate.

Her eyes landed on a silver compact and she laughed. "You chose that?"

"Nah, I think it chose me. I'm not a fan."

"Can you endure it for a few more miles? I'm staying at . . ." she almost said home then stopped herself. Even though the house was gone, she still thought of the place that way. "Danielle and Cooper's. I've actually got something I'd like to show you."

He nodded, opened his mouth, then hesitated. Iris sensed a weight resting on his mind, but he didn't seem ready to talk. She silently prayed, *Please, God, not more bad news.*

Lincoln took hold and held her flush. The kiss he planted without warning made her gasp and pulled his essence into her mouth. He deepened that kiss with the taste of questions and promises. Just as she melted, he let her go.

Stroking a thumb over her lower lip, he said, "Lead the way, I'll follow."

***

Lincoln shadowed the dusty plume that trailed her bike over the gravel road. He searched his mind for details of every conversation they'd had about her brother. Never once had she hinted that Ian lived only in her past. Yet, she never referred to him in the present, either. Perhaps Ian had been stuck in a half-way place until Iris could find a way to say goodbye.

In a small way he understood. He had no memories of his mother, but somehow, she still existed on a different plane. She'd become a collection of wishes and dreams, fashioned to describe a woman he'd never know, a stranger who blessed him with one hell of a name.

Iris slowed and took a turn onto a narrow road that separated one identical field from another. The pungent scent flowing in Lincoln's window strengthened, then they passed a few dozen cows loitering near a barbed wire fence. As they pulled up to the farm, a red barn crowded the horizon, casting a shaded rectangle toward a low, modern house. Iris parked in that patch of shade, lifted from her bike, removed her helmet, and waited for Lincoln to join her. Other than the buzz of insects, the farm was quiet.

"What do you think?" she asked as he met her.

"Is this where you grew up?"

"Yeah. The barn is the same, but not the house." With a tilt of her head, she looked beyond him. "My two story house was white with black trim." She pointed to something that wasn't there, but the light in her eyes remembered. "And my bedroom window faced this big red barn."

He nodded. "I can imagine you here in pigtails, playing hide-and-go-seek."

Iris laughed, her eyes flicked across the land, seeming to retrace happy memories. He reached for her, wanting a physical connection and she laced their fingers. "Come on." A tug got him moving, then Iris pulled him to a jog toward the barn.

Going from bright to dark disoriented Lincoln for a moment. He trusted her senses until his eyes adapted. Golden dust motes floated in thin shafts of sunlight that sliced in between shrunken boards. After his eyes adjusted, he spotted a row of stalls along one side, and ahead of him, a solid wall which supported a sturdy wooden ladder leading up to a loft.

To the right of the rungs, a wide door, secured by a handmade latch concealed a closed-off storage area below the loft. Iris pulled him to it, then released his fingers to lift the primitive handle. The door creaked open and she led him through while searching the air with her touch. She found what she was looking for and yanked a long string. A bare bulb suddenly lit the room.

"Ta da!" Iris giggled.

Lincoln staggered and blinked. An early Triumph Bonneville sparkled in the yellow light. "Fuck me."

Iris bumped him with her hip. "We can get to that later."

His eyes swung to hers and she blushed. Hope and plans merged but couldn't distract him from the sexy-as-shit bike. "Is this Cooper's?" he asked, trying not to hate the guy.

"Um . . . no. It was Ian's. So, I guess, it's mine now. Cooper rides it from time to time, and Dani's *not* thrilled. She's hoping I'll find a way to get it home."

"Find a way to get it home?" he repeated, but his words begged, *Pick me, pick me.*

"Could I talk you into helping me with that?" she teased.

"Angel, right now, you could talk me into anything."

Iris pulled him toward the machine, but keen need took over. He wanted her. But until a moment ago, he wasn't sure they were on the same page. When she gave his arm another tug, he planted his feet and used her built-up momentum to spring Iris into his arms. With an oomph, she crashed against his chest.

Earlier his kisses had been tentative, but this was desperate. Stored passion clutched her body to his as his lips captured her breath. Securing her torso, Lincoln devoured, taking everything she was willing to give.

Iris buried her fingers in his hair and pulled with exquisite force. As she wriggled, Lincoln grasped the back of her thigh and lifted her leg, opening her hips to imprint the evidence of his desire. She gasped when his cock raked over her center. In response, she writhed and teased. Frantic hands dipped from her waist to her ass—trembling, wanting—yet the grip stalled.

This wasn't the place to stake a claim on her future. They'd chased reckless passion before, and that lust burned hot and dangerous. If he wanted forever with Iris, he'd have to nurture a slower burn.

His kisses calmed. He released his hold and settled her feet onto the floor. Palms cradled her face and he controlled the descent of his passion, each touch of his lips promising more.

"I missed you," she whispered against his mouth.

"I know." He couldn't say more. If he began, his words wouldn't stop until he said, *I love you.* Before that revelation, she deserved the details and the chance to make her own decisions.

A diesel truck rumbled to a stop and the faint smell of oily exhaust seeped between the barn's ancient boards. Iris stepped away, smoothed her blouse and then her hair, but remained close enough for Lincoln to sense her tempting heat.

Footsteps approached the barn. "Hey, Iris, are you in here?"

"Yeah." Her words came out breathy. She reached for Lincoln's hand and held on.

Drawn by the incandescent light bulb, boots approached until a guy who could have answered a John Wayne casting call stepped through the door. "I saw that car outside. You must be Lincoln," he said.

Releasing Iris, he extended a hand. Cooper took it and sent a message with a painful squeeze—*Don't hurt her, or I'll hunt you down.*

"And you must be Cooper." Lincoln tipped a nod. *Message received.* Dropping the hand, he took a step back, then Iris leaned into his side.

Heavy boots stirred dust as Cooper widened his stance. "Welcome to Kansas."

Was he really all that welcome? "Thanks."

"It took you long enough to get here."

Iris screeched, "Coop, would you shut up?"

Cooper tipped a smile. "What?"

Lincoln snaked an arm around her. Gears of understanding aligned—she had wanted him here all along.

"When did you get here?" Steel eyes assessed him then glanced at the bike.

"This morning."

Iris turned. "Did Maggie tell you where to find me?"

Lincoln shook his head. "No. I just knew."

That seemed to satisfy Cooper and he laughed. "Come in the house. I'm starved. Dani and the kids will be home soon. Let's grab something to eat before they inhale everything in the kitchen."

As they followed Cooper out, Iris reached over her head for the string attached to the light bulb. She snagged the thin white cable, and Lincoln blinked as the vintage Triumph vanished like a dream in the dark.

THRITY-ONE

A dark blue minivan filled with three kids, their mom, and nine bags of groceries pulled up. Everyone poured into the house, tripling the volume. After quick introductions, Danielle brought Lincoln a beer and disappeared with Iris.

Laughter bubbled from the kitchen, tempting Lincoln more than the baseball game on the TV. Turning, he discovered Cooper's scrutiny. His fingers twitched, wanting a cigarette, but he'd abandoned his smoking vice at home.

Lincoln scrubbed his hands across his jeans. "I'm gonna grab another beer. You want anything?"

"Sure." Cooper followed. "I'll find us some chips. Dinner will be awhile."

Iris had her back to him, washing lettuce in the sink. Her shoulders shifted when he walked over and stole a slice of yellow bell pepper. The vegetable crunched, then he swallowed, leaned, and whispered, "Delicious."

As she turned, her jade eyes sparkled, knowing the compliment was for her, not the food. She gave him a quick kiss. "You're in luck. Dani's putting together her famous lasagna."

Fresh ingredients spread across the counter. Besides the usual meat and cheese, she had eggplant, mushroom, and spinach ready. "Looks awesome. I may steal the eggplant idea for a vegetarian pizza."

Danielle grinned. "I remember the first time Iris told me about *you* and *your pizza*."

"Really?" He settled a hip against the counter, ready for this. "When was that?"

Iris' eyes targeted Dani, yelling *Shut up* without a single word.

237

Grinning wider, Dani looked at the ceiling and tapped her chin. "Well, let me think. As I recall, she called me to complain about a big sign you'd put up on your building. And when I asked if she'd tried your pizza she just moaned."

"Moaned?" He laughed.

"Stop!" Iris launched a slice of pepper missing Dani's nose by a few inches.

"What? I'm only telling the truth."

Lincoln bent to kiss Iris on the cheek and gloated, "I can't help it if I'm irresistible." At least he'd learned they were even. Iris had floored him from the moment they'd met.

She placed her lips next to his ear and whispered, "Honey, it's all about the *sauce*."

His jeans tightened and the kitchen heated, Lincoln inched toward the refrigerator looking for a drink to cool off.

Cooper's scowl deepened. He opened the refrigerator and handed over a beer. Lincoln grabbed the longneck, thanking his host with a nod. It gave him something to hold when he'd rather have his hands wrapped around Iris.

With a beer in one hand and chips in the other, Cooper headed for the kitchen doorway, then paused at the threshold. Lincoln took the hint and followed. The kids had taken over the living room, dumping a mountain of Legos all over the floor. The youngest looked up and asked, "Daddy, do you want to help?"

"In a bit, sweetie. Lincoln and I were about to take a walk."

Great. Time for the inquisition.

Cooper tossed the chips on the coffee table on his way to the front door. Lincoln took a deep breath and followed, ready to let the man have his say. They walked away from the house, down the gravel lane, under a massive sky he'd never get used to. A thick line of clouds on the southern horizon hinted nasty weather from the south. The potential storm heightened his concern.

He was studying the looming cloud formation when Cooper blurted, "What are your plans with Iris?"

The blunt question stopped Lincoln's feet. He thought for a moment and answered, "To make sure she's happy."

"Happy? So far, I've gotta say, I'm not impressed."

She'd talked to her friends about him. Usually, he didn't give a rat's ass what anyone thought, but Cooper seemed to speak for all the men in Iris' past who weren't around to see to her future. He respected that and nodded. "I've messed up and Iris knows that, but I'm beginning to hope she's willing to try again. If she does, I'm not wasting that second chance."

Cooper hooked his hand over the back of his neck and kneaded. "She's had enough heartache for two lifetimes." The way his boot kicked the ground acknowledged his role in a portion of that pain.

"She hides it too well." Lincoln's voice lowered. "I didn't know about Ian."

"That doesn't surprise me."

"What was her brother like?" He had to know but wasn't ready to ask Iris questions he knew would hurt.

"Ian . . ." Cooper smiled and gazed into the endless horizon. "His presence was big. The energy that drove him was even bigger. This town was too small to contain him. Even if he wasn't bound for a major league team, he'd never have stayed, not here, not on this farm."

"Was he really that good?"

"Without question. There was an intensity, coupled with raw talent. Ian could have gone directly into the minors. He had offers but wanted a degree. So, he went that route instead. I think he was looking long-term. Management, shit, with his drive, he might have owned a team someday."

Lincoln laughed. He'd underestimated Iris. If this was the twin she'd fought with and won, his woman was fiercer than he'd imagined. "And Ian never wanted this place?" Lincoln asked, scanning the land, the expanse of it, knowing everything he saw should have belonged to Iris.

Cooper squeezed his forehead, pulled his rough hand across his features, then stared far over the horizon. "Iris and I, we made sense . . ." He coughed and took a breath. "Everyone knew this place would eventually be ours someday. That went from the future to reality when her dad passed. When the storm hit, we were engaged—she had a ring, we'd already picked the date, but the invitations hadn't gone out. She wanted a fall wedding, something about the colors. Anyway, the storm hit, her dad died a couple of weeks later, and her mom didn't have it in her to stay. She moved to Texas when my family bought this place, but essentially it was ours—Iris' and mine. We set her third of the sale aside to build our home after she recovered."

"How bad were her injuries?" Lincoln asked.

"It wasn't the broken arm or the stitches. It was here." Cooper spread his hand over his chest. "And here." He tapped his forehead. "Her strength crumbled after her dad died. Then her brother left, running from his guilt and joining the army. Iris postponed the wedding and managed to get by for a few months. She made it through winter, but then the early spring thunderstorms rolled in, and I didn't know how to help her, couldn't convince her to stay. When a tornado outbreak hit Oklahoma, she packed her things, and by Easter she'd moved away."

The pain in Cooper's voice echoed from the past—a wound healed by time, new love, success, and family. But the scars left something behind, a heightened awareness that everything he love could be stripped away in a moment.

Lincoln turned in a slow circle, surveying everything she'd given up. "I can't imagine letting it go."

When he finished his circuit, his eyes landed on Cooper. Iris had lost her future with this guy too—like a child holding tight to the strings of a hundred balloons, she'd opened her fingers and let everything bright in her life drift away on the breeze. How could anything or anyone ever replace that? An overwhelming weight threatened. All at once, he felt inadequate, unworthy, imperfect.

A heavy step brought Cooper into Lincoln's hazy line of sight; his vision obscured by a wash of rare tears. "Thank you for bringing Iris back to us," Cooper said, slicing into the bleak moment, cutting away a thin layer of Lincoln's uncertainty.

"I didn't do a thing." He squeezed his eyes shut and shook his head.

"Don't bother denying it, Lincoln. She's different with you—open, vulnerable, unguarded. Iris needed all of that to return to herself. I've never seen her like this with anyone, not even me."

Hope pushed against Lincoln's ribcage, but fear pressed back. "She's facing changes in Ashwood and may choose to move again, but I'll be there for her for as long as she'll have me."

Cooper's eyes bored in. "Take care of her."

"I will." A slow breath escaped as he grappled with contradictions. He wanted the best for Iris, but still wasn't convinced he was that man. They stood in silence for a long moment until the wind picked up, spiraling dust from the fields. Cooper turned toward the house. "Looks like we're not gonna dodge that storm."

"Need some help?"

"Sure. Follow me to the barn."

***

Iris pushed back from the table, thanking the lycra-gods for stretchy jeans. She pretended not to notice when Dani and the kids crept into the kitchen. Cooper stretched across the table and topped off four glasses of wine. An off-key version of the birthday song burst in with the kids, Dani, and a cake blazing with thirty-four candles. Blue wax melted into the frosting and Iris pressed her hands over embarrassed cheeks.

Lincoln's low bass finished the song, then he said, "Make a wish, Angel."

One wish. How could she choose only one? To get Northside Grill back. To find a way to stay in Ashwood. To have another chance with Lincoln. She simply couldn't pick one fantasy. Smiling, she hoped for it all and blew out the candles. While everyone clapped, Iris found her lips covered with Lincoln's quick kiss. Cooper whistled, and Jacob mumbled, "Yuck."

The kiss heated more than her face. When her gaze hit Cooper, his laugh boomed with genuine joy. Something had changed—her oldest friend had accepted Lincoln. Iris had another reason to celebrate and blurted, "I better cut this cake!" Taking up the knife, she started the destruction.

"Let me get the ice cream." Dani dashed away and returned with a stack of decorated paper plates and vanilla ice cream. Iris sliced through blue flowers and white frosting, revealing rich chocolate layered with raspberry. She wondered if the same woman still baked all the desserts for the local market. Years ago, two names would have covered the cake—Happy Birthday Ian and Iris. His name always came first. Perhaps because he was a few minutes older, or more likely, because he'd made a bigger impact.

As Iris plated each slice, she wondered where Ian would be now, if he was alive to celebrate the day. Lincoln seemed to notice the slight curve of her spine as she contained the thought. He slid his hand over her shoulder and gave her a reassuring squeeze. She returned a smile and a silent thank you. They finished dessert at a table loaded with the remnants of a perfect night.

Even though it was her birthday, Iris kicked Dani and Coop out of the kitchen and took over the clean-up duties. They fought her until the kids admitted they had homework and needed help. Lincoln scraped plates, and they savored their first quiet moment together since this afternoon in the barn. When her apron came loose, he retied the strings and whispered in her ear, "I'm so glad I could be here. But I bought my ticket so quickly, I didn't have time to buy you a present."

"Bought your ticket quickly? Why?" All at once, she felt foolish. Lincoln hadn't rushed here for her birthday; no, something bigger had propelled him to Kansas. Disappointment shifted her features and he went blurry as her eyes swam.

"Angel, there's no reason to cry."

His soft kiss attempted to erase her fear, but she couldn't contain it. "What's happened now?"

"Come here." Lincoln wrapped her in one arm while the other shut off the water filling the sink.

His hand at her spine coaxed her to the mudroom where he lifted her to the dryer and nestled between her knees. "Listen. I've got great news. But even if I didn't, I'd still be here. I'm exactly where I want to be."

"With me?"

"Angel, it will always be you."

Lincoln held her eyes until she accepted, nodded, and inhaled a steadying breath. He placed one hand on each thigh, nerves concealed beneath a smile. "You have two options for The Grill."

She closed her eyes then slid them open slowly, shifting her vacation brain to business. "Okay. I'm ready."

"You have an all-cash offer and it's amazing. Someone from California is looking for an opportunity in Washington."

"How much?" She held her breath.

"Five hundred and sixty-five thousand."

She choked on a number that made her light-headed. "That's more than asking price." She'd have enough to pay off Dale, Ruth, the line of credit, and still have plenty left over to start something new.

"I know. He doesn't want a bidding war with the others who are taking an interest."

Her voice went up an octave as a smile stretched across her face. "There are others? Has he seen the place?"

"Yeah. Twice."

"Hot damn." Iris knew she should secure that offer, but as she thought about it, her joy began to fade. "And the other option?"

"Much more risky." Lincoln squeezed her thighs. "But if I remember right, my girl likes to take risks. So the question is, do you trust me?"

She shook her head no, but said, "Yes," with a teasing grin.

He covered her giggle with a quick kiss. "Good, because I'm counting on everyone in Ashwood to come through."

Iris scrunched her nose. "What are you talking about?"

"Paige, Maggie, Ruth, and I came up with a plan, and it's caught on all over town." His nerves bled through a tight chuckle. "You know that fishbowl you collect change in?"

"The one for the busted jukebox."

"That's the one. Ruth bought a bunch of them, Maggie made labels, and everyone's tossing donations into the *Keep Northside Grill Greene* fund."

"As in my last name?"

He chuckled and grinned. "Catchy, right?"

"Lincoln, a few collection-plates at the grocery store won't save my business." Disappointment caved her hopes and her body shrank.

"To be honest, I thought it was a long shot at first. But then Wade put one at the taproom, and the Rafting Outfitters south of town added a bowl. There's one at the school, the salon, the llama

Farm, and when I made a run to Hood River, I saw your fishbowl at the grocery outlet checkout counter, too."

"In Hood River? That's over thirty miles away. That doesn't make sense."

"Yeah, I asked the guy about it. I guess he stops in at Northside Grill when he's cross-country skiing. He loves it and wants it to stay exactly the way it is."

"How did he find out?"

"I don't have the first damn clue."

Shock stole her ability to speak and Lincoln slid his hands up her arms, grasping her shoulders. "I won't blame you if you take the sure bet. It's a shit-ton of money, and at last count, we were only halfway to collecting what you owe Nash. But either decision is covered because the flyers have a disclaimer. If we don't meet our goal, we give the funds to the food bank."

His dark eyes held her gaze. "The food bank needs that money more than I do," she admitted softly.

"Maybe. But I think Ashwood needs Iris Camellia Greene more." Her smile spread as she considered her options and his grin reflected hers. "Do it, babe. Take another risk." When she hesitated, he added, "Angel, you already gambled big on me."

Iris didn't deliberate long. Northside Grill was more than an investment—it was her second home. "I hope this gamble pays off faster than we did," she said.

"Then you'll do it?"

"I guess . . . if you think I have a shot." He didn't give her an answer, instead he devoured her buoyant laughter with a kiss. A tilt of his head took the contact deeper, rasping the tender skin around her mouth with his goatee. Iris wrapped both arms around his neck, not caring if his passion left marks.

As he eased away, regret rumbled. "I guess we still need to deal with that mess in the sink." He touched his forehead to hers. "Baby, you have no idea how much I've missed you."

Iris did know—she'd ached for him and held tight to the last spark of hope. It warmed her again, radiating from his inked skin and the depths of his eyes. Lincoln might be ready for complicated.

They barely talked as they rinsed dishes and loaded the dishwasher, but their bodies nudged often. Before they left the privacy of the kitchen, Iris grabbed his belt loops, pulling him close. "Dani asked me if she needed to make up a bed for you on the couch."

He lifted his eyebrows. "And?"

"I told her you were with me. I hope that's okay."

"More than okay," he whispered against her mouth, sweeping his tongue over the seam.

She hummed. "Just so you know, the boys share a wall with our bedroom."

His brows crinkled. "Hmm. That's unfortunate."

She squeezed his butt with both hands. "If you can't handle it, the couch is still available." Lifted brows dared him to accept the sleeping arrangements.

"You dish it, I'll take it." He kissed her neck and came away eyes glittering with sinful intent. "How many days until I have you to myself?"

After biting her lip, Iris set her idea free. "Are you willing to extend your vacation for a long ride home on my brother's bike?"

He nodded. "Absolutely."

Iris kissed him again. "Then I think we should head to Wichita tomorrow and return that gutless rental car."

"And take the Triumph for a test run?"

"You didn't plan for a road trip. Let's pick up a few supplies."

"Babe, you're on."

"If the weather looks good, we could plan to leave the next day."

Lincoln mirrored her excitement and squeezed her waist. "Perfect. Two nights here. I think I can handle that."

She squirmed against him, making the challenge—and Lincoln—harder.

Dark eyes took control and he whispered, each word almost a growl, "Two days might be too long. Wasn't there a hayloft in that barn? I'll just chase you up that ladder and live out a fantasy."

Iris stared, wide-eyed, as his words took shape in her mind. Her hayloft thoughts evaporated when the kids stormed into the kitchen, and Jacob yelled, "Hurry, Iris. Our homework's done. We want to play Settlers of Catan!"

Tugged into the living room, she took a spot near the coffee table. Lincoln hung back, his eyes on the board game—the same game he and Russel had brought home from the Stop-n-Shop.

Jaw tight, his eyes skated to hers. "I need to make a call."

She nodded and he headed for the front door.

"Hun?"

Her word turned his head. "Yeah?"

"When you talk to Russ, see if he'd like us to visit on our way through."

His eyes glimmered as he grinned, dipped his chin, and ducked outside.

THIRTY-TWO

The guest room door snicked shut. Iris spun and found a sexy grin on his lips, but he didn't speak. Her cheeks heated as his eyes scanned the double bed. Damn, this night, trapped in that tiny bed with him was going to kill her.

An involuntary sigh hissed from her lips as his shirt disappeared, baring muscled symmetry and beautiful ink. Closing in, she gently traced the intricate lines with her fingertips. Neck bent, Lincoln watched her hand move, but those inquisitive fingers halted when he released his jean's top button. Iris swallowed hard, remembering he went commando, and just how impressive that was.

He reached up and covered her trembling hand with his. "Breathe, baby."

Air whooshed out, her gaze traveled, and he said, "You keep looking at me like that, and I'm gonna drag you into the hayloft tonight."

"Oh." She blinked, gave him a sweet smile, then struggled to find a safe topic. "What did Russel say?"

His son's name put a smile on his face, and Lincoln placed a chaste kiss on her forehead. "He was really excited when he heard we were coming." Releasing her, he stepped back and toed out of his boots. "But Russ wanted to know why we weren't bringing Zippo. It won't be long before that mutt will need to get used to the bike."

"What?" Her eyes scrunched, confused.

"Remember that day when you saw me at the Harley dealership?"

"Yeah."

"I was there hunting for a sidecar, and I talked to a custom shop in Seattle. I'll have a sidecar ready not too long after we get back."

248

"That's amazing. And the sight will turn heads in Ashwood."

"Maybe I'll put a logo on the side." He stretched his hands in the air. "Cascade Cannabis."

"Or Lincoln's Pizza," she added with a nod.

The talk of his business sent his gaze to her feet. "I forgot to tell you something earlier . . ." His eyes lifted. "To raise funds for *Keep Northside Grill Greene*, I traveled with Mosquito Creek Brewing to a festival. Took the food truck."

"For me?"

"Yeah."

"Thank you." She tried to sound cheerful, but the fact that he'd officially opened still hurt.

"I shouldn't have made that deal with Wade," he said, taking her hands in his.

"It's fine."

"No, it's not. But I can't undo it, at least not for a while. And shit, the entire weekend trapped in that sweatbox . . .It sucked."

She chuckled. "That wasn't supposed to make me happy, was it?"

He snaked his arm around her waist and attacked her neck with his kisses and his beard. "So, you'd like me to suffer?"

She held up her thumb and index finger separated by an inch. "Maybe just a little."

His whiskers tickled, and Iris clasped her hand over her mouth, smothering the squeals she was afraid would wake the boys in the next room.

A suck on a tender spot coaxed heat. "I give, I give," she moaned through clenched fingers. Once she could breathe again, her mind raced with questions. "Wait a second, without a proper kitchen, how did you prep for the festival?"

"Maggie worked up the crust ahead of time, and I took care of everything else in that sweltering sardine can."

Her eyes widened. "*No way*. Did you reveal your crust recipe to Maggie?"

A smirk worked his lips and he nodded, a slow, deliberate tease.

"Why do I feel like you cheated on me? I've wanted that crust recipe almost as much as your secret sauce."

His grin took a devilish slant. "You can have that right now, if you're willing to follow me to the loft."

Heat pulsed between her legs and she threaded her fingers into his hair, drawing him in. His lips coaxed surrender matched by the rhythm of his hips. A low satisfied hum rumbled in his chest and her body melted.

"Want you," he whispered and her hips pivoted.

She froze when shuffling footsteps passed by in the hallway. The barely audible click of a bedroom door, opening and shutting, gave away movements. Danielle and Cooper were checking on their kids. Iris inched away, licked her lips, and found his eyes watching her carefully.

Lincoln inhaled and closed his eyes. "Maybe you should get ready for bed."

She smoothed her rumpled clothes, then turned to search through her duffel for something to wear to bed. Quietly, her bare feet rushed to the bathroom to do her thing. Needing a thin layer of armor, she left on her panties and slipped into a cotton tank top and matching sleep shorts.

After they traded places, she plumped the pillow and crawled onto her side of the bed. When Lincoln returned, he clicked off the light, and the room went dark. Her eyes didn't adjust right away, but a zip and rustling fabric let her mind wander. Lincoln climbed in, snagged her with one arm and pulled her flush. She wiggled her bottom. He growled and she smiled—her rock-hard man still slept naked.

***

A low rumble woke him. Then a flash widened Lincoln's eyes. "Iris." His fingers hit warm sheets, but not his woman. The next roll of thunder moved him to his feet. He pulled on his jeans and padded down the hall toward the living room. The lights were off, but the outdoors blew in, bringing an earthy scent into the kitchen. Iris stood on the other side of the screen door watching the storm. Another flash illuminated her outline in the dark.

The hinges squeaked as he slipped through. "Babe, are you okay?"

"Yeah, I'm good. Really good."

Her eyes stayed on the sky as he wrapped his arms around her. A closer bolt streaked cloud to cloud, illuminating the breadth of the storm. Thunder rolled and she shivered but she held her shoulders taut. "I'm so glad this happened tonight," she said, her voice steady.

Amazed by the transformation, Lincoln squeezed her hip and wondered, *Why?*

As if she'd heard his silent question she added, "I wanted to replace that awful memory with something good. I needed a storm, but it had to happen here. It's not as wicked as the one that flattened my house, but this will do." Drops of heavy rain descended in a rapid sheet. The air chilled, wind swirled, and she nestled into his warmth. Her body relaxed, fear gone, completely beautiful.

***

Morning light slanted through the window. The Triumph revved three times, a loud and effective alarm clock. She rolled, her head on his pillow taking in his scent. It was missing something—the rich tobacco.

After a quick shower, Iris found Danielle in the kitchen. "Want a warm-up?" she asked from the coffee pot.

Dani looked up from her laptop, eyes glazed. "Sure. Anything to distract me from these blasted books." Iris remembered her mother doing the same thing, handling the farm's expenses. Those spreadsheets had her missing Northside Grill. Now that she had a chance to keep it, she was anxious to get home.

When the engine revved again, Dani cornered Iris with a knowing look. "So, Lincoln's hot, but he's not exactly what I had expected."

She'd always been attracted to safe and predictable. "Unexpected, but kind of perfect." Iris wrapped her hands around her coffee mug. "I still can't believe he showed up here."

Dani lifted an eyebrow. "I told you so, feels so good sometimes."

"How did you know?"

"When you said you were coming to Kansas, I knew something *big* had happened. That man tinkering with your brother's bike was the only explanation. A guy who helped you get over all that stuff wouldn't leave you to deal with your difficult family reunion on your own."

Iris swallowed. "Well, he knew about the tornado and my dad, but I never told Lincoln about Ian. Nobody in Ashwood heard that part. I guess I couldn't face it myself."

"Wow. I'm sorry." Dani shook her head, "But somehow that makes his visit even more . . . special."

"No one has ever dropped everything to be with me before."

Danielle gave her a watery smile. "It's about time someone did. Now I almost feel guilty. Cooper should have been there for you when you needed him most."

"Dani, don't. You know that's not what I meant. When I see what the two of you have built, I'm glad it was you and not me."

Nervous laughter bubbled from her friend. "Thanks, I guess. I'd be lost without Cooper and our kids. But what you went through. . ."

With a sweep of her hand Iris tried to erase the sorrow. "Let's not go there. Not on my last day." The motor outside rumbled again, and Iris turned toward the perfectly-timed sound.

"Thanks for taking the bike." Dani worried her lip. "Cooper's getting that restless look again. Last time his eye got that gleam, he bought a fishing boat. I think I better suggest a Caribbean cruise before it's too late."

"Good plan." Iris nodded but couldn't relate. In her case, the motorcycle wasn't dangerous. No, the machine unleashed powerful magic and granted freedom.

"Will you be back tonight in time to catch Jacob's baseball game?" Danielle asked.

"Probably not. After dropping off Lincoln's rental we've got to shop for some gear. When he bought his ticket, he wasn't planning to ride Ian's bike home."

Dani nodded. "That's too bad. I guess we'll see you both for dinner."

"Hey. It's not fancy, but could I treat us all to a night out at Buddy's?" Iris wanted to finish her trip at their old hang out.

"Yeah. That sounds great. I'll need a beer or two after this." Dani's eyes flicked back to the screen and she scowled.

"I'll let you get to it." Iris rose, refilled her coffee, and poured a cup for Lincoln. The screen door creaked when she pushed outside into the cool morning air. Dark eyes met hers then landed on the cup, steamy furls containing hot caffeine.

Lincoln straightened, wiped his hands on a rag, and accepted the mug. "Thanks, babe."

"How's the bike look?" she asked as she circled the machine.

"Great. I cleaned a little corrosion from the points and changed the oil, but it's obvious that Cooper's been keeping it up. He must be riding some."

"Yeah. I think that's why Dani wants it gone. She won't go with him because of the kids."

He acknowledged the danger involved with a quick nod. "Tread looks good, so do the brakes. I want to get it on the road." As he took a sip, he watched her with eyes as dark and smooth as his coffee.

THIRTY-THREE

The bike handled beautifully, not like her Harley—the Triumph had a gritty feel all its own. Her brother's voice hummed a little louder on the ride to Wichita, blending with the sound bouncing from the pavement.

You know, I really hadn't planned to give you this bike.

"Well thank you, anyway, bro. Where did you find this gem?" Iris asked as the engine propelled her. She gave Ian time to answer and let her mind search. Maybe he'd bought it off a friend on-base. Maybe he found it in London while on leave. Details from the last years of Ian's life were as tangible as the wind blowing across the plains—real, yet unseen.

His voice murmured regrets she'd heard before. *I'm sorry I wasn't there to dig you out of our wrecked house. I should have spent more time with you at the hospital.*

"That's okay. You had to get back to school."

Dad needed my help on the farm. If I hadn't been playing ball for Missouri, he'd still be—

"Hey, don't do this. The coach put pressure on you." She'd dealt with her anger this way, letting Ian's voice say all the things she wanted to hear. Eventually she'd offered him an apology, too.

Hours after their father's funeral, Ian went to the army recruiting office instead of back to school. He was at boot camp a few weeks later, then training somewhere in Georgia. The army eventually sent him to Germany where he handled logistics, not a rifle. Iris relaxed when he got that assignment, but anger kept her from picking up the phone. She figured she had time. It turned out, she didn't.

A gun didn't kill Ian . . . a knife did.

It was a random attack at a train station. They took his wallet and his life. Iris had been pulling a late shift at Northside Grill when her mom called with the horrifying news. She'd never forget the sound of her mother's voice, stripped of all emotion. *"Ian . . . He's gone."*

"I tried to get to your funeral. Hell, I even bought a plane ticket," Iris confessed.

I know. It's okay. I saw what you went through.

"I felt awful. Mom handled everything alone. But when I got to the airport, the roar of airplanes taking off scared me senseless. I was crouched in a goddamned bathroom stall when they made the last call for my flight."

Mom wasn't alone.

"I know. The rest of our family was with her."

Dad and I were there, too.

She blinked hard behind the visor of her motorcycle helmet, praying this was true.

She'd contributed what she could, from a safe distance.

Half the nation separated her from his memorial, but Iris put all her sorrow into the design of Ian's headstone, then had the same image inked onto her skin. The small personal tribute hadn't been quite enough until she stood over his grave and said goodbye.

The leading edge of Wichita came into view.

So, how do you like the bike? The voice in her head asked.

"I love it. This Triumph is the bomb."

Are you really gonna let this Lincoln guy ride it home?

"That's the plan."

I'm not sure I trust him with it or with you.

"Get used to it, I love him."

The traffic increased, and she had to pay attention. She barely heard her brother's voice over the sound of a nearby semi.

Will you at least take it slow?

With a quick glance in her side mirror, she spotted Lincoln hanging back several car lengths. The view gave comfort. "Yeah. I'll take it slow. I promise. Tell Dad I said hi."

Bye, sis. I love you.

"Love you, too." They never said that while growing up, not once. If only she could rewind time and undo all the little mistakes.

Traffic near the airport silenced the conversation. Lincoln pulled ahead of her at a light. By the time she parked in front of the rental office, she'd forced her thoughts in a different direction. Still, she was thankful when he jogged inside. It gave her a moment to peel away her helmet and wipe a few stray tears from her cheek.

She was smiling when Lincoln pushed through the door and approached her at the curb. To make him worry, she kept her butt planted on the Triumph's leather saddle.

He cocked an eyebrow, folded his arms across his chest, and leaned back on his heels. The man clearly didn't intend to climb onto this bike behind her. He smiled *after* she released the grips and lifted her ass from the seat.

As much as Iris enjoyed the feel of controlling her brother's vintage Triumph, she loved the way her body molded to Lincoln even more. After picking up supplies for the trip, he chose a less traveled route back to the farm.

Iris clung to his torso, trusting him as the road dipped and curved. Cottonwood growing in dense clumps near a shallow stream sheltered the pavement and damp air swept a chill beneath her leather jacket, penetrating her jeans. She shivered until the road took them into the heat again.

The sun stayed on her back the whole way to the barn. He stopped the bike; the farm was quiet because Jacob's baseball game had just started. As much as she wanted to see him pitch, she couldn't force herself on that field again. Ian's presence would just be too strong.

A soft tug on his hand was all it took. Lincoln's grin widened as Iris pulled him a few steps closer to the barn.

"Where is everybody?" he asked, calculating how much time they had alone.

"At a baseball game. We've got nine innings."

"Perfect." He tugged her close then covered her smile with his lips, coaxing her pleasure with his tongue. She moaned as his hands traveled to her butt, squeezing and massaging buns that still tingled from the ride. He satisfied her need for a thorough kiss and she writhed, wrapping her arms around his neck. His hands slid to her thighs, lifting her onto his trim hips. Lincoln's long steps carried her inside the barn.

"Nine innings should be enough . . . What I have planned might take some time."

She trembled, aching for him in every way.

"The ladder. Does that head up to the hayloft?" he asked.

"Mm-hmm." Her feet landed on the dirt floor and her arms left his neck.

"Start climbing, babe." As she went from one rung to the next, Iris put extra swing in her hips.

His deep voice rumbled below her. "View's awesome. But damn, I wish you were wearing a skirt."

"Might be a little awkward on a bike."

"Ah, shit. Now you've planted another fantasy."

Her feet left the last rung and landed in a familiar place. Sun streamed through the partially opened window, giving the stacked hay a golden glow. A breeze kept the loft bearable, but it was still too warm with layers on. Leather creaked as Lincoln shucked out of his jacket behind her. Iris spun to the sound and followed his lead.

Her fingers stopped on the zipper of her jacket when he said, "Don't move. Let me." The space between them disappeared. He reached for her, lowered the zipper notch by notch, guiding her anticipation.

She shivered as he tossed her coat onto the bale next to his. Lincoln surprised her when he pulled his phone from his front pocket, swept the screen, and filled the loft with music. After setting the phone down, his hands took hers and wrapped them around his neck. "Can I have this dance?" he asked.

She nodded as his hands led her hips to the rhythm of U2.

"Why this song?" she asked swaying to *With or Without You.*

"Angel . . . don't you remember?"

Her feet stilled. "Oh, my God . . . our first dance."

"I'll never forget the way you looked that day. Those silver shoes. That flowing blue skirt. And shit, the way you moved. I wanted to flip you over my shoulder and drag you out of that party. But I couldn't figure out what was going on—"

"With Wade," she whispered.

"Yeah. I know I didn't hide it well, but Wade's claim on you really pissed me off."

"Is that why you were—"

"Such an asshole? Yeah. You were unexpected."

"Mmm, you surprised me, too." She tilted her face and waited for his kiss. Warm lips met hers, soft and minty. His tongue charted the contours of her lower lip—tracing, sucking—then he paused as the song finished, but he'd set it for repeat. When Bono started singing again, Iris hummed the tune against Lincoln's mouth. His hips added more to the sensual rhythm of the dance. A sinewy thigh fitted between her legs, crowding her stance with lean, muscled heat.

Leaning in, she let him take her anywhere he wanted to go. He didn't break the tempo as he stripped her layers away, then bent forward to taste the top swell of her breast just above the lace edge of her cotton camisole. Her head tilted back, giving him room to work his magic with his lips and hands.

A gentle tug coaxed the delicate cami from her jeans. She lifted her arms and he slipped it off.

"Gorgeous." Blunt fingers trailed down her ribcage. "You wore blue today." His tongue traced the piped, indigo edge of her simple bra, which was far more sensible for the trip. A ribbon of desire tracked her clavicle as he spread his hand to slip the thin strap away. Her shoulder lifted to his nibbling teeth where he'd just stripped her bare. Patient lips meandered down her arm, lingering on the sensitive bend at the middle. Lincoln paused and sucked. That erogenous spot transmitted an electric throb to her center.

He began the route again on the other arm, but this time he pulled her bra away and tossed it on top of her shirt. Her nipples tightened, aching for his attention, but she had to wait. Greedy kisses covered her mouth—a sample of what his cock intended to do. Panting, she pulled away to gasp a breath, giving Lincoln time to cover one peaked nipple with his lips.

The top button of her jeans opened. He teased the zipper down and added pleasure. Gliding his hand beneath her panties, Lincoln pressed two fingers inside.

"Oh, God." Her knees shook and he gentled his caress, then slowly pulled his wet fingers from her center to pulse an easy rhythm over her needy nerves. Perfection saturated her body, taking her to the edge of bliss. But Lincoln intended to give her more. He eased her a step back and led her to the bales of hay where he'd tossed both leather jackets.

"I have to taste you," he said as he lay her body down. The warmth in the hayloft caressed her skin with gentle heat. Iris kneaded her lips as he stripped away his shirt. Her interest sharpened as he pulled his leather belt from the loops.

In moments, she knew what he had in mind. The soft leather trapped her wrists together, then he stretched her prone over the bale of hay. She hadn't noticed the coil of rope hanging from the post behind her, but Lincoln had. He used the tether to his advantage and stretched her out, arms over her head.

"Are you comfortable?" he asked, a growl more than words. The raspy tone sent another surge of wet heat to her center.

She nodded, her eyes locked on the bulge of his eager cock straining against his jeans.

Her eyes slid to his again as Lincoln stood and admired his handiwork. "My God, I've never seen anything so beautiful. In this light, your skin looks like liquid gold."

When the song repeated a fourth time, he bent to his phone and swept the screen. The sultry throwback play list continued—*Wild Horses*, The Rolling Stones.

Lincoln's eyes traversed her body as he settled at her juncture. Broad shoulders pressed her open, strong hands caressed, and warm lips placed a petal-soft kiss. She sighed and strained against the tether at her wrists. His palms smoothed the inside of her thighs, spreading her wide. A deep inhale seemed to intoxicate him before he gave her center a long, slow lick. The rough glide of his tongue drove her insane. She tossed her head back and cried out when soft precision plunged inside.

He gripped her hips and lifted her higher, changing the angle for a deeper taste. Teasing and licking overwhelmed her senses and her thighs began to tremble. Lincoln lifted her legs and placed them over his shoulders, letting her ride him to a sensual release. On the precipice, she yanked against her restraints. His tongue pulsed deep and euphoria hit with an epic wave. Bliss crashed and she went slack, panting, nearly sated.

"Please, I need you inside me," she begged between breathy gasps.

"Greedy girl." He smirked as he lowered her legs and placed soft kisses over her mound. "You're in luck, because that's exactly what I intend to do."

A hiss reflected the sting as his belt disappeared from her wrists. His deft massage teased the tingling away until she sighed. He hovered over her lithe body on his hands and knees, and her eyes slid open to find him watching. Patience controlled his mouth's descent to her lips. Angling the connection, his tongue mapped the contours, yet no other part of his body made contact until Iris begged once again, "Please."

He pulled his mouth from hers and watched as she licked the musky-sweet taste of her arousal from her lips. She grasped his bicep with her trembling fingers and waited. Muscles shifted beneath her fingers as he lowered his torso against her sensitive breasts.

The shaft pressing at her juncture pulsed and Iris squirmed. He chuckled, canted his hips, and pushed in, stretching her taut with one steady glide. *So full.* She forgot how easily this man could strip her senses bare. But now, she wanted him to take everything—she needed to trust him that much.

A sigh of complete surrender slipped from her lips as he pulled his shaft away then pressed his girth back in, impossibly deeper, sensuously stretched. Lips merged, tongues plundered, her fingers grasped, and he repeated the path, speeding the cadence each time.

Lincoln's thighs quaked and his sweaty torso slicked against her breasts. "Angel, you feel like pure heaven, but I'm not going to last."

She nodded and canted her hips, and he took the movement as a sign. Grinding a little harder, the next penetration stacked insistent need. Her pelvis circled as his cock surged, withdrew, impaled, recoiled, then rushed forward in a frantic release.

Guttural grunts and incoherent words bounced from the rafters. She layered a higher-pitched cry over his. Light shimmered as Iris claimed the last fragments of pleasure from the crest. Her body sank into the hay and he settled with a groan, giving her his weight. Her arms and legs wrapped around his sweat-slick torso, fastening his body to hers.

He hummed, satisfied, then kissed the sensitive spot at the bend of her neck. "I could spend a lifetime with you and never get enough," he said against her skin.

"Mmm. I'm counting on that."

He hadn't confessed love, but he claimed her future. And because they were taking things slow, that was enough.

THRITY-FOUR

Hot water streamed down her back. "Hold still, looks like I missed one." Her knees—on the floor of the tub—ached, but she didn't budge while Lincoln picked another bit of straw from her hair. Iris was surprised the man had enough strength to stand. A moment ago, he'd come so hard that she'd grasped his thighs to keep him secured in her mouth.

They had shared the shower to remove all remnants of their recent literal roll in the hay. The most efficient search positions led to other things. Lincoln took advantage of the proximity, leaving her senseless with his plundering tongue. Years of yoga practice paid off when he stretched her leg over his shoulder, spread her wide, and devoured her until she came undone.

She'd returned the favor from her knees. His hips sped, and his fist gripped her hair, while the other hand braced against the tile. Satisfied echoes filled the bathroom and Iris held on.

Lincoln gave her his hand as the water cooled. "Better hurry," he said, and Iris dove beneath the spray for a final rinse. They climbed from the shower and she peeled her eyes from his lean physique long enough to grab two towels and a washcloth. After draping the towel over his shoulder, she used the cloth to wipe condensation from the mirror. "Wow, we really steamed up the bathroom."

"Not surprised. That thing you did to my balls scorched my senses."

Iris licked her full lips, plumped by the attention she'd lavished on his cock. She loved taking him in her mouth, directing his pleasure, until he completely lost control.

With a towel wrapped around her, Iris eased open the bathroom door. She listened for a moment. Silence. Yup, they were still alone.

Steam escaped when she flung the door wide. Chill bumps popped as she dashed into the guestroom to choose clothes from her meager pile. She loved traveling two-wheeled, but it had one drawback—packing light.

While she dried her hair, Lincoln got dressed and jogged back to the barn to retrieve his phone.

Movement in the bathroom doorway turned her head and she flicked the hair dryer off. "Did you find it?"

"Yeah, my phone was right where I left it, scrolling through my Iris playlist."

She blushed and tilted her head. "I inspired a list of songs?"

"Of course. You're always surrounded by great music. And that subtle thing you do with your hips when the beat hits . . . Damn it kills me every time."

"Can I listen to a little more?"

Lincoln shrugged and held up his phone. "Later. My battery's low and it looks like we've missed a couple of calls."

Worry tightened her stomach. "Who's trying to reach us?"

"Maggie, then Paige, and about five minutes ago, Ruth."

They both knew that it wasn't about the sale, because Iris had already pulled Northside Grill from the market. Ruth had sent a celebration video with three members of Iris' posse tearing down the *for-sale* sign.

"Who should we call first?" Lincoln asked, his fingers hovering over the screen.

"Maggie, just in case something happened to Zippo."

His phone beeped a low battery warning and Iris dashed to find her phone instead. Maggie picked up on the first ring. "Iris, thank God, you called. Let me put you on speaker. Ruth and Paige are here."

Fear weakened her knees, and Iris sank to the bed while she hit the speaker symbol on her screen. She reached out and Lincoln took her hand. "Tell us what's going on."

Paige spoke first. "We've had more vandalism."

"What happened this time?" he asked.

Iris released his hand. "This time?" she whispered only loud enough for Lincoln to hear.

He tilted his head, eyes on hers, mouthed *I'm sorry* and apologized for concealing essential details.

Tilting her head, Iris shut him out while she stared at the phone in her hand.

Paige cleared her throat, but it didn't keep her voice from shaking. "Like before there's a couple of broken windows. But that isn't all. Someone set the contents of the dumpster on fire, and with as dry as it's been, that big Cedar caught, too."

Iris gasped. "Oh, no. I love that big old tree."

"At least it all happened after hours. No one was at the Grill, and the fire department got it under control before there was any damage done to the restaurant."

Iris covered her mouth to hold back a sob. As her shoulders curled, Lincoln inched closer on the bed, sitting just near enough to share his body heat.

Maggie sighed, "Well, no damage except for the broken glass. Rick and Seth boarded up my shattered window then moved on to the mess at Northside Grill."

Anger replaced her fear and Iris said, "Hold on. Goldfinch Bakery got hit, too?"

"Yeah. A rock with a flyer attached, just like Lincoln's shop the night before he left for the airport."

"Oh, my God."

"Wait, you didn't tell her?" Paige lashed over the phone.

Iris shook her head and bit her lips together.

Lincoln reached out and took her hand. "Iris, I'm sorry. I didn't want to worry you. And to be honest, since I arrived in Kansas, I haven't given my businesses much thought."

A long silence stretched between the friends, until Iris inhaled a staggered breath. "I guess I haven't either." She squeezed his hand and he relaxed. The cocoon they'd been in took a hit, but neither one of them was going to let this outside force destroy it.

Maggie smoothed everything over. "It's fine. Jerrod's investigating, and it won't be long before he brings someone in."

Ruth huffed. "That someone being Daryl Nash."

Iris couldn't contain her frustration. "I hate this. You've all become targets because of me."

A comforting arm stretched around her and pulled her close. "Angel, it's not you he's after, it's me. And the man isn't using a scope. He's taking a sawed-off-shotgun approach."

Iris sighed and leaned into his torso. "I feel so helpless. I bet Daryl thinks he's got us on the run."

"Let him," Ruth said with vindication in her tone.

Maggie agreed, "Now that he's getting careless, Jerrod will have more evidence."

"Do you think we should skip our visit with Russ and hurry home?" Lincoln offered, his shoulders rounding.

His clear regret made Iris' decision easy. "Not a chance. Russel's counting on a visit, and Daryl can't do that much damage in two extra days."

"She's right, and after this round of vandalism, Daryl's got the entire town of Ashwood watching his every move." The calm in Paige's voice eased the tension on both ends of the call.

Finding comfort in that, Iris couldn't stop her smile. "Thank you. I don't know what I'd do without you."

"Goes for me, too." Lincoln cleared his throat. "We leave early tomorrow morning, I'll send an itinerary, and we'll check in often."

"Okay, then." Ruth's clap echoed over the speaker. "Enjoy your road trip."

"And be careful," Maggie said. "Zippo misses his mommy and daddy." Iris held her breath, waiting for Lincoln's reaction.

"Will do," he said right away, unflustered.

Iris exhaled, but those words wouldn't fade. *Mommy and Daddy*. Either Lincoln didn't catch it or he didn't mind. But the label resonated in Iris, igniting a tingle of curious want. *A baby. With him*.

The ache remained and it stayed with her on the ride over to dinner and didn't fade when Jacob and Zach fought over the biggest half of a giant cookie. The sensation expanded when Lilly climbed onto her lap for a sip of shake through a large-bore straw.

She wanted all of this—the noise, the cuddles, the early mornings and late nights packed with the exhaustion she knew came with kids. And most of all, she wanted it with Julius Caesar Lincoln.

That night, they crawled into bed and slept hard, slack with satisfaction, still lingering from time spent in the loft. Lincoln woke first the next morning, showered, then headed out to pack the bikes. He balanced the load between the two machines and took each one for a short test-run.

After a light breakfast, promises to return mixed with a tearful goodbye. In a flurry of activity, the kids left for school, Cooper climbed in his truck, and Iris followed Lincoln down the long gravel drive. Overnight, rain had settled the dust and chilled the air. A blue cloudless sky stretched into the west, leading them home.

THIRTY-FIVE

Lincoln didn't mind taking it slow on the two-lane highways. Better riding gave him time to absorb the land. He'd always been a West coast guy, rarely straying from the states that touched the Pacific. Visits to see Russell pulled him inland a couple of times a year, but he'd always traveled by plane. Soaking in the open landscape with Iris felt right.

They passed an abandoned gas station with two rusted pickups parked beneath a catawampus canopy—a predictable marker of the next town. A speed limit sign appeared in the distance. Lincoln eased off the throttle and flexed his hand, then signaled his intent to stop—a station sharing a lot with Mama's Diner checked off two needs.

They each chose an empty pump. Iris stretched and bent, unaware of her supple allure, while filling her tank. "How's the Triumph feel?" she asked.

"Great, but I miss cruise control." He wiggled his numb fingers.

"Want to trade for a while?"

"Not today. The scenery keeps me from noticing the pain." He chuckled, while hanging the nozzle back on the pump.

"I love the open, but I was raised under this big sky." Her shoulder shrug asked if he loved it just as much, and he smiled. The way she talked without speaking intrigued him more than a thousand perfect words. "Mama's Diner looks busy," she said when the silence stretched.

"Always a good sign. Let's get a bite." After parking the bikes, he took her hand and led her inside.

All eyes landed on the newcomers when the bell rung over the door. He took the scrutiny in stride. The tattoos always collected side glances, but during summer, when his tan deepened, the looks lingered a few seconds longer.

A few eyes cut from him to Iris then back again. His neck tightened. *That's right, stare all you want. She's damn near perfect, and she wants me.*

Iris looked up, gave him a sexy smile, then tugged him toward a table. The booth wasn't that big, but he slid in next to his woman, put an arm around her, and rested his hand on the top edge of the golden vinyl seat. She tucked into his side while pulling a paper menu from the spot between the ketchup and a bottle of Tabasco. Menu flat on the table, Lincoln leaned in to scan the choices.

"What looks yummy?" she asked.

"Besides you? Probably the chicken-fried steak." He was a sucker for gravy.

"I think I'll get the taco salad, but I'm gonna order a side of fries if you'll let me dip them in your gravy."

He squeezed her and growled, "Fine with me."

The lone waitress appeared, took their order with the abrupt efficiency of a drill sergeant, and barked their orders over her shoulder. He ordered a Mountain Dew while Iris got an iced tea. Drinks clunked onto the table, served with plenty of ice in giant plastic cups with a faded Coke insignia on the side.

"You still okay with pushing all the way to Colorado?" he asked, knowing the road would feel longer as the day progressed.

"Sure. I'm not too sore. Maybe tonight we can find a place with a tub. I'll take a bubble bath and soak the miles away."

He shifted. "Damn. Now I'll be picturing that for miles."

When their food came, she plunged her fries in the pool of gravy, which covered most of his meal. The chicken-fried steak was great, but there was a lot of it. Lincoln was thankful for three thick slices of fresh tomato that came on the side—the only healthy thing on his plate.

He took care of the bill, and Iris stopped in the bathroom to strip out of the thermal layer she'd needed this morning to keep warm. While he paced near the bikes, two guys wandered over to admire his ride.

"The English model?"

"Yeah. That's right, but it's not mine. My old lady inherited it from her brother. I guess he picked it up overseas."

"Inherited." The quieter guy nodded. "Honor ride?"

"Something like that." Lincoln hadn't thought of it that way until now, but he felt closer to Ian through miles spent on his machine.

"Are you stayin' on this road?"

"We hope to make Colorado."

The more talkative guy stared west. "There's this spot across the state border and they like travelers on two wheels. It's a motel, bar, and restaurant all rolled into one. The place is called Fool's Gold. They got the best rib steak I've ever had. And your woman will like a fancy room if you can get it. My wife thought she'd died and gone to heaven when she sank into the big clawfoot tub."

Lincoln thought he'd won the lottery. Information from those he met on the road never disappointed. "Thanks. I'll look for it."

As they headed off the quiet one muttered, "Keep the rubber side down." They climbed into a well-used pickup and drove away. Lincoln glanced back at the diner and saw Iris closing in, wearing lighter layers and a smile that warmed him as much as the summer sun.

"You ready?" she asked, kissing his cheek.

"Just a sec. I gotta answer a text about the pot shop," he said, needing to buy a little time.

"Mind if I wander into the mini-mart?"

He nodded. "Grab me a water?"

"Gotcha."

"Appreciate it, babe." While she shopped, he found Fool's Gold, gave them a call, and reserved a room with a clawfoot tub.

***

Iris couldn't contain her smile when the kitschy two-story establishment came into view. Her squeal echoed in her helmet when Lincoln backed his motorcycle near the welcoming stairs. Those steps led to a broad porch where rocking chairs begged everyone to stay. Still straddling her bike, Iris lifted off her helmet, closed her eyes, and inhaled a thick aroma of beef, onions, and deliciousness. Her stomach rumbled. "Please, can we eat dinner here tonight?"

"We can do better than that," he said with a sly smile. "I've already reserved a room."

"Seriously?" Joy bubbled, and she couldn't get off her bike fast enough to give him a thank you kiss.

He came away chuckling. "Let's get our shit inside."

Uneven floorboards creaked as they stepped up to check-in. There wasn't a computer in sight, just a paper registry and an old manual credit card machine—the kind with a carbon copy. When Iris leaned against the wide counter, the woman at the desk noted her interest and said, "This old thing's reliable. The power goes out nearly every time we get a stiff breeze."

"Your place is beautiful. Every detail oozes vintage charm." Iris spun to take in fifteen-foot ceilings, single-paned windows encasing distorted glass, and a massive curved staircase which led to the guest rooms on the second floor.

"It's been in the family for a long time, and we have a faithful following. Here's your key, Mr. Lincoln." The woman grinned, enjoying the name. "Just go up the stairs and take a right, follow the hall around to the Canyon Suite at the back."

A tiny yelp caught in Iris' throat when she heard the word *suite*. Lincoln's chuckle covered his grunt as he slung the heaviest bag over his shoulder and grabbed another in his other hand. Iris took the rest and followed him up the wide staircase. A rustic iron and antler chandelier lit their way to the second floor.

"When did you do this?" she asked, stunned by her surroundings.

"A guy I met at lunch recommended it."

"This could spoil a girl," she whispered.

"You need more spoiling. And I plan to do that once I get you alone."

A shiver sped down her spine at his words. Anticipation coiled as he fitted the key into the door. The hinges creaked when Lincoln pushed it open to reveal a room dominated by a massive four-post king-sized bed. The fluffy comforter looked as soft as a cloud.

She hauled her bags inside and stopped at the foot of the bed. "Oh, my God, that looks too pretty to sleep in." Iris didn't want to touch the beautiful creamy linens until she washed away the dust and sweat from the road.

Lincoln pushed the door shut with his shoulder. "I plan on doing a lot more than sleeping in that bed tonight."

"Can I take a shower before we . . ." Her gasp echoed in the luxurious bathroom, her feet frozen at the threshold. "Look at this! There's a deep, clawfoot tub with room for two."

Her spin found Lincoln smiling, joy swelling his chest. She crashed into his embrace and he kissed her thoroughly. "Glad you like it, Angel."

"Now I'm torn. When I passed the restaurant, I wanted to ditch our bags and claim a table."

"It did smell great."

"But now I want to sink into that tub and never leave."

Strong hands dropped from her waist to her butt, gripping, easing her hips forward. Iris sighed, loving the sensual strain. Lincoln touched his forehead to hers and suggested, "Why don't we test out this bath and see where the night takes us. We're gonna need fuel at some point—a little energy for what I have in mind." His lips descended, adding temptation.

Her toes squirmed when his tongue slipped in and danced. The massive tub suddenly seemed less important than the fluffy bed. Kissing distracted her while he peeled away layers. Her leather, shirt, jeans, camisole, and panties fluttered to the floor. Between kisses, he spun on the water, dug through a basket loaded with essentials, and poured something sweet in the turbulent bath. She sighed when the room filled with vanilla-scented steam.

"Just a sec." Iris turned toward the mirror and secured her hair in a tie from her wrist.

Lincoln followed, staring at their reflection, his eyes only on her. "So stunning, my biker goddess." He bent his neck and savored the soft skin she'd revealed.

While he sucked the tender spot, their eyes met in the mirror. Her nipples tightened and Iris blew out a breath. "How do I always end up naked while you're still completely dressed?" she asked, giggling.

"Magic hands." Tanned and rough, his fingers covered her soft breasts, creamy white in contrast. He squeezed and she sighed.

"Stop distracting me. Gear off," she said. "I'm not enjoying this decadent pleasure alone."

"Shit, babe, I haven't taken a bath since I was a kid."

"You'll love every minute, I promise."

He tossed aside his leather jacket and boots. She stripped his shirt, then popped the buttons on his jeans. "Commando. Thank you, God."

A throaty growl rumbled when she stroked his smooth as velvet length.

"Gotta shut off the water," he said on a groan. When she released his girth, he turned off the faucet and extended his hand.

Iris lowered into the foam like a water sprite and hissed, "Ooh, it's so hot." She slid toward the center of the massive tub. Looking up, her eyes surveyed his naked body, pausing on his urgent erection. "There's plenty of room. Get in."

"If you say so." Lincoln stepped over the rim, nestled behind her, water lapping the edge. His arms swept around her and she sighed, completely content.

"Now for the good part." His words rumbled against her spine. To the left of the tub, a white wicker shelf held a stack of washcloths and bars of fancy soap. The washcloth rasped in contrast to the soap's heavenly glide. His hands covered her breasts as her feather light touches traced his forearms, caressing the details of his ink.

Hot water relaxation coaxed a question from Iris. "When did you get your first tattoo?"

He answered without hesitation, "When I was thirteen."

The water sloshed when her body reacted. "Isn't that a little young?"

He smoothed away her concern with a stroke of his hand across her stomach and then lower. She barely heard when he added, "It was done by a close friend."

"Which tattoo?"

He twisted his free arm and her fingers shifted to the exact spot. "Right there."

"So many shades of black and gray." She outlined the waves, the moon, and the detailed rocks.

"It wasn't my intent at the beginning, but as time passed, adding color just didn't make sense."

Lazy fingers parted her center and Iris had to work to think. She flipped his free arm and traced a different scene, one without joy—a splintered shipwreck battered by angry waves. "And this one?"

Lincoln hesitated, then his hand left her core. "I had that done later, when Dad got sick and everything came apart." She missed the sensual contact but didn't react. Learning more about him overshadowed her quest for pleasure.

"Dad was part of a motorcycle club—that's where he met my mom. She split a month or two after I was born."

"How could she?"

"Don't worry, babe, I had an instant family in the club."

"Why aren't you still with them?"

"There was a shift in power years later." He hummed, rubbing his calves against hers as he brought back the details. "I think I was about fifteen when Dad chose the losing side of the split. Not long after, Dad started feeling like crap. First, he had a cough that wouldn't go away, then he couldn't seem to breathe well at all. He'd smoked a couple packs a day for years. Shit, everyone did. Aggressive lung cancer spread and took him quick."

Iris laced his fingers over hers, hiding her hands beneath his palms. Warm tears fell into the water and he wrapped his arms around her body. "Don't cry, Angel."

She leaned her head against his shoulder. "I'm just so sorry."

"It was a long time ago. And you know better than anyone, hurt eventually fades."

"Yeah, but it never goes away." She released his hands and turned in the water to gaze at the man who had collected the broken fragments of her life, knit the shattered wreckage together, and somehow made her whole again.

Lincoln took her face in his palms, smoothed his thumb across her lips, then pulled her in for a kiss. Water sloshed as she straddled his hips. With an intent all its own, the broad crown of his cock sought her entrance, then merged their bodies on a slow impale. Taking in the heat of his breath, she shared his bliss.

***

He needed fuel after the round in the tub. Yet, his hunger dissipated when Iris gave him that look. Knotting bathrobe belts, he tied her to the four-post bed, keeping her trapped in their room until seven-thirty.

The extra exertion increased his appetite and Lincoln ordered sautéed mushroom appetizers with their wine. After one bite, he asked the server to add another serving to the top of his twenty-two-ounce rib steak.

Iris suffered from the same shaky state until she bit into a slice of warm bread. Instead of adding extras to her main dish, she held out for dessert. He didn't refuse when she fed him bites of her mile-high chocolate cake. It was still too much sweet, so they brought what was left of the dessert and the bottle of wine back to their room.

Too stuffed to do anything more than snuggle, Lincoln pulled her against him in bed and spooned. At three, Iris woke him again, exploring his torso in the dark. Her hand drifted over his abs, and her mouth followed the path to his cock. With a growl, Lincoln kicked off the comforter, inverted their bodies, and thanked her for sharing her cake.

THIRTY-SIX

At sunup, Lincoln left the most comfortable bed he'd ever slept in to check the bikes. Iris turned as he slipped into his boots but she didn't wake. She tucked her hands under her pillow, sighed in her sleep and murmured *Lincoln* as she settled. Her dark hair splayed across the pillow, sexy and messy, the color of chocolate.

He backed from the room slowly, he had to, or he'd crawl over her again. And damn, they had a schedule to keep—to cross the continental divide before finding another place for the night. But today's stretch of road brought them one day closer to Russel, then closer to home.

Forty-five minutes later, Iris brought him a kiss, a coffee, and a breakfast burrito from the restaurant. They packed the bikes and headed out. Before noon, the highway passed between steep-sided mesas—nature's monument to a decaying mountain range. On a rugged pass, the air thinned, and dark pines clung to barren rocks beside white-trunked aspen shimmering bright green.

Lincoln slowed, lowered his hand, and signaled a stop to Iris at an overlook above a wide emerald valley. Another group of leather-clad bikers hiked out onto a rocky pinnacle, posing for pictures near a crumbling ledge.

Iris reached for his hand. "If they take another step back, they'll disappear forever."

He gave her a reassuring squeeze, pulled her close and whispered, "I won't drag you out there, but I wouldn't mind a picture of us together. You know, to prove we were here."

She lifted her eyes to his and smiled. "It'll be our first couple's selfie."

Lincoln wanted all those silly things with Iris. Holding hands, kissing in public, their faces pressed together on Instagram, even a couple's Halloween costume suddenly didn't seem so bad. Iris peeked behind them, chose a backdrop then tipped her head to his shoulder. She held her phone at arm's length and touched the screen, then changed the angle and took a couple more.

As she checked her shots, he snaked his arms around her waist and rested his chin on her shoulder. Iris scrolled through the pictures. "What do you think?"

He laid a kiss on her cheek. "Just what I wanted."

"I'll send you a copy." Her fingers flew over her phone, his buzzed in his pocket, then she put her device away. When Iris lifted her face again, he stared for a long moment.

She flinched and smoothed her hair. "What, do I have helmet head?" She laughed somewhat self-consciously.

"God no. You're gorgeous. Surrounded by all this beauty, babe you still stand out."

Stunned by the unexpected compliment, she blushed and her mouth popped open a fraction. Chuckling, he covered her surprise with a kiss.

A few hours after the continental divide, the sun dipped and shadows lengthened. Lincoln spotted a flashing vacancy sign posted along a narrow gravel road that disappeared into the trees. He took the turn and found a campground with a dozen cabins clustered along a stream. Iris angled her bike next to his, and they walked into a building that doubled as a small market.

Inside, a young woman stocking the beer case yelled, "I'll be right with you."

Iris tipped her face to his and whispered, "Let me get our place tonight." He bristled at the suggestion, but she reached out and squeezed his forearm, "Please."

When he nodded, she moved in front of him at the counter.

The woman's ponytail bounced as she jogged to her spot behind the register. She scanned the ink on his neck, then her eyes darted toward Iris. "Can I help you?" she asked.

Iris flashed her sweet smile. "We need a place for the night."

"You're in luck, we had a cancellation. We've got a place with a kitchenette. and you can use the laundry if you need it."

"That'd be great."

"Oh, and the Wi-Fi password is broncos." She fisted her hand, gave it a cheerleader pump, and giggled.

While digging her wallet from her pack Iris laughed, and said, "I guess I'm more of a baseball fan,"

Lincoln wandered away, shaking off his irritation as Iris put the cabin on her card. He admired her independence, but the little things—like letting her pay—bothered him. It felt like rejection.

The only person who accepted his love without condition was Russel, and that brought him unending joy. But Iris wanted something different, something equal, and he'd never learned to love like that. He wasn't certain he knew how to give her everything she needed. If he couldn't figure out the give and take of it, he might lose her, and *that* would kill him.

Before he forgot the password, he plugged it into his phone and stepped toward the door. The snappy pine and thin mountain air smelled too clean, and he hoped a cigarette and a little space might patch the holes in his mood. At the last gas stop, he'd bought a pack and stowed in under the Triumph's seat. He'd made it to the bikes when his phone found a thin signal and alerts filled his screen with missed calls from Maggie, a couple texts from Wade, and even an email from Natalie. *Shit.*

Lincoln glanced over his shoulder and found Iris at the counter chatting with a woman who seemed to crave girl time, even with a stranger. Always friendly, Iris indulged the young girl's need for conversation.

He dialed and Maggie picked up on the fourth ring. "Goldfinch Bakery. How can I help you?" she answered, breathless.

"Hey, Maggie, it's Lincoln. Is everything okay?"

"It's all good. Wade helped me solve the problem. Fed-Ex dropped six boxes next door, and I didn't have a key."

"What? They just left them there?"

"Yeah. I guess they thought Cascade Cannabis was open. Probably because Wade didn't replace the paper when he and Seth installed your new window."

"I didn't need or expect that. Damn, by the time I get home I'll owe everyone in Ashwood a kidney."

Maggie laughed. "Don't be silly. We're happy to help. Oh, and Jerrod armed the security system. I hope that's okay."

"Yeah. That's great." *Shit, now he owed the sheriff, too.*

"Are you expecting any more packages?"

"I am. And I'm not sure I can stop them. I'd have Kara come and deal with it, but she's under twenty-one and I don't want to risk it with Daryl and his minions watching."

"No worries. I'll take care of it."

With the way this was going, he figured he'd owe Maggie his next child. *Next child?* The thought sent panic through his limbs, right down to his feet. He stumbled to the grocery store's bottom step and took a moment to breathe.

"Are you still there?"

"Yeah. I'm here. Thanks, Maggie, for everything. I owe you."

"You don't owe me a thing. I thought you'd be used to it by now—the way we look out for each other in Ashwood."

Lincoln didn't know if he'd ever get used to it. Deep down, would he ever really belong? "Hey, Maggie, I gotta go. I appreciate the help."

A small, disappointed hum leaked into his ear. "Be safe. And thank you, Lincoln, for taking time to bring our girl home."

Home. The word tightened his chest. He really missed that place. Shit, when had Ashwood become more than another dot on the map?

***

The screen door creaked as she pushed through. "Is everything okay?" Iris asked when she found him crouched on the bottom step.

"Yeah. I needed shade so I could see my screen." Quick fingers swept, replacing text messages with his gallery, yet his hands were shaking. Iris needed to know why.

"I was just looking at the pictures we took on the pass." He tipped the phone so she could peek, but his voice betrayed his lie. What was he hiding?

Her butt and two bags landed next to him. Tilting her head, she settled her cheek on his shoulder for a better look. "Not a bad pic. But maybe we can do better." She touched the camera icon, snagged his phone, and extended her arm. "Smile for our travel log."

An unexpected, perfectly timed kiss landed on his cheek as she took the shot. Iris giggled, satisfied. "Russ will want a copy of this."

"Thanks," he mumbled and pocketed the phone. He grabbed the bags and left her sitting on the porch.

She followed a few paces behind, watching his shoulders hunch, pressed by a burden he refused to share. Last night, his confessions in the tub confirmed one thing—she didn't really know Lincoln that well. High points stood out and she could tally them on one hand—Mom named him then left, Dad raised him and died, the woman who gave him Russel married another man. Who did Lincoln have? Only her. But would he accept the shelter she offered when he endured life's storms?

In silence, they crossed a wide lawn—a public area dotted with a couple of barbecues, a fire ring, three picnic tables, and a horseshoe pit.

"I love this." Iris jogged a few steps and caught up to Lincoln, but he had his arms through the grocery bag loops and his eyes bent to his phone. Iris pulled ahead and checked the number on the cabin. "This is our place."

She took the steps two at a time. He lumbered up, boots thumping. After fishing the key from her pocket, she slid it into the lock and turned the handle, but the door stuck. Iris gave it a shove with her shoulder and stumbled in.

"Whoops!" Laughter carried her inside.

"You okay?" Lincoln asked, but didn't bother with a visual check. He just followed her into the cabin and plopped the grocery bag's down.

"I'm fine. Isn't this great?" She spun and checked out the tidy room—a bed, two nightstands, a small kitchenette, and a round table with two chairs. No TV. *Halleluiah.*

Lincoln loaded hamburger, cheese, and beer in the refrigerator. Chips and hamburger buns landed on the counter. "Looks like burgers tonight." He gazed, eyes blank—maybe irritated— then added, "Thanks for picking this up."

"Not a problem." Iris tilted her head toward the bathroom. "I'll be a sec, then we can get the bikes."

She found him outside, fingers flying over the screen. The stubborn cabin door needed a tug to get it shut. Lincoln stuffed his phone into his pocket when he heard the thump.

A dust plume lifted from Lincoln's boots as he ambled toward the bikes. As they climbed on, a pair of two-wheeled travelers pulled in. Customary nods exchanged a quick greeting, and she knew they'd probably be hanging out with them later by the grill. She looked forward to the company—her traveling companion wasn't talking much. No, scratch that, he wasn't talking at all.

He parked the Triumph in front of their cabin, and every chance he got, he'd stab a few more words into his phone. Iris grabbed her gear from the bike, then bit the inside of her mouth as she unloaded his stuff too.

"You want to take a walk before dinner?" she asked, hoping the Wi-Fi would fade as they wandered away from the cabins.

"Yeah, sure."

"Great," she said to a man who'd lowered himself to the edge of the bed, not listening. A hike with him wouldn't be any better than hiking alone.

"Give me a minute." Iris searched her bag and found her favorite shorts, the ones that made her butt look awesome. When she stripped her jeans and he didn't lift his head to steal a glance at today's sexy panties, she stifled a nugget of worry. Maybe something serious was going on at home.

Lincoln looked up on a slow blink, noting her clothing change. He grunted, glanced at his heavy clothes, and wandered to his bag. Iris ducked outside and called Paige. Everything was great at Northside Grill. Iris kicked the dirt while texting Ruth but got nothing but a smiling emoji from her friend.

By the time Lincoln wandered out, Iris couldn't take anymore and tried a covert approach. "Were you making plans with Russel?" she asked, knowing he wasn't because his son never put a scowl on Lincoln's face.

"Uh, no . . . do you think I should?" he asked.

She shook her head. "Oh, never mind. He's probably still in school."

Confusion shifted Lincoln's features, but he'd emerged from his tech-trance long enough to take the hand she extended his direction. Iris coaxed him with a tug toward the trails and hopefully, away from the Wi-Fi. They walked in silence for a while, then he stuffed his phone into his pocket and circled his shoulders.

Iris inhaled the piney scent and tilted her head, watching the aspen leaves shimmer.

Lincoln raked his hand through his hair and huffed. "I'm sorry, I've been so distracted. Some shit's going down at home." His rough exhale eroded another layer of stress.

"Bad shit?" she asked, knowing there wasn't any other kind.

He slowed his steps. "Not really, no. This trip has insulated me from stuff I've been avoiding. I guess it's time to deal."

"Maybe I can help?"

"That's the thing. It's already carved in stone, and I can't weasel my way out."

He still hadn't told her a thing, but he didn't need to. It had to be Mosquito Creek Brewing and Wade, a man she hadn't thought about in ages.

Lincoln huffed, "It's the food truck."

Just as she guessed. "And?"

"Wade's putting pressure on Kara. She's dealing with the startup crap on her own. Then I get an email from Natalie. She's wanting approval to add pictures of the food truck and menu to Mosquito's website—it just seems so fucking official."

Iris nodded, concerned but not surprised. "Paige has been adjusting Kara's schedule, helping her with the transition."

He stopped so quick his boots left skid marks in the pine needles beneath his feet. "You knew about this?"

She shrugged. "Of course. Paige and Kara both work at Northside Grill."

"Then why didn't you bring it up?" Irritation serrated his words and the birds fell silent.

Iris raised her eyebrows and counted to ten but didn't soften her opinion. "First, I assumed you knew. And second, I guessed that you wanted me to stay out of your business. Looks like I guessed right."

Lincoln stepped back, looked past her, then dropped his head and stared at his feet. "God damnit. I'm sorry. I'm such a fucking fool."

She didn't argue that point.

He kept his head down as she took a step toward him. When the toes of their shoes nearly touched, her fingers skated over his sculpted arms. His forearms rippled with tension under her loose grip while she waited for Lincoln to bring his eyes to hers. "Just tell me what I can do to help."

His hands grasped her hips and he steadied himself in her stance. "When I followed you out to Kansas, I put off the soft opening of the food truck. It wasn't a big deal."

"But Wade got nervous."

"Yeah, and he showed up at Northside Grill. Without talking to me first, he put Kara on Mosquito's payroll. Now she's stuck in the middle. That poor kid will drive herself crazy trying to make everyone happy. I've never liked the idea of her working so close to the taproom, especially in a food truck near the highway. It just doesn't feel . . . safe."

No wonder he'd been distracted . . . Iris smoothed the stress from his features with her fingertips. "Are you telling me I might get to keep Kara on at Northside Grill?"

"You'd be okay with that?"

"Hell, yes. Lincoln, you've got to trust me enough to talk this out. We don't need to tangle our businesses—we just need to co-exist."

Lincoln pulled her body flush and blended their lips. The simmering contact didn't resonate need—it only realigned what had gone off-kilter between them.

When the kiss cooled, Iris let her hands fall from his neck to entwine their fingers. She'd come to crave this simple mating of their hands. They parted and moved silently farther down the trail, walking in silence while the birds began to chirp again. "Do you want to go back?" she asked at a fork where the paths narrowed.

"Yeah. And I promise to silence my phone."

Iris laughed. "Don't. Russel might call."

His fingers squeezed, transmitting anticipation. "I'm loving this road trip, but damn, I can't wait to see my boy."

"Me too. I know we'll be riding through some amazing scenery tomorrow—arches and canyons I'd love to explore—but I think I'd enjoy it more if—"

"If Russ was along." He smiled and finished her thought.

"Exactly. Do you think his family would drive from Salt Lake and meet us in Moab tomorrow?"

Fresh excitement sped Lincoln's steps. "I'll give Wendy a call. It's mid-week, but I think they've already planned some time-off for our visit."

When the cabin came into view, they broke into a jog. As she slipped the key into the lock, he spun her to face him. "Angel, are you sure about this? I feel like I've hijacked your vacation."

"Are you kidding?" A playful slap landed in the center of his chest. "I'm dying to spend more time with Russ." He captured her excitement with a kiss, then released her to let her spin the key.

They got on the phone and plans came together quickly. Wendy loved the idea and suggested a place with a pool. Lincoln passed Iris his phone and credit card and she worked with Wendy to lock down reservations for two nights. Her fingers trembled, as she anticipated this opportunity that would give her a glimpse into Lincoln's past.

A late dinner came together cooked on the barbeque outside. Lincoln flipped burgers and shared a beer with a couple of other bikers who rolled in late. The campfire turned into an impromptu party when a guy wandered from his cabin carrying a guitar. Haunting music blended with conversation while the orange firelight bounced from Lincoln's chiseled features. He laughed, she reached for him and he tugged her close. Stories blended into a murmur, punctuated by bouts of laughter while the fire shrank to a bed of hot coals. The musician went quiet and no one bothered to add another log. Lincoln and Iris strolled back to their cabin after midnight. They heard the hiss of water turning to steam when someone drowned the fire.

In bed, Iris snuggled against him to get warm. Lincoln wrapped his leg over hers. "Damn, you should have told me you were getting so cold."

"It was worth it—I can snuggle closer now." She burrowed into his torso and his cock stirred. A kiss wasn't enough, and Iris pivoted her body, landing on top of him. Pressed against his chest, her alert nipples pearled and ached. Iris sat up, her legs riding over his hips, his hot tempting girth trapped between their bodies.

Lincoln's hooded gaze slowed her momentum, and the way his hands caressed her face made her feel bold. "I've been thinking about something, oh, for about a hundred miles or so." She knew he understood the clarity gained by miles spent on a motorcycle.

"Babe, that sounds serious."

"I guess it is. I've realized that I'm addicted to loving someone." He stopped breathing for a fraction of a second, but Iris couldn't stop the truth from bubbling like an artesian spring. "And this addiction, it immerses me easily. I sink too fast." She took a deep breath. "I'd like to slow things down this time."

"Angel, I don't like the sound of that."

"No. Let me finish. If I can take it slow . . . then maybe, I'll learn how to love deeper."

His hands skated over her torso, gripping her waist, fingers pressing in. "Are you saying you love me?" A vein of fear stained his words.

She couldn't say it, only gave him a nod. "But it's different with you. I sense something more, something that might dig in."

"In a good way?"

"Yeah. In a very good way." She snuggled closer and he covered her nape with one hand, her lower back with the other. Both points of contact controlled his kiss, slow and patient. She hummed then wriggled an inch away. "And while I'm working on this deeper thing, it might give you time . . ." she whispered.

Lincoln kept the volume low, but cranked up the truth, "To figure out how to catch up."

Iris lifted her eyes enough to study his face in the gray-scale light. His features, while always handsome, seemed bolder as if an artist had sketched his brows, eyes, and goatee with coal. The pads of her fingers traced his lips, and he snaked out his tongue, touching her thumb. Iris sank forward, meeting his kiss. He painted her lips, licking, savoring, moaning. Patiently, he lifted his hips on a slow impale. Iris cried out, penetrated and completely owned.

Her position on top gave her no advantage as his hands and shaft took control. The climb was slow, lips to her breasts, teeth to her nipples, hands covering her ass while deft fingers explored. Each time her body trembled, he'd slow his ministrations and teased her away from release.

Eventually, he gave her the ecstasy she sought, and her body shattered pleasure into a million fragments. The orgasm released a kaleidoscope of bliss—tumbling, spinning, and settling, merging rapture with love.

THIRTY-SEVEN

Iris woke first, slipped silently from bed and climbed into the shower, taking time to process the previous night. When she came out of the bathroom, coffee sputtered in the pot and he was loading the bikes, probably also needing space for his thoughts.

After a quick breakfast of fruit and granola bars, they rolled down the highway where miles stretched and she could think. Still, even on separate motorcycles she sensed a strengthening tether. The lines separating them had blurred and disrupted her sense of order because the man leading her unleashed her sense of freedom. She'd never been comfortable coloring outside the lines. When she was a kid, she always traced thick borders with dark crayon, pressed hard into the paper to create a waxy edge. The method kept her world contained, safe. Unpredictable things left her breathless—storms, motorcycles, *Lincoln*. What would happen if she let go?

Trusting her balance, she released the grips on her handlebars, then sat up straight and rode without hands. Pure momentum carried her forward. The bike drifted slightly to the right, her body leaned, instinctively correcting for a slight sidewind. A sense of freedom sped her heart, but as she focused on the road, the dashed line, and the man riding a few yards in front of her she absorbed a new sense of calm. Eventually, a sharp bend in the highway coaxed her hands to the handlebars again. Laughing to herself, she vowed to keep a sense of wonder as she rode on.

The land flattened as they came out of Colorado. For a while, Iris felt like she and Lincoln were the only people on Earth. But the traffic increased in proportion to the arid, red-rock beauty that surrounded them.

South of Moab, she pulled ahead and led the way to their condo. The modern place wasn't as welcoming as the cabin, but with a playground and a pool, it was perfect for the kids. After she slid the keycard, anticipation sped Lincoln's steps to the kitchen. Cupboards banged and she found him holding a beat-up cookie sheet in one hand. "Hey, babe. They won't be here for at least an hour. Why don't I run to the store? I promised Russel pizza tonight."

He didn't try to hide his excitement and she laughed, wagging a finger. "Oh, no, you're not going without me. This is my shot to figure out your recipe."

Lincoln chuckled. "It won't be the same. I probably can't even buy some of my key ingredients in Utah."

"What?" She paused when realization hit. "No wonder it's so good. You're putting drugs in the sauce."

When he gave her his sly-grin, Iris knew she wasn't far off the mark.

***

Not long after they returned from the store, a knock rattled the door. Lincoln jogged from the kitchen to open it, while Iris stayed in place, nervous, using meal prep as a distraction. Everyone converged. Emotion crowded her throat when Russel caught both arms around her neck and said, "I missed you."

Awkward introductions didn't last long. The kids took over, loud and impatient, eager to check out the pool. Swimsuits seemed to appear from nowhere and Russel tugged Lincoln's hand. "Come on Dad!"

David smiled, easily adjusting as roles shifted. "I brought another suit if you need one," he offered.

"I got it covered just give me a minute and I'll help you get this wild bunch to the pool."

Iris caught a glimpse of Lincoln's ink before he ducked out. Her eyes lingered on the door as it closed, tempted to follow. But she wandered back to the kitchen where Wendy remained, unloading the last of the groceries, clearly wanting time alone to talk.

"Where would you like to go for a hike?" Iris asked, searching for a safe topic.

"Oh, anywhere at all. More than anything, the little guys want to swim, and Russ wants time with you and Lincoln. It makes sense for you to steal him and hike. The younger kiddos won't be able to keep up."

The honesty put Iris at ease. "Wendy, I have to ask. Do you think I should hang back and let Russ have his dad for an afternoon?"

"No, that would break Russel's heart. He talked about you and that fishing trip non-stop after he got back."

"That was a magical day. I just wish Lincoln had been along."

Wendy went silent, then took a deep breath. "If we had more time, I'd try to be subtle. Please forgive me if I'm nosing in . . . I was surprised when Lincoln called from Kansas. I thought you two had gone separate ways."

"He surprised me, too. It's not been easy, especially since we're both so competitive. In a small town, with similar businesses, it's . . . intense."

"But just the restaurants?"

"That's right. I don't know much about the marijuana industry. He's doing every business in Ashwood a favor by opening a local shop."

Wendy's nervous laughter filled the room. "I'm not sure I'll ever get used to that. Even in my wild years, I never tried the stuff." A giggle gave Iris a glimpse of the girl Lincoln was drawn to—her curious innocence must have been irresistible.

"Has Lincoln told you how we met?" Wendy asked, taking a diet soda from the fridge.

"Not yet." Iris found a raspberry iced tea and popped the top. "He's pretty careful about his past." She followed her to the living room where they each curled on opposite ends of the couch.

"I met Lincoln through his dad. I'd bought this awful car, trying to be independent, and to prove to my parents I could handle life on my own. His dad was working on that clunker when his health took a turn. Lincoln took on the project, but I think he was just trying to keep the cost down for a girl he'd never met."

Iris smiled. "Sounds like Lincoln."

"Mm-hm." Wendy pulled her knees to her chest, bare feet on the couch, arms wrapped around her legs. "When Lincoln took over the repairs, he called to explain and glossed over the bad stuff. I brought cookies over to thank him and wound up staying to make dinner. He and his dad needed more help than I did."

Iris hid jealous ache behind her smile, wishing she was the girl who'd been there for Lincoln.

"My parents didn't approve when he rode up on his motorcycle for a visit."

"Besides the bike, what set them off?"

"Oh, it was the tattoos. There weren't so many then, and he didn't have a beard either, but even at eighteen, he was still all Lincoln." Wendy laughed.

"I get that." Iris relaxed and chuckled, liking this honest woman more and more.

"After his dad died, I moved in with him for a while. We needed each other for different reasons. We'd only been living together for a few months when I got pregnant. Lincoln had so much going on and adding a baby to that didn't seem right. To be honest, I was really scared. I broke things off and went back home. He was at the hospital when Russ was born, but so was David, and we were already engaged." A hum, tight with guilt, bled from Wendy.

Iris couldn't even imagine how much that hurt Lincoln, knowing another man would raise his son. "This was in California?"

"Yeah. David's job brought us here four years ago, but Lincoln visits at least twice a year. And even when I knew he was sacrificing everything, he never missed a support payment—most of the time he adds extra."

"He's a good man."

"And a great dad."

Wendy shared more about Russel—his interests at school and a girl she suspected her son had a crush on. Iris listened, laughed, and envied that journey of watching a child discover the world. When the front door opened, Lincoln's eyes found hers and she wondered if he might consider going down that road again.

**

After pizza, Wendy gave Russ a kiss and left him to stay at Lincoln's condo. His son had his leathers slung over a chair three feet from his twin sized bed.

Russel squirmed. "Dad, I'm too excited to fall asleep."

Lincoln kissed his forehead. "Close your eyes and morning will get here faster."

"It seems that way, but I'm not a baby. I know that's not true."

He ruffled his son's hair, knowing that at some point in the not too distant future his son wouldn't want to be tucked in anymore. The thought stuttered his heart and Lincoln swallowed hard to deal with the runaway emotion.

Slow steps gave him time and the dim living room masked any lingering unease from Iris. Her eyes skimmed across the screen of her e-reader, the device she preferred on the road. "You think that late night swim will let us all sleep in?" she asked when she glanced up.

"Don't count on it." He reached for her hand, ready to take his woman to bed.

**

A little after dawn, a solid knock at the bedroom door woke them. Iris stifled her laugh with her pillow when Russel hollered, "Dad! It's time to get up! We've got tons to do!"

Lincoln stretched. "Be right there."

Rolling to his side, Lincoln kissed Iris quickly, sat up in bed, and scraped his hand over his goatee. "I'll get breakfast started."

"Mm-kay. Sounds great. I'll just stay right here and wait for my coffee," Iris teased. "And don't forget the cream."

Lincoln's feet landed on the floor and moved him to the foot of the king-sized bed. His eyes targeted her messy, gorgeous disarray. "That's your plan, my queen?"

"Yup. I'm on vacation." She smiled and threw a pillow at his head.

He caught it mid-air, tossed it back, and in the same swift motion, flung the blankets to the floor. She squealed when he gripped both ankles and tugged her to the end of the bed. Her silky sleep shirt rode up, baring her tummy. Tempted by soft skin, Lincoln leaned in with an evil smirk.

"No, no, no!" Laughter bubbled from Iris as he pinned her arms to the mattress.

Bent in half, Lincoln kissed the soft rise on her stomach. Her giggles bounced as his prickly beard grazed against her sensitive skin. "Oh, please stop, that tickles."

Heat shaded her words and her soft body beckoned, but he didn't have time to repeat what he'd done to her last night. Instead, he widened his mouth and blew a raspberry-kiss on her belly. Iris twisted and kicked. Her glorious laughter did as much to his cock as her jostling breasts.

Across the hall a toilet flushed, the water ran, then the bathroom door squeaked. A moment later, Russel yelled through the locked door, "Dad, are you playing with Iris?" His son's voice halted Lincoln's attack.

"Not anymore," he mumbled. Standing over her, he stared—dark hair surrounded her head in a tumbled halo, sexy as hell. He groaned, located his jeans on the chair, and shifted his dick while wrestling the eager anatomy into his jeans.

Lifting her eyebrows, she laughed and said, "That's not my fault."

"Oh yeah, Angel, it totally is." Flashing a wolfish grin, he licked his lips, ready to pounce as he stepped closer.

She held up her hands. "All right. I'm getting up."

Breakfast came together fast. They locked the condo in less than an hour.

As Russ approached the bikes, he asked, "Can I ride with Iris?"

She shook her head. "Maybe another time. Your dad has more experience. I'd feel better if you rode with him."

"Where did this old motorcycle come from?" Russ asked as he zipped up his leather jacket. "Is it special?"

Lincoln put his hand on Russel's shoulder. "Yeah it is. It belonged to Iris' brother."

Down on one knee, Iris got eye-to-eye with his son. "I had a twin, and when he died, he left me this bike."

Russel's eyes swam, "Y-Your brother died? That's sad."

Iris held out her arms and the boy fell in. "Hey, it's okay. He passed away a long time ago. I'm just happy that I can finally take his bike home." He pulled away and she brushed two tears off his cheeks.

"Because of my dad?"

Iris nodded, glanced toward Lincoln then back to his son. "If it wasn't for your dad, I'd still be in Ashwood, missing all this awesome stuff."

Russel's smile bent in confusion. "Why?"

"Well, he helped me. Until I met him, I was too afraid of thunderstorms to travel very far from Ashwood."

"Thunderstorms. Wow, Iris, that's sorta silly."

"Russ," Lincoln scolded.

Still crouched, Iris looked up and grinned, okay with the curiosity. "No, he's right. It was sort of silly. And I'm really glad I'm not afraid anymore."

"Me too." The explanation satisfied Russel, and he was ready to move. Lincoln spread a colorful paper map of Moab on the Triumph's seat and let Russ choose the destination. His finger landed on a sketched collage of three spectacular stone arches. Helmets secured, they headed for adventure.

After getting off the bikes, Russ took both their hands, hurried them to a map, and pointed at the red dot. "We are here." Iris squeezed Russel to her side, and Lincoln couldn't get over how right this felt.

They scrambled rocky paths together, taking pictures of stone formations carved by wind and water and time. Iris hung back, giving Lincoln extra time with Russ. He tried to ignore the clandestine pictures she snapped from a distance but looked forward to seeing them later.

A mob of tourists asked Iris to take a group picture of their unruly family. It took a while for her to squeeze them all into the shot. She lifted her chin and smiled as Lincoln looked her way, then waved him on, encouraging them to wander down the next path. He and his son rambled on, but not too far ahead.

Russel kicked a rock and asked, "Do you think we'll see any cougars, Dad?"

A smile spread across Lincoln's face. "Probably not. There's a lot of people around."

"And cougars are skittish."

Lincoln huffed a laugh. "Yeah. They're skittish."

"How about snakes? Will we see any?"

"I hope not." He scanned the rocky environment, cringing as Russ tapped into a hidden fear.

"Snakes are cool. I hope we see one."

I don't. Before his nerves imagined rattlers that weren't there, Lincoln changed the game. "Well, would you rather see a snake or a dinosaur?" With that, a familiar pattern began.

"Dinosaur for sure, but it has to be a big one . . . a Triceratops." Russel sidestepped and made a frill behind his head with his arms, making sure his dad got the picture.

Lincoln gave him a thumbs up. "Gotcha."

Russel skipped a few steps. "My turn. Would you rather shake hands with a zombie or an alien?"

"Alien for sure. I'm not touching a zombie. I might get bit."

"Good thinkin'. Now you."

Lincoln took his time. His son's creative mind demanded it. "Would you rather ride in a sidecar with Zippo or with Iris?"

"A sidecar?" he squealed. "Did you get one for your motorcycle?"

"Yeah. I thought it'd be fun. And I like having Zippo with me, but when you're ready for your dog, I'll bring him out."

"A sidecar sounds totally awe-some. And I guess you can keep Zippo since he's not sad anymore."

Lincoln stopped walking and waited for Russel's eyes. "Why was Zippo sad?"

"Didn't he tell you? He didn't like it when you left Iris all alone. Zippo wants you and Iris to be a family."

A family. His ribcage tightened and he couldn't speak.

"Can you do that, Dad? Iris needs us. She needs a family."

A cough cleared Lincoln's throat. He hadn't realized—until his son pointed it out—how much he wanted exactly that. "I'll see what I can do."

***

"Russ crashed."

"I'm not surprised." Iris spotted something besides satisfied exhaustion on Lincoln's face. "Are you okay?" she asked as he settled next to her on the couch. Having already caught the weather on the local news, she muted the sound and twisted her body, lifting Lincoln's arm to settle close. Her legs stretched, long and tan, across the cushions.

"I'm good. Today went by so fast. And tomorrow will be our last full day on the road."

"And it'll be long."

He nodded. "It seems like Ashwood—and all the crap that goes with it—is closing in." Lincoln squeezed her tighter. "I don't want to mess this up. What we've got is good. Still, it's easy here, but back in Ashwood—"

"We become competitors again."

Lincoln sighed, worry heavy in the exhale. "Please, no matter what, don't let me ruin us. I'm in new territory here."

"Believe it or not, I am, too." Iris wouldn't let him take all the blame. "For years, I thought I'd failed in relationships because I compared everyone to Cooper."

His body tightened behind her, but she snuggled into his chest and pushed on. "This trip demolished that. All this time, I haven't really been searching for another version of my first love. I hate to say it, but I think I blamed him when he couldn't protect me from that tornado. Then after Dad died, I developed a dangerous sort of self-reliance. I drove away anyone who threatened my independence. If I was in control, nothing bad would happen."

"Then why me?"

She considered his question, making sure the words came out right. "Maybe because we turned our attraction into a game."

He chuckled. "An addictive, high-stakes gamble. Why me? I'm definitely not a sure bet."

She laced her fingers through his and spoke softly. "You couldn't be more wrong. I thought I was searching for someone who wanted what I had to offer. But it turns out, I was waiting for the one man who had all the qualities I desperately needed. Lincoln, I was waiting for you."

His breath hitched, then a kiss pressed the sensitive spot where her shoulder curved into her neck. "Angel, if you haven't noticed, I love simply, because simple was all I ever knew. When I was a kid, my dad gave me what I needed—food, shelter, clothes."

"He gave you love, too."

"He did. Then as I got older, he was my best friend. We hung out, laughed, and joked around. It was uncomplicated. Angel, I like the games and the friendship we've built, but for our love to grow, I need you to need me, too."

Love. Iris pushed an all-in wager and risked her future on this brooding, unpredictable man. "Lincoln, do you love me?"

Inked arms trapped her against his galloping heart. "I'll go to my grave loving you."

She spun to face him, hips straddling his, arms on either shoulder. "Julius Caesar Lincoln, I love you, too."

THRITY-EIGHT

Iris didn't know if she'd ever get used to the sight of Lincoln marching into Northside Grill. His eyes scanned the room like a heat-seeking missile landing on her. He closed in on his target, snagged her waist, and met her lips, claiming her publicly as his. Oh, God, she loved it—but she might not ever get used to it.

Lincoln pulled away, but his touch lingered, with his hand spread across the base of her spine. "Missed you, babe. Couldn't wait until tonight to tell you what Jerrod had to say."

She nodded, loving this change, too. It settled comfortably without discussion when they arrived in Ashwood. They were a team—a single unit facing challenges as one.

He tipped his head toward her office. "Probably shouldn't talk out here . . ." he said.

"Okay." He released her and she led the way. Iris sensed his eyes on her ass, heating her butt as he deployed x-ray vision. Now that she had full access to her lingerie drawer, the guessing game was on.

He shut the door to her office and joined her behind her desk. Keeping things equal, they both squeezed into the small space together. Lincoln propped against the smooth wood and caged her with his long legs. Dark eyes scraped over her once, but he didn't touch her. His news wouldn't get very far if he did. "Jerrod couldn't be specific, but he knows who's behind the vandalism. He just doesn't have enough evidence to make an arrest."

Iris frowned, disappointed. "Even with the video?"

"Nope. Couldn't get a positive ID. The plates were smeared with mud or maybe grease. And the most likely suspect doesn't own the vehicles we caught on film."

"Crap. That old man probably drove a rig he was repairing to throw everyone off."

"He checked on that, too. Jerrod got a search warrant to go over Daryl's records. That's why we got the head's up—he's worried about potential retaliation."

Iris smoothed concern from her features. With each passing day, Lincoln took on more and was stretching himself thin. "I'll add extra cameras," she said. "You can't keep an eye on every business in town."

He shrugged but she knew he'd try to do exactly that. "The sheriff's increased his patrols. This will all settle once the *Keep Northside Grill Greene* party happens."

Iris blew out a slow cleansing breath. She'd need another yoga session to deal with her tension. "Only one more week of chaos, and then we know if the efforts collected enough."

Lincoln leaned forward, steadied his hand against her chin, and made a promise. "No doubt, babe, whether you like it or not the Grill is yours."

The long shot had morphed into a regional event. They'd seen the evidence when they rolled into town. Each place with a fishbowl displayed a flashy banner, made and donated by the guy who designed the *Welcome to Ashwood* sign. And every person Daryl bullied over the years found a different way to help—that list of irate victims was long. They'd already coordinated with local foodbanks, knowing there'd be surplus to share. When that word spread, donations poured in to meet a greater need.

With the publicity, Daryl had closed his establishment. Nobody knew where he was, but Iris figured his garage would open again on payment day. She couldn't wait to write that check and put this behind her.

Lincoln stroked her cheek. "It won't be long. Angel, you look a little tense. I can help with that. Are you ready to play?" His grin lifted the corners of his mouth and his eyes took on a predatory glint, eager to guess the color of today's lingerie.

Iris squirmed, instantly wet. "Three tries." Her fingers teased, wiggling in the air.

One sneaky eyebrow lifted and Lincoln guessed, "Pink?"

She shook her head, "Nope. Strike one." Her fingers released a button, but she was careful to show only skin.

"Hmm. Your blouse is pale. Is it lavender?"

"Nope. Strike two. Last try." Another button opened, displaying just a little more flesh.

Lincoln closed his eyes, waited, and opened them slowly. "Today," his finger stroked the hollow of her throat, "my angel . . ." desire drew a heated line to the swell of her breast, "wore white." He pushed the fabric aside and grinned. "I win."

Iris smiled and rolled her chair from between his legs, earning a scowl.

"Hey, wait . . . where are you going?"

She flicked a glance over her shoulder. "To lock the door."

The last two buttons parted as she turned. Facing him, Iris tossed the blouse away.

"Fuck, babe, I love it when you're naughty."

***

Lincoln could get used to the sight of his woman coming to see him on her bike. She looked sexy as hell as she tossed aside her helmet. Confidence propelled her across Mosquito Creek's gravel lot, her gaze on him. Iris didn't even shift her attention when Wade appeared at the taproom's wide bay door.

In one jump, Lincoln exited the food truck then met her by the picnic tables. Zippo scrambled from his resting place in the shade and beat Lincoln to hello. After Iris greeted their dog, she raised on tiptoe and gave him a kiss—sweet, warm, perfect.

She pulled away and whispered, "Yummy."

He never hoped for a woman like her. Someone who loved him as he was—attitude, tattoos, and the occasional cigarette. She needed him, flaws and all, even flaunted their couple status in town.

Pride puffed his chest as her lips targeted his. With a sigh, she melted into his frame, fitting as if she were made for only him. His cock swelled, too eager. Lincoln needed a few feet of physical distance or he'd be forced to lock the food truck and take her home.

Iris leaned away from the kiss. "Missed you." Heat in her eyes, she softened her words and whispered, "I need you again."

He liked hearing that but chuckled. "You had me only three hours ago."

"I know, but I felt that delicious ache when I revved my bike."

"Shit. Angel, you're killing me." Lincoln backed her a few steps and coaxed her to the seat of a picnic table. He claimed the opposite spot and asked a silent question with his eyes.

A half-smile gave her away. "I had to come over when you didn't pick up my call."

Lincoln pulled his phone from his pocket. "Sorry about that." A look at the screen put a smirk on his face. She'd only called twenty minutes ago. His woman was gone for him.

Iris reached across the table and covered his phone with her palm. "Paige informed me that I'm taking a vacation day."

"I meant to tell you tonight."

"Do you mind filling me in on our plans?"

"I thought you'd like to come to Seattle with me."

"Seattle? Oh my, the sidecar's ready!" Her excitement overflowed for a moment, but then she groaned, "Wait. Am I just ballast?"

Lincoln shrugged but didn't feel the least bit guilty. "This is part of needing each other more. And I need your—"

Iris held up both hands. "Don't say it. Even though I know you can't ride safely with an empty sidecar, I will not have my weight compared to Zippo's." Hearing his name, the dog barked and nuzzled her hand.

Iris scratched behind his ear. "What are we doing with this big monster while we're gone for the day?"

"He'll be fine at home. I asked Ruth to swing by and check on him."

She nodded. Their group had tightened, watching out for each other, waiting for Daryl's next move.

***

The custom sidecar fought Lincoln until he let go of his motorcycle instincts, stopped trying to ride and just drove. He practiced on side streets before taking on Seattle traffic. If Iris felt nervous, it didn't show. Regal in her sleek black chariot, she waved at people who honked in appreciation as they rolled by. Every so often she'd lay her hand on his thigh, stretching her fingers over his muscles as they flexed with the bike.

They stopped for lunch at the half-way point, and he offered to give her control of the machine.

"That's okay." She stole another fry and teased, "You know I like watching you ride."

He chuckled, noted the heat in her gaze, and tallied the miles until he could get her home.

Back on the bike and with a full tank, he maintained a leisurely pace until movement stole his attention for a moment. Iris hid her phone beneath the protective sidewalls and windscreen, fingers flying, tapping out a message. Lincoln came out of a curve and her hand landed on his leg again, this time squeezing. A rapid glance caught her signal, and he searched for a wide spot to stop.

As he slowed, Iris raised her voice over the engine, but he only heard the last few words ". . . can't find him."

Lincoln fought panic and pulled over. "Can't find who?"

"Zippo. Ruth went to our place and the dog wasn't there. She called and called, but he didn't come." He hadn't wandered at all since they'd settled together again, and they knew something was off.

"Shit. Let's go."

Iris tightened her helmet and zipped her jacket to prepare for a different type of ride. Speed replaced their former leisurely pace, but he couldn't cover the ground fast enough. Lincoln pushed the throttle and the engine bled heat into his legs.

Ten miles from Ashwood, he went on alert, figuring the dog couldn't have wandered any farther from home. On a side glance he discovered Iris had already begun her visual quest. Her head pivoted, scanning shadowed places alongside the two-lane road. The search tightened his stomach as they approached their gravel drive. Parked in front of their house, Ruth's red Cadillac sparkled. Iris peeled her helmet off before Lincoln stopped the bike.

Ruth appeared on the porch and Iris yelled from the sidecar, "Any word?" She climbed out and Lincoln stayed in place, not wanting to waste any time.

The engine masked Ruth's words, but they read her lips, "No one's found him."

Lincoln focused on Iris. "Babe, I'm gonna go start the search."

She covered his hand with hers and gave it a squeeze. "I'll talk to Ruth, then get back on the road in my bug. Maybe he's just visiting the Grill."

"Looking for his mom and dad," Lincoln blurted, but knew immediately he shouldn't have added those tender words. Iris sniffled and a single tear fell. He lifted his gloved hand and swiped away the drop with a gentle touch. "I'll check Northside first. It'll be okay."

Iris slapped the handlebars, yelled, "Go, go, go!" then backed away.

Lincoln gave the Harley fuel and swung wide. He gritted his teeth as the bike and empty sidecar bumped over uneven ground. On the smoother road he twisted the throttle and strange physics coupled with acceleration. The sidecar's wheels lifted from the pavement like an airplane wing, taking him on a wild, barely controlled ride.

THIRTY-NINE

Ruth waited for Iris on the porch. "It has to be Daryl."

"I don't know . . . Maybe Zippo got lonely and wandered to the taproom. Zippo would rather dig under the house than go anywhere with that awful man." Iris tried to convince them both and failed.

Ruth caught her in a hug. "Kara and the pizza delivery drivers are out searching, along with most of the senior class."

After a squeeze they let go. "I hope they're being careful. The last thing we need right before graduation is a wreck."

"They only want to help."

Iris spun in a circle, unable to decide where her attention should go. A strange guitar lick echoed inside her house.

"That's my phone!" Ruth rushed for her purse as Iris rattled her keys, eager to leave and begin her search for her dog. Her friend came away from the short conversation with information that could help. "That was Kara. She spotted Daryl on the river road."

"Any sign of Zippo?"

"She couldn't see, but she's following."

"Crap. I hate this. No one knows what that man's capable of." She ran for the door and yelled over her shoulder, "Stay here, and call if you hear anything."

Tumbling into her car, Iris guessed where Daryl might be headed. A gut feeling pointed her Beetle toward the wilderness north of town. A web of single-lane roads zigzagged between lakes and skirted ancient lava flows. The unpaved tangle could get the best navigators lost, but that chaos had a few pinch points where routes came together. Iris drove toward the closest one.

The pavement ended and her Volkswagen rattled hard enough to jar her teeth. In rutted spots her green car fishtailed then caught air a few times as she mashed the accelerator toward the floor. Dust billowed in her wake, but her dirty cloud wasn't alone. In the distance, through gaps in the trees, Iris glimpsed similar plumes. And those curling gray spirals led to the crossroads ahead.

"Yes!" Her hand pounded the steering wheel, celebrating. She'd guessed right. Rounding a bend, a dual-wheeled pickup appeared, skidding so hard into a curve that the back end whipped like a tilt-o-whirl.

At the apex of the arc, a brown and black mass hurled out of the truck's bed. Iris screamed as she watched Zippo launch from the bed of the truck into a dense stand of pine. Only a miracle would keep him from injury. Daryl spotted her, aimed his truck, and in seconds the chromed grill crowded her view.

Her only option was using her Beetle's small size to her advantage. She took the little car off-road, crashed over the embankment, and squeezed between trees where Daryl's massive vehicle couldn't follow. Metal crunched and the side mirror flew off as her precious car ricocheted from tree to tree.

"Oh, shit!" A towering boulder blocked her path, but the soft earth wouldn't grip her wheels. Momentum stopped with a jolt, but the airbags didn't deploy. A quick assessment of her physical condition told her everything was fine.

Using hands and feet, Iris shoved her driver's side door open, snapping branches as she carved out enough room to escape the ravaged car. Two engines still echoed in the distance, and over the noise she heard a loud bark. Thank God, her big, goofy puppy was alive. Both hands cupped her mouth and she yelled, "Zippo. Come!"

Shoving brush aside, Iris climbed over a fallen tree and scrambled toward Zippo's excited bark. Through the branches, she spotted a black and brown furry mass bolting toward the road. She tried again, whistled, clapped, and yelled, "Come, Zippo, come!" But the dog ran the other way.

Blackberry vines tore at her ankles and a large branch caught her shin, splitting the skin as she closed in on the steep gravel berm that led to the road.

"Zippo. Stop." Frustration sharpened her command from the base of the embankment as she watched her dog's hind feet scramble out of sight.

On all fours, Iris dug into the gravel, made it halfway up loose scree, then slid backward several feet. Desperate fingers gained purchase, bleeding as she gripped the sharp rock. A foot at a time, she climbed until her head popped over the rise just as a Subaru sped by. Iris held her breath and watched Kara's car edge the road's shoulder. She'd barely avoided Daryl's pickup as he wheeled his truck around for another pass.

Oblivious to the danger and apparently unharmed, Zippo jogged down the middle of the road, with his tongue lolling from his big rottweiler mouth.

Daryl Nash paused and took aim. He seemed to enjoy the evil sport and revved his engine twice. Gravel sprayed as he pressed the accelerator and his knobby tires dug in. Kara honked, Iris shouted, but her dog trotted on. Nash sped past Iris on his path toward the dog. Kara honked her horn and Iris screamed, "Zippo!" from her spot by the side of the road. But when another growling engine pulsed through the air she froze.

In moments, a Harley—gleaming sidecar attached, careened around the corner, straight into Daryl's path. Iris trembled as fear for her dog twisted into terror for her man.

Every sense heightened, just as it had during the storm. She tasted dust, smelled fuel, and above her heartbeat, heard Zippo's bark stacked above the vicious growl of a pegged motorcycle engine. Iris couldn't take her eyes off Lincoln as he put his body and his motorcycle directly into the massive truck's path.

The Harley's motor revved, and the sidecar lifted from the road like a wing. Daryl hit the brakes and sent his pickup into a sideways skid. Lincoln's maneuver vaulted the sidecar and motorcycle up the nose of the diesel rig. Black metal, spinning tires, and glistening chrome collided with the monstrous truck. When the sidecar hit the windshield, glass burst and rained around Iris like jagged, horrific hail.

Through all the chaos, Zippo barked.

***

Lincoln groaned. *Dog breath, why did he smell dog breath.*

"Sweetheart, don't move." Iris smoothed her hand over his good leg and took his hand, the other limb pulsed with white hot pain. Shit, he'd lived through that motorcycle flight.

He blinked twice, but the flashing colors didn't change—blue, red, and purple reflected against dark evergreens.

A voice he recognized said, "Give us room." Kara grabbed Zippo and hauled him away by his collar. A guy in a uniform put his hand on Iris' shoulder. His woman touched his cheek then slowly backed away. Hands went to work, taking his vitals, putting a tight contraption on his neck, but nothing hurt as bad as his leg.

"Sorry, but you're gonna feel this." He grimaced as Rick rolled him onto a backboard. His friend, who worked for Seth and volunteered for the fire department, hadn't lied. He'd never felt so much pain.

"Ah, fuck." It took all he had not to puke when they positioned him on a narrow gurney. He closed his eyes as the wheels bumped over the uneven road, adding to the grinding agony.

Opening his eyes, he huffed at the familiar face. Jerrod gripped his shoulder. "Shit. You are one lucky dude," he shook his head and chuckled, "and stupid, really stupid."

"Thanks. I guess I must not be dying."

"Not today. I'll catch up with you at the hospital and ask what went down."

The shriek of metal against chainsaw shifted Lincoln's eyes, but he couldn't turn his head in the constricting collar. When the sound quit, he heard Daryl yell, "Get me the fuck out of here."

Lincoln questioned Jerrod with a look and the sheriff shrugged. "That sidecar's wedged in his windshield. Somehow your Harley detached and landed upside-down in the bed of the pickup. Craziest thing I've ever seen."

A hard swallow changed Lincoln's expression. "Jesus, I didn't mean to..."

Jerrod shook his head. "Don't worry. Nash will be fine. He should thank you for every meal he gets to eat in the hospital. The food in jail is even worse."

The sheriff stepped away. Pain doubled as the medics lifted his gurney into the ambulance.

"Where's Iris?" he yelled as Rick cut away his pant leg.

"Right here," she called.

He raised a hand and groaned, "Don't leave me, Angel."

"I'm climbing in after they get you settled."

Hearing her promise, he could breathe again. Lincoln closed his eyes and waited for her touch.

Iris covered his hand with battered fingers and blood-covered knuckles. Leaves and twigs hung from her disheveled hair, and tears carved channels through the dirt on her face. She was stunning, perfect, and meant everything.

"I love you," he whispered.

"Love you, too."

The road jostled his busted leg, and a squeeze from her hand helped him endure the pain. He faded out and came back again, coaxed from a groggy place by her touch. "Hang on. We're almost there."

"Never letting you go," he whispered. Lincoln would hold on to Iris forever.

FORTY

Lincoln turned off the television when he heard Iris' sunny voice greet the nurses on the floor. His heart rate sped as her footsteps approached, and he huffed relief—at least they'd taken away the heart monitor. The whole floor didn't need to know how much his woman affected him.

His eyes hit her at the threshold, and he greeted her with a silly grin. "I'm sorry I missed your big day. Give me all the *Keep Northside Grill Greene* details."

Iris closed the curtain around his hospital bed, creating a private cocoon. He couldn't wait to get out of this place. But so long as his angel visited every day, he'd endure.

"First, tell me how your leg is feeling."

"Starting to itch, so it must be healing. And today, the physical therapist cranked up the torture so I can get out of here. Enough with the hospital shit. Spill. I need something to think about besides the Price is Right." Watching the news only pissed him off, and daytime television was driving him out of his mind.

"Okay." She held his face in her hands and bent forward to give him a kiss before taking a seat. He reached for her hand and knitted their fingers. The innocent touch twitched his cock—yet another reason to get back home.

"I'll start from the top. Ruth forced me to hide in my office until everyone was settled in the bar. And let me tell you, it was a crowd."

Lincoln chuckled. "Ruth must have loved that. She always likes the big reveal."

Iris grinned and nodded. "She does. Paige led me out, and I found at least seventy-five fishbowls lining the bar . . . every single one stuffed with cash."

"Damn. I would have liked to see that."

She squeezed his fingers. "You can, at five, on the local news."

He laughed. "Shit, Ruth must have loved that, too."

"Oh, she did, but I was so nervous. People came from everywhere—Hood River, Stevenson, The Dalles, Yakima. Some I recognized, other's not at all. There was even this guy from eastern Washington; Ryker, a random person I met at a bar when I first got out on my bike."

He gave her a look, and Iris just smiled and shook her head. Tugging her hand, Lincoln pulled her to him. When their lips met, he threaded his fingers into her hair, coaxing her toward his bed. "Stop. The doc hasn't cleared you, for . . ." she whispered.

He growled and didn't care if the nurses heard his frustration. "They didn't put a cast on my cock."

As he released her, she laughed and licked her lips, tempting him with a peek of her slick pink tongue. "I'll make it up to you when we get home," she promised.

"Counting the minutes, babe." She settled again and Lincoln waited for her hand. "Who else was there?" he asked stroking her warm, silky skin with his thumb.

"Everyone. Maggie, Paige, Ruth and her posse, Kara's friends, the entire Michaels' clan, even Natalie's brother Ben came in from Portland. Northside Grill was packed. A team of bank tellers went to work on the spot and the checks were cut. Every county and town that pitched in collected funds. And those food banks had never seen such generous donations."

She glowed. Iris loved her town, and when she'd needed them, they'd showered love and overwhelmed her with support.

"What's the latest on Daryl?" she asked, knowing Jerrod stopped by nearly every day. Through this ordeal, Lincoln had found a close friend.

"Nash has one more surgery. Recovery time, then when he's fit enough, he'll spend a few months in prison and serve his time."

Her jaw clenched at the short punishment, but it was part of the plea deal that had erased Iris's debt.

"When can you come home?" she asked. "I want you in our bed."

He liked the sound of that and knew they'd never spend another night apart again. "Three more days, but maybe we should hire someone to help." He looked down at the cast that stretched from mid-thigh to his foot and wiggled his toes.

"Nope, once I get you home, you're mine. Paige has Cascade Cannabis under control. Kara's running your pizza business out of Northside Grill. Ruth will cover the bar for me until you get comfortable with your crutches."

After Iris tallied off his concerns, he crossed out another. "And Wade already found a replacement. I'm officially out of the food truck business."

"Halleluiah." She kissed him, deep and hard.

His fingers wrapped around the back of her neck to keep her lips from escaping too soon. A knock against the metal doorframe moved his woman, and a nurse appeared with a stack of white towels and a washcloth in her hand. "Mr. Lincoln, are you ready for your bath?"

Iris stood, eyes on the young woman at the door. When the nurse hesitated and backed up a step, Lincoln tried not to laugh.

Iris closed in on the blushing nurse and reached for the bathing supplies. "Thanks . . . but I've got this."

"Are you sure?" Her fingers gripped the towel tighter, like she didn't want to let go.

"Oh, yeah. I'm sure." Iris won the tug of war still smiling her sweet smile. The nurse released the towels and turned with a huff.

Iris watched the nurse sashay down the hall then closed the door. She spun to Lincoln. "How many times has that girl seen you naked?"

He chuckled. "Four."

"Seriously? You've only been here five days."

He feigned innocence as he lifted his hands. "Hey, she's just doing her job."

"Yeah, right," Iris mumbled something about cold water while she searched the drawers. She came back with a shallow basin, set it on the counter, and put her hand on her hip while she let the warm water run.

A FEW MONTHS LATER

Zippo barked when she parked her cherry red Beetle in front of Lincoln's Garage.

She barely got her door open before his big head pushed inside. "Hey, boy." Iris kissed the top of his head. "Where's Daddy?" she said and the dog backed enough to let her escape her car. Dry leaves crunched under her flats on the way to the wide-open bay. Iris glanced above the door, taking in the round logo. Vintage letters surrounded a sleek blue iris in masculine script. *Lincoln's Garage*. She loved everything about that sign.

Her man emerged from the shadows—long, lean, and sexy. He wiped his hands on a rag, hooked it in his back pocket, and grinned. She didn't know how he balanced everything—Lincoln's Garage, Cascade Cannabis, and his portion of Northside Grill.

A slight limp lingered as he crossed the clean concrete floor on his way to her. "Hey, Angel. How are my babies feeling today?"

Iris smoothed her hand over the slight swell. "Mama and the kiddos are fine." Twins ran in the family, yet two heartbeats at their first prenatal appointment had been a surprise. "I'm craving some of your special sauce, with kalamata olives, and artichoke. Should I bring pizza home from the Grill tonight?" She snaked both arms around him, not caring if grime from the Ford he was working on got on her clothes.

"Sounds perfect," he said before he gave her the kiss she craved.

"Three guesses?" he asked against her lips and she laughed, wondering how much longer she could make her current lingerie work with her pregnant body. Not that Lincoln complained about the way her boobs overflowed her ever-tighter bras. Iris nodded and held up three fingers.

Hands at her waist, he leaned back and deployed his x-ray vision. "Black?"

"Nope." One finger tucked under her thumb, leaving two in the air, counting his tries.

His eyes flicked over her sweater, a mixture of rich greens that brought out her eyes and welcomed the cooler weather that came with autumn. He hummed for a moment, thinking. "Red."

"Wrong again. Last guess."

"Either way, I'm dragging you into my office."

She smiled, counting on that. There were only winners in this game.

Lincoln slipped his caress beneath her sweater, feeling for clues. Rough fingers skated up her spine, found the clasp of her bra, and released it with a snap. "Dark blue."

"How did you know?" she asked on a giggle.

A shrug hitched his shoulders. "I'm very good with my hands." She wriggled knowing this was true.

His eyes darkened. Lincoln lifted her into his arms and crossed the garage. Iris laughed on the way and hit the button that lowered the bay doors as they passed.

The sleek new counter welcomed her butt. He dashed to the window to switch off the neon *Open* sign, then he spun the rod on the blinds and shut the rest of the world out.

Her sweater landed on the shining vinyl chairs as Iris peeled his T-shirt away. Strong hands eased her hips forward, thighs spread, making room for him. Lincoln watched her fingers trace his most recent tattoo—the only color etched into his skin. Indigo blue stood out from the sharp blacks and gradient grays. Her delicate touch traced the edges of the iris, and her lips followed, kissing his chest.

"You're always with me, Angel—completely under my skin." Lincoln covered her mouth with an urgent kiss while his hand spanned her tummy, covering their babies. He eased away and the look in his eyes confessed his love again. "I didn't have my grandmother's ring to give you. And your father couldn't walk you down an aisle."

She smiled, remembering simple vows spoken at their overlook where nature and a few friends stood witness. "It's just us, and so much more than I ever imagined." Her hand covered his and the tiny hearts beating in her womb.

Lincoln's touch trembled. "Everything I am is yours. My heart. My life. Permanently marked by my Angel."

*****

- -

Also by Kinney Scott

In Ashwood
Inheriting Trouble
Trouble Brewing
Chasing Trouble
Addicted To Trouble

Watch for more at https://kinneyscott.com.

About the Author

Kinney Scott writes contemporary romance from her home near Puget Sound on the rainy side of Washington State. Her steamy heroes and complex heroines feel most at home in the rugged and uniquely romantic environments of the Pacific Northwest. When she has a moment away from her computer, Kinney escapes to her garden or spends a few hours hiking trails near her home.

Want to know more? Visit Kinney at https://kinneyscott.com
Read more at https://kinneyscott.com.

"I grew up here," he said. "As I said, people in this town don't have a lot. Maybe they have someone they care about serving time up the hill," he told me as he referenced the large prison just outside of town, his smile fading. "Most others work at the racetrack or its attached casino, and neither of those places pays well. This isn't a place where many people have spare resources to spend to get their fortune told."

"Well, that's good, because I don't tell fortunes. I'm not opening a fortune telling shop."

He looked confused.

"Mystic Moon Gallery is an *art* studio, Officer," I told him as I pointed to the boxes of charcoal, watercolors, acrylics, and oils. "Classes in the back, supplies, and art for sale up front, and a fancy coffee maker with free coffee to bring people in. I hope, anyway."

"What's all this, then?" Gabe Wilcox motioned toward the goddess statue and selenite crystal ball on my display table.

"Art?" I answered him as patiently as I could.

"It's a crystal ball."

"It's selenite. It looks like a moon," I told him, pointing toward the full moon in the sign behind the counter. "Mystic *Moon* Gallery. A ball that looks like a moon. Understand?" I decided not to mention the fact that selenite was also used for good luck and protection.

"So, this is an art studio and coffee shop," he drawled, raising his eyebrow. "You will not try to gouge these people for money so you can give them the lottery numbers or something?"

I glared at the officer again.

He glared back.

Finally, I decided to just come clean. I *did* want these people to trust me, and being cagey with the man's questions about what I used to do for a living might be causing more suspicion than necessary.

And who knows *what* the Mickwac sheriff said.

"Yes, Officer, I used to travel with a circus and give people readings," I explained as I hopped up to sit on the counter. "Yes, I follow a spiritual path that might be termed "witchcraft." But *if* I do a reading, I don't tell people anything they don't already know, honestly. I help them work through their own thoughts and feelings so they can come to their own decisions. Or recognize when they've already made them."

"And people pay you for that?"

"They used to," I smiled. "Now, I do it for fun. Here? I'll give away awesome coffee and sell baked goods. I'll have classes in the back, sell paintings, art supplies, books. But no one will pay me hundreds of dollars for an egg unless it's a replica Fabergé."

"The bath splash my grandmother uses?"

"That's Jean Naté."

"Yeah, right, right," Officer Wilcox said, but then he froze. Turning to me with a shrewd glance, he asked, "Wait a minute. *How* did you know that?" He reached up and placed his hand on his head as if to assure himself his brain was still protected by his skull.

"Because many grandmothers use Jean Naté if they're of a certain age," I told him as he rolled his shoulders. "Lots of older folks came for readings at the circus. I learned to recognize the scent of Jean Naté pretty quickly. Not a supernatural vision of your grandma, sorry."

"What kind of coffee?" he asked with feigned enthusiasm, changing gears.

"Come by Monday. First one's free," I grinned and winked.

A real smile cracked his heretofore rather inexpressive face. "You know who says that?"

"There's nothing illicit in my coffee, Officer Wilcox, I promise," I told him as I held up my hands. "Besides, *all* the coffee is free in any case. As I said, I have nothing to hide. You're free to check out everything in the store if you like. I want to have an open and honest relationship with law enforcement as a business owner in Mystic's End."

"If that's true, Ms. Delphi, you may be the first

in this town to feel that way," he said as he nodded his head and bid me a good night. Halfway across the room, he turned back to face me. "By the way, it's *Detective* Wilcox. *Not* Officer Wilcox. Been a while since I've been on the beat. I would have guessed you'd know that, being psychic and all."

"Detective," I acknowledged as I walked forward and held out my hand again, ignoring his snarky observation. "Come by anytime."

There was a longer pause than I would have liked, but Detective Wilcox finally reached out and grasped my hand to shake it firmly. His hands were soft, like he moisturized them at the end of each day. My telepathic tingle went off as he wrestled with a slight attraction that he couldn't help but broadcast. Tilting my head to look up at him, our eyes met.

Within seconds, he coughed and drew his hand hastily from my own.

Images filled his head as he walked toward the front. Gabe Wilcox visualized himself walking back into the store again and again.

And once again.

And one more time as he stepped through the archway to leave.

* * *

S urveying the storefront, I was pleased with myself and everything I had accomplished in just a few weeks. After having lived in the Magical Midway, I had come to enjoy Charlotte's ability to accomplish great physical tasks with a wave of her hand. Without being able to rely on her for the first time in a while, I hadn't been sure I could manage setting everything up on my own.

I mean, I am a witch, but not *that* kind of witch.

Well, technically she and I were the same kind of witch.

Technically.

Sort of.

Okay, truthfully? I was probably the *least* of all witches. Every time I tried to get witch lessons from Gunther (who was probably the *most* of all witches, along with Charlotte), something came up. A dead body. An attack from the Witches' Council. Something. Something more pressing, something more important.

When Charlotte gave me the chance to become a witch, a real one, to thwart the murderous intentions of the Witches' Council, I had *jumped* at the chance. I believed it was the thing that would make me feel like I belonged, finally—and I was admittedly dazzled by the idea of having powers.

Well, more powers beyond my telepathy, anyway.

But I never learned much after I got them, and so I was usually left out of all the exciting and dangerous things Charlotte and her pack of paranormals did.

That's actually how I wound up learning to paint. I needed something to pass the time once the circus shut down to visitors.

Anyway. I was what Charlotte was, but I couldn't do what she did.

Even without magical powers (or, more precisely, magical powers I didn't have much of a clue how to use) I had really pulled the place together.

It was just one big open room with a counter in the back, though, so it really hadn't been a massive undertaking. To the right were shelves of books on all different kinds of art—painting, ceramics, drawing, tapestry, mosaic. Every book contained positive, uplifting messages designed to help encourage people to express themselves through creativity and crafts.

Next to the books were supplies like sketch pads, blank canvas, charcoal and pastels. I had wax to make candles, beads, crushed glass. I wanted to ensure that there were multiple tools and mediums for people's self-expression, and so I tried to have a little bit of everything. You could buy it and take it home, or buy it and use my tools in the back to create right here.

On the left side of the shop there was room to display art for sale. Shelves for pottery or crafts, plenty of wall space for paintings. I hoped that our location in the town square would encourage out-of-towners visiting the gambling establishments to stop by and bring some art home with their winnings.

In the center of the room toward the front, I had placed comfy couches so people would feel welcome, invited to sit down and enjoy the carefree and easy-going atmosphere. Perhaps with a cup of coffee from behind the counter and a book they could peruse.

After shutting off the front lights, I walked through the door behind the counter into the second gathering room. I called it the Muse Room. An open, airy room with tables and easels that could accommodate classes of twenty, or be used by anyone whenever they decided to create art. A decent sized gas kiln sat in an alcove off the side, a feature I had desperately wanted—but which had cost me an enormous amount of my seed money.

Charlotte and Gunther had given me more than enough resources to get started on this little adventure. I was luckier than most new business owners.

Switching that light off, I felt up to the task I set for myself, despite my nerves. Sandwiched between the town post office and the town salon in the downtown square, I hoped tomorrow would bring those that needed me to my door.

TWO

The glass shattering startled me awake.
As I swung my head toward the only glow in the room, the digital clock blared brightly that it was 4 a.m. My eyes burned from the lack of sleep.

Still dark.

I listened.

More glass crashed to the floor somewhere down below.

I jumped out of bed and wrapped my hands around a bamboo stick I kept *just in case*, and raced through my apartment. Reaching out to see if I could sense anything, I saw images tinged with red flashes of fury as I descended the stairs. Whoever was in my store was clearly angry.

Well, I'd barely had any sleep so, frankly, I wasn't exactly in a pleasant mood to cheerfully greet a guest, either. "I have a gun, so you'd better get out of here!" I hollered, lying through my teeth. I gambled that I could scare whoever it was away with the lie before I made it down the stairs and things got confrontational.

"Get out!" a raspy howl echoed in my ears. It felt like it came from all directions. "This is *my* home! Get out!"

Sounds of destruction grew louder as I landed with a clunk on the floor and took off across the Muse Room. I magically flicked the front light on (an act of magic I *could* perform) as my bare feet slapped across the wooden floor. With a mighty shove, I flung the entry to the storefront open expecting to find everything I had so carefully put up the night before broken on the ground.

I did not.

I found a glowing orb of light floating in the center of the room casting an ethereal glow.

"Oh," I sighed with relief, dropping the upraised bamboo stick to my side. "It's just a ghost. Hey there. What are you doing here?"

"Just a ghost? Just a ghost!" the orb shouted as it pulsed like a disco ball. "I am a terrifying ghost! I am haunting this place and it's mine! Mine, mine, mine! I will *kill* you if you do not leave my home!"

The orb whizzed and jetted across the room as the sounds of glass breaking and chains rattling grew louder—despite the fact that not so much as a feather moved.

"I'm a witch," I told him as I placed the bamboo stick on the counter and wiggled my fingers toward the personal coffee maker. "The rattling chains, glass breaking, glowing pulse orb thing?
It's *really* not going to work on me."

The pulsing stopped as if stunned.

"Maybe you should just introduce yourself?" I asked the orb. "Here. I'll start. My name is Fortuna Delphi. I just moved here."

"Well, I know *that*," the orb pulsed as it spoke. "I've lived here for years, and no one has been stupid enough to rent a haunted townhouse. Not in this town."

"I've bunked in a haunted house before in the middle of a paranormal circus," I shrugged. "Doesn't bother me."

"Wonderful," the ghost said as the ball melted into a twenty-something young man with a Mohawk, black leather jacket, and motorcycle boots. He stomped over to the couch and let out a string of four letter words as he sat down.

"Hey, there's no need for that," I told him. "Don't spit your ghostly negativity into my store. I just cleaned the energy of the place."

"My store," the punk snapped back.

"Granted, I've been in the paranormal side of the world for quite a while and I may be a *little* out of touch with some things," I told the ghost as I poured myself a cup of decaf coffee. "But I'm still pretty sure you can't own property once you're dead. Not there, and not here in the human world. What's your name?"

"Spike," he told me. I raised an eyebrow.

"Okay, so what's your real name," I asked.

"Someone by the name of Fortuna Delphi is giving me crap about my name? That's *rich*. That *is* my real name," he said as he stood up. "I don't go by my *slave name*."

"You...don't go...by your...slave name?" I stared at the guy as pasty white as a ghost could be and tried to figure out that one.

"That's right."

"But you've decided to wear a dog collar for all eternity?" I asked him, pointing to the black collar with silver spikes around his neck. He didn't seem to understand the irony.

"I didn't *decide* to wear it, witch. I died dressed like this. I was coming back from a concert," he answered. Standing back up, he held out his arms to show off his outfit. "Twenty years ago, this outfit looked good, I'll have you know."

"You decided to wear *that* for twenty years?"

"What do you mean *decided?* You keep saying that like I have any power to decide a damn thing anymore," Spike asked me as he rolled his eyes. He tugged his leather jacket trying to remove it, but it stayed on as if glued to him. "Again, witch, *I died in this*. Right upstairs in the store room. What choice did I have?"

Spike seemed unaware he had the ability to change clothes. Heck, he could change his face, his body, his voice—ghosts could appear as anything their ghost-mind could conjure, really. But no one seemed to have ever told my hardcore roommate over there.

"Am I the first person you've spoken to since you've died?"

Spike glared at me for a while as if contemplating whether to tell me more, or resume his chain rattling. With a sigh, he leaned back against the chair.

"First living person, yeah," he said as he slumped over, the red flashes of anger fading to pink, then white. "I used to try to get people's attention when they came into the shop, but it just freaked 'em out."

"Then no one would rent the place because they thought something haunted it," I said, recalling the real estate agent's excitement in showing me the property. Spike nodded. It's no wonder she was so eager to get me a stellar deal even though it meant a lower commission for her. She must have figured an out-of-towner was the only person that *would* buy the place.

"Something does haunt it. *I* haunt it," Spike told me sullenly. "Not like I *want* to, though. I've tried to leave. I can't get out of here." The fierce looking punk gazed backwards over his shoulder and looked at the town square just beyond the glass. "I've tried. I can't go out the front door, the back. I even tried to jump off the roof. No dice."

"You can," I told him. "You just have to learn how. I mean, you turned into an orb. So, you can. Trust me." If I was the least of witches, Spike seemed like he might very well be the least of ghosts. How on earth had he gone so many years without leaving this building? I shuddered.

"Naw, I don't think I can," he shook his head. As Spike relaxed, I could see the dimple in his chin, and high cheekbones. Under the spiky, multicolored hair and the snarly attitude, Spike was *kind* of cute. "No one's ever found my body. It's still up on the third floor. I figured until someone finds it and buries it or something, I'm probably stuck here."

Did he say his body was still here?

On the third floor?

The third floor where my bedroom was?

I froze. "Your body is still here?"

"Yeah," he nodded. "I got killed on September 10, 2001. Bad timing on my part, right?" he laughed sadly. "People were so freaked out about what happened I guess they just didn't look very hard for me. I kept trying to get through to Busy, my coworker, but she just stayed glued to the television. She was so sad, so preoccupied. After that, people stopped coming in the shop. A month later, they closed," he explained. "I've been pretty much by myself ever since."

"How were you killed?"

"That's the weird part," Spike said tilting his head. "I have no idea. One minute I remember coming into the store on the way home from the show, the next minute I was dead. I don't remember anything for, like, a whole day."

"Why were you coming back by the shop? Do you remember?"

Spike's expression twisted and then he slumped again, shaking his head no. It wasn't surprising. People often blocked out trauma if it was too much for them to handle. That was true for live people and dead people.

"Well, you seem pretty together for someone who's been alone for decades," I told him as I rubbed my forehead. If I didn't get some more sleep I would wind up with a wicked headache tomorrow. "Aside from the whole shouting in my ear, glass breaking, chain rattling demand to get out we started our relationship with."

"Yeah, um...sorry about that," he said as the corner of his eyes crinkled. Spike's posture was loose and he seemed far more relaxed than when I first met him. "You made this place all girly and, honestly? It's easier to be alone when you're not reminded of just *how* alone you are every single day. I didn't actually think you'd be able to hear me..."

Spike's voice trailed off as he gave voice to his loneliness. As if his state, and his dislike of that state, was still something he wasn't comfortable with feeling yet. My heart went out to the punk ghost.

"Well, if you promise to let me get some sleep, I promise tomorrow we'll call the Mystic's End police. They'll find your body if there is a body to be found," I said as I yawned and he nodded. "Where is it exactly, by the way?"

"On the third floor, in the west wall in that far corner room," he answered as I dumped the fresh coffee I just made down the sink.

My bedroom.

Of course the corpse was in my bedroom.

* * *

Detective Wilcox was looking at me as if I'd grown another head.

"So, you just *sensed* he was in the wall last night? Just woke up in the middle of the night because of a feeling?" he asked for the third time. I nodded again as two men secured the bones from upstairs in the small body bag atop a stretcher. "You've spent multiple nights here, but last night before you opened for the first time, that's when you suddenly realized there was a dead body in the room with you?"

"You can ask me again, Detective, but the answer won't change," I said. Spike floated nearby watching the scene intently.

"Over the years I've learned that people hiding something often can't keep their answer straight when asked the same question multiple times."

"I'm not *hiding* anything," I rolled my eyes.

Which wasn't precisely true. I decided before ringing the police that I would not mention Spike's spectral visit. The detective was already suspicious of me. I didn't want it getting around town that the hippie gypsy could speak to the dead, or that my gallery was haunted.

"You were hiding a body," the detective pointed out as the bag was zipped up.

"I wasn't *hiding* a body. You can't *hide* something you didn't know was *there*." I rolled my eyes. "I'm sure after your forensic investigation you will realize who this person is and that they are not connected to me in any way."

"You're sure about that, are you?" his eyes narrowed.

"I'm sure about that because I didn't stuff a dead body in my bedroom wall," I said as I was shouldered out of the way. "Hey!"

"Stand on the side," the gruff technician from the coroner's office grumbled at me. "Hard enough to get these bones out on a stretcher without people standing in the way."

Detective Wilcox placed a gentle arm in front of me and swept me to the side. "Sorry about that. Bobby's bedside manner is much more appropriate for the dead than the living."

"That's Bobby Newsom," Spike said with amazement. "I went to high school with him. Man, he looks worse than I do. And *I'm* dead."

Bobby Newsom couldn't have been over forty if he went to school with Spike, but the man looked like he was in his mid-fifties. He was heavy, so heavy that he grunted as he walked, and his greasy hair was shot through with heavy grey. His rough, calloused hands gripped the stretcher tightly as he pushed it through the front of my shop.

"Don't need you to apologize for me, Wilcox," Bobby said with a sneer as he passed us. A shorter, younger man flashed his eyes over to me and smiled quickly. He had incredibly long, brown hair pulled back in a ponytail. His long mustache would make any other man look fierce, but his eyes were so kind that he looked playful. "Ollie, let's go!"

"And that's Ollie Kane!" Spike exclaimed. "I went to school with him, too!"

Okay, maybe he *wasn't* younger than Bobby Newsom.

"Let's go over what happened when you woke up one more time," Detective Wilcox said.

With a sigh, I repeated the story, sans ghost, once more.

THREE

The Mystic's End Police Department surprised me. It was a bustling, modern building too vast for a city as small as this. At least that's what I would have thought before Detective Wilcox asked me to visit it.

"You can sit down right over there," Wilcox pointed to an aged vinyl-padded chair next to an industrial gray metal desk. "I just need to get what you told me typed up so you can sign it. You own the building, right?"

I nodded as an older man with a badge walked by and gawked at me.

"Sorry, I didn't hear you," Detective Wilcox said as he spun around.

"Yes, yes, sorry, I do own the building.

Outright," I told him as I sat down. His eyebrow raised, but he let my confession pass without comment.

"The town will compensate you for the cost to repair your wall," he said as he sat down at the desk opening and closing drawers distractedly. "I have a sheet around here someplace that tells you how to get your money back."

"What if I couldn't afford to get the wall repaired first?" I asked him.

He glanced into my eyes and smirked. "Somehow I doubt a single woman that could procure a brownstone with cash needs to worry about that."

"I don't," I acknowledged, blushing. "I was just curious what would've happened if money had been an issue."

"Someone in town would've done it for you once we confirmed you're due a remuneration," the detective replied. "This is a small town, Ms. Delphi. Everybody knows everybody."

"With a huge police staff for a small town where everybody knows everybody," I observed, craning my neck toward the forty or so men that milled about the main room. About half were in standard officer uniforms, the other half plain-clothed with badges on their belts. All of them were armed. "I thought there were only a few thousand people in this town? Why would you need so many officers?"

"The casino and race track are within the town limits," he explained as he jerked his thumb toward the southern window that overlooked the gambling campus. "They have their own special security force, but they keep us busy."

I turned toward the bay window and scanned the vast casino and enormous racetrack. "Is that a horse track?"

"Greyhound," he responded as his eyes scanned the paper in front of him.

"They race pet dogs there?" I asked, dismayed.

"You're one of *those*, huh?"

"If you mean someone who doesn't think we should make animals run around in circles so we can bet on who wins, yeah, I'm one of those."

"So says the woman who traveled with the circus," he raised his eyebrow. "From what I hear, it wasn't Cirque du Soleil you ran with."

The detective had caught me there. The Magical Midway had almost no actual animals anywhere on its fairgrounds—they were all shapeshifters. That wasn't something I could explain to Gabe Wilcox, however. The humans thought they were animals and I couldn't reveal they were were-creatures.

"We treated our animals well," I told him. "I

hear that greyhound racing tracks are not noted for treating their dogs with much care or kindness."

"The ones that win are treated fantastically," a man with blond hair and a wrinkled shirt called out from the desk behind Detective Wilcox.

"And the ones that don't?" I leaned forward to meet the man's stare and raised my eyebrow.

"The ones that don't should've run faster," he shrugged, dropping his gaze. I frowned.

"The only jobs in this town are at the track or the casino," Detective Wilcox told me in a softened voice. "Sure, there are shops here and there. For an hourly job? People here don't have too many options. Most folk won't take too kindly to an outsider criticizing the two largest corporations in Mystic's End. If you get my meaning."

The room dimmed as the sun slipped behind a cloud. The natural light let in by the huge bay windows disappeared. It made the place seem dreary.

"Yeah, I get your meaning," I said as he looked me over and tilted his head.

"You still strike me as trouble, Ms. Delphi."

"I would never strike a member of the police department, Detective Wilcox," I said lightly. He gave me a half laugh and then turned back to his papers.

"Hey, Gabe," Ollie Kane said pleasantly as he

strode up on the other side of the desk across from me. "Bobby confirmed what you thought. The body we pulled out of Miss Delphi's bedroom wall? It was Willy Mason."

"I figured," Gabe Wilcox sighed. "Poor kid must've been stuck in there for over twenty years until Fortuna here raised up his ghost."

I froze, astonished at the detectives accurate sense of precisely what had taken place. "I did *what* now?"

"It's just an expression," Ollie said with a smile at meeting my bewildered face. "At least that clears him of those burglaries years ago. Anyway, I'm sure if that place really was haunted the way everybody says? You'd know it by now."

"I'm sure I would," I responded while forcing my face into the blandest expression imaginable. "So who is...was Willy Mason?"

"I went to school with him back in the day," Ollie said leaning on the desk, his waist-length ponytail dragging across the metal top. "I hung out with the skaters, he hung out with the punks. We were music *adjacent*, if you know what I mean."

I didn't, but I nodded anyhow. The private schools my adopted parents had dispatched me to before I ran away didn't have cliques divided by music or interests. It had cliques separated by household cash and class.

"He disappeared over twenty years ago," Detective Wilcox continued. "He'd gone to a show in Little Rock but never arrived home. The police suspected he'd run away because the kid went poof just after a series of burglaries from the record store. I don't think anyone thought he made it back to Mystic's End at all. There wasn't much in the case file."

"What kind of burglaries?" I asked.

"Oh, you know, money missing, that sort of thing," Ollie frowned as he grabbed a mug off of Detective Wilcox's desk and poured himself a cup of coffee without asking. "His mom had died, and his Dad was friendly as a bramble bush. And I don't mean a little grouchy, either. His dad had a reputation for beating the crap out of people first and coming back to beat you up again later once you healed. So everyone assumed he just had enough and skipped town."

"Joe Mason has called every couple of years to ask if we've heard anything," Detective Wilcox told Ollie. "He sounded concerned."

"Maybe he just wanted to make sure he was still in the clear," Ollie said thoughtfully, sipping his coffee. "Just because he's interested doesn't mean he *didn't* do it. In fact, as bad as they got along—"

"You think Will's *father* murdered him?" I gasped.

"I think—" Ollie began, but Gabe cut him off.

"We're just beginning the investigation," Gabe Wilcox told me as he glared at Ollie. "We barely know anything at this point."

"Of course," I nodded. Ollie snorted.

"Well, I have to inform Joe his son was found," Wilcox sighed, and gestured to me. "Let me run and get a printout of this so you can get out of here."

* * *

Just as Detective Wilcox and Ollie disappeared toward the back of the room, a silvery-haired old woman poked my shoulder. Her wrinkled and spectacled face thrust down two inches from my own. "Are you my grandson's girlfriend?" she demanded with a look of determination, her watery blue eyes sparkling. "You're sitting at his desk, and you don't look like a criminal to me."

"Now, Bessie, that any way to introduce yourself?" a female voice challenged from behind her.

"Claire, I'm eighty-four years old. I don't have time to fiddle-fart around with subtleties. They just waste time," Bessie snapped without withdrawing her face so much as a millimeter from mine. "Well, girl? Speak up. Are you Gabe's sweetheart?"

"No, ma'am," I explained politely while leaning ever so slightly away from the woman.

"You're not a hooker, then, are you? Pretty girl like you, that's the only kind of criminal I'd guess you are," her eyes narrowed. My eyes widened.

"No, ma'am!" I answered again, horrified.

"That's good. Good girl," the old woman stood up and nodded. "Too many hookers in this town. We don't need no more of them."

"Bessie Baker, you stop harassing this young lady," a short, stocky woman with short hair said as she walked around and lightly grabbed Bessie's arm. "Let's go over to the bench and wait for your grandson there."

"I wouldn't have to hassle her if you would go out with my grandson!" Bessie pouted as she yanked her arm out from Claire's grasp.

"Miss Bessie, I've told you a hundred times, I don't like men," Claire lifted her eyebrows at the old woman.

"Well, I don't like men, either. I don't see what that has to do with anything!"

"She's gay, Miss Bessie," the golden-haired man at the next desk told the old woman. "That's why she wouldn't go out with me in high school."

"I know that she's gay, Beau Conroe!" The old woman spat at the disheveled detective. "I spend all day and every day with Claire, you think I don't realize she's gay? I see that she's gay. I watch *Ellen* at the nursing home. I'm modern!"

"Then why are you trying to get Gabe to go out with Claire, Miss Bessie?" Beau asked her as he leaned back in his chair with a smirk.

"You respect your elders, Beau, and don't ask me ridiculous questions," Miss Bessie snapped as she waved her hand at the man.

"Grandma, what are you doing here? Claire," Detective Wilcox nodded to Ms. Bessie's keeper as he stepped around his chair to welcome the prickly old woman. "I've got a murder case today so I can't do lunch. I wish you would've called first."

"If I'd have called you would've told me not to come and I never would've met your new girlfriend," Miss Bessie told him as she whacked a palm on my back. I flinched.

"I'm not his girlfriend, Miss Bessie," I started, but the old woman whirled on me quicker than I would've expected her capable of at her age and condition. With a flourish, she jabbed a finger in my face.

"Did I say you could call me Miss Bessie?" she cracked.

"No ma'am," I shook my head no, eyes large.

Turning back to her grandson Gabe, she put an arm around me and pointed with her other hand. "This one's not a hooker, Gabe."

"I'm absolutely not, no," I concurred with dizzy velocity.

"Grandma, this is Fortuna Delphi. She's launching an art shop in the town center. In the old record shop building. Ms. Delphi, this is my grandmother, Bessie Baker. She was born in this town, so if there's anything you want to know about your new home, she'd be a great resource to ask," he said rapidly with a yearning glance toward the exit. "In fact, why don't the two of you go to lunch at *Mr. Rice Guy* and get to know each other? It's your favorite, Gram."

Why did this guy think I wanted to go out to lunch with his grandmother? I needed to get back to the brownstone so I could talk to Spike now that the police had cleared out of my place.

If he was still at my place at all. I hoped now that the body was removed he could leave the location.

"It's nice to meet you, Ms. Delphi," Claire said reaching out her hand. "My name is Claire Chaplin. I'm Miss Bessie's personal caregiver."

"And I'm Miss Bessie," the old woman stuck her hand out to shake mine after Claire and I exchanged pleasantries.

"It's nice to meet you both," I responded, shaking her exceptionally strong wrinkled hand. "What would you suggest that I call you?"

"Well. Miss Bessie. What the hell else would you call me, girl?"

"But you said—"

"Mrs. Baker makes me sound like a schoolmarm, and Bart's been in the ground over twenty-five years now. I've been the Widow Baker longer than I was Mrs. Baker. But if anyone calls me the Widow Baker, I'll smack him in the head," she raised her voice while crossing her arms. As she glared from man to man around the station, all the men buried their heads in their computers.

"Miss Bessie it is, then—"

"Anyway, back to the reason I came," the old woman flapped her hands. "Are you going to go out with her, Gabe?" Miss Bessie asked her grandson as she punched me on the back yet again. "She's cute, and you get first crack at her before the other fellows in town."

"Pardon me?" I sat back in my chair trying not to blush.

"Grandma, I have to get Fortuna to sign the statement and then go let Joe Mason know that we found his boy," Gabe told the old woman. "I promise, I'm not trying to duck you or avoid this conversation. Though if I didn't have an actual case, make no mistake—I would be."

"The sweet one with the crazy spiky hair?" Miss Bessie asked. Gabe nodded. "Did he pass on?"

Gabe nodded again. "Poor Joe. First his wife and then his boy."

"Well, Grandma, Willy Mason's been gone for a *long* time. I don't think it will come as a shock to Joe that Will's dead. I'm sure he'll have some questions, though, that I can't answer just yet."

Detective Wilcox pointed to the bottom of the paper. I skimmed over the statement and signed it. Handing the pen back to him, I asked if the police would have any more need of my bedroom, and he shook his head as Claire stopped Miss Bessie from interjecting an off-color comment.

"I doubt there is any evidence left after this many years," he said.

"Okay then!" Miss Bessie exclaimed and snatched my arm. "Come with me, girl! Let's go get some lunch."

"I wanted to—"

"What? I can't hear you," she said as she turned away and dragged me toward the door.

"It's really better to just go along with it," Claire leaned toward me and murmured. "You may think she'll forget about you by tomorrow if you beg off now, but I assure you that old woman's brain is like a sieve."

"Oh?"

Claire nodded as we followed Miss Bessie out. "Sure, a lot of stuff leaks out but the important stuff is locked in there, and once she decides something will happen? You won't be filtered out as a priority until she gets what she wants. And you don't want to be a priority."

"No?"

"No. Trust me."

FOUR

"So, where are you from?" Miss Bessie asked me as we slid into a booth at *Mr. Rice Guy*. "California originally," I told her as I grabbed a sticky plastic menu. Despite the Southern decorations strewn around the intimate (small) dining establishment, the menu consisted of a variety of Asian-inspired rice bowls ranging from bland to spicy. "My parents sent me to boarding school in New York, though, so I grew up on both sides of the country."

Claire moved the glass of ice water slightly outside the range of Miss Bessie's animated arms as the old woman squinted at me. "Coastal elite, are ya? What are you doing in some podunk town in Arkansas?"

Miss Bessie hadn't impressed me as someone that could hold a confidence. Since I barely knew the woman, I decided not to tell her about my history with Mystic's End. I gave her a generic answer about the beauty of the Ouachita Mountains, the Hot Springs, and the low cost of living.

"It's low because no one wants to live here," she sniffed.

"Now, Miss Bessie, that's not true and you know it," Claire chided her.

"*I* don't want to live here. Do *you* want to live here?" she asked impatiently.

"If I didn't want to, I wouldn't," Claire responded as she smiled across the table at me. "Mystic's End has a lot of charm, or at least it used to."

"I think it's an adorable little town," I said.

"That's because you haven't gotten to know it yet," Miss Bessie said as she peered behind me. "Gangsters at the casino, Mafia at the dog track, shady politicians at the penitentiary." She leaned back in the booth and flapped her hands in the air. Leaning over, she whispered. "There are even corrupt *police* officers. They're on the *take*. Though *not* Gabriel."

"Miss Bessie, you'll scare poor Fortuna," Claire told Bessie.

"I *should* scare her," Bessie said pointing a finger at me. "She'd be wise to be terrified before this town sucks all the marrow from her bones and leaves her a shell of the woman she was meant to be!"

Claire grabbed her hand and tenderly lowered her finger. "Miss Bessie! Where are your Southern manners!"

"Ellen wouldn't care about my Southern manners," she grunted.

"Miss Bessie would like to apologize for her behavior," Claire said as she tilted her head in my direction. I smiled and struggled not to laugh at Miss Bessie and her dramatic take on the intricacies of the town's shadow narrative. My telepathic sense gave me a clear picture of the old woman. She was far more concerned with her performance in presenting the risks than she was my safety as a potential victim of them.

"That's all right, truly," I said as I replaced the menu at the end of the table. "At eighty-four years of age, I think Miss Bessie's more than earned the right to her own unique take on things."

"Damn straight I have. I like you," Miss Bessie slapped her palm on the table and shot an accusatory glance at Claire. "Why can't you be more like Fortuna, girl?"

"Because I've worked for you for three years,

Miss Bessie," Claire told her, smirking. "After three years with you I've got my own particular take on things, too."

"You're never any fun," Bessie grumbled.

"I'm way more entertaining than the nursing home," Claire countered.

Miss Bessie harrumphed and fell silent, scanning the patrons of *Mr. Rice Guy* and softly cataloging any new pairings she came across for later nursing home gossip.

"When are you planning to open the art studio?" Claire asked after the waitress left to put in our orders.

"I expected to open today," I told her as I sipped my iced tea. I explained that though the damage was on the third floor of the brownstone and out of sight of the public, I wanted to have the wall fixed before launching the shop. "The second and third floors aren't really that detached. I wouldn't want someone creeping up to get a peek at the wall and wind up getting hurt."

"Why not just lock up your bed chamber?" Miss Bessie demanded.

"I like the open staircases," I told her, explaining that putting up walls and a door now would be just as much work as patching the wall the police damaged to remove Spike's bones.

"Who's Spike?" Bessie asked, her eyes narrowing. Her mind closed to me.

"That was Willy Mason's nickname, Bessie," Claire told her.

I sipped my tea again to cover my slip up. No one had told me much about Spike's past. I was sure no one other than Spike himself had told me his nickname.

"*I* know. But how did *she* know?" Bessie pointed with her omniscient finger.

"Gabe must have told her."

"I wish he would go by his full name," Bessie complained as she ricocheted onto a new subject. "Gabe sounds like a middle-aged man that has given up on life. Gabriel is an *angel*. A Christmas angel, in fact! That's where Mary got—" Bessie abruptly closed her mouth and looked out the window.

"Who's Mary?" I asked. Bessie turned to me and narrowed her eyes. Images of an elegant young woman laughing and hugging a little boy flipped through the old woman's mind. Then, suddenly, the young woman lying still. I startled a bit as I realized the young woman was dead.

"Move, Claire," Bessie barked. "My bladder ain't what it used to be." Claire asked if she would need help, but the old woman shook her head forcefully and shoved the younger woman away.

Shuffling toward the back of the restaurant, she paused to say hello to almost everyone she passed despite her sudden sour demeanor.

"Miss Bessie raised Gabe from the time he was ten years old. After her daughter, Mary, drowned," Claire confessed quietly. "It still troubles her greatly. Mary was her only child."

"I'm sorry, I didn't know," I apologized.

"Don't worry about it. How could you?" she smiled and ran her hand through her close cropped hair. "You're not a mind reader."

* * *

"Let's go see her studio," Miss Bessie said as she opened the door and clambered out of the car. "We took her out to lunch, it's the *least* she can do."

I waved off Claire's concerns as she struggled to persuade Miss Bessie to get back in the car. "That's not a problem at all," I told them both as I glimpsed Spike's ghostly face peering out at us through the front window. "It seems like Miss Bessie knows everyone in the town. She'll be free advertising."

"I don't come cheap, girly," the old woman said as she followed me to the front door. "If you want me to talk up your little shop, you better inspire the dickens out of me or tickle my palm. If you get my drift."

As soon as I pushed open the door, Spike pelted me with questions about what had transpired at the police station. "Are they going to come back here? Do they know who murdered me? Does my father know someone found me?"

I glared at the ghost and then stared at the two women pointedly.

"Why don't you just tell them you can talk to ghosts?" Spike asked with irritation. Closing the front door, I welcomed the two women in and dropped my purse on the crystal ball table in front. "Miss Bessie knows all the secrets, anyway. She'll find out yours, too."

"Fortuna, did you do this painting?" Claire breathed as she looked at an oil landscape of a flowered field in pinks and blues. "It's so soft, almost like...I don't even know what it's like, I've never seen anything like it."

"It's in an Impressionist-like style," I told her. A burst of gray zipped across the front window of my shop. I leaned down and searched the street, but saw nothing.

"What's wrong?" Spike asked.

"I thought I saw something."

"What did you see?" Bessie asked as she pressed her face against the clean, streak-free glass. "Was it Gabriel?"

"No, ma'am," I said as I locked the front door.

"Are you locking us in here? Maybe I'm wrong about you, girl," Bessie said as she trudged up and stuck her face in mine. "Are you a crazy person? Are you taking us hostage?"

"Miss Bessie—"

"She's just teasing you," Claire told me as she leaned down and looked into the selenite crystal ball I kept at the front of the store. "Is this a crystal ball?" I nodded.

"It's a selenite sphere from Morocco."

"Why do you have it in your shop?"

"Because she's a witch, and she sees ghosts," Spike said as he hovered around Claire. Claire scratched her head and waved her hand around her face as if a fly was buzzing near. "You're in a haunted brownstone!" Spike laughed and flew toward the front door only to ricochet off as if it was made of elastic. "And so am I," he laughed. Then his face fell. "Probably forever."

I glared at him but couldn't say anything out loud.

"What? They can't hear me," he shrugged.

"What causes you to assume *that*, young man?" Miss Bessie asked looking straight at the twinkling, mohawked Spike. The ghost skidded to a stop and froze, gawking at the old woman. His mouth pulsed open like a fish out of water. "Close your mouth, you look like a moron."

Spike closed his mouth.

"You, too," she gestured to me.

I closed my mouth.

"I'm sorry, this must've been a long day for her," Claire said as she put a gentle arm around Miss Bessie. "Sometimes she just talks gibberish. It's not often, though. I should probably get her back to the nursing home."

"She doesn't know," Miss Bessie told me plainly as she let Claire lead her toward the door. "You know, though, don't you?" she said as she sent an impression of an infant squalling on the step of a police department directly into my mind.

"Wait, please—" I gasped, stepping forward.

"I honestly can't, Fortuna. I really need to get Bessie back so she can lay down."

"Come see me, Fortuna," Bessie sang as Claire hustled her out of the door and back into the station wagon.

"I can't believe it," Spike said as he watched them drive away. "That woman could see me through this window for over twenty years and she never came in to say hello. How *rude*."

I waved my hand to silence Spike and stepped through the front door. Standing on the pavement in front of my new home, I watched Claire and Miss Bessie drive down Main Street toward the nursing home south of the square.

Did she know that I was a witch? Was she a witch?

Although I was a telepath, the old woman had concealed what she knew about me the entire afternoon we were together. I never picked up so much as an inkling in her mind she was a psychic, or that she knew who I was.

I was off my game.

Turning to go back in the shop, a gray dog barred my doorway. The soft brown eyes peered up at me, head angled, as he sat on the step. A step much like the one in the psychic image Miss Bessie had sent me.

"Where d'you come from?" I asked the dog. He barked. "Go on. Go back home." It thrust a vision of my front door into my mind. "Did you do that? Did you send me that?" He flung an unusually excited image of me opening the door and accepting the dog into my store into my mind. "Ow!"

The gray dog yapped and skipped forward to press his body against my leg. I reached down and patted his smooth, long head and sighed.

"Come on," I told him and opened the door.

Though with far less excitement than the dog had hoped.

FIVE

"I'm allergic to dogs," Spike said as he gawked at the barrel-chested greyhound.

"You're a ghost," I informed him. "You don't even have a nose. You're not allergic to anything anymore."

"I don't *like* dogs." He launched himself onto the counter and settled atop it like a nervous elephant that had just seen a mouse. "That's one of the racing dogs, anyway. You *don't* want to get caught with them. Some of them are worth a lot of cash."

"I found him on my front stoop."

"Doesn't matter *where* you found him," Spike said. "He's not a normal dog, he's a racer. Someone's probably looking for him."

"He doesn't have a collar," I said as I kneeled down in front of the sleek greyhound. He nuzzled my cheek, wagged his tail, and licked my face with a loud slurp. "He's probably a stray."

"He has a tattoo," Spike said as he glided over the dog and waved toward his ear. "Identification numbers."

"Which ear?"

"Both."

I flipped over the dog's ear and found blue-gray letters and numbers on the soft skin inside. "So. That's kind of horrifying." They looked similar to *certain* tattoos I'd seen in history books, and my stomach churned a little in revulsion.

"Some of these dogs are worth a lot, like I said. That's how they keep track. They tattoo their ears as puppies."

I shuddered, and the dog shuddered. Then he barked as the bells on the front door announced a visitor.

"Where did you get the dog?" Gabe Wilcox asked as he strolled into my studio.

"He was on the front step after your grandmother left," I said as I stood up.

"Looks like he's from the track," Gabe said as he stepped over to the large greyhound and kneeled in front of him. The dog hopped on his front paws and whimpered faintly. "Have you checked his tattoos?"

"I saw that he had some," I said, grateful to Spike that I sounded knowledgeable.

"You can look up who he is on the data site for greyhounds," Detective Wilcox said as he pulled out his phone. Tugging on the dog's ear, he mumbled what he read to himself and then stood back up to type something into his phone. "Uh oh."

"Uh oh?" Gabriel's face showed a level of concern for the dog's ownership that he hadn't bothered to show for Spike's murder.

"Well, as long as you get him back to the track, you shouldn't have a problem," Gabe said glancing up at me. "But that's Reverend Dexter Kane's greyhound. He just won a race three days ago, so they *will* miss him for sure. I wonder how he got so far from the track," Gabe said as he scratched the dog again. An image of the dog jumping the fence flashed in my mind.

"I guess I can't just keep him?" I asked the detective hopefully. Within a very short time I'd become attached to the dog. This was, incidentally, the reason I had been reluctant to allow the dog in. As soon as he navigated the threshold of my store, the dog was pretty well mine. The dark-colored dog whined as he stared at the detective and wagged his tail.

"In this state, an animal's property," Gabe shook his head. "Greyhound ownership is pretty well documented, Ms. Delphi. Probably the best documented animal ownership there is around here."

The dog barked.

"I spent the entire afternoon with your grandmother—just call me Fortuna, Detective," I told him as I considered what to do. Greyhound racing was distasteful to me, but provoking the town preacher by telling him that didn't seem very neighborly. "Well, he doesn't *look* like they have harmed him."

"He's a winner, so that's unlikely." Spike nodded and concurred with the detective.

"If he was a loser, it would have been okay to abuse him?" I shot back.

"Slow down there, Greenpeace. That's not what I mean," Gabe said with an eyebrow lifted and a half-smile. Well, we went from Ms. Delphi to a snarky nickname awfully quickly. "A winning racer? He's making someone money. Reverend Dexter will not treat his cash pup poorly. Dog probably has one of the larger kennels and better food at the track. At least that'd be my guess judging by his racing wins."

That the dog had a slightly larger cage than his buddies didn't make me feel any happier about returning him.

"You have a kennel to transport him back?"

I shook my head no. "Can't they just come and get him? Why should I return him back there? Don't you have an animal control department that deals with strays?"

"That's *not* a stray. That's a racing greyhound. I, um...I wouldn't want some of those guys in *my* shop, if you know what I mean," Detective Wilcox said, looking uneasy. "Pretty girl, living alone. If you called animal control and let them know that you have a found greyhound, they'll just call the track to come get the dog. Get me?"

"Let's just pretend that I get you," I observed while struggling not to blush after he called me pretty. "That dancing around the point thing you do? That's the exact *opposite* of your grandmother, by the way."

"Yeah, about that," Gabe Wilcox smiled. "Sorry about pushing you into lunch with her. I really thought she'd be a good resource for you, and she loves art."

"Does she?"

The greyhound barked.

"She painted a lot when she was younger," he nodded. "Before..." His voice trailed off and his eyes took on a distant look. After a few seconds, they cleared. "Well, anyway, it's not something she's done in a really long time. I thought getting hooked up with you might help keep her out of trouble."

"That little old lady? Trouble?" I chuckled, but he didn't respond with a laugh.

I didn't need to reach out with my telepathy to pick up on the recollection of his mother floating in the air between us. My powers were something I could extend out and pull in at will, but I didn't need to reach for his pain. The look in his eye was enough to get a sense of his ache for her.

"I'll definitely see if I can get her involved in the shop," I assured him. "Maybe I should talk to the nursing home about starting an art class over there. I'm sure she can't be the only one that might enjoy it."

"Have you been over there to meet some folks at the nursing home?" he asked, his eyebrow raised. I shook my head no. "Go over there and meet a few of the old folks first. Decide if you would want to teach them in a group altogether. If you get my meaning."

"Your meaning suggests that the aged in this town are unruly when in a group?"

The detective coughed. "It'd be best if you, ah, went over there and saw for yourself."

"You just don't like to say anything very specific, do you?" Gabriel looked shocked, but then conceded my point with a nod.

"I never really noticed it before," Gabriel shrugged. I stared at the cautious man with my eyebrow raised. The dog barked again. "I have a crate in the back of my SUV. I could drive you over to return him if you want."

"Can't you just take him back?" I inquired with some regret. The dog's tail drooped, and he whined.

"Yes, cop, take the dog back," Spike said with a heavy dose of mockery. The greyhound narrowed its soft brown eyes and rumbled in the ghost's direction. "Oh, you can't see me so just cut it out." The hound growled louder.

"I...um...well, I'm not that popular with the boys that work at the track," Gabriel responded. "I'm happy to give you a ride over there, but if I show up with a missing dog I'm likely to be blamed for his removal. Especially considering he's Kane's dog."

I noted the shift in Gabriel's phrasing, and the dropping of the honorific when speaking of the Reverend. "Do you and the Reverend not get along?

"The right Reverend Dexter Kane is not fond of me, no ma'am," Detective Wilcox shook his head. "He believes I led his son on a corrupt and damned path of sin."

That took me aback. Gabriel Wilcox was so clean cut with a well-ironed shirt and perfectly cuffed slacks—I couldn't picture him leading *anyone* toward corruption. If I had learned anything at the Magical Midway, however, it's that looks can be deceiving.

"Are you just going to leave me hanging?"

"I encouraged his son Ollie to join the police department."

"The long-haired guy from the police station? His father owns this dog?"

Gabe nodded.

"That's it? His son got a job he didn't like and he blames you?" That didn't seem like much of a reason to accuse someone of stealing a dog.

"Well, and I introduced Ollie to beer."

"That's it?"

"And motorcycles," Detective Wilcox added. "And I took him to get his first tattoo. After the tattoo, he grew his hair down to his rear end and his father wasn't all that pleased. I don't think that's my fault, though."

"I suppose not," I smiled.

"Reverend Kane *hates* all that stuff," Spike told me. "Dude tried to perform an exorcism on me because I got a mohawk one night when I slept over at Ollie's. He is *seriously* out of his mind."

"I guess it didn't work," I muttered to Spike.

"You guess what didn't work?" Gabriel asked.

"Um, the Reverend's attempts to blame you," I blurted out to cover I was talking to a ghost. "It seemed like you and Ollie are still friends and he's still working at the police department."

"Yeah, no, that's true," he said sounding unconvinced by my attempts to cover.

The greyhound walked toward the back of the room, found a pile of textile scraps and pawed at them until they made a suitable mound. With a sigh, the dog dropped his spindly body on top of them and laid his head down to go to sleep. One eye popped open to stare at us defiantly.

"Are you sure I can't keep him?" I asked hopefully, but the detective shook his head no. "Well, then we probably should get him back to the track. I have nothing to feed a dog and it will probably be his dinnertime soon."

"You're right," he nodded. "Let me go pull my truck around and I'll drive you over there.

"Thanks, detective, I appreciate you helping me," I told him as I leaned down to pet the dog again. "I still don't have a car. I probably should get one."

"Just call me Gabe. You don't have a car?" he paused and stared at me, shocked. I shook my head no. "How did you move here if you didn't have a car?"

"Teleportation," Spike laughed.

"I came with the moving vans," I told him. I just didn't tell him the moving vans were teleported here by Charlotte. "Since there's a small grocer in the square and I live in the store, it didn't seem like it was super important. I could just use my app if I need to go further than that," I shrugged as I waved my phone.

"I could take you to go look for a car if you like," he offered while standing in the archway.

"You want to help me go look for a car?" I asked him. I realized when his face took on a defensive look I may have sounded more incredulous than I intended to. "Look, it's not that I'm not grateful—I just figured you probably had a lot more important things to do."

"My grandmother really enjoyed her lunch with you. I got a call as soon as she pulled away," he said leaning against the door. "Honestly, it's been a long time since I heard her that excited about anything. And if you don't have a car? You won't be able to go over to the nursing home to visit her."

"So you have an ulterior motive, then?" I laughed.

The dog barked.

"I do," he nodded. "Though this is a small town, Fortuna. We help each other out." We stared at each other for longer than was strictly necessary, and I wondered if the handsome detective had another motive he wasn't divulging. I thought about reading his mind but I stopped myself.

The quickest way to end a relationship of any type? Read the mind of the person you're interested in even though they believe their thoughts are private.

No one is on their best behavior in their own mind.

"I'll go get the truck." He smiled and headed out the door.

SIX

With a kind of astonished horror, I gawked at the imposing metal fencing that surrounded the back entrance to the Greyhound track. The runaway pooch in the back barked unhappily as we pulled up.

"What do *you* want?" a rugged-looking security guard asked Gabe through the window. His expression was sharp, even suspicious, as he leaned down and glanced at me across the front seat. "Entrance to the strip club is on the other side of the lot," the man laughed noisily at his own joke.

It was clear the man was trying to imply *I* was a stripper and Gabriel was dropping me off for work, but I decided that he *had* to have meant something else. Because if he meant what I first thought he meant I would have felt compelled to deck him, and doing that in front of a cop would probably be a bad idea.

"This is Fortuna Delphi, she just opened an art studio in the square," Gabe said as a muscle in his jaw twitched. "Dexter Kane's dog must have wanted to paint." Gabe leaned forward and hitched his thumb toward the backseat where the dark-colored greyhound glared at the guard. "Check the fence line. Must be a hole in it."

"Gideon-Jerubbesheth-the-Valiant?" the man choked, his face white. He gestured wildly to another tough looking guard watching from a station and the barbed wire topped fence clanged open to let us in.

All suspicion and aggressive pretense had drained from the guard. He now looked panicked. "Go see Hoyt at the end of the stall, quick-like. My cousin Jeb is supposed to be taking care of the dogs today, and he'll lose his job if Dexter finds out that hound's been missing. My Daddy'd *kill* me if that happened."

"Look, Bart, I don't want to go into the track—"

"Come on, Gabe, don't be a jerk about this," Bart said as he stood up and peered around desperately. After assuring himself that we were not being watched, he leaned down again. "I got no wagon or golf cart to get the dog back to where he needs to be. I can't lead him. I got no reason to be around the dogs. Someone sees me, I'm *toast*."

"Okay, okay, but you get whatever hole he ran out of patched up," Gabe said as he stepped on the brake, and put the car into drive.

"You're a good man, Gabe."

"Yeah, that's why you gave me such a pleasant reception, right?"

"Oh, that, yeah," he said with an uncomfortable grin. "C'mon, man, *you* know how it is here." Gabe nodded. "Thanks again, man. I owe you one."

"If I ever collected all the beers you owe me, Bart, I'd have alcohol poisoning," the detective said as he pulled away, window still down. Looking in his rear-view mirror, he informed the greyhound, "Gideon, your adventure's practically over. We'll have you back with your mates in a few minutes."

The hound whined sadly. I sighed.

"If he ever stops winning, you *could* always adopt him at one of the rescue adoption days," Gabe said as we pulled toward a huge gray building with hanger-size double doors. The setup was so vast it looked like you could hide a passenger jet in there without a problem.

"What do you mean?" I asked.

"Their owners don't want them for pets. They want them for competing. When they stop winning? They're *finished* with 'em. Want 'em gone as quick as they can get them gone so they can stop paying to feed and house them."

"That's awful!"

"Not really," Gabe pulled up next to the door. "When these dogs are retired, they finally get a family and a home," he added as he shut off the car and opened his door. "If the greys knew the life of leisure awaiting them, they'd probably just lay down and sun themselves when the gate opened."

I peeked back at the crate. Gideon's head shifted and I *swear* it looked like that dog was smirking.

* * *

"Stupid dog," Hoyt Abernathy said as he snapped a lead to Gideon's collar and yanked just a little too roughly.

"Hey!" I objected and stepped forward without thinking. "It's not his fault there was a hole in *your* fence and he got out! Don't jerk on him like that. That's just mean."

"Aren't *you* tender-hearted," he scoffed and yanked again. My face burned with indignation as Gideon's tail wrapped itself up underneath his belly and the dog sank his head. I mentally rushed through my limited repertoire of witchcraft skills to see if I could remember being taught a spell for boils. Big ones.

"Hoyt, she found the dog and called the police to get help returning him," Gabe lied as he casually stepped in front of me. "You owe her a debt of gratitude that we could bring him back before Dexter Kane knew—"

"Before I knew what?" an imperious, heavily Southern voice reverberated from within the drab building. The four of us (including the dog) turned to the open rolling door just in time to see a tall, gray-haired man in an ill-fitting suit walk out. Behind him another followed, all dark hair, white teeth, smoldering eyes and cologne. I coughed.

"Reverend Kane, sir," Hoyt bowed and scraped so much that I thought the man would fall over onto the cleric's dusty leather shoes. "I didn't know you were here, sir. I was just takin' your Gideon for a walk to keep his legs supple and this girl here stopped us, sir, and I told her not to disturb him because you would be mad and I said she should be glad—"

"Dear God, you ignorant buffoon, just stop your talking," the Reverend drawled to Hoyt, his scorn for the lying track worker clear. "You could wear the horns off a billy goat, son." Reverend Kane turned toward Gabriel, his face puckering. "What are *you* doing here, boy? Run out of real police work?"

"Actually, we were here to ask Hoyt about Will Mason," Gabriel lied smoothly as he gestured toward the nervous track hand while ignoring the preacher's disrespect. "Maybe you all hadn't heard, but Will's body was discovered this morning. In her wall, in fact," he said, pointing to me.

"After all this time?" the heavy-lidded man next to Reverend Kane asked in a deep voice. His outward expression was steady and indicated neither surprise nor concern.

"Yes, sir," Gabe nodded.

"Well, his father will be happy you found his son's body. Some closure, at least," the man replied.

"Perhaps the intervening years have ensured the hideous hairstyle has decayed with that dishonest boy," Reverend Kane sneered. The two men chuckled. Kane's comment and laugh were far more callous than I would have expected from a man of God. "Hoyt here had the same issue as that Mason boy, but we disabused him of his folly right quick. Didn't we, son?"

"Yes, sir," Hoyt said with a strong bow, his face aflame.

"Get my dog back to his kennel," Kane barked before Hoyt's head was upright again. The worker jumped and stumbled quickly into the dusty building dragging Gideon behind him. The dog gave me a last yearning glance over his shoulder and then disappeared. "That dumb dog. If he didn't run so fast I wouldn't put up with his ridiculous independent streak."

"He's a dog, sir. Maybe he just doesn't appreciate being in a pen all the time." Six eyes swung to me, one pair concerned and the other two clearly astonished that I had opened my mouth at all.

"What would an out-of-town artist know about racing greyhounds, I wonder?" Dexter's companion said as he inspected me. It wasn't clear whether his statement was a conclusion or a question.

The man watching me was elegant, but harsh. There was an unstable energy about him, an intensity that put me on guard even more than Dexter Kane's obvious aggression. The preacher seemed like an alpha bulldog off his leash. This man was like a coiled snake patiently waiting to strike.

"I know being caged and then coming out to run in circles doesn't sound like an enjoyable life, that's all," I said, dropping my eyes down so the man wouldn't see the tears that had sprung to my eyes. Poor Gideon's life seemed so dreary and he looked so sorry to be back.

And his owner seemed like a *complete* jerk.

A CB radio on the snake man's hip crackled. *"All units, we're en route to a grass fire at Harvard and Blossom in the east parking field. We expect traffic to be impacted, please reroute to west parking field."*

"Well, I must check on that. Dexter," the man said as he reduced the volume on his walkie talkie. "You let me know about that fund-raising dinner, and we'll get everything set up for you."

"Thanks, Martin, the church appreciates the discount," the Reverend nodded as he shook hands.

"Hope your Gideon recovers enough from his experience to place tonight," Martin slapped the Reverend on the shoulder. "You two can show yourselves out, I take it?" His dark brown eyes met mine, and he stared at me with intensity. "Or do you need an attendant to show you the way?"

"No, sir, Mr. Salvi," Gabe told him. "We've got it." Martin Salvi nodded back and spun around to walk away. As if suddenly struck by an idea, he paused, turned back and called to me. "Come to the races tonight! Come as my guest. Perhaps I can change your mind about greyhound racing."

"I doubt it, Mr. Salvi," I called back.

"You doubt that you'll come, or you doubt I can change your mind?" I opened my mouth to speak, but he raised his hand to stop me. "Don't tell me.

Surprise me. I *love* surprises, Miss Delphi. They're hardly ever disappointments."

He winked at me and strode away.

* * *

As soon as Martin Salvi left, Dexter Kane had dismissed us without so much as a polite goodbye and left us standing alone on the dusty road.

If he treated *people* this poorly I didn't even want to contemplate how he treated Gideon. If he even thought of the dog at all, beyond whether he had won a race.

"How did he know my name?" I asked Gabriel once we were back in the car.

"How did *who* know your name?" Gabriel asked distractedly as Bart let us back out of the gate. The security guard looked at Gabe hopefully, and Gabe flashed him a thumb's up sign. With relief, Bart pumped his hand in the air and grinned.

"Martin Salvi," I said as we pulled out and started back toward my shop. "How did he know my name? You said that I owned a shop, but I don't think you ever said my name to him. Which *was* kind of rude, by the way."

"Martin Salvi knows everything that happens in this town," Gabe said as we drove through the tree-lined streets, traffic on the opposite side already building for the greyhound races in a few hours. "He's the head of the track, and the restaurant there, and the bar. The track is a full entertainment complex."

"So I heard. A strip club, too, hmm?" I asked casually as I looked out the window.

"Yeah, that…Yeah, there's one there. It's an adult playground, I guess. Whatever you want you can get at Mystic's End." The mocking tone of his voice made it clear this wasn't something he was happy about.

"Well, it *is* legal, at least." Unless that was where the hookers his grandmother complained about congregated.

"Not all of it," he countered under his breath.

"Maybe someone should tell the cops."

"If it would do any good, people probably would," Gabe said indignantly, and I shifted away to look out the window. I had hit a nerve and since I didn't know him very well, I didn't want to hit another one. He drove silently, clearly aggravated.

After a few minutes of silence, Gabe spoke again.

"Look, I'm sorry," Gabriel said. "Seeing Dexter Kane or having to go to the track just puts me in a bad mood."

"Don't worry about it. I—"

"So, my day off is tomorrow. Want to go look for that car?" he asked, cutting me off and changing the subject abruptly.

"That would be really kind of you," I nodded. "Thanks."

We drove the rest of the way back making small talk and studiously avoiding any discussion of Dexter Kane, the Mystic's End Racetrack, or Gideon.

As I walked into my shop, I glanced at the pile of textile scraps. They were still dented in the center from Gideon's warm body and as I picked them up and resettled them, I tried to push thoughts of the greyhound from my mind.

SEVEN

"Well, get in the car, 'Tuna, we don't have all day," Bessie demanded through the back passenger side window the next morning. Despite the humidity, they'd rolled down the windows. Gabe smiled at me from the driver side as I opened the door. "You don't mind if I call you 'Tuna, do you?" she asked me as I slid in.

"I don't prefer it," I told her, surprised that the old woman was in the car. I hadn't forgotten about the fact that she was able to see Spike (or her invitation to come see her), but I hadn't decided yet exactly how I wanted to handle it. I was hoping to avoid the old woman while I contemplated how to deal with her.

No such luck.

"Well, how do you expect an old lady to recall such a peculiar, newfangled name like yours," Bessie muttered more to herself than to me. Claire sat quietly in the backseat next to Bessie. She nodded and mouthed an apology. I shrugged and grinned.

"It's not a *new* name," I told her as Gabe pulled the car away from the curb. "It's an archaic name, actually. Fortuna was the Roman goddess of fortune and luck."

"Well, that's not pretentious at *all*, now, is it? Who in their right mind would name a helpless baby that?" she observed as she slapped her hand against Gabe's seat. "Taking the name of a goddess! My goodness. My name is old, too, you know. The Hebrew name Elisheba. And you thought *Fortuna* was a mouthful," Bessie laughed vigorously at her own joke as she slapped Gabe's seat even harder.

"Since you said both just fine, Miss Bessie, how about we just call Fortuna by her actual name instead of 'Tuna," Claire told her charge. "I doubt anyone wants to be called a fish."

"Some fish have really pretty names," Gabe said as he glanced into the rearview mirror. "There's Koi. Cisco. Goby. That's not to say I think 'Tuna is a good nickname."

"How about For, then?" Bessie asked. "I don't know what on earth your parents were thinking namin' you *Fortuna*. We'd have made fun of you a damn sight more than most in school, child."

"Maybe everybody wanted to sit next to her during tests hoping that she would bring them luck," Claire suggested as we traveled down Main Street.

"That wasn't my name back then," I told the car without realizing. I immediately regretted the words as the old lady's nose twitched in the backseat as if I had just waved a red knitted afghan in front of an old bull.

"Oh, it *wasn't*, now? It sounds like there's a tale here," Bessie said with a smile as she elbowed Claire. "What was your name when you were a little one?"

"Heather Addington," Gabe murmured. I stopped breathing, astonished that Gabe knew the name I had before my present one. At the Magical Midway, anyone could be a telepath and so I supposed everyone knew everything about me.

Since coming back to the human world, I wasn't prepared for it. On top of that? Someone learning about my past *wasn't* coincidental.

"How did you know that?" I threw the question at him as the skin on the back of his neck pinked up. "I haven't told anyone, and my legal name is Fortuna Delphi. So how did *you* know?"

"When you showed up, I did some background

checking—"

"Stop the car," I told him as I reached for the door handle. He stared at me in surprise.

"Fortuna, wait, I—"

"I said stop the damn car!" I repeated hotly, cringing that Bessie and Claire heard me curse. The car slowed its speed gently, too gently. I was so indignant I didn't even wait for the car to stop rolling before hopping out. I was halfway down the block before Gabe had it in park.

"Fortuna!"

I heard a car door open behind me but I kept walking. We couldn't be more than a mile from my shop thanks to the super-slow center of town speed limit, and it wasn't that hot out. I could walk.

"Come on, Fortuna, wait a second!"

I spun on my heel and stomped back to the detective, who was sprinting to catch up with me.

"That was a complete and utter infringement of my privacy!" I shouted at him as the two of us met on the walkway in front of a small community church. "How *dare* you dig into my past without even *speaking* to me? And how dare you divulge my original name without talking to me about it first!"

Gabe looked at me, obviously baffled that I was furious. "You told my grandmother it wasn't your original name, so I thought...Look, I didn't...I wasn't trying to—" He struggled to figure out what he was expected to explain or apologize for, and that only made me angrier.

"My past is *my* past!" I told him. "You had *no right*."

Part of me couldn't believe I was as angry as I was. Gabriel was a police officer, and I was new in town—with a dead body in my bedroom to boot. Of course he looked into me.

The other part of me knew that old tapes were playing in my mind. Children teasing me that I had been dumped as a newborn, cousins bullying me because I didn't look like the rest of the family. Gabriel blurting out such an intimate detail, a name that still made my heart seize up in anguish, was producing a fierce reaction in me.

"Now, wait a minute," he said, crossing his arms and adopting a businesslike tone. "That information is public, and this town *isn't* one that lends itself to privacy. When people *are* secretive? That normally means that they're hiding something."

"Are you accusing me of hiding something?" I demanded, even though I was.

"Well, aren't you? You were *trying* to," Gabe replied.

"Not telling you my *no longer legal* name isn't *hiding* something. And frankly, even if it was, it wouldn't have been any of your business, anyway!"

"I'm a cop, everything's my business," he

chuckled.

"Okay, *George Orwell*," I told him with a snort.

"I got a call from the sheriff in another town about you! Why *wouldn't* I look into you?" Gabe asked me incredulously. "Fortuna, you're completely overreacting to this."

"I'm *overreacting*, am I?" I spat back, even though some outrage had drained from my words as Gabe reminded me of the Mickwac sheriff's phone call. And, well, I knew I was overreacting a little.

I just wasn't sure how to stop.

"Is everything all right here?" Martin Salvi asked from a black sports car so silent I hadn't even heard it drive up next to us. His head leaned out of the rolled-down driver's side window, his fancy watch glinting in the sun.

"It's fine," Gabe told him quickly. "We're fine."

"Miss Delphi?" Martin asked as he purposely ignored Gabe. "Can I give you a ride someplace? I'm headed toward your shop, and the short trip there will give me another opportunity to persuade you to come to the track and see the races. I found myself disappointed by your absence last night."

Gabe's frown at the proposal was *all I needed* to turn on my heel and accept Salvi's invitation. "That'd be great, Mr. Salvi," I said as I shot a sullen glance at Gabe. His jaw stiffened as he watched me walk over to the sleek, expensive car. Martin jumped out and beat me to the passenger door, opening it like a gentleman.

"It would be my pleasure," Martin grinned as he gently closed the door. "Please, call me Martin."

I tried not to gloat too much as I saw Gabe's frown deepen as we pulled away.

* * *

After I unlocked the door to my shop, Martin Salvi followed me in. The aura of danger that had surrounded him was no longer detectable, and I wondered whether I had sensed it at all.

So far, he had been all rich person manners and smoldering sexiness. If Gabe Wilcox was jeans, beer, pool and hiking, Martin Salvi was pressed silk slacks, champagne, opera and 3-star restaurants.

"Would it be too forward of me to ask what that exchange was about in front of the church?" Martin asked as he dropped into an armchair without being invited.

"Gabe is nosy," I responded as I grabbed two bottled waters from the fridge, handing one to Martin. He took it gratefully and smiled, all perfectly white teeth evenly displayed between soft, well-moisturized lips. "I like my privacy, I guess, and he pushed a little too far into it without a green light."

"Good to know. It *is* a new era for men these days," he said with a head tilt. "We are all getting used to the new rules of engagement with women we are interested in."

"He's not *interested* in me," I replied. "He was just taking me to go look for a car. I don't own one. Probably should, though."

"Is that so?" Martin asked casually, his eyes twinkling as they focused on me. For a small, tiny, itty-bitty moment it seemed as if I'd forgotten how to breathe.

I inhaled deeply trying to break his spell...

...and realized he smelled *fantastic*.

"Well, I would like to help you get a car *without* making you feel obligated," he said as he stood up. "I will send one of the track limos over with a driver to transport you to the dealership."

"You think sending me a limo and driver to use will somehow make me feel *less* obligated than someone giving me a ride to a dealership?" I asked him with a lifted eyebrow.

"I don't want you to feel obliged to spend time with me, Fortuna," he told me, a slightly amused look in his eyes. "Just think of this as one local business helping another out. Not personal. After all, we have to support one another in this town."

"Look, Mr.—"

"Martin," he cut me off as he stepped closer to

me. Closer than he was, but not close enough to *really* be invading my space. Just near enough for me to mull over whether I would be comfortable with him coming closer.

I hadn't decided.

"Martin, I appreciate the offer, but—"

"Good, then that's settled," he nodded as he turned from me and reached for his phone.

"Martin, I—" He held up his finger as he began speaking to the person on the other end of the call. I fell silent as I heard him demand a limo be in front of my shop along with a directive they take me wherever it was I wished to go.

I wondered if he stole the line from *Pretty Woman* by accident, or on purpose.

* * *

"Damn," Spike said as I watched Martin Salvi slip into his preternaturally silent sports car after waving. "I am totally and absolutely straight, but even *I* could see *that* guy was smokin' hot."

"He owns the racetrack. Or he runs it. I'm not sure if he owns it or runs it," I said distractedly as I watched him drive away. "But yes, he was pretty hot."

"Barely here a *week*, girl, and you have two guys trying to snag you," Spike grinned. "Leave with one, come back with another, and all in the same hour! You work *fast!*"

"That was an accident," I dismissed him as I grabbed the empty water bottles and tossed them in the recycling. "Gabe really ticked me off."

"How?" Spike asked as he hovered from one side of the room to another like a pendulum.

"It doesn't matter," I shrugged. Spike turned and gave me a funny look, but I just shrugged again. "I didn't come here to find a boyfriend, anyway. I'm here to find out where I came from, and I don't need either of these guys to do that."

Three even knocks echoed from the glass front door. I turned and saw the driver waiting politely. He was dressed in a perfectly tailored suit, his face expectant but oddly impassive.

"I have to go get a car either way," I told Spike as I grabbed my purse. "Once I have wheels, I won't need anyone to take me anywhere, and both of them can go back to whatever they were doing before I got here."

"That's how you think this will go, hmm?" Spike asked skeptically.

"That's how it has to go," I told him before I opened the door. "I'm a witch. They're human. It's not like it could ever work out with either of them," I lied.

EIGHT

I drove up to the back of my shop with a shiny new Mercedes-Benz Sprinter. Instead of a car I opted for a cargo van. I figured it would be easier to lug around art supplies, especially if I started running classes at the nursing home.

As I locked it up and moved toward the back door a woman approached from the corner of the building. "Excuse me," she called loudly as she saw me. "Are you Fortuna Delphi?"

"Yes, that's me," I answered.

"You own the Mystic Moon Gallery?" she followed up, pointing to the heavy metal door to our right. "The one where Spike was found yesterday?"

"Who are you?" I asked, my voice wary.

"Liz Dalton," she said as she drew closer, her

heels clicking on the concrete. Liz looked to be roughly my age, her hair perfectly coiffed in a modern look that shined. A single purple streak curled around her face, and it matched the shade of her silk outfit perfectly. Her eyes were a *striking* amber color. "I'm the owner of Magic Cuts. Over there." The woman pointed to the back door next to my own.

"Nice to meet you," I nodded, still wary of the woman's mention of the dead body. I had no idea who she was, but on the off chance Liz really was just a friendly neighbor and not some murder-tourist, I didn't want to be rude.

"I used to work here in college," she told me as she joined me near the door. "Back when it was a grungy music shop."

"Oh! Are you Busy?" I asked.

"Nope, I'm done with work for the day!" Liz laughed and whacked me on the shoulder. I grinned back. "Okay, sorry, sorry. If you're asking if I was the girl that worked with Spike in the record shop when he disappeared, yes," the woman nodded as the friendly grin faded from her face. "That was me. I guess the police told you a little about the town when Spike disappeared?"

"A little," I told her, though I didn't know about her from the police. I knew about her from Spike. Not something I could explain, though.

"Crappy way to welcome you to Mystic's End, I guess," she laughed awkwardly. "Welcome to town. Here, to make you feel at home let's make sure you're assigned a role in an unsolved murder. Typical, frankly."

"Are there *typically* unsolved murders in Mystic's End?" I asked her as I pulled out my keys and unlocked the back door.

"People that disappear rarely make it into an *actual* murder investigation. They just remain an unsolved mystery, a missing person," she said as I opened the door. "That Willy's body was found at all is pretty unusual, actually. No body, no crime. No crime, no case. No case, no criminal," Liz scowled.

"I'm sure prosecutors can gather evidence and prosecute cases without a body," I told her as I balanced the heavy door against my hip. "If television is to be believed, anyway."

"Not *here*," she shook her head no. "Well, I'm sure that they *can*. They just don't. Not in Mystic's End."

I wasn't sure what to say to that, so I invited her in.

"Sure, thanks!" Liz said as she grabbed the door. "I'm really curious to see what the old place looks like now."

* * *

Spike looked at Liz Dalton curiously as he followed her around the shop. Liz's forehead creased as she examined the shelves, walls, and rooms. She was seemingly unaware that her old friend's ghost hovered behind her silently, watching.

"The whole place feels completely different," she murmured, the expression dark on her delicate features. "I haven't been in here in over twenty years, but since it sat empty, I thought it would still feel familiar somehow. It doesn't, though."

"Is it *that* different?" I asked her as I threw my keys on the counter. "I left the walls where they were, more or less."

"The store was dark," she looked away. "It feels so much more airy and open. Hopeful, I guess? Like, the aura of this place when I worked here?" Liz shuddered. "It wasn't grungy because of the music, I'll tell you that much."

"I know her. I think I know her. Do I know her?" Spike whispered as he continued to float behind her. I grabbed a pad, wrote her name, and tapped the edge of the pen on the paper. The ghost floated over, tearing his eyes from Liz to glance down at the pad. "*That's* Busy? But she's so *grown up!*"

Ollie and Bobby had been all grown up, too, but where Spike seemed happily surprised by their time-propelled adult transformation, Busy appearing as a grown woman was having the opposite effect on the frozen-in-time punk.

"I appreciate you saying that, that it feels airy," I told Liz as I watched her from behind the counter. "It's what I was going for."

"Of course, now you're the art studio in the haunted building where the dead body was found," Liz told me easily, her half-grin friendly. "So, you might need *more* pink. Maybe a streak in your hair right in the front." Liz pointed at my head.

"Um...no, no streaks of color in my hair. Just on the canvas," I said. Liz's face fell in disappointment. "Yours *is* beautiful, though. I'm usually covered in paint, and I'd hate to spend money on something like that only to scrub it out of my hair," I added quickly.

"Luckily, you have a hairdresser just one door over that could fix anything," she grinned widely. I smiled back, but then her face fell slowly. "I shouldn't laugh. Honestly, it feels a *little* wrong, laughing in here. Poor Spike. I can't believe he was just stuffed in a wall all these years."

"Well, thank goodness *someone* feels bad about that," Spike snapped as her words pulled him out of his hazy amazement and back into his annoyed indignation. "That's the first scrap of emotion I've seen out of *anyone* since they found me!"

"I've been wondering about that," I said as I handed her a bottle of water and motioned for her to sit down on the couch at the front of the shop. "Someone mentioned that you worked here at that time. How did someone *not* notice a freshly bricked-up wall upstairs?"

"I don't think *anyone* searched this place, to be honest," Liz said as she squinted at the ceiling. "Spike had gone into Little Rock for a show, and everyone just assumed that if something terrible happened to him, it must have happened in Little Rock. Besides, the top floor was really the shop owner's storage. We hardly ever had any reason to go up there."

"Shop owner?"

"Jeff Abernathy," she said, and then shuddered again. "Real piece of work, that guy. One of the *biggest* hypocrites in this town, and *that's* saying something. Rich, always in the front pew at Holy Grove Church listening to Dexter Kane blather on and *on* about the evil of gambling and music and who knows what else, but the guy's construction company built the Mystic's End Racetrack."

"Wait a minute," I said as I held up my hand. "The Reverend preaches *against* gambling?"

"Loudly, and with *great* passion," Liz said as she nodded.

"I just saw him down at the racetrack. One of his dogs wound up on my front porch and Detective Wilcox drove me over there to return him."

"*Owning a beast is not gambling*," Liz said in a grave voice, her back ramrod straight as she mimicked the Reverend.

"But the church is having some sort of dinner there—"

"*We must go to the places where the sinners congregate to save their souls*," she rasped again, her eyes wide. Then she coughed. "I said Abernathy was *one* of the biggest hypocrites. I didn't say he was the biggest, or the only."

"Your town is more complicated than I thought it would be," I said as I glanced warily out the window.

"It's about to get even more complicated," Spike warned me as he hovered in the window. I looked at him and raised my eyebrow. "Claire and Miss Bessie are headed this way, and Miss Bessie *doesn't* look happy."

* * *

"What did you think you were doing? Leaving my Gabe on the side of the road to go off with that Martin Salvi fella?" Bessie screeched at me as I unlocked the front door to let Bessie and Claire in.

"You know Martin Salvi *already*?" Liz asked, her eyebrows shooting up. "That didn't take long. Hey, Claire."

"Hey, Liz," Claire nodded at the hairdresser. "What are you doing here?"

"Just introducing myself to my new neighbor," she smiled as she pointed at me. "I was hoping to get to her before the wolves started sniffing around, but if she's *already* met Martin Salvi, I guess I'm too late."

"There's an *awful* lot of women in my house," Spike complained as Bessie waddled over to the glass fridge and helped herself to a bottle of water. "I think maybe I liked it better before all this."

"Shut up, boy, you should be so lucky as to have this many beautiful women around your rooster-looking rear. You're *lucky* Liz can't see you, she'd laugh herself silly," Bessie snapped as she waved her water bottle at him. "A ghost with a mohawk. *Ridiculous*," she muttered as she waddled back and plopped down on the couch.

"A ghost?" Liz asked as she glanced around nervously. "What do you mean, ghost?"

"Miss Bessie's mind drifts here and there occasionally," Claire told Liz in a whisper that

Miss Bessie could surely hear. "Just smile and nod."

"My mind is a *steel trap*," Bessie snapped. She clapped her hands together to demonstrate, and water shot up from the open bottle.

"It makes you wonder, though," Liz mused as she glanced around the shop.

"Wonder what?" I asked.

"If no one *knew* that Spike's body was here, how did this place get a reputation for being haunted?" she asked. "I mean, it is right smack in the center of town. It's almost like anyone that thought about buying it just *felt* him here somehow. But that's impossible, right?"

"Right, impossible," I nodded as if I agreed with Liz wholeheartedly. "Anyway," I said as I moved quickly to change the subject. "What can I do for you, Miss Bessie?"

"You can call up my Gabriel and apologize for leaving him on the side of the road the way you did," Bessie said forcefully as she leaned over and put her hand firmly on my knee. "No one cares what your name was before you picked this carnival barker one. No one cares, I tell you."

"*I* care, Miss Bessie," I told her as I gently removed the death grip of her hand. "He had no right to tell you and Claire without talking to me first. It was inconsiderate at the very least."

"You're going to date that *Martin Salvi* now *instead* of my Gabriel? Aren't you?" she snapped again with a shake of her head.

"I'm not going to date anyone!" I told her, blushing.

"Damn, Miss Bessie, with a matchmaker like you, Gabriel Wilcox is going to die *alone*," Liz snorted. Bessie twisted her head around on her wrinkled neck and dialed in on Liz Dalton. Liz stared back without fear, but I noticed her muscles tense ever so slightly.

"What about *you*, Miss Dalton? Forty may seem like it's far away, but you're still without a man!"

"I *was* married, Miss Bessie," Liz told her as she got up from the couch and walked over toward the garbage can. "You know that."

"Ain't married *now*, are ya?" she snapped. "What happened?"

"I realized I played for the other team," Liz told her as she tossed the water bottle into the recycling. "You probably know that, too, since you know all the gossip in this town. Ma'am," Liz added respectfully.

"Don't you *ma'am* me, Liz Dalton. For goodness' sake, how many lesbians *are* there in this town?" Miss Bessie exclaimed as she threw her hands up in the air.

"Clearly not enough considering I'm single," Liz said wryly. Claire chuckled.

"No *wonder* my Gabriel can't find a woman to settle down with! The whole town is filled with lesbians!"

"Now, Miss Bessie—" Claire warned her, but she whirled on me.

"Are you a lesbian, too? Is *that* why you stormed off?"

"Um. No, ma'am," I answered.

"Damn it," Liz said, and then she winked at me.

"Well, *thank* goodness!" Bessie Baker shouted, raising her arms.

"This is bordering on offensive," I warned Miss Bessie. She waved my concern away. "I'm serious, Miss Bessie. You're starting to make me a little uncomfortable with the way you're talking about Liz and Claire."

"If I'm only making you a *little* uncomfortable, I must not be working hard enough," she shot back.

Claire chuckled as she reached a hand out and placed it on my shoulder. "I'm sure Liz and I appreciate you saying something, but Miss Bessie is honestly one of the least bigoted folks in town."

"She is. Next to Dexter Kane, Miss Bessie should be nominated for an award," Liz nodded. "Mostly, this is an accepting town, Fortuna. Live and let live and all that."

"Yeah, um, hey, no, it's not," Spike said as he pointed his two thumbs at his chest. "Dead guy that was not allowed to live, yo."

"No one dies for no reason," Miss Bessie told him. "You must have made someone want to stuff you in a wall. Hell, your hair alone would have done it for me," Miss Bessie told Spike. Spike frowned at her.

"I think it's time for Miss Bessie to head back to the home," Claire said as she reached down to help the old woman up. "Dinner's soon, and she's talking to thin air again."

"Hey, Claire, why don't you head back over here and we can take Fortuna out to dinner? Give her the lowdown on the town?" Liz said as she bounced out of the chair. Claire nodded as she wrapped her arm around a frowning Bessie. "Awesome, we can take her over to the complex and show her the bright lights of the track."

"You two are taking her out?" the old woman asked as Claire pushed her toward the door. Claire nodded again, and kept pushing. "No turning *her* into a lesbian, ya hear? I like her. I want her saved for Gabriel."

"Are you talking about her heterosexuality or her virginity?" Liz called after Bessie cheekily as I blushed.

"*Perceived* virginity," Claire murmured as my cheeks burned even hotter.

"Miss Bessie, it doesn't work like that," I reassured her as Liz opened the door for her and Claire.

"Don't tell me how it does or doesn't work, missy," Miss Bessie called behind her as Claire lead her out of the store. "If I lived in Mystic's End now and was looking for a man, I might be tempted to go for a woman instead, too!"

NINE

"This place is *unreal*," I breathed as I got out of Claire's car and looked at the front of the Mystic's End Entertainment Complex in all its neon-lit glory for the first time. The huge, shiny building with offshoots of smaller buildings and well-manicured pathways snaking around in between it all was so enormous it was breathtaking.

Liz smiled and nodded as I stared. "There's a lot of issues with the track, and I'd be the first one to admit it," she said as she came around to stand beside me. "One thing you *can't* say, though, is that it's run-down."

"I think they go for a Vegas vibe," Claire said as she locked her car.

"I expected something more...sketchy, I guess?

When Gabe and I took Gideon back, the place was dusty. It looked kind of cheap, if you want to know the truth," I said as the three of us began walking toward the superstructure. "It was just a big metal building. With holes in the metal."

"Right, that's for the dogs," Claire nodded as she glared at a tourist that had just rudely pushed past her. "If it mattered to revenue, I'm sure they'd upgrade the back end. Since it doesn't, they don't. The owners don't care," she shrugged. "There *are* worse places, though. Most of the people that work in the back are local folks we know. They love the dogs and try to do right by them."

"*Most* of them. *Not* all of them," Liz interjected.

"Let's keep it to the good parts of town first," Claire told Liz. "Plenty of time to fill her in on the rest."

The three of us fell silent as the crowds grew thick. I could see the large, high, stadium-like building through the space between smaller buildings. It looked to me as if the huge track had smaller, entirely separate buildings jutting out in all sorts of odd directions, almost as if it was *designed* to disorient people looking for their destination. In between there were well-manicured pathways, concession stands every hundred feet, and loud music blared from speakers along the walls.

My head began to throb from the press of so many people and the thumping of the bass. Everyone was so excited to go clubbing, slotting, betting or eating that their energy was crashing over me like waves. "Is it always this loud?" I shouted above the din as I tried to push the energy of the crowd out.

"Just in the front!" Claire shouted as she grabbed my arm and pulled me closer to her. "We're going to the Club, and it's not noisy at all, I promise! Sorry, I should have warned you it gets like this in the evening!"

I grimaced and pushed on.

* * *

We headed toward a wide opening between an exterior building that could be an ice cream shop or a bordello (depending on what the massive, licking neon tongue signified). Above the shadowy archway, a big blinking sign said *Centre Tunnel* in sinister, creepy lettering. A velvet rope stretched across the archway, and a serious young man in a tuxedo stood to the right.

"Jack!" Liz waved as she thrust herself in front of the crowd. "Open up, we have reservations!"

"We do?" I asked, puzzled.

"We do," Liz responded.

"Good evening, Ms. Dalton. Lovely to see you again," Jack said as he elegantly unclipped the velvet rope to steer us in. As we stepped through, protests erupted from the waiting horde of hopeful patrons.

"How did they get in?"

"They don't follow the dress code!"

"Ladies and gentleman, Ms. Dalton has the honor of styling the luxurious tresses of Ms. Evangeline Laroux," Jack said as he turned to the crowd and narrowed his eyes. "She and her guests are *ever* welcome at the Centre Supper Club *with or without* reservations, *with or without* proper attire."

The crowd quieted down, but grumblings were still heard here and there.

"Since she is a personal and *favored* friend of Ms. Laroux, it would *behoove* you to quit *hooting* at her like a parliament of irritable owls," he told them with the most exquisitely elegant menace I had ever watched in my life.

The crowd quieted instantly.

"Jack, this is Fortuna Delphi," Liz said as she tugged me to the front and held out her hand to Jack. "She just opened the gallery in town. You should go by there, I know how much you like to paint. Fortuna, Jack Stewart," she said pleasantly as she hitched her head toward Jack. "As you've probably guessed, he's the security guard at the Centre Supper Club."

"Nice to meet you," I smiled as he clutched my hand. Looking up I noticed his eyes were as green-grey as my own. The tall, slim man must have had a foot on me in height, maybe more. He was in his mid-twenties with stylish stubble on his face and he shook my outstretched hand smoothly, but decisively. Jack's eyes smiled far more than his impassive face did.

"You as well, Ms. Delphi," he inclined his head and released my hand. "I trust that you three ladies will enjoy your evening, and Ms. Laroux will *appropriately* dazzle Ms. Delphi." He nodded at Claire and glanced meaningfully at Liz.

"I know the drill, Stew," Liz said as she whacked him on the shoulder. He flinched. "We'll give Fortuna a run-down of Angie's...ah, eccentricities?"

"Very well," Jack responded as we started our plunge into the darkened tunnel.

"What eccentricities?" I asked as soon as we were far enough away from Jack that he couldn't hear my question.

"We have a lot of interesting folks in this town," Claire explained as we passed by an oil painting of a mysterious fog-encapsulated house. I winced at the beautiful oil being exposed to the open air like this. "Angie's one of the *most* interesting."

"She's in her mid-thirties, and I'll grant you she's completely, positively *starlet-level* stunning," Liz breathed as we advanced down the dimly lit tunnel. "She went off to Hollywood after she finished high school, got a few parts as an extra, married a ninety-year-old billionaire. Lucky for her, he kicked the bucket a few months later. Left her all of his money."

"That doesn't sound lucky, *that* sounds calculated," I pointed out.

"They investigated," Claire said as we walked. "Never could discover any reason to believe she murdered him. Well, other than the fact that she was in her twenties at the time, and he was old and rich."

"I truly don't think she killed him," Liz said as the path began its ascent toward two glass doors surrounded by softly glowing white bulbs. "I think she married him for his money, don't get me wrong. But I don't think she could *kill* anyone."

"Oh, come on," Claire scoffed.

"She didn't really *need* to. He had no kids, and he let her spend whatever she wanted. All she had to do was stick around until he croaked. And really, how long would *that* have been? The guy was *ninety*."

"And all that is what *she* said. *He* can't corroborate," Claire snorted.

"Anyway, she moved back here so she could be the big, famous, brilliant fish in the miniature pond," Liz continued with a pointed glare at Claire. "So, treat her like a famous movie superstar, even though she isn't. Always act gobsmacked about how pretty she is, which admittedly isn't hard. She's naturally bewitching, if I say so myself."

"Pretend she's famous, gush over her beauty. Got it," I told her, nodding.

"Oh—and the food's always delicious," Liz said as she held open the door.

"Even when it *isn't*," Claire whispered.

* * *

They settled us at a half-circle table looking over a section of the greyhound track in the back of the Club. The table faced outward so anybody in the booths along the walls had a clear view out the huge floor to ceiling windows. It was spacious, with high backs to provide a tremendous amount of privacy. You'd have to work really hard to peek in any of them to see what was going on.

"Oh, my gosh," I said as I noticed a low rumble and a slight shift outside. "Are we *moving?*"

"Cool, isn't it?" Liz said, grinning widely. "The

building is a circle, and it rotates completely once per hour. The view booths are the hardest to get."

"But nevah, evah hard to get for mah secret weapon," a tall woman purred in an exaggerated Southern accent as she slithered around the right side of the booth. Her hair was gleaming platinum, and it draped around her face in a perfect combination of silky coils. Her eyebrows were dark brown, proudly announcing Liz's *impeccable* bleach work. A choker of pearls, five strings high, covered her throat.

Liz was right. She was *striking*.

"It's always appreciated, Angie," Liz smiled affectionately. Evangeline Laroux was wrapped in pure white silk, her black bra stylishly visible beneath the thin shirt fabric. "You look stunning as always."

"Ah, this old thing?" Ms. Laroux feigned humility as she swung her glowing white hair to the side and blushed delicately. "Why, Lizzie girl, you always make me lament that I was born as straight as an arrow, I'll tell you what, now." She blushed even more deeply as she dropped her heavy-lidded eyes in Liz's direction. "And who are these lovely women with you? Oh, my Claire, I didn't even see you there!"

Angie said *Claire* and *there* as if they were two-syllable words, her Southern lilt doubling their sexy impact. I had no doubt this was the famous non-celebrity Evangeline Laroux. Ms. Laroux smoldered flirtatious seductive sensuality at such a high degree it astounded me the wooden table didn't catch on fire due to her proximity.

"Ms. Laroux," Claire said with a friendly smile. "Wonderful to see you again, Angie."

"And how is our *lovely* Miss Bessie doin'?" Angie inquired. "I hope that she's able to get out and about now."

"That's my job, Angie," Claire answered. "I expect she'll be happier now that Fortuna's come to town. Angie, Fortuna Delphi," Claire said with a wave. "Fortuna owns the art studio that opened in the town square. You know how much Miss Bessie loves art."

"I *do* declare!" she exclaimed in five, not four, syllables. "I thought an artist would be much more vivacious!" Angie laughed musically as she leaned back against the thick glass window. "Why, you are such a shy *mouse* of a *girl*, now, aren't you?"

I stared at the Southern belle Marilyn Monroe wanna-be unsure of exactly how to respond. She gaped at me, judging me, and I could read that her choice to call me a *girl* (as if she and I weren't the same age and as if the word had two syllables) was no accident.

My telepathy continued to tally away at the

mentally transparent blonde as she made quick calculations in her perfectly coiffured head—how much of a threat would I be to her? Which man would be interested in me? Was I a lesbian and therefore easily dismissed?

I tried not to roll my eyes.

"I tend to be a bit quiet in new situations," I told her as I stretched my hand across the table. "It's nice to meet you, Ms. Laroux." She shook limply without answering.

"Fortuna's had an awful few days, Angie," Claire told her as she and Liz exchanged looks. "They found Will Mason in the wall of her bedroom just two days ago. Apparently, someone murdered him after he came back from Little Rock all those years ago. He didn't run away with the money. Isn't that *crazy*?"

I *felt* the defensive wall shoot up from Angie Laroux telepathically far more than I saw it. No one at the table would have known how rattled the blonde was just by looking at her.

But I knew.

Claire's announcement had come as a jolt to Angie.

"Had you not heard?" I asked her as I raised one eyebrow. "This town is so small, I would have expected everybody had learned by now."

"Of *course*, I heard," she snapped at me, her eyes narrowing.

But she hadn't.

She was lying. She was lying her perfectly make-upped, powdery, crimson-lipped face off. Evangeline Laroux hadn't known they recovered the body until the three of us came here and revealed it.

And something about it?

Something about it scared the heck out of her.

TEN

"You don't recall someone named Evangeline Laroux at all?" I asked Spike as I dropped my purse off on the table in the hallway of the second floor. Claire almost had to roll me up the stairs, I was so full from the seven-course dinner the ladies had taken me to. "As soon as I mentioned they found your body, it was like every cell sparked with *shock* or something."

"If there was someone in town as I was growing up named Evangeline Laroux, I *assure* you, I'd remember. That's not a name that would blend in, if you get my meaning," Spike said as he flickered in a wingback chair with his spectral face in his hands. "This *is* a small town."

"Yeah, I don't know if I'd call it a *small* town," I

told him as I kicked off my flats and shoved them against the wall. "Sure, not many people live here, but that greyhound racetrack? That thing is *huge*. There were thousands of people there tonight."

"That place wasn't around when I was alive, but I overheard the agents when they'd show *this* place," Spike mused as his eyes followed me. "The track was only built like 15 years ago. It was like overnight this place was awash in construction and money and then BOOM. There it was."

"Why would someone build something like that *here*, in the middle of nowhere?"

"Big cities are close, and people travel, I guess," he shrugged. "This Evangeline person probably moved here with the rest of the rich people."

Rich people like Martin Salvi, no doubt.

"From what Claire and Liz said, it didn't sound like it." I looked at the time on the wall. It was only ten, though it felt a lot later than that. "They told me she finished high school and then went off to Hollywood. Maybe you knew her as Angie. Angie Laroux?"

"Nope, doesn't ring a bell," Spike said as I grabbed an old t-shirt and my hands moved up to unbutton my blouse. His eyes widened. Pausing, I glared at him pointedly. "What? I'm dead. You won't even give me a peek?"

"Out," I told him.

He disappeared but I could still feel his spirit in the room.

"Come on, Spike, downstairs while I change."

No answer, no change in his energy. I waited impatiently with my comfy shirt in hand. If this whole haunting-my-home thing was going to work, Spike would have to recognize some boundaries, and since he could make himself invisible, it would be super-hard for me to enforce those. Then an idea came to me.

"You know, I *know* a couple of genies. They can make other genies from ghosts. If you think living in *this* building for years was tough, try living in a lamp the size of a teapot for eternity."

I felt Spike's energy withdraw from the room. I could still sense his closeness, but he was much further away than before.

* * *

"Come here," I called to Spike as I came down the stairs and went into the back studio. I placed a small canvas on the easel as he floated in from the storefront, stopping in the door.

"*What* in the Sam Hill did you do to yourself?" he asked in dismay.

"It's a face mask," I told him as I picked up tubes of acrylic paints and squirted globs of each color on the palette. Placing it on the table, I stepped back and whispered a spell to myself. With a flip of my fingers, the paint snaked up in slivers toward the canvas and threaded themselves down in thin lines. "Give it a few minutes."

"What did you do to yourself?" Spike asked me again as if I hadn't answered him. It amused me that the ghost was far more fascinated with the mysteries of female beauty than he was the mysteries of magic creating a painting automatically with no hands.

"I put a honey mask on my face, and a clay mask on my hair," I told him. "Relax, I'll wash it off in a few. What, you never had a sister?"

"No! Geez, you don't have to worry about me wantin' to see you undress," Spike said with disgust as he turned his face to the magic painting. "I don't want to anymore. You look like you were dragged out of a mud pit."

"I would pay good money to roll around in a mud pit of Bentonite Clay, honestly," I confessed to him as I jabbed my hardening hair with my finger. "I love this stuff."

"That's Rowena Clutterbuck!" Spike gasped as the painting solidified into a portrait of the slinky woman I met at dinner. "I mean, she's older in that picture, and she didn't have that color hair when I knew her. But her *face*? I'd recognize *that* face anywhere."

"I guess Evangeline Laroux is her stage name or something?" I mused as the last of the paints fell into place.

"Would *you* hire 'Rowena Clutterbuck' to star in a Hollywood movie?" Spike asked. "How on earth would they even fit it on a movie poster?"

"Stop, the name's not that bad. I'll grant, though, Evangeline Laroux is far more glamorous sounding than 'Rowena Clutterbuck.'" I did not point out that as *Fortuna Delphi*, I had very little room to criticize anyone's exotic name change. "Okay, so now that we know who *she* is, why would she have a reaction to *your* body being found?"

"I don't know, actually," Spike answered quietly as he squinted at the painting. "We weren't really *friends* at all. I mean, I knew her. We had some classes together. But she was a cheerleader dating a football player. *Obviously*," he said as he pointed to his tall, spiky mohawk, "we didn't run in the same crowd."

"Undoubtedly," I agreed as I swung back to the painting and looked at it, considering. "She and Liz seemed pretty close. Well, in a *master and servant* kind of way, a little. It was clear Evangeline liked her, but also clear that she thought of herself as a *bit* higher on the social food chain than Liz."

"Busy...um, Liz ran around with *my* crowd," Spike said, turning to me. "She wouldn't have been caught dead hanging out with the cheerleaders. Besides, she—Rowena, I mean—was Hoyt's girl."

"Hoyt?" I asked, thinking back. "You mean the guy that works at the track taking care of the dogs?"

"Why do you ask me things like that when you know I can't escape this stupid building?" Spike responded with a glare. "I don't know who works at the track! For years I didn't even know there *was* a track!"

"Right, right, sorry. Um...Hoyt Abernathy? Was that his name?"

"Yeah, that's him. His Dad owned the shop."

"Hoyt's *father* owned this record store? You mean the one you worked in? Like, *this* building?" I spun toward Spike in surprise.

"If it's the same guy, yeah," Spike shrugged.

I tapped my finger against the easel as I thought about all the strange, spider-webby connections of Mystic's End. I'd barely met anyone here, and yet everyone's history seemed all wrapped up in everyone else's.

"Do you know if he owned the *store,* or the *building?*" I had acquired the building from a corporation, but I didn't know who ran the firm at all. At the closing, I never met the sellers, and we communicated through the real estate agents.

"Both, probably," Spike shrugged. "His family owns the Mystic Construction Co. I think they built every single house, building, street, and doghouse in this town going back to the beginning."

"Why would a kid from an affluent family be working at the greyhound track taking care of dogs?" I wondered. Then I yawned.

"You're asking one of those questions that I couldn't possibly know the answer to again," Spike said with an eye roll. His face softened then, and he looked at me, worried. "You look exhausted, anyway. And I think that stuff on your head has turned to concrete. You look silly now, but you'd look even weirder bald."

I put my hand to my head and nodded.

"If you think of anything else, let me know," I told him as I turned toward the stairs.

"Why?"

"Huh?" I asked him, turning around.

"Why do you want me to tell you if I remember something? I mean, *why* do you care?" he asked, tilting his head. "I'm dead. Why I'm dead...I mean, who cares? If someone knew something, who cares?" he asked glumly. "No one cared until now. Heck, I doubt anyone cares *now*. You didn't even know me then. Why do you care?"

Poor Spike. Feeling trapped and forgotten all

those years must have been so difficult for him. I smiled at him.

"Humans need closure in their lives. They need answers. I realize that from all the years I gave readings to people. It's a deep, emotional need," I explained. "Even if the answer isn't the right one, people still need *some* answer, some *why* they can live with."

"I'm dead, though—"

"You're *still* a people," I told him softly. "I doubt dying changes your emotional need to know what happened to you. Why someone wanted you dead. What you lost your life for. I guess I want to help you get that. If I can."

Spike looked at me, his expression softening.

"And honestly, we're stuck with each other," I told him brightly. "Now you're *my* people. I hope we can be there for each other even if we wouldn't have *chosen* to be friends in any other circumstances."

Disbelief colored his face in a pink haze, and the corners of his mouth slanted in a frown as if he wasn't sure whether he could quite trust me. I stood by quietly, and the haze slowly dissolved to white as he contemplated what I'd replied.

Finally, the corner of Spike's mouth turned up slightly. He gave a brisk nod. "Thanks, Fortuna," he told me gently.

"That still doesn't mean you can watch me take a shower," I informed him as I turned to climb the stairs.

I heard a chuckle behind me.

* * *

One of the greatest feelings in the world is stepping out of a hot shower into the muggy air squeaky clean and smelling like flowers. I brushed my thick, wet hair as I studied myself in the mirror and sighed.

This little human town could give the Magical Midway a run for its money. What crazy drama.

I spotted the hole in the wall of my bedroom in the mirror as I brushed. Spike's tomb remained open, but the police had not been back to examine it at all. No one told me to stay out of my bedroom. They barely left with any evidence.

Truthfully, it seemed like Spike was right. No one looked to care about his murder so many years ago.

No, that *wasn't* true, I thought as my eyes narrowed. Evangeline Laroux cared. She cared something fierce.

I yawned again and put the brush down. Time to worry about this all tomorrow. I was weary from being filled full of steak and lobster and little mashed potato flowers and…I inhaled so much food at the Club I couldn't even recall all of it. My vision was a haze of whipped desserts and buttered rolls as I turned out the light on my nightstand.

The bed squeaked as I slipped my legs between the cool sheets…

…and I stopped as my leg struck something warm.

I froze, listening.

Something shifted to my right.

I held my breath…

…and yet the heavy rise and fall of breath could still be heard.

It was close.

Too close.

Either I was glutton-drunk and paranoid and imagining things, or *something* was in bed with me.

Faint heat brushed against my cheek as the breathing echoed, and I didn't know whether to scream or run or reach out telepathically to find out what was here.

The latter idea, let's face it, would be ideal. I mean, I'm a witch and I can poke into someone's mind to uncover their thoughts, feelings, memories. It's an *awesome* skill if you can muster up the fortitude to use it in times of vulnerability.

There's that aspect of it, though.

Having the *bravery to act.*

Which I was struggling with, if you want to know the truth.

I used to freeze in my bed and ignore all the ghosts trying to talk to me as a child until they would go away. Eventually, they always did. So, in my panicked mind, that *seemed* like a wholly valid option here.

A cold nose nuzzled my cheek as a gentle tongue traveled intently from my chin to my hairline leaving dripping slobber as it went.

I shrieked and bolted straight up out of the bed. The dog barked excitedly, and the bed creaked as he bounced. Spike appeared instantaneously in my bedroom looking haggard. "What, what happened? What's going on?"

I switched on the light to gawk at Gideon-Jerubbesheth-the-Valiant on all fours, his tail up and tongue lolling out of his grinning mouth. The dog sent me a vision of myself as someone standing on the track would have seen me that night—through the window of the Club awkwardly chatting with Liz and Claire.

"Oh, my gosh, I think I peed a little," I panted as I held on to the wall for support. "Gideon, what on earth are you doing here? And how did you get up here?"

An image of the dog standing on its hind legs

teaching a class (with a graduate's cap on his narrow head) burst into my mind.

"Yes, yes, you're a very smart dog, but you're *not* supposed to be here," I explained to him as I stepped closer to the bed and rubbed him behind the ears.

"Hey, Dr. Doolittle, you *have* to get that dog back to the track," Spike warned me. I looked at him, bemused. I raised an eyebrow. He shrugged. "Well, that's what the cop said before. It seemed smart to remind you in this situation."

Gideon growled at Spike.

"For years, *no one* could talk to me, now *everyone* can see me, and everyone's a *critic*," Spike grumbled.

Gideon barked.

"He's right, though," I told the greyhound. Moving closer, I noted that he still had a collar and leash on him. "Did you just run away from your handler?" I scanned the filthy leash and unclipped it from the dog to get it off my nice, clean sheets. "Gideon, you're going to get someone in trouble."

An outraged Hoyt Abernathy chasing the dog blazed in my brain, and the dog rolled over with his feet up and smirked again. At least I assume he was smirking. I mean, the dog *totally* looked like he was smirking.

Gideon sneezed.

"Yeah, well, if Hoyt gets fired, I won't lose much sleep over it," I conceded. Whatever else the guy was, he was mean to dogs. I immediately disliked anyone that wasn't nice to animals.

"What are you going to do?" Spike asked me.

"Well, it's the middle of the night, so at the moment, I'm not going to do anything," I said as I snatched a decorative ceramic bowl from my shelf and went to the bathroom to fill it with water. "It's not *my* fault they lost their dog or that he came here. I'm tired. I'll take him back in the morning."

After I lay the bowl on the floor, I grabbed some extra blankets and deposited them next to the bowl. "Come on, Gideon," I called, snapping toward the blankets. Gideon got up, glanced at the blankets I placed on the floor for him. "You can sleep there. Come on, pup."

The greyhound tilted his head at me. Then he turned away, stepped to the head of the bed, and walked in three circles until he plopped down on the pillow next to mine. Placing his head down, he let out a contented sigh and closed his eyes.

I stared.

One eye popped open and stared back at me.

I pointed to the blankets on the floor.

The eye closed, another contented sigh.

"You've got to be kidding," I complained as I leaned against the wall.

"I don't think he is," Spike said.

"Oh, forget it," I said as I turned off the light and crawled into bed. "I have to get some sleep."

Spike's ghostly glow dimly illuminated the bedroom as I settled in next to Gideon. As soon as I stopped moving, the greyhound nosed under my arm and inch-wormed to rest his hard head on my chest.

Spike faded away as the greyhound began snoring.

ELEVEN

"Come on, you, let's get you something to eat," I told the dog as I exited the lavatory. Gideon splayed out across the top of my bed. The dog's extremities were so long that all paws just about hung off the borders of the big queen-size on both sides. "Come on, lazy, let's *go*."

Gideon yawned, groaning as he exhaled.

"I thought you guys liked to run. Doesn't that entail standing first? Come on. Up!"

I heard a heavy clunk behind me accompanied by the frantic scraping of claws against the wooden floor.

"Hey, Fortuna? That cop's at the front door," Spike said as he sparkled in front of me.

"I didn't hear the bell."

"I don't think he rang the bell," Spike said as he drifted in front of me backwards keeping pace with my stride. "He's just standing there looking at the front door to the store. Hey, mutt," the ghost nodded at the greyhound.

Gideon barked.

"Ugh, I haven't even had my coffee yet," I said as I went down onto the second floor and crossed the living room to what passed for the kitchen. Pushing the switch on the coffeemaker, I heard the familiar gurgle as I turned and continued my descent downstairs.

"Don't you want to change?" Spike asked pointedly as he eyed me up and down.

I lowered my head and surveyed my twenty-year-old stained Depeche Mode concert T-shirt, tattered black sweatpants, and bare feet. I shrugged. "What's wrong with how I look? All the bits are covered," I told him, not mentioning that I would be sleeping in clothes from now on since my place was haunted by a guy. "I just woke up."

"That's what's wrong," Spike warned.

"Oh, *please*, like I care if Detective Nosey sees me in my old sweatpants," I said as I hit the bottom floor. Walking through the studio, I reached out and plucked a band out of the basket to pull my wild hair into a pony-tail. I didn't care if he saw me in my sweatpants, but a girl has to look a *little* presentable.

Gideon barked as I trudged up to the front glass door. Gabe turned around, his eyes large as he sighted the greyhound happily wagging his tail behind me.

"Did you need something, Detective Wilcox?" I asked formally after I cracked open the front door. I did not open it wide enough for him to come in.

"It's Detective Wilcox now, is it?" Gabe asked with a half-grin. He clearly expected his dazzling charm and sunny smile would smooth over what he'd done. I nodded and shot him a look without replying. His grin faded as he realized I was still angry about the day before. "Look, can I come in?"

"Do you need to examine the crime scene for something, *Detective*?"

He looked amazed. "No, I wanted to talk to you about what took place yesterday. Can we talk?"

"We *are* talking," I countered, my arm rigidly gripping the glass door so it was an accurate example of my not giving so much as an inch.

He frowned. "Come on, Fortuna. I'm trying to make amends here." He looked puzzled as he glanced at the dog. "Besides, you'll need someone to drive you to get Gideon back to the track. That dog sure seems to have become attached to you."

"Clearly. I'm easy to become attached to. Oh, just come on in," I gave in as I shoved back from the door. My arm was throbbing, anyway. "I don't need you to help me get Gideon back, though. I got a van yesterday."

"The white, windowless kidnapper-looking van in the back?" he asked.

"Is it hard work being *that* suspicious of everything, or does paranoia just come easy to you?" I asked him pleasantly as I walked through the door to the studio and made for the stairs. "I just bought it yesterday. I have to find a place that can paint the store logo on it, thanks very much. I'll stay away from school zones until then. Just in case."

"I can't tell whether you're being sarcastic or sincere," Gabe said as he followed me into the second floor kitchen.

"I haven't had my coffee, so if I were you I would err on the side of sarcasm for the rest of this conversation," I told him. Opening my cabinet to grab a mug, I turned and raised an eyebrow.

"Please, that would be great," he said to my implied question. I pulled down an enormous mug for me, and a tiny espresso cup for him. Placing the cream and sugar on the counter between us, I held out the itty bitty cup of coffee.

He did his best to stifle a laugh.

To his credit, Gabe sipped the abnormally small cup like nothing was odd about it. He even complimented me on the quality of the breakfast blend I served him as I microwaved a pound of bacon for the dog.

* * *

"So, look. I didn't mean to hurt your feelings, insult you, invade your privacy," Gabe said as we sat at the table and drank our coffee while the dog destroyed the bacon in three violently jerky gulps. Well, *I* drank my coffee. *He* taste-tested, really.

"Okay," I told him.

"I...I wish I hadn't said anything."

"You wish you had said nothing, or you wish you hadn't dug into my past like I was a suspected bank robber?" I asked him without looking at him. It wasn't shyness, though; Gideon was writhing into a pretzel as he desperately tried to lick the bacon fat off his own chin, and it was hysterical to watch.

"I absolutely wish I hadn't *said* anything," he answered. "I can't say that I'm sorry I looked into you. Newcomers to this town...well, let's just say that we *used* to be more welcoming to outsiders," he revealed. I raised my eyes and saw Gabe looked pained. "It's not your fault," he said as he met my eyes. "But I *am* sorry if it hurt you, or it made you feel—"

"Violated?" I finished for him. He winced.

"I would say unwelcome, but I guess that works, too," Gabe smiled sincerely and took another tiny sip of his comically small coffee cup. "I get defensive about Mystic's End. It's not something I apologize for."

"Well, of course you do," I said, nodding. "You're in law enforcement. It's your *job* to protect people."

"Is it?" he asked softly, gazing at the dog. Then as if realizing he had spoken out loud, he said, "Of course, that's correct. Anyway, can you forgive me?" Without waiting for my answer, he added, "It will be *exceedingly* awkward at Thanksgiving dinner if you don't."

I raised an eyebrow. "Why's that?"

"Miss Bessie told me last night that we're having it here," he said, as if I knew that Thanksgiving dinner was taking place in *my house.* He slanted his head as *his* eyebrow raised. "You didn't know?"

"Nope. I'm cooking *Thanksgiving dinner?*" I asked, my voice breaking just a little. I mean, I just *microwaved* a pound of bacon for the dog. That should give you a sign of my cooking skill level. They don't teach rich girls how to cook in Home Economics when you're sent to a rich person's boarding school.

They teach them how to give commands to the

house staff.

"You don't cook?" Gabriel asked.

"I, um...I mean, I have all the things I would need to cook, I think. I mean, I *guess*," I said as I looked around the kitchen. Gabe's gaze drifted over to the counter-top convection oven and the hot plate. "Right?" I asked him hopefully.

"A turkey that will feed me, Bessie, Claire *and* you won't fit in there," he pointed to the tiny oven. "Not to mention all the sides."

All the sides? The sides of what? I gulped.

"Why didn't you have a full kitchen put in?" Gabe asked me.

"It's just me in here," I explained to him, ignoring Spike hovering in the corner and the grinning greyhound sitting at my feet. My *live-alone* plan had ballooned a bit more than I expected. "How much equipment do you really need to warm up a TV dinner? I worried more about the shop than the living area," I told him as I waved my hand towards my meager living room.

"I don't want to overstep again because when you take offense, you take a *healthy* bit of offense," Gabriel said, pausing to drain his tiny espresso cup. "But if you'd like, you can come look at my house to get some ideas. Cooking is actually a hobby of mine," he said proudly. "Let me make you dinner, and you can see how useful real kitchen equipment can be."

Gideon rose to his feet in excitement, his tail wagging so hard it made loud clunks against the chair. "Sorry, bud," I told the dog as the tail drooped. "You can't come. You have to get back to the track."

They greyhound whined loudly as my cell phone rang.

"Just a second," I told Gabe as I hit accept. "Hello?"

"Fortuna, it's Martin Salvi."

* * *

I held up my finger to Gabe and stepped across the room so he couldn't hear my communication with the sexy operations manager, but I couldn't for the life of me figure out what possessed me to do it.

It wasn't like Gabriel and I were dating.

Or Martin and I were dating.

But still.

"Good morning, Mr. Salvi," I answered quietly. "How are you this morning?"

"Martin," he corrected. "Disappointed that I didn't run into you last night," Martin's smooth as silk voice hummed in my ear. "Ms. Laroux related to me you visited us and dined at the Club last night. I wish you had let me know you were coming," he purred. "I would have *ensured* you an evening to remember."

Well. One thing this guy wasn't.

Subtle.

"Some friends invited me at the last minute, Mr. Salvi—"

"*Martin*, Fortuna. I *insist* that we be on a first name basis," he said warmly but insistently. "Honorifics put far more distance between the two of us than I aim for there to be."

Wow.

"Okay, Martin," I said, and I saw Gabriel's head snap up as he played with Gideon. Our eyes met for a moment across the room, and then I turned my back on him to face the wall again. "Is there something I can do for you?"

"Oh, many, many things, I suspect," Martin chuckled, and I cringed a little bit. "On this morning, however, I am calling to find out if one of our dogs made his way to your home again. Dexter Kane is *beside* himself with concern for his prized hound."

"Yes, Gideon's here," I confirmed. "He's perfectly fine, unharmed, and I was just getting ready to bring him back over to you."

"Oh, please, don't put yourself out any more than you have, Fortuna. I'll send some of my men over to pick him up," Martin volunteered, but remembering Gabe's warning about not having strange men in my house from the track, I demurred. "If you're sure, I look forward to seeing you within the hour, my dear. If you've not eaten, I'd love to take you to breakfast as a thank you."

Without agreeing, I told Martin Salvi I would see him within the hour and hung up the call.

"You've definitely made some interesting connections for your first week out and about," Gabe said as he stood up. "I'm not trying to be judgmental or get in your business, but you're swimming in the deep end of the pool here."

"He just called about the dog," I said dismissively as I thrust my phone into my pocket. "There's nothing going on between me and Martin Salvi," I told him. Crossing my arms, I looked pointedly at Gabriel Wilcox. "And even if there *was*, Gabe, I wouldn't need to explain it to you."

He studied me, his face tightening. After a few moments, Gabe exhaled loudly and held up his hand. "You're right. I'm sorry. I just...Martin Salvi's not a good guy, Fortuna."

"How so?" I asked him, my arms still crossed. For a moment, it looked like Gabe would say something, but then he turned away and grabbed the leash I had placed on the counter. When it was clear he wouldn't respond, I turned my attention back to Gideon and changed the subject. "Do you still have that crate? I don't want him riding free in the back of my van. It's dangerous."

"I do, but I can't let you use it. It's bolted into the SUV," he said regretfully. Okay, with *apparent* regret. I don't think he really regretted it at *all*, if you want to know the truth. "I'm happy to take you both over there. Or drop him off for you since Salvi knows I didn't steal Kane's dog this time."

"I'll go, too. Just give me a minute," I told him as I ran up the stairs to change and get my purse. "I want to find out when Gideon's going to be retired. I think I may be as attached to that dog as he is to this place. Maybe I can put myself on a list or something."

And it was a great chance to get a look at Hoyt Abernathy again.

Just before I reached the third floor, I looked down at Gideon, and saw his head hung low. Unexpected tears sprang to my eyes.

I had become attached to that spindle-limbed comedian, and for a second I wondered how much a Grade A champion racing greyhound cost if you wanted to buy him from his owner in the middle of his winning streak.

TWELVE

This time, Bart waved us through cheerfully as if we were scheduled. Gabe waved back at the man as we pulled through. When the gate clanged shut behind us Gideon whimpered quietly.

"If you were up for adoption, buddy, I'd grab you in a heartbeat, I promise," I told the hound, my breath catching again. I'd gotten used to having animals around living at the Magical Midway (even though they were all were-animals.) Once the Magical Midway and the Makepeace Circus joined, there were cats and dogs around every nook and cranny until things got worked out.

"You could make an offer for him," Gabe said as he drove slowly toward the big gray building.

"I was thinking about that back at my place," I told him. On the drive over, I'd sifted through the data site for info on racing greyhounds. Gideon was winning Grade AA races, the top races, and from what I could tell that meant he was earning decent money.

Greyhound racing was complicated, with different grade races, different tracks, different kennels, different owners. I wasn't sure that I understood it completely, but one thing was clear. Every human involved seemed to be able to profit off one dog running in a circle *if* he won a race.

And Gideon was a champion.

"Hey, Gid—do you *enjoy* racing?" I asked as I turned around in my seat and reached my fingers through the wire cage to scratch behind his ear. My mind crowded with images of the dog laying on my bed as the sun spilled through the window. "Well, *I'd* rather lay in bed all day, too. But isn't there any part of it you like?" A quick vision of Gideon watching another greyhound be lead away as Gideon cried jarred me. I exhaled.

"I don't think he's going to answer you," Gabe told me.

"Anyone with compassion can understand the answer of another creature whether they communicate in the same language or not," I told Gabe as I turned back around. "It just seems like everyone benefits from greyhound racing *except* the greyhounds."

"Look, he's healthy, and this track doesn't put down the dogs when their career is over. That's something, at least," he told me as he pulled up next to the gray building and put the SUV in park. It may be something, but it didn't seem like enough.

"But he's so skinny," I protested as we got out.

"Greyhounds are bony," Gabe chuckled. "Pat his rear, Fortuna. That dog is solid muscle where it counts, I guarantee you. He wouldn't be winning otherwise." As Gabe opened the door to the crate, I reached out to scratch Gideon down the length of his body. I hadn't really noticed before, but the detective was right. The dog was all ribcage, legs, lungs, and muscle.

"If you think about trying to buy him, a word of advice," Gabe whispered as Martin Salvi, Hoyt Abernathy, and a man I didn't recognize came out of the barn-sized doors. "Don't let on that you want him for a pet, even if you do. The kennel makes more cash than the owner does off the dog. Make it sound like you'll keep him there and make sure that Kane agrees to pay any buyout fees with his kennel contract."

"If Kane owns Gideon, who owns Gideon's kennel?" I whispered back.

"Jeff Abernathy," Gabe told me as Gideon jumped down. "The guy behind his son, Hoyt."

* * *

Martin frowned for a split-second at Gabe before bursting into a wide grin. "Fortuna!" he said, his arms wide as if he would hug me. Which he didn't. Thank goodness.

"Hello, Martin," I smiled coolly as I grabbed Gideon's leash. The dog jumped down and walked next to me, his dark eyes glaring at Hoyt. A nearly imperceptible growl rumbled in his throat. "I brought back your little escape artist, but before I hand him over, I wanted to ask—is he for sale?"

"That depends on how much money you have, little girl," a voice thundered as Dexter Kane strode out of the building and glowered at the hound. Gideon pressed against my leg, and I could sense the dog shaking slightly. My eyes narrowed. "That dog's a winner, at least on the track. Off track, he's *a nitwit*, but God gave all creatures a purpose. Running in a circle is evidently his."

"He's brighter than my *stupid* son," Jeff Abernathy said as he whacked Hoyt in the back of the head. "No one can catch a greyhound once he gets away, but the point is *not to let them get away*."

"Gentlemen," I said as I took out sunglasses

from my purse and slipped them on hoping they would hide my distaste for the three men. "While interesting, none of this is getting me an estimate for the sale of this racer," I told them. "I'm a superstitious woman, and it seems if God keeps leading him to my back door, maybe He's trying to tell me something. So, Mr. Kane, if you absorb any kennel fees left on your contract, what would be your walk out price?"

Now Dexter Kane's eyes were narrowing.

"You're a God-*fearing* woman, are you, Ms. Delphi?"

"Let's just say I read the signs that are put in front of me," I told him. "As far as fear? I fear very little," I told him confidently. Gideon sneezed, but I was almost sure that dog sneezed to cover a laugh. "How much?"

"Dexter, you're not *seriously* thinking about selling him to this girl," Jeff Abernathy scoffed. "She came from a circus, for God's sake. She's probably some kind of carnie running from the law!"

"She's *literally* standing next to the law, Dad," Hoyt told his father sarcastically as he rolled his eyes.

"You shut your mouth, moron," the elder Abernathy responded as he thumped his full-grown son again as if he was a misbehaving five-year-old.

Martin Salvi stood behind the three men, his

arms crossed and head bent, observing me with amusement.

"Price," I said haughtily as I pulled out my phone, opened my bank app, and poised my finger over the screen. "I can transfer it to you in minutes with Zippy as soon as you provide me the contract. You'll have it in your bank before I leave the grounds. Why buy *anything* if it's not the best? Gideon's the best at this track, isn't he?"

"Well, now, Ms. Delphi, I *like* the dog," Reverend Kane said, lying through his fancy capped teeth. "Granted, the hound is three years old, and he's due to retire in the next year or so, but he's won quite a bit of money for me. Not to mention the satisfaction I get out of owning the best. I doubt my price will make it worth it to you to run that dog for only a year, even if he is earning now. He's practically at the end of his usefulness."

Jerk.

"Try me," I told him.

"Fifty-thousand dollars," Dexter tried. Gideon whined.

"Done," I responded as both Gideon and Gabe turned to gawk at me as if I were ridiculous. "Where's the contract?" Dexter Kane's eyes enlarged, and the three men rushed into the barn like their pants were on fire before I could change my mind.

"I knew there was something unusual about you, Ms. Delphi," Martin Salvi's eyes gleamed as he studied me keenly. Gabe leaned down to pet Gideon as Martin looked at me, and when he leaned back up, I discerned he had closed the distance between us. "You're going to take that dog home, aren't you?"

"I don't know what you're talking about, Martin," I lied.

"What I'm talking about is *I* expect you just offered $50,000 to Dexter Kane for a pet," Martin Salvi chuckled.

"As I said, I don't know what you're talking about," I turned away from his stare and hurried toward the kennel building. Gabe hurried to accompany me, and Martin Salvi followed.

"I am rarely surprised by anybody, Fortuna," Martin said, still snickering. "But you? You confound me."

* * *

"And done," I signed the transfer papers for Gideon's purchase. Clicking two buttons on my phone, I turned over a *huge* chunk of the financial safety net Charlotte and Gunther had given me to Dexter Kane.

The dog wagged his tail enthusiastically.

"Now, here's the contract for his kennel," Hoyt said as he laid another paper in front of me. "He's got a pretty fancy kennel, so it costs a bit extra, of course. Since you only have one dog, we had to raise the rate to remove Dexter's volume disc—"

"That won't be necessary," I told him as I laid the pen down without signing. "I'll be taking Gideon home with me."

Martin Salvi watched with that bemused grin, but didn't react.

"You're going to *what?*" Hoyt asked. He and his father met each other's gaze, both men mirroring the other's shock. "You said you would race him! Are you going to another kennel? We're the best—"

"No, I didn't," I shook my head.

"You did, you said you wanted the best!"

"I *said* that, but I didn't say I wanted the best so I could race him," I told Hoyt as his mouth opened and closed like a fish trying to get oxygen from air. "All I said was I wanted to buy the dog."

"He's the top racer in this kennel, young lady," Jeff Abernathy told me, a nasty edge to his voice. "If you take him out, we'll take a large hit to our points."

"I don't know what those are, and honestly, I don't much care," I shrugged. "I own the dog now, and I can do whatever I like with him. Right?" I reached down and scratched Gideon's head while he chuffed, the tail wagging so fast it was a blur.

"Dexter, what the hell did you do?" Jeff Abernathy slammed his hand on the desk and yelled at the pastor, infuriated. "Do you know how much this will cost us?"

"Sorry, Jeff," Dexter Kane shrugged without looking up, his eyes glowing with the number reflected from his phone as he gazed lovingly at his bank account. "It was a lucrative deal. And let's face it," he looked up. "Your son couldn't keep the cursed dog at the track, anyway."

"You witch!" Jeff said, shaking his finger at me.

Oddly accurate.

Gabe turned to step between Abernathy and me, when the operations manager of the track spoke. "Settle down, Jeff," Martin's warning came from the side of the room, his voice low but threatening. "It's just business. There's no need to be ungentlemanly."

Jeff Abernathy quieted instantly. When no one else spoke I concluded this would be the ideal time to get the heck out of here.

"Martin, I know you asked me for breakfast, but I really have to run to the pet store and get stocked up for Gideon. Hoyt, what does he eat?" I turned to the surprised trainer.

"Raw meat and dog food," Hoyt said after

looking for guidance from his father as to whether he should answer. "High protein. Sometimes we add pasta. Vitamins. But on race day—"

"That won't matter," I told him as I patted Gideon on the head. "He won't be racing anymore."

"Jeff, why don't you go get Fortuna a bag of dog food from the kennel as a reparation for your outburst a minute ago," Martin told the barely calm kennel owner. "Maybe two bowls as well. An A racer is retiring. We should send him off with our thanks."

"A double-A racer," Jeff grumbled as he walked out of the office.

"Forgive Mr. Abernathy, he was caught by surprise," Martin told me. Then he winked. "Is there anything else we can do for you, Fortuna?"

"Actually, perhaps the Reverend can," I said as I gestured to Dexter Kane while keeping Hoyt in my line of sight. "I wanted to attend Sp—um, Will Mason's funeral. Is that taking place at your congregation?"

"*You* want to attend?" he asked, startled. "Why would you want to go to that boy's funeral? You didn't even know him."

"No, but they found him in my bedroom wall," I explained as I leaned against the desk. Snapping as if I just recalled something, I turned to Hoyt.

"You knew Will, though, didn't you? In high school?"

"I...uh, no, I didn't know him," Hoyt said as his eyes shifted over the room and he pulled back from the desk. "I didn't, no."

"But he worked at your father's music shop," I prompted him.

"So?"

"I just thought since you worked here at one of your father's businesses now that wasn't new for you. Did you ever work at the music store? You must have."

"No." He glanced at Dexter Kane with apprehensive eyes.

"You didn't work there, but you were friends with those spiky-haired punks," the Reverend said as he leaned toward Hoyt. "Your father was beside himself when you started hanging out with those thugs and tuning in to all manner of the devil's music."

"Nah, I don't think I was," Hoyt shook his head forcefully. "I was on the football team, I didn't have a haircut like Spike did."

"I thought you said you didn't know him?" I inquired.

Hoyt glared at me indignantly.

"Did your girlfriend, Rowena, know him?" I pushed further. Almost as soon as the words left my lips, I felt Gabe's hand grip my elbow tightly. Turning to him, I could read the warning in his eyes.

"How do you know Rowena?" Hoyt asked me as he started, fists balled, around the table toward me. Gideon yelped and hugged closer to my leg.

"I think we're getting a bit far astray here," Martin Salvi interrupted as he glided into the center of the exchange. "Reverend, the funeral?"

"Ah, yes, tomorrow," he said as he stared at Hoyt, his face revealing his confusion. Whether he was confused about Hoyt's answers or actions, though, I wasn't sure. Slowly turning to me, he peered down. "You're welcome to come, of course. It will be at 10 a.m."

"Do you need a ride?" Martin inquired.

"She does not," Gabe spoke up for the first time and glared back at Martin Salvi. If he moved any closer to my position he would step on poor Gideon. I nudged him.

"If I do, I'll call you," I told Martin, and he inclined his head briefly.

"In the cop's car," Jeff Abernathy said as he came back into the room, red-faced and sweating. Despite being in construction, it didn't seem to me that the elder Mr. Abernathy was used to physical labor much. "Dog food, bowls, leash, muzzle—"

"Muzzle?" I asked as I looked down at Gideon, concerned.

"Thank you for everything," Gabriel said as he thrust me toward the exit. For a flash of a second I was tempted to push back, but I realized I really wanted to leave. No reason to question anyone here when I could mingle at the funeral tomorrow.

"Of course," Dexter Kane said with more happiness than I had heard the edgy preacher express so far. The $50,000 deposit seemed to satisfy him like a fat leech after feeding. "Good luck to you, Gideon!" he called as if he cared.

Which he didn't.

After loading up the ecstatic greyhound and climbing back in the car, Gabriel Wilcox confronted me as soon as the car doors slammed shut.

"Just what *the hell* is it you think you're doing?" Gideon growled.

THIRTEEN

"Don't *talk* to me like that," I snapped at Gabe as he backed the SUV up faster than anyone should back an SUV up. The car lurched forward spinning its wheels in the gravel. "I'm happy to talk to you about anything, but I don't respond well to arrogance."

"You seem to respond to Martin Salvi just fine, so not sure I believe that. Besides, I'm not arrogant, I'm concerned for you!" Gabe countered hotly.

"You don't sound concerned. You sound ticked off," I told him as we waved to Bart in the guardhouse. "I suppose you are ticked off, though, watching an art studio owner ask questions that you should be asking. How do you have so much time to chauffeur me around the town, anyway? Don't you have a *murder* to investigate?"

"No," he told me as we pulled out of the complex and onto the road. "No, actually, I don't have a murder to investigate. They ruled Will's death accidental."

"Will *accidentally* bricked himself up into a wall for 20 years?" I asked as I crossed my arms and stared at Gabe in shock from the passenger seat. "That's the most ridiculous thing I ever heard." Gideon barked in agreement.

"Whether or not it's ridiculous, they have ruled the death accidental, so there's no investigation. Look, if there's no investigation, there's a reason for it—so don't go poking around where you shouldn't."

My eyes narrowed. "What does that mean?"

"What does *what* mean?" Gabe asked as he turned into the center of town.

"That there's a reason there's no investigation? You have a dead body, someone shoved him in a wall and bricked it up to *hide* the *dead body*...I mean, isn't that *enough* of a reason for an investigation?" I asked as we pulled up behind my store. "How do you know it was accidental unless you talked to the person who shoved him in the wall? Have you?"

"Have I what?" Gabe asked distractedly.

"*Talked* to the person who bricked him up in

the wall!" I exclaimed in frustration as we got out of his SUV and walked to the back to get Gideon. "Am I in the twilight zone or something?" The temptation to rummage through the deliberately-being-obtuse detective's brain was strong, and it took all I had not to peel his thoughts apart like an onion.

"*No. Investigation*," Gabe drawled. He emphasized each syllable as if I were a small child. "I don't know *how* he died, *who* put him in the wall. The case has been *closed*. Death ruled accidental. No crime committed. Nothing to investigate. If the Chief says the case is closed, the case is *closed*."

"I can't decide whether your over-sized police department is obtuse or corrupt," I said as we walked in the back carrying the bowls, leashes, and dog bed that Martin Salvi had demanded Jeff Abernathy give me.

"He's just not well-known enough for anyone to spend time on figuring out what happened to him, Fortuna," Gabe tried to explain. The skeptical expression on his face when I turned to face him told me that even he wasn't convinced he'd be able to defend this.

"Who's not well known enough?" Spike said as he floated in the art room and smiled widely when he spotted Gideon. "Hey, pup! Are you going to be staying with us?" Gideon barked as he wove in and out of the easels sniffing everything and getting to know his new home with determination.

"So, answer me this. Who would Will have had to know in order for his death to be investigated? In order for what happened to him to have enough meaning to someone that the police would want to look into why a teenager lost his life?" I asked Gabe angrily. "Would he have had to be a member of a certain family? Have a certain income? Not have a mohawk? What?"

"Why do *you* care so much?" Gabe shot out.

"Why do you *not* care at all?" I shot back.

"You're making an assumption I don't care just because I can't *do* anything," Gabe said, an edge to his voice. He plopped down in front of a blank canvas and looked at it wistfully, his eyes examining the empty white space as if he was searching for the image that should be there. "I care," he said quietly as he turned to face me. "That doesn't mean I can *do* anything."

"Do anything about what?" Spike asked, his smile fading as he looked between us.

* * *

Claire and Miss Bessie knocked just after Spike's question, which was convenient. It enabled me to explain to the ghost what Gabe and I were arguing about while seeming to explain to the new arrivals. Miss Bessie had no such concerns about anyone wondering if she could see ghosts, and she openly glanced at Spike repeatedly as he listened.

"Are you sure you don't remember what happened to you, boy?" Miss Bessie asked Spike. His sour expression deepened as he concentrated, and then he shook his head. "Well, what *do* you remember?"

"Gram, maybe you should—"

"Young man, if you even *think* about interrupting me, I'll bend you over my knee and whack your behind until your skin's as red as that stoplight in the center of town," Miss Bessie said as she pointed a gaunt finger at Gabe, who had made the mistake of interrupting Miss Bessie's exchange with the ghost. "You ain't too old for it," she harrumphed at the thirty-something detective.

I realized that Miss Bessie wasn't strong enough to snatch Gabe to literally, you know, do it. The old woman needed Claire's aid to walk from the car into the shop. Gabe also wasn't altogether weak—I could see his muscles flex when he turned in a certain way. He wasn't a gym rat, but I could absolutely see him as a gym hamster, maybe.

Despite all that, Gabe fell mute.

"You should tell him," Bessie told me. I turned

from Spike and raised an eyebrow at the old woman. "You should tell him what we're both doing here."

"She's starting early this morning," Claire murmured. "Ma'am, do you want to go back to—"

"Tell you what, you tell him," Bessie jabbed her finger toward Gabe, who was now inspecting the portrait of Evangeline Laroux I magicked last night. "I'll tell her," Bessie poked at Claire. "Besides, if we're going to be friends, honey, ultimately she will figure it out with two of us rushing around yapping with the invisible. It was funnier when it was just me," she shrugged. "Now it feels like *work* instead of amusement to try and keep them from thinking you're one can short of a six-pack."

"What feels like work? I don't understand," Claire asked as she looked at me skeptically. Looking over at Gabe, she inclined her head. "Do *you* know what your grandmother is talking about?"

"Did you know my grandmother before I introduced you?" Gabe asked as he pushed up from his chair. Gideon trotted leisurely across the room, his nails clicking on the concrete floor. Once he was in front of me, he planted his slender legs on the ground like a guard dog and peered up at Gabe, a low growl growing louder as Gabe advanced. "Fortuna?"

"Damn, with friends like these," Spike murmured.

"Oh, he doesn't know that we can hear you," Bessie snapped at the ghost. "Or see you. Or that Fortuna and I share a gift that long died out in the rest of them. Take out that part and I'm sure she and I look like there's a light or two burned out in our string, if you get my meaning."

"You've *always* sounded a little strange, Gram," Gabe told her. "But Fortuna's new, she bought a building with a dead body in it, she paid an irrational amount of money for that dog only to keep it as a pet, and she used to be a fortune teller—"

"I was never a fortune teller!" I protested indignantly. "And your grandma and I are talking to Spike, if you must know. Your grandmother isn't crazy or suffering from dementia. She and I can see and speak to ghosts. That's all."

* * *

"Over here?" Gabe asked, his arms swinging widely in front of him as he sought to feel where Spike was. Spike, on the other hand, was ping-ponging around and through Gabe snickering.

"Just tell him he can't feel me already," Spike

told me. "He looks like a moron. And *you*, old woman—"

"You're a brassy, spiky haired little urchin," Bessie snapped at the specter of rudeness. "Fortuna's got enough cash that if she gets sick of you, she can pack up and move this whole shebang across the street, Mr. Mason. I'd be a little nicer to people if I were you. You're riding a gravy train with biscuit wheels after being sealed up here all alone. Be grateful, son, before the lot of us decide you're more trouble than you're worth."

Spike looked at the old woman.

"How did I never know you could do this?" Gabe breathed, gawking at his grandmother as if seeing her for the first time. "Wait, could you do this? Before Fortuna arrived here?"

"Because people dismiss women all the time, and of course I could," Miss Bessie told him. Claire sat beside her, her jaw dropped and mouth wide, staring at the old woman in shock. "Even women dismiss women," she added, hitching her thumb toward Claire. Reaching over, she pushed Claire's chin up. "Close your mouth, dear."

"Gabe, you won't be able to feel him," I told the detective as Spike tornadoed around him. "He's traveled through your head at least five times. If you didn't feel *that*, swinging your arms in the air will not help." Gideon barked.

"Can the dog see him?" Gabe asked, looking at the greyhound. Gideon wagged his tail and sauntered over to nuzzle Gabe's hand.

"It appears so," I responded.

Gabe froze again, and sat down, shocked. He glanced from his grandmother's face to my face, and then finally to Claire's face (which was the only other face in the back room that was echoing the bewildered confusion in his own.)

"Look, I—"

"Fortuna, maybe I should be the one explaining this to the two of them," Bessie interrupted me, her eyes softening and her gaze sympathetic. "These two have known me for a long time. I let them assume I was just a mad old lady because it was simpler. It was easier than revealing that Mystic's End got its name legitimately. And that I was the last of my kind."

"The last of *what* kind?" I asked, wondering for the first time whether Miss Bessie could be my birth mother if she was the only one with a witch talent in the town. Adding up the years in my head, I dismissed that as impossible. The woman was far too old to have given birth to me.

Gabe's mother on the other hand...

I looked at Gabe and tried to see some resemblance between us.

"Fortuna!" Bessie snapped me out of my reflections.

"Yes! What?" I asked as I re-focused my attention on her. Her eyes narrowed. "Sorry! I was just thinking about—"

"Why you're really here," Bessie finished. Claire and Gabe glanced at one another.

"What do *you* know about why I'm really here?" I asked Bessie, my eyes narrowing.

A small smile curled up at the corner of the old woman's mouth as her gray hair fell into her face. With a toss of her head, she moved it back into place. "I told you to come see me, didn't I?" Bessie said as she leaned back. "Anyone else realizing there was *one* other person with the same power in the town she was searching for her relatives in would have come. Quickly, too, I imagine."

I stared at Miss Bessie. Our eyes locked, my dark green-grey and her watery blue.

"But you didn't."

I hesitated. "No. I guess I didn't."

"Why do you think that is?" Bessie asked me pointedly.

"I, um...I was busy."

"No, you were frightened," Miss Bessie said as she nudged herself up. "Afraid of what you knew to be true." The woman shuffled toward me, and though I felt some kind of threat, Gideon seemed indifferent. Although I could scarcely breathe. "I've waited for you, child. Waited for you to find your way back to us," Bessie wheezed.

I felt held in stasis, hypnotized by her shining eyes.

Claire and Gabe watched quietly.

Finally, the old woman stumbled up to me and whacked her hand on my shoulder. A crack reverberated through the room as if a hot ceramic had just exploded in the kiln. I felt a heat race through my veins. Gideon barked.

"You're it!" Miss Bessie chuckled as I grabbed onto a stool to steady me.

And that is how I became the last mystic in Mystic's End.

"I've never heard of it, Fortuna," Charlotte's voice assured me through the phone. "I told you I thought that town's name was a little sinister."

"Miss Bessie said that there is only one at a time, and that sounded similar to the ringmaster thing, so I thought I'd call you," I told Charlotte as I peered out the window of the second floor. Gabe, Claire, and Miss Bessie were still standing on the street corner talking energetically. I had pushed them out soon after the change of sovereignty, or anointing, or assault... whatever it was.

"It may be like the ringmaster thing, but I've never heard of it," Charlotte insisted again. "Did she tell you anything about what the role is, where it originated?"

"I was a little ticked off at the time," I said. In fact, this may have been the understatement of the year. Charlotte had turned into the ringmaster of the Magical Midway by choice. I had gotten slapped by an old woman without my permission. Then I was passed some kind of magical power without my assent.

I might've consented to both things, but Miss Bessie didn't bother giving me the chance.

"I know that you're upset about what transpired, and believe me, Fortuna, I know all about winding up at the center of something you didn't agree to and you don't understand," Charlotte said, her voice sympathetic. "That doesn't change the fact that your first order of business is to find out as much as you can about the power you've just been given. It sounds to me like Miss Bessie is your best resource in the situation."

"I know you're right," I sighed. I didn't mention that whether or not she was right, I wanted to dig on my own before talking to that old woman further. Another thing I learned from Charlotte? Everyone's got an agenda.

"Of course I'm right," she answered playfully.

"Still cocky, are we?" I chuckled.

"Look, if you tap on your arm and you don't

echo like the tin man from the Wizard of Oz, you're already doing way better than I was," she reassured me. Though I knew it was an attempt at marginally sarcastic wit, I raised my left arm and slapped myself just to be sure. Relief surged through me as no telltale metal clang rang in my ears.

"There is no shield on me," I told her.

"Well, that could be a good thing and that could be a bad thing," she reasoned. "Sure, the armor made the relationship between Gunther and me pretty complicated, but it obviously came in handy when people were trying to murder me."

"This is a small town in Arkansas, Charlotte, not a fight for the mountaintop of the paranormal world," I told her, alluding to her long tug-of-war for power with the Witches' Council. "I doubt anyone will try to kill me."

"Yeah, I could've said the same thing," Spike called from the other side of the room.

"Anyway, thanks, Charlotte. I guess I just wanted to hear a familiar voice, and talk to someone who had been through something like this."

"I haven't been through what you're going through, Fortuna," Charlotte said, her voice growing thoughtful. "You've gone to the town where you were born and later abandoned—and now you've been handed a power by an old woman that says she's been waiting for you. I always knew, more or less, who I was. I don't think you have that same luxury at the moment."

As I said goodbye to Charlotte, her words echoed in my ears. She had always had the aid of her family, whether it was her parents or her Uncle Phil. She had a sturdy support, a deep awareness of where she came from before she dealt with the strange paranormal goings-on at the Magical Midway.

I came to this town with questions.

Now, I had even more questions.

And no answers.

* * *

"What do you know about this mystic thing?" I asked Spike as I heated up a microwave dinner. "Does the town have some kind of history that might give me some insight into what I just got myself into?"

"Honestly, it's not that complicated," Spike said as he sat cross-legged on the kitchen table. "Allegedly, during the witch hunts early in this country's history, a coven of witches escaped to Mystic's End. The women who were witches, or claimed to be witches or whatever, established an area they hoped would keep them safe."

"I understood the Abernathy family founded

the town?" I asked him as my processed dinner dinged.

"This town used to be called Mystic," Spike explained as I sat down in front of him and gave him my full attention. "I mean, when the women showed up here, they called it Mystic. The rumor was that they called up some kind of protection spell to keep them safe."

"This sounds vaguely familiar," I told Spike as I took a bite of spaghetti. "I wonder if all power like that has to be vested in a person?"

"What do you mean?" he asked.

"My friend Charlotte was the ringmaster of the Magical Midway, and essentially the power that kept the circus safe was invested or imbued in her," I clarified, leaning back to look up at him. "She was the fulcrum point. Before she was, her Uncle Phil was. And before him, his father. With their family, though, there was a hereditary magic. It was about their lineage."

"You know nothing about your bloodline," Spike pointed out.

"Thanks for reminding me," I rolled my eyes.

"No, what I *mean* is, you might be related to Miss Bessie."

"Maybe, but let's not get ahead of ourselves," I told him as I twirled my fork. "So, witches came, they founded a town, it was called Mystic. Other people showed up. So then what happened?"

"A group of women living together with no men?" Spike rolled his eyes. "What do you think happened?"

"Humor me," I answered.

"So, as the story goes, the Kanes showed up first. Dexter's lineage goes back years in this town, and the founding Kanes were missionaries, too. They established the church," Spike told me. "When they started the church, they demanded everyone attend. Anyone who didn't?" Spike held up his hands.

"Satan possessed them. Or they were influenced by whatever evil preachers claimed people were possessed by in that time," I predicted.

"Satan works as good as anything else," Spike explained. "Irma over at the library, though, has a different take on it. She believes that the new folks that rolled up in this town found farmland and already-built homes and unprotected women. That the witch story was just that. A story to cover for what the missionaries had done."

"Much easier to point at somebody and make an accusation against them to take their land, I guess?"

"You got it."

"Well, if people showed up and stripped the

land of the first coven (if there is real magic and a coven at play here), it doesn't suggest to me that whatever protection magic they had was all that useful," I pointed out as I stood up from the table and threw away the plastic tray into the garbage. "So, did I just take over a meaningless title or something?"

"I don't ever recall seeing Miss Bessie do anything magical that made people stand up and notice, to tell you the truth," Spike shrugged as he followed me back up the stairs to the bedroom floor. "I mean, if she had magic? I think she would've saved Gabe's mom in a heartbeat."

"What was Miss Bessie like when she was younger?" I asked as I strode into my closet to change into my pajamas. "Was she a stay-at-home mom or did she have a job?"

"Oh, she *had* a job," Spike laughed on the other side of the door. "Her job was making the city council, the mayor, the school board, and the police chief miserable. And the more people in power she could make miserable in the same moment with the same issue? The *happier* she was."

"What do you mean, make them miserable?" I said as I walked out of the closet. Spike stared at me as if I had grown another head. "What? Why are you looking at me like that?"

"Um...*why* are you wearing your pajamas?" he asked me.

"Well, I just had dinner. Now I want to huddle down in my jammies on the couch and watch a movie, and then I'll sleep," I told him as Gideon wagged his tail and eyed the bed. "It's been a stressful day and I just need to force *all* of this out of my mind."

"So, I guess you can *do* that, but I would pick more than one movie."

"What do you mean?"

"You didn't just eat dinner, you ate lunch. It's barely 1 o'clock in the afternoon," Spike told me as he pointed at the window. "Sun is straight up in the middle of the sky, Fortuna."

I walked over to the window and looked. Sure enough, the sun was bright and people were out and about in the plaza. Gabe was still standing in front of my store leaning against his SUV, lost in thought. Miss Bessie and Claire were gone.

"I...um...well, this is a *little* awkward," I smirked at him sheepishly. I walked over to my hamper and stared down at the balled up clothes I had scarcely worn for a few hours. Miss Bessie's whack had really discombobulated me. Clearly. Since I was standing in my bedroom in my pajamas at one o'clock in the afternoon.

"It's been a peculiar day," Spike nodded.

I took another shower and resumed my day.

First thing I wanted to do was visit the Mystic's End Library. They must have archives of newspapers. I'd been meaning to go by there and look up any information on my own foundling, but now I needed to dig around into Spike's disappearance, too.

And, of course, check out a history book or two on this strange little town.

* * *

Irma Sperling hunched over the desk, her finger following the words on a page at a pace I doubted most mortals could read. I stopped before her in the quiet, empty library waiting for her to finish. When she flipped the page and continued, I cleared my throat.

"Oh! Goodness gracious, dear, you shouldn't sneak up on a person like that!" she exclaimed as she squinted up at me. The woman was old. Not as old as Miss Bessie, but old enough to have a room at the assisted living center if she wanted one. Her hair was sprayed so thickly that it looked like sticky cotton candy. "You're that new artist woman, aren't you, dear?"

"Fortuna Delphi," I told her as I reached my

hand across the desk. "Pleased to meet you, Ms. Sperling."

"That's *Mrs.* Sperling, Fortuna, but you can call me Irma. *Everybody* just calls me Irma," she told me gaily. "Everybody that comes into the library, anyway. Which is, surely, only about twenty people in the entire municipality. And one of *those* is the postman," she said as she looked distractedly off into the distance. Refocusing on me, she gave me an immense grin. "But you're now one of the library people, so welcome! Welcome! What can I do for you?"

"Well, I was looking for—"

"Let me just stop you there, my dear," Irma said as she pushed herself out of her chair and narrowed her eyes. "If the rest of your sentence is 'the bathroom,' I'm going to get very, very unhappy. You won't like me when I'm very, very unhappy. Now," she added smiling broadly again. "You were saying?"

"I need a few things, actually," I said, and her smile became an inch wider with each thing I needed. "I'd like to look at archives of old newspapers going back twenty years or so, maybe a bit more. I'd like a history book or two on the official, accepted founding history of Mystic's End, and I'd like a book on the history of Mystic's End from back when it was just called Mystic," I told her leaning in.

"You want to know about the magicians," she murmured breathlessly, her eyes peering around to insure no one could overhear us.

Which, you know, they couldn't. There was no one in the place.

"I have just the books for you," she told me heartily. "Which would you like first, the newspapers? The history books? The *real* history books?" she clapped her hands.

"Well, it will possibly take me some time to look through the newspapers," I told her. "So why don't you take me to the periodicals section so I can start searching through them, and you can get me the books you think I should read."

"Do you want me to pick them for you or would you like me to bring you a choice?" Irma asked, her eyes gleaming with delight.

"You're the librarian of Mystic's End," I told her. "If you could get me one or two of each viewpoint, that would be awesome."

"I know just the books," she said passionately, clapping her hands together anew. "Let me just take you to the periodicals room, and then I'll find those books for you right away. If you need any help at all finding something, you just holler."

"Well, I would come find you," I told her. "It's

not right to holler in the library. It seems...just unacceptable."

"Oh, *poppycock*," Irma frowned as she led me toward the back of the library. "It's not like there's anybody else in this place to annoy, anyhow."

FIFTEEN

The room was old, and dingy, and enclosed a huge microfilm system. "You know how to use one of these?" Irma asked as she flapped her hand toward the massive, old monstrosity.

"They're not digitized?" I asked as my eyes roamed over the knobs and dials.

"The library has not been a recipient of the gambling money flowing into Mystic's End," the old woman frowned as she tenderly patted the metal appliance. "We're lucky we have auto-Irma, here."

"Auto-Irma?" I asked, trying not to smirk.

"Well, I can't be everywhere at *once*, dear," she said as she pointed over to the large metal drawers.

"The films are in there, filed by month and year. You just take out the roll, like so," she said as she pulled out a roll of film and walked it back to auto-Irma. "Place it on this roll right here. See the green button next to the roll? Push that, and slide the film down this little chute here, just like so, until it's under the glass," she showed me. "Close the lid, hit the load button, and you're good to go!"

"How do I make it go forward?" I asked, stabbing on the screen to no avail.

"That's not a touch screen, dear," she advised me as she lightly patted my hand away from the screen. Irma showed me the dial to make the film go, how to change the orientation, how to zoom and focus. "That button right there will print for you. Just make sure what you want to print is within that box," she pointed to the screen.

"You mean those lines?" I asked, touching the edge. She slapped my hand again, a little harder this time. I pulled my hand back.

"Don't touch the screen, dear, but yes," she acknowledged as she pressed her glasses back up on her nose.

"I probably won't need to print anything, actually, I'm just curious about some things."

"Are you wondering about that boy that was found in your wall?" Irma asked, nodding, as she pushed the button to forward the film. Her bony finger waved toward the screen. "I grabbed *that* roll for you. There wasn't much about poor Will, unfortunately. That was right around the attacks, you see, and people were...well, people were just overwhelmed, glued to their televisions."

"I'm sure," I told her, squinting down at a tiny corner mention of Spike's disappearance. It was a small mention, just two paragraphs. It wasn't even an article about him. They folded his disappearance into the news that the music store would be closed indefinitely.

"Well, if you need no more help, I'll grab those books for you, dear," Irma patted my back and hitched her sweater closer around her shoulders. "You'll also need a library card, of course. I'll bring you the application. We have a wonderful art history shelf."

Just a *shelf?*

"That'll be great, Irma, thank you," I said as I slipped into the chair to dive through the reported history of Mystic's End.

* * *

T hree hours later, I exhaled noisily and slouched back in my chair. This town?

This town was *nuts.*

There was almost nothing, nothing at *all,* written about Spike's disappearance. No follow-up, no interviews with townspeople. A young man that had grown up in this small town, who had gone to school with the children of police officers, city council members and other citizens, just disappeared one day never to be heard from again, and no one seemed to care.

Spike's *mother's* death, on the other hand, got more ink. They found her hunched over her steering wheel late at night, unconscious, in the town square. After being rushed to the emergency room, they pronounced her dead from a heart attack.

Only it didn't seem like one reporter, Pepper Stanford, accepted that.

Ms. Stanford wrote a string of articles examining Mrs. Mason's life years after she died— more precisely, the town's chatter about an inheritance from Mrs. Mason's own parents that arrived only a week before they found her dead. It was juicy, dense stuff yet nothing seemed to come of it. The articles just stopped.

It was a pattern, in fact, that seemed to keep repeating. Gabe's mother, too, died—this time in an accidental drowning, but no mention of where or how. A lake, a bathtub? Pepper Stanford begins investigating years later, pokes and then just when it seems like the story would come into focus—poof, gone, and Ms. Stanford refocused her articles on bake sales and school dances.

Aside from this, I found the barest hint of my own story.

A baby found on the steps of the police department, the police chief asking for any information, the mayor quoted as assuring the public that the mother *will* be found, the child will be taken care of.

And then poof—my story disappeared from the paper, never to be written about again. I searched to see if Pepper Stanford had revisited that story, but it didn't seem so. That meant there was very limited information about me.

One thing I found out.

The police department used to be housed in the large building in the middle of the plaza. I could *see* the steps they (whoever they may have been) had left me on out of my bedroom window.

"Did you find what you were looking for?" Irma asked me as she sailed into the periodical room. The librarian peered at me over her glasses, a friendly smile on her face. "I've been checking on you now and again, but your brow was furrowed so *intently* that I didn't want to interrupt you."

"I don't know that I found what I was looking

for," I mused as I looked up at Irma. "I'm not sure it's there to find. It seems like every crime in this town goes unexplained, at least as far as the newspaper is concerned."

"You caught that, did you?" Irma asked eagerly. "You're not the only one that's noticed our newspaper seems to have an inherent pattern of stopping stories just before we are to get to the resolution." She walked over and opened up the storage drawer. "Check any major story of the last twenty years, you'll find the same thing."

"Why do you think that is?" I asked her.

"I couldn't tell you," Irma said as she glanced out the door. Looking back she lifted an eyebrow. "Most people cognizant of it couldn't tell you, either."

"Are you telling me you know and you won't tell me? Or that you don't know?"

"Dear, I'm the town librarian. There is very little that happens in Mystic's End that I *don't* know," she told me haughtily. "You see this, though?" she asked as she pointed to the creases on her face, pinching and pulling them to make sure I understood. "I got those because I've lived a long time, young lady. And I've lived a long time by not telling tales I shouldn't be telling."

"Well, that's not much help."

"It's more help than you know, dear," she replied without a trace of irony. "This is a town that's very fond of its secrets. If they needed those secrets known? They would've put them in the local paper," Irma said as she studied me. "If you want to get along in this town? Take my advice. Learn to deduce the truth from the things that are known so you're not caught unaware, but leave the things that are unknown buried where they belong."

* * *

Irma's voice and cryptic counsel echoed in my head as I drove back to my shop. I was so lost in thought I almost didn't see Gabe standing in my parking spot. I wondered how long the story in the newspaper would run if I ran over a detective.

"You're back," I said as I banged the driver's side door to my van. "I would've thought you'd be asking your grandmother twenty questions about her phantom-chatting abilities."

"Oh, I did, and she told me almost nothing," Gabe replied as he accompanied me toward the back door. "Now, I want some answers from *you*. You didn't just come upon Spike's body, did you?"

"Well, clearly *not*," I told him bluntly as I

swung the back door open. "You couldn't put that together on your own? You had to drive all the way back here to *ask* me, the person who can talk to ghosts, if a ghost told me where his body was?"

"I swear, I think you're having fun with this," Gabe said accusingly as he glowered. There was nothing in his tone of voice or his posture that denoted he felt I should be having any fun with this whatsoever. In fact, he seemed a little judge-y that it entertained me.

"I'm not having *fun* with this, I mean, I don't think it's funny that I had to lie to you," I said after he followed me in. "I come from a place where I'm used to everybody knowing what I can do and what I can't. I also just moved from a place where what I can do isn't *exactly* unique."

When his face turned white, I knew I had communicated a little too much for him to handle.

"What do you mean? *What* does that mean? There's a town somewhere just full of ghosts and people that can talk to them?"

Oh, if only you knew, buddy.

"There's an entire world you can't see, but that's beside the point," I said as we wandered to the front of the shop. "That crystal ball? That painting on the wall you looked up at on the first night? *I* didn't say none of it was real. *You* are the one that said you didn't believe in any of it," I pointed out.

"Then why didn't you just tell me Spike's ghost told you about his body?"

"You had already told me you didn't believe in any of it. Besides, would you have *really* wanted to put that in a police report?" I quizzed him.

With a melodramatic sigh, Gabe sank down into a chair. After two seconds, he rose up again and paced.

"Well, I don't believe in any of—okay, didn't believe in any of it. To tell you the truth, I probably still wouldn't if my grandma hadn't told me she has the same gift, too," Gabe's gaze lingered on the crystal ball. "What are you here for, really?"

"Because I can talk to ghosts I must be here because I have some agenda?" I asked him fiercely as if I wasn't here in his town because I had some agenda. He ceased pacing directly in front of me and shifted to meet my eyes.

"I may not have known about any of this yesterday," Gabe said as he leaned forward and crossed his arms. "But you show up *and* my grandmother comes clean about being some kind of mysterious psychic woman a few days after meeting you? *That* doesn't strike me as a fluke."

"What did your grandmother say?"

"Um...well...that it, uh, wasn't a fluke," he said sheepishly.

I stared at him wondering why he couldn't see the ridiculousness in the statement he just made before he made it. At least enough to have stopped himself from saying it altogether.

"I'm surprised anything strikes you as a coincidence in this town. I just came from the library and it seems like your police department is manifestly *incapable* of closing any cases," I told him, crossing my arms and leaning forward until we were practically nose to nose.

"You were checking up on me?"

"I was checking up on the *township*. Why? Is your close rate *below* average at the Mystic's End Police Department? Because I have to tell you, from what I've seen? *That* would be a hell of a feat."

He drew back and put his hands on his hips. "You're the stranger in town. You're the one who showed up here and turned my grandmother into some nutty psychic woman. Since that's the case, how did *you* wind up turning this discussion around on *me*?"

"Because I'm super smart," I told him, putting my hands on my hips and lifting my chin up.

"Not smart enough to avoid being slapped by my grandmother."

"That's not about brains, that's about *reflexes*," I

shrugged. "I didn't say I had good reflexes. I said I was super smart," I tilted my head and tapped my temple.

Gabe looked for a second like his head would explode. Clearly, that wasn't the response he expected.

I was, undoubtedly, having a lot of fun teasing him, but I dropped my arms and looked at him with a more serious face. "Look, Gabe, I *assure* you I'm not here for any kind of nefarious anything."

"My grandmother just gave you some super duper inherited psychic power thing, and you're telling me you didn't know she was going to do that?"

"I don't even know *what* she did, Gabe. I don't feel any different from before," I said as I sat down. He continued to look at me with some suspicion but I noticed his hands had relaxed some. "I got some books from the library that may explain to me what this is, but I don't know what it's all about yet."

"Why not just *ask* Bessie?" Gabe asked as his gaze went to the hardback books I placed on the desk.

"In my previous life, I found an old woman with a plan can't be trusted sometimes. Books, though? Books give you a lot more information with a lot less attitude."

"I don't know if I can trust you," Gabe said after a few moments of silence.

"Gabe, who are you kidding? You *never* trusted me," I told him with a snicker. "Knowing I can see ghosts? I bet it barely moved the needle with you."

"Oh, it moved the needle," he declared, scrutinizing me. "I'm just not sure which *way* it moved the needle."

SIXTEEN

When I walked into Holy Grove Church, the peals of laughter struck me as they rang out from all corners of the chapel. The atmosphere wasn't so much a funeral as it was an ice cream social. Only there wasn't any ice cream.

"Are all funerals in Mystic's End so cheery?" I asked Gabe, whose arm pressed against my back.

"Not usually, no," he murmured as we made our way down the pew aisle. "It has been twenty years, though. A lot of Will's classmates may have moved away, or their memories of him are distant."

"My memories of my grandmother are distant and not particularly full of fondness," I whispered back. "I still don't think I would attend her funeral to catch up on the town gossip and laugh about... well, whatever those people are laughing at."

"Is he here?" Gabe asked quietly.

"Is who here?"

"Will."

"You mean Spike?"

He hushed me after glancing around to make sure no one had overheard me. "You're not supposed to know his nickname, remember?"

"Why isn't she supposed to know his nickname, Detective Wilcox?" a clear voice rang out. An athletic woman dressed in all black marched toward Gabe and me as if she had been waiting for us to arrive. I opened my mouth to answer, but she gestured for me to be quiet. "I'd like the *detective* to answer my question. If you don't mind."

"Pepper, can't you drop the twenty questions until the end of the funeral?" Gabe asked her fiercely.

"I'm *always* doing *my* job, Gabe," she answered back just as fiercely. "Are you *ever* doing yours?"

"Not *here*. I don't want to do this now," Gabe responded under his breath. The way the two of them looked at one another I was sensing a bit of history here. It practically crackled in the air between them.

"Did he say your name was Pepper? As in Pepper Stanford? The reporter?" I asked as I pushed in between them. Gabe rolled his eyes and threw up his hands.

"I am," Pepper turned on me and tilted her head. "And *you* are Fortuna Delphi. You just moved here from Texas after having traveled with the Magical Midway."

"That's correct, it's nice to meet—"

"You're in your mid-30s, single, and for years you made your living giving psychic readings to people that visited the various fairs that you worked for," she continued in a low but almost aggressive flow of words. "You've never had a romantic relationship with anyone, at least not that I could find. You were adopted at birth, and you moved here because you're looking for something or someone," she finished.

If Pepper Stanford *wasn't* psychic, she certainly could pull off a cold reading at a fair *pretending* to be. At least, if she was given enough time to do research beforehand.

"*That's* pretty impressive," I told her.

"It's her only talent," Liz said as she came up to the group and embraced Pepper. "Hey, girl, I didn't expect to see you here."

"Well, that's a total lie, now, isn't it?" Pepper responded sarcastically.

"That it's your only talent, or that I didn't expect to see you here?"

"Both," she nodded. "As entertaining as this is and as much as our new resident interests me, I don't think she has anything to do with Mason's murder. Someone else chatting around here might, though," she said as she turned and began to step away. "Off to mingle before the service. Meet for coffee after?"

Pepper Stanford was gone before anybody could respond to her question. I watched her sidle up to the next clutch of people and interject herself in the conversation without missing a beat.

"Can I join you two for coffee?" I asked Liz. "I was doing some research yesterday in the library and I noticed that—"

"You want to talk to Pepper about something you found while doing research in the library yesterday? I can guess what you noticed," Liz said as her face flashed a look of contempt. "But yeah, sure. Pepper will be happy to bend somebody's ear that hasn't heard it all before."

"I, um...maybe I shouldn't go," Gabe said hesitantly. His eyes were still following Pepper across the room and it hit me out of the blue in a flash. Pepper Stanford and Gabriel Wilcox had been an item in the past. My ears were practically itching with curiosity to rummage around in one or both of their heads to find out their history, but I refrained.

"You'll go," I told him as I scanned the room. "I'm sure you and your ex-girlfriend can be civil for the time it takes us all to drink one cup of coffee."

"How did you know that Pepper and I used to—"

"You're still not believing all the psychic stuff, are you?"

"*What* psychic stuff?" Liz asked curiously.

Before I could answer, Evangeline Laroux walked into the chapel of the Holy Grove Church. Dressed in a tight-fitting black power suit, a hush fell over the assembled gossips as all heads turned. Her platinum hair glowed as if an evening star had come out during the daytime. Her ruby red lips shined a pout even as dark sunglasses hid her eyes.

"Well, that *is* unexpected," Liz murmured. "She ran off to chase her Hollywood dream the day after Spike disappeared. And before she left, she didn't know Spike that well at *all*."

I glanced quickly again over the guests in the pews before their reactions faded away. I spotted Hoyt Abernathy's red face and clenched fists as he stared at what used to be Rowena Clutterbuck.

* * *

"We are gathered here today as a community to remember a fallen young man,"

Reverend Dexter Kane began in his deep, booming voice. "A young man who traveled down the wrong path, and to find at the end of that path there was nothing but a brick wall. A brick wall that he could *not* knock down," Kane said as he bowed his head.

I couldn't help it. My jaw dropped.

"William Mason was born in our town, a child born with promise as all children are. As he grew, he took that promise and painted it with hair dye, and draped it with black leather and spikes," the cleric said as he slammed his hand down on his pulpit, his voice growing louder and more offended as he went on.

The large picture at the front of the chapel on the dais was of Spike as a young boy, smiling. Clear-eyed and fresh-faced, he must've been twelve or thirteen.

As soon as Dexter's hand slammed on the pulpit, though, a mouse of a woman shuffled up and flipped over the picture. A snarling Spike in full punk regalia stared out over the crowd.

"This is what happens when you defy the norms of the community," Dexter thundered as he stepped out from in front of the pulpit and stared down at his flock. "The twisted wreckage of your soul is first visible outwardly. This makes it easier for God to *pluck* you from the field of flowers like the *weed that you are.*"

"Is he saying that Spike was killed because of his fashion and music choices?" I whispered to Gabe, but he shushed me. I was getting a very *Children of the Corn* vibe from the right Reverend Dexter Kane.

"Conformity, my friends," Dexter shouted, his eyes wide. "We base this community on the understanding that it rewards obsequious bowing, and the *rebellion* against those standards and norms is punishable. Now," he dropped his voice and half smiled, "perhaps not with entombment for years upon years."

He paused and raised himself up, throwing his shoulders back. "But perhaps, as the young brother William has shown us, just perhaps..."

A silence thick with judgment descended into the pews of the Holy Grove Church as Dexter's sentence hung in the air unfinished. I glanced around at the parishioners and noticed most were barely paying attention to the pastor's thunderous lecture. A few others, however, gazed up at him with sycophantic grins and shining eyes.

One of those faces was Hoyt Abernathy.

Another, I was told later, was Joe Mason.

* * *

"That was the most disturbing funeral I've ever been to in my entire life," I said as Gabe, Liz, Pepper and I slid into a booth at the Mystic Diner. "Are funerals in this town typically that full of fire and brimstone?"

"I suspect the mohawk and brick wall was just far too convenient for Dexter. Why let an allegory against individuality pass when it falls into your lap. Or out of a wall," Pepper said as she grabbed her ice water and took a sip. "Besides, Joe Mason, Will's father, is part of that cult they have. I don't think poor Will stood a *chance* of getting a decent funeral. Not in this town."

"Are there no other churches or funeral homes?"

"Are you *kidding* me?" Pepper scoffed. "Dexter Kane owns the soul of this town. Well, at least the people who believe, I guess. This is a strange town."

"How so?"

"Okay, we have this super conservative Holy Grove Church, right?" Liz explained. "But we also have this gigantic entertainment complex just on the edge of town that can cater to any sin you could think of."

"That's a lot of sins," I said.

"Right?" Pepper jumped in. "You would think if Kane wanted to go on some kind of spiritual warpath or something, he would do it against the sin and debauchery complex, right?" she continued as she played with her bendy straw. "But nope. The tourists? Not a concern. The townsfolk? Well, that's another story altogether."

"And if the townsfolk are at the sin and debauchery complex," Liz added. "That's okay, too. Which makes no sense to me. Like, they can sin *there*, but not on Main Street?"

"You've been remarkably quiet since we sat down," I turned to Gabe and raised my eyebrow. "You have nothing to add?"

"He can't," Pepper told me. "The church owns the police department."

"That's not true," Gabe protested, his face tensing.

"Come on, Gabe, we *all* know it," Liz told him.

"Just because we have expanded the police department over the years to ensure that we can take care of any crime at the complex *doesn't* mean that we're owned by anyone," he protested hotly. "Least of all the church."

"Gabe gets very *defensive* when we bring up the subject," Pepper tilted her head and met my eyes. "Mr. Wilcox likes to believe that he's on the side of the angels, what with his shiny badge and blessing from the church and all."

"Pepper, don't start this, not here," Gabe warned her.

"Detective Wilcox believes that I'm *paranoid,*" Pepper continued, ignoring Gabe. "He sees nothing particularly odd about the number of people that have gone missing, the number of things that have been stolen, or the number of people murdered in Mystic's End."

"I never said that, I just don't want—"

"He's *especially* unconcerned about the fact that most of these crimes? They are *never* solved," Pepper whispered loudly in my direction as if she was confiding in me. "They just get tossed onto the open case pile or, like with poor Will Mason, get explained away as just *another* odd coincidence in old Mystic's End."

"Look, Pepper, it's not that—"

"It's especially frustrating for poor Gabe over here that his ex-girlfriend, who is *not* on the police force, *always* seems to turn up information that *he* doesn't know—"

"She can talk to ghosts," Gabe blurted out at Pepper, looking like the cat that swallowed the canary, so proud of himself that he knew something she didn't. "Bet you didn't know *that,* did you?"

Pepper stared at Gabe in shock.

I slowly turned my head to stare at the detective.

"Sorry," he said without meeting my eyes.

SEVENTEEN

"I really am sorry," Gabe said as he pulled up in front of my gallery's back door. "Pepper and I dated in high school, but we broke up after she started working at the paper. She always seems to know just what to say to get under my skin."

"How long ago did the two of you break up?" I asked.

He veered around and looked at me. "It was a long time ago, and before you even go there, I do not have any feelings for Pepper Stanford," Gabe said quietly.

"I didn't say anything about whether you have feelings for her, Gabe," I told him as I stopped in front of him. "I just asked a question. Whether or not you still have feelings for Pepper isn't really any of my business."

"Well...I was kind of hoping that—"

"Hey, Liz!" I whirled around, cutting off whatever Gabriel Wilcox was about to say. Which, okay, being a mind reader I kind of knew. Actually, I didn't need to be a mind reader. I knew where his statement was heading, and I didn't want to be confronted with it. "Want to meet at your place or mine?"

"After Gabe spilled the beans on your ghostly talents, you really think I want to go to the unhaunted hair salon? Besides, I want to see this fifty-thousand-dollar greyhound you purchased," Pepper said as she shut the passenger door and walked over. "Your purchase was the talk of the park last night."

"Do you guys have a formal gossip tree?" I joked as I let everybody in. "Or does the information just flow through the town naturally?"

"You would think with the way people gossip, more secrets would spill out into the open, wouldn't you?" Pepper shot Gabe a fierce glance as he looked away from her and ran his hand through his hair. "So, is he here?"

Gideon skidded across the storage room and slammed into me, jumping from his front to his back paws as if he was a bucking horse. His tongue lolled out of the side of his mouth as he chuffed excitedly.

"Gideon, meet Pepper and Liz," I said as I pointed to each one. He tilted his head and considered Pepper, then Liz. After a few seconds, he ran over to them and pressed his body against their legs.

"Okay, I've seen the dog. Where's the ghost?" Pepper demanded after petting Gideon for a less than adequate time. At least, according to him.

"Have you been able to see ghosts before?" I asked her as we made our way to the front of the shop and its comfortable seating area.

"No," she shrugged. "But I knew Will pretty well. I'll be able to tell if you're talking to him or not."

"You don't believe her?" Liz asked, surprised.

"I don't believe anybody," Pepper replied, her arm shooting out and grabbing Liz. "You're about to step in dog poop."

"Gideon!" I sighed, turning toward the greyhound. I had assumed since he and I could communicate a bit he had understood when I would be back. Which wasn't long, really.

Gideon sent me images back. The first was he and Spike chasing each other through all three levels of the building. I winced as I watched Gideon skidding toward the stairs. The second was Jeff

Abernathy's face pressed against my front window. I glanced up and could see the smears from his hands on the glass.

The third image was of Gideon looking over his shoulder at Jeff Abernathy and taking a dump on the floor in front of the window as the kennel owner glared at him.

"Okay," I told him as I cleaned it up, grateful that I had opted for painted concrete floors in the shop. "I understand why you did it, but let's not do it again, okay? You get one pass here, buddy."

"Are you talking to the dog?" Pepper asked, her eyes narrowing.

"Sort of. I mean, I'm talking to him, but he's not talking back at me in words," I told her as I dropped Gideon's floor art in a Ziploc bag and sealed it to contain the smell. "He can communicate to me a little, in a way. He sends me images and movies."

"Can you do that with any animal?" Pepper stepped forward and crossed her arms.

"Probably, I guess," I shrugged, dropping the Ziploc in the trash. "Gideon seemed to be the one intent on communicating with me, though. I would suspect it's the animal's choice whether they want to talk to me."

"Pepper, she's got a business to run," Gabe warned as he watched the wheels turning behind

Pepper's eyes. "Don't get her involved in your stuff, she doesn't have time and—"

"Are you actually talking to *your* ex-girlfriend *about* me...no, not even about me. You're talking *for* me without talking *to* me?" I asked Gabe, my expression incredulous. Gabe's shoulders stiffened.

"He has a habit of doing that," Pepper confided.

"This is the second time you've done something like this, Gabe," I told him. "I'm happy to have met you, I'm glad that we're becoming friends, I really like your grandmother. But I didn't move here to find more people to tell me who I am or what I should do," I explained frankly.

"It's not gallant, Gabe, or chivalrous. You know that, right?" Liz jumped in.

To give Gabe some credit, he didn't run screaming from the gallery in the face of three annoyed women. His expression, though, was a little like a protective mother being confronted by three dysfunctional children.

"Fortuna, I know more about what Pepper gets into than you do, and I wasn't trying to control your life or be some kind of misogynist, controlling—"

"Stop," I told him firmly. "Just stop. Doesn't matter what you were trying to do. I just told you *again* not to do it. The only proper response to what I said should have been an apology. Come on—"

"I think I need to go," Gabe frowned as he

turned and walked back through the gallery. I sighed as I watched his back retreat toward the exit.

Pepper's face lit up with a smile. "You needed to do it. Trust me, if you don't give him strong boundaries? He crosses them without thinking."

"Wait a minute, what kind of boundary crossing are we talking about, here?" I asked her, startled. "You're not talking about any kind of violence, I hope."

"Not violence. Valiance, really," she said as she gazed at the closed door three rooms away through the archway. "He's a valiant man who wants to protect everybody he cares about from everything. He would lie down on glass if you were about to walk over it. Sometimes he protects first, respects later."

"You sound like you still care about him," I pointed out.

"Pepper and Gabe are not good as a couple," Liz said as she shuddered. "They're like brother and sister. Or cat and dog. Or oil and water."

"I'll always love him," Pepper smiled again. "I want nothing but the best for him—despite the hard time I always give him. But Liz's right. He and I are just not good for one another."

"I concur!" Spike said as he floated into the room.

* * *

As soon as I let Pepper know that Spike was here she turned to make her way to the couch, pulling out a micro-cassette recorder, note pads, and several sharpened pencils. "This is an interview with Fortuna Delphi, who claims to be able to speak to William Mason, deceased," she said into the microphone. "She has asserted that William Mason is here."

Pepper Stanford did not mess around.

"You want me to stay?" Liz asked. "I have an appointment in ten minutes, but I could get one of the other girls to take it."

"No, it's fine," I waived her out. "Maybe at some point I'll open this place up and have appointments, too, I hope," I said, only half joking.

"And why haven't you opened up your gallery?" Pepper asked me as she placed the micro-cassette recorder between us.

"Well, I was planning on opening the Monday they found Spike," I told her. "But then they found Spike."

"But they, meaning the police department, *didn't* find Spike, did they?" Pepper prodded looking up at me from the pad she was scribbling on. "You are the one that reported the body in the wall. So, *you* found William, not the police."

"I suppose so."

"Why do you call him Spike?"

"Because that's what he said his name was," I told her.

"The ghost told you his nickname?"

"He just introduced himself as Spike," I explained as Spike floated over her shoulder and looked down to see what she was writing. "I didn't know his legal name until the following morning when the police arrived."

"What did he tell you about the night he died?" Pepper asked.

"Almost nothing. He doesn't remember."

"What *does* he remember?"

"Spike?" I looked up at him. "What do you remember, exactly?"

"I told you, almost nothing. I came back from the show in Little Rock alone, and dropped by here to do something," he shrugged. "I just don't remember what it was." I related what he said, word for word, to Pepper.

Pepper looked up and narrowed her eyes. "You're talking to him right now?" I told her I was. "Does he remember me?" I related Spike's answer that he did. "What happened to me in kindergarten that was completely embarrassing?"

Spike's easy smile slipped into a frown. "Oh, man, that was so sad. It was snowing out, and her

Mom had put her in this one piece winter coat thing. You know, the kind with legs and arms?" I nodded. "The zipper got stuck when she got to school and she couldn't get it off. She really had to pee, and, well...she was a little kid, you know? It wasn't really her fault, but she got teased mercilessly about it for years."

I related the story, trying to be as general as I could in my description. Her face remained steady, unmoved, but a little pain leaked out as she compared Spike's explanation with her own memory.

"Yeah, you couldn't possibly know that," Pepper said as she sat back. "Not something adults mention to each other. Well, I guess you could. Maybe they're still talking about Tinkles Stanford and the Kindergarten Pee Pool," she half-smiled and leaned forward.

"They called you *Tinkles*?"

"Oh, worse than that. I also got Pee-per a lot," she said as she reached over and turned off the micro-cassette recorder. "Kids can be cruel. That's how Gabe and I got together, actually. He used to stick up for me in school. It happened so often, we wound up dating. Are you a witch?"

"I'm sorry, what?" I choked out trying to follow her whiplash-inducing questions.

"So, here's the thing. The reporter in me wants

to rake you over the coals six ways from Sunday," she said as she leaned forward, elbows on her knees. "You're a new person in town, you paid fifty thousand dollars for a pet, you discovered a person who had been missing for over twenty years in your wall. Add to all that the fact that you can talk to ghosts? You're a walking story, Fortuna, and I don't trust people with this much intrigue around them," Pepper smiled. "Oh, and the name."

"Well, so far, it's been a gentle raking, so thanks," I told her.

"The *human being* in me senses that I can trust you—and that's rare for me. Like I said before, I don't trust anyone."

"I'm a trustworthy person," I told her.

"*Are* you, though?" Pepper tilted her head. "You're not being honest about why you're here, I'm pretty sure about that."

"I *haven't* lied about why I'm here," I disagreed. "I just haven't made all the reasons I'm here public. That's all."

"That's a mighty fine split hair you have there," she chuckled. "Anyway, are you using some kind of magic or pheromones or something to make me *feel* like I can trust you? Like I said, I don't trust easily. But there's something about you."

"I am not doing anything artificially to inflate your sense of trust in me. No witchcraft, no oxytocin perfume," I promised her as Spike rolled his eyes. "Though if I did that for some nefarious reason, do you really think I would tell you?"

"See, that's just it," Pepper drawled. "I think you would."

"Well, I *would*," I assured her. "But I don't know how you can believe that. We just met."

"I don't know, either," Pepper shrugged. "But my instincts have never failed me, and I never lose when I follow them. So, are you going to help me figure this out?"

"I...wait, what now?" I said, struggling to follow her again. "Figure out what?"

"How Spike wound up in that wall," Pepper said as she got up and started walking toward the back of the store. "Is it this way?" she asked without waiting to be invited upstairs.

EIGHTEEN

"People find you a little hard to take, don't they?" I called as I hurried after her. Gideon followed us both, wagging his tail.

"I do everything right all the time," she said as she climbed up the stairs toward my living area uninvited. "People find that a little intimidating."

"Do they, now?" I began taking the stairs two at a time. Pepper moved like a gazelle, sailing up the stairs with a speed that spoke to her single-minded purpose. "Maybe it's your intense humility that puts them off."

"I promise you it's not that," she responded with a wave as she reached the landing and stood examining my bedroom. "A bit of a minimalist, are we?"

Why was everyone so concerned with the interior design of my living space?

"The safe was in that wall," Pepper murmured as she walked across the room toward the hole.

"She's right, actually," Spike said as he floated toward the dark hole covered with crime scene tape. "This is where Mr. Abernathy kept the wall safe. The hole matches the dimensions almost exactly."

"Do you remember when it was removed?" I asked him.

"Did he follow us up here?" Pepper asked me. I nodded without looking at her. Spike was staring at the hole intently, his face twisting as he stared at the break in the wall in front of him. "What's he doing?"

"Staring."

"At?"

"The hole," I pointed.

"Does he remember when he was put in the wall?" Pepper asked.

"I was always in the wall, from the moment I woke up dead," Spike squinted, thinking. "Eventually I realized that I could float out of the darkness, but that's what I thought death was for a bit. Just...just darkness. And sounds."

"What sounds? What did you hear when you were in there?" I asked him as Pepper looked at me curiously.

"Well, everything was muffled," he said as he floated back and forth. If his limbs had still had muscles, they would have been tense and twitching. In death, they sparked with Spike's frustration. "It was dark, and I was..."

"It frightened you," I told him softly.

"No!" he snapped, lying. "I wasn't scared, I was...It was confusing, okay? I didn't know what happened to me."

"Are you going to clue me in here?" Pepper asked with some exasperation as she stood poised with her pen over her pad. I outlined for Pepper what Spike had said so far which, to my mind, wasn't a lot. She saw it differently and perked up when he related he heard voices. "He doesn't remember...Ugh, this is ridiculous. Spike, do you remember being put in the wall?"

"No," he told her, and I related his answer as if I was a ghost-to-mortal translator. "I told you, the last thing I remembered was coming in the store that night. Then I woke up in the wall."

"Well, you didn't tell *me* that, you told *her* that," Pepper said. "No matter. When you say you woke up in the wall, do you mean you woke up while you were still alive, or you found yourself in the wall after you died? Like, when you woke up dead. You know what I mean, Spike?"

"I know what you mean," he told her. "I think it was when I died."

"You're sure you don't remember being in there in pain or having trouble breathing or anything like that?" I asked him. He thought for a minute and shook his head no. "And did you remember September 11th, or did you learn about it later?"

"I remember watching it over Liz's shoulder downstairs," he said. "I saw her arrive that morning. I'd been out since the middle of the night already."

"They put him in that wall the night he disappeared," I told Pepper. "Ghosts orient themselves pretty quickly to the fact that they're dead and not anchored in their body anymore. Spike, this is really, really important," I said turning back to him. "The day you died, was the safe here?"

"Of course it was," he told me. "I remember distinctly because we hadn't made a deposit for a month or so."

"Was that typical?" Pepper asked after I related his answer.

"No," he shook his head. "Mr. Abernathy was nervous about keeping a lot of cash in the place. The safe wasn't all that strong, really, and we didn't have a security system."

"So, why didn't you make a deposit for a month?" I asked him.

"I don't know," he shrugged. "One day when I

came in, Busy... um, Liz told me we weren't supposed to make the bank runs anymore and someone else would handle it."

Pepper and I looked at each other.

"I hope Liz is done with that client," she said as she walked toward the stairs.

* * *

"What do you think?" Liz asked the woman sitting in the chair. The woman's hair was curled tightly against her scalp, so tightly that I had to fight the urge to tug on a curl to see if it made a *boing* sound. "You said you wanted tight curls," Liz reminded her.

"I did, I did," the woman said as she leaned forward and squinted. "Are you sure your girl didn't make them too tight?" she asked with uncertainty.

"Well, you asked for the smallest rollers we had, June," Liz told her as she fluffed through the wretched hairstyle with a pick. "It will relax over the next few days. It looks to me like exactly what you asked for," she reminded the woman again as she turned her back to her, looked at Pepper and me, and rolled her eyes.

"If I decide I don't like it, what can we do?"

"Shave your head and buy a wig?" Liz suggested.

"You're such a snotty young woman," June responded as she pulled the cape from her neck with as much attitude as she could muster. "I don't know why I keep coming here."

"You keep coming here because the spa at the complex banned you for life after you threw a hot iron at your hairdresser, June," Liz told her as she stepped behind the counter and rung the woman up. "That, and because you don't want to drive to Little Rock to get your hair done. That's fifty for the cut, and a hundred for the perm."

"That's *awfully* steep!" June said, shocked.

"Mrs. Johnson?" Liz said as she held her hand out. "I don't have time for the games today."

"Horrible young woman," June grumbled as she shoved a wad of cash into Liz's hand and stalked out of the front door. The bells jangled violently as she left.

"Wow," I commented as I watched her slip into a Jaguar and peel out of the parking space (nearly hitting another car in the process.) "Who *was* that?"

"*That* was June Johnson, a Southern belle and society social climber," Liz said as she pressed a few buttons on the cash register. The drawer popped out, and she began sorting the cash into the proper places in the till.

"Does she climb the hill on the bones of her defeated enemies?" I asked.

Liz laughed. "Probably. What's hilarious is she complains about everything, but she comes back here every two weeks. And she tips well," the salon owner said as she held up three one-hundred-dollar bills. That was *besides* the multitude of twenties I'd already watched her sort.

"That's not just well, that's obscene," I blurted out, and then quickly apologized. "Not that you're not worth it or anything. I'm sure you are. I just don't understand why someone would—"

"Complain about the price and then pay triple?"

I nodded.

"She saw Angie do it once," Liz said as she shut the drawer. "Once. *Just* once. But that's all it took. June did not want to be shown up by Evangeline Laroux. Anyway, what's up? Pepper looks like she's got something on her mind."

"I'm thinking Pepper's always got something on her mind," I told Liz as she motioned for us to follow her to the back of the salon. The three other hairdressers and their clients watched us quietly. Well, watched me.

I wondered how long it would be before I wasn't the town's new bright and shiny curiosity.

I guess finding the body in my bedroom didn't help.

* * *

"We're curious about the safe," I told her, and explained what Spike had told us back at my place. She thought back and nodded.

"Yeah, now that you mention it, the safe disappeared a week or so before the store closed for good," Liz said. "Hoyt moved it out on September 11th. I remember it distinctly because he was in the store with it—at the back door, actually—when things started...well, when they started," her eyes clouded over.

"You're *sure*?" Pepper asked.

"Absolutely. I remember it distinctly because when they announced that flights were grounded Hoyt cursed up a *storm*. His father was in Boston for business and was due to fly back that day. Through New York."

"He must have been awfully worried," Pepper gasped.

"Heh, no, not really," Liz shook her head. "He wasn't worried at all, he was angry that his father wouldn't be back that day. Said he needed his help with something unexpectedly."

"Unexpectedly, huh? When did Mr. Abernathy finally make it back?" I asked her.

"Not for days," Liz said. "In fact, when he showed back up, he closed the store down. Never reopened it. He didn't even issue me my final check. Paid me off the books for the last two weeks."

"Wait a minute—Abernathy senior paid you off the books just for the final two weeks? You're sure?" I asked her again. Liz nodded. "And the safe was there the last day you worked with Spike, on September 10th, but Hoyt moved it out September 11th?" She nodded again, her face falling.

"You don't think when I came to work the next morning, Spike was..." Liz trailed off and then turned, eyes wide, to look at Pepper. "He was there that whole day? That whole week?"

"I think they killed Spike September 10th on the third floor of that building, sure. And bricked him up in the wall that night. We knew all that, though," Pepper pointed out.

"I didn't!" Liz protested hotly.

"It was the only logical time. Didn't you wonder about it when they found him? I mean, after—Liz? Liz!"

Liz's eyes filled with tears and her breathing became ragged, shallow, as she reached out frantically to support herself. "Was he...was he *alive*? Could I have saved him? Oh my god, was he *dying* upstairs while I was sitting and watching *the news*?"

"Liz, no. No. Liz, look at me," Pepper said as she grabbed the stylist by her shoulders and shook her. "Snap out of it. You couldn't have done anything. Spike died and became a ghost before the sun rose on that day."

"Are you *sure?*" Liz asked tearfully, her expression hopeful.

"He remembers some things distinctly. Spike knows he went to the show in Little Rock. That puts him back here at around eleven or midnight," I assured her as Pepper continued to hold her. "He remembers noticing his death while it was still dark, and he remembers hovering behind you as you watched the news on September 11th. So, no, Liz, there's *nothing* at all you could have done to help him. I promise."

"Okay. Okay," Liz breathed shakily as she leaned against her bookcase. Pepper continued to look at her with concern. "You can let go, I'm okay. Just...the idea that I just sat downstairs while he suffered and...it just overwhelmed me a little, that's all. I'm okay." Liz rose to her feet.

"Good, because we need your help," Pepper said as she pulled away. "Tell us everything you know about Hoyt Abernathy from the time of the store closing. *Everything.* Leave nothing out."

NINETEEN

As Liz went over all that she recalled of that last month Spike was alive, she revealed that the police had investigated a series of robberies at the store in August and September. "It was a typical Mystic PD job, though," she said as she rolled her eyes. "They came, they marked a report, and they took off."

That sent Pepper straight to the library, me in tow.

"Irma!" Pepper shouted as she stormed into the library like a force of nature. "I need the crime reports for September 2001, pronto! What aisle in the cage?"

"Four!" came a holler back from someplace in the stacks.

"Thank you!" Pepper shrieked back across the vast, silent building.

"Anything for you, dear!" came the final boisterous bellow.

"If Hoyt said *not* to transfer money into the bank, he had to be looting the cash," Pepper said as she pulled out a set of keys and pointed toward an old cage in back. It enclosed a portion of the library corner, the cage making it a separated room of files and books. "Him, or someone that he knew. I want to know just how much cash disappeared. And *when*."

As I followed Pepper into the archived police records cage, I became vaguely worried that Pepper was looping me in to a conspiracy that would remain with me all the rest of my days in Mystic's End. I mean, let's face it—I was already pretty memorable.

And not in a good way.

It wasn't enough that my new home contained a ghost. Or the top racing greyhound had resolved to telepathically communicate with me to ensure I knew he wanted to move in with me. Or that a detective and his nosy grandmother had taken a special interest in me (which may be the understatement of the year).

Now the town busybody had concluded *I* was her new best friend and I wasn't *entirely* sure we hadn't just illegally broken into police files. Even if she did have the keys.

This wasn't starting off well.

"What?" Pepper asked looking up from a file cabinet as she observed my expression.

"I just feel like I'm poking into things that will make me *a little* unwelcome here," I told her as I leaned against the file cabinet. "I didn't move here to make trouble or make waves or tick everybody off, you know? I've noticed that when you move toward people to speak to them, they move away *pretty* quickly," I told her as her face hardened— even though that may have been the other understatement of the year. "Look, I'm not saying this to be—"

"If you don't care that this town is crooked from the mayor to the street sweeper in front of your shop, then that's *fine*," she snapped back scornfully and turned her back to me. "You don't have to get involved in this. To tell you the truth, Fortuna, *nobody* really does. Get involved, I mean. That's why we have 90% of murders unsolved, 70% of missing persons unfound, and 95% of thefts unrecovered."

"Look, I didn't mean to—"

"You did, but that's fine. I understand," she snapped again, cutting me off, but I could hear the hurt in her voice. "You're not locked in here. If you

don't care about how Spike died, there's the door."
She pointed toward the open cage door without
facing me. "Your shop is two blocks away. I'm sure
you can find it."

"You're taking way more offense at this—"

"*Someone* has to." Pepper went on shuffling
through the file folder as she looked for the police
records for September 2001. "If it's not me, then it's
not anybody," she rambled into the dusty files.
"Everybody talks about it. No one does anything
about it. Well, *I'm* not like everybody else. If *you*
are, go."

I watched as she grabbed a file and moved over
to the table beside the cabinets. She was ignoring
me. Pepper had said what she had to say, and that
was it. She wouldn't beg me to stay. She would just
challenge me to feel good about leaving.

I watched her begin sifting through the
information with single-minded determination. I
chuckled silently to myself. She was like a dog with
a bone.

I *liked* Pepper.

Then I frowned.

I could also understand where this was going.

Hoyt Abernathy likely killed Spike, or he knew
who did. Pepper had said nothing yet, but I realized
Hoyt probably told his father about the body
upstairs. At least if his agitated demeanor regarding

needing his father's help the day after Spike died was any sign.

Implicating Jeff Abernathy would put me *even higher* on his poop list than I already was for acquiring the prized greyhound that I then took home, costing his kennel money.

And if Pepper accused Jeff and Hoyt Abernathy, *they* might be close enough to the Reverend Kane that *he* would be resentful.

Maybe Ollie Kane, too.

Then maybe Gabe.

And then there was still Evangeline Leroux's anxiety that Spike's body was revealed at all.

In short, it seemed like I would suspect or accuse fully half of the people I had met in Mystic's End before this was over, or be standing next to the town troublemaker that would shout the same allegations.

Or...

You know, I *could* just take off.

Leave Pepper on her own to accuse the town because, frankly, it *sounded* like the town was used to that.

Go back, open my art studio, start teaching classes, paint pictures and look into my birth mom in my spare time. I *still* didn't know which family in this town would turn out to be connected to me. If any. It would be *seriously* awkward to find out later I had accused my own birth family of murder.

That settled it.

It wasn't a good idea to make waves two weeks after I came to town. Especially since I could be related to any of the people I would be accusing.

(Yes, okay, I bought Gideon and in doing that I made waves. But I got a dog out of it and he wanted to come home with me, so that's *entirely* different.)

I bit my lip and stared at Pepper pouring intently over page after page of entries, wondering how to tell her I had to go. I was done. I didn't want to be involved in this.

"Are you going to just stand there and stare at me or are you going to help? Because if you're *not* gonna help, I'd rather you just *go*," Pepper said without looking up from the paper. "I get stared at enough by the people in this town, I don't need to add you to the list."

I took a deep breath.

* * *

By the time Pepper and I were done going through all the reports—

Yes, okay, I *should've* just gotten up and walked out. I should have pushed myself off the file cabinet and walked out of the cage, then walked out of the library, and back to my place to play with my new dog.

I wanted to. You do not understand how much I wanted to.

In the end, though, my time at the Magical Midway and all that we had done and all that we had faced wouldn't allow me to turn my back on injustice. The next time I spoke to Charlotte on the phone, I would have felt such shame at shrugging off unfairness for my own convenience.

Because that's what it was.

Ignoring something because I would be more comfortable not having to deal with it.

Yes, I wanted the people in this town to like me. But I was getting the impression that would be challenging regardless of what choice I made here. I wasn't the only one with secrets.

I had to decide *who I was*.

And I wasn't someone that could ignore this. So I sat down with Pepper. For Spike, yes—but because it was the right thing to do.

"Can you double check my numbers?" Pepper asked as she passed over the paper. I grabbed the adding machine on the table and re-added the column of numbers she laid out. "Yep, that's the same thing I got."

"How does anyone make half a million dollars in a small town record store in a month?" I asked.

"There shouldn't have been that much cash in there, not if it was *just* from that store's sales. CDs were what, ten dollars a pop?"

"If it was in twenties—the cash, I mean—it would have been heavy, too."

"Too heavy to carry?" I wondered.

"Depends," Pepper said as she scribbled out a mathematical equation on a blank piece of paper with a pencil. "That would've been fifty-five pounds. Hoyt's strong, but even so, that's a big duffel bag. And heavy, too," she said as she scratched out another equation. "Only twenty-two pounds if it was in fifty dollar notes, but fifty dollar bills at a *record store* makes little sense at all. You make some bills fives and tens and that thing gets *way* too heavy to carry all at once."

"I still say half a million dollars at a record store makes little sense, but even so, it *wasn't* all at once," I told her. "They took it in four separate robberies."

"*What* are the two of you *doing?*" Gabe asked as I jumped, startled.

"*Your* job," Pepper deadpanned without looking up at her ex. Pausing only to take a breath, she continued as if Gabe wasn't there. "If half a million dollars was picked up in four separate robberies, and each time the crooks made off with a hundred and twenty-five thousand dollars almost on the nose...I mean, those are some *really* meticulous thieves, right?"

"Unless they *weren't* robbers. Not in the traditional sense," I murmured as I grabbed all four of the police reports and arranged them out in front of me. "All four happened in the middle of the night. All four were discovered the following morning. All four have almost the same wording—"

"You guys aren't even supposed to have *access* to this cage," Gabe said as he began picking up the reports and bundling them back in the folders. "*Or* these files."

"Wait a minute, give that back—" Pepper said as she yanked the papers out of his hand with a scowl and laid them back out. "Look at this, Fortuna. You're right, all four of them have virtually the same wording," Pepper said as she put the first two reports and the last two reports next to one another in a square. "No, look—they have the same exact wording. Same handwriting. Same detective. Same everything."

"Except the dates," I marked out.

"Right," Pepper noted and leaned over, squinting. "It's not a copy, though. These are the originals."

"Who's the detective that signed them?" Gabe asked as he leaned in, now curious.

Pepper looked down and sighed. "Great. We

may as well just give this up right now. Even if we solve this, nothing will happen."

"Why?" I asked her.

"The detective on the case was Terrance Clutterbuck." Gabe and Pepper shared a glance I couldn't altogether read.

"Wait—is he Evangeline Laroux's father? Brother?" I asked.

"Father," Pepper said.

"And the current chief of police," Gabe added.

"Good afternoon, Chief!" Irma practically screamed from the front of the library not two seconds after Gabe finished his statement. "Need something from the cage, do you?!"

"*Hide*," Gabe whispered as he pushed Pepper out of the chair. Pepper grabbed my hand and tugged me toward the back, propelling me behind the stacks so I'd be out of sight. Once she forced herself in after me, she looked at me and held her finger up to her lips.

Just in case I couldn't figure out talking right now was a bad idea, I suppose.

* * *

Pepper and I watched Gabe looking through the papers we had laid out on the table as if he had been there all along. The chief, a big, muscular lumberjack of a man, strolled in and stopped short in dismay when he saw Gabe seated at the table.

"Detective Wilcox, what are you doing here?" he asked as he strode up to the table and looked down. As his eyes skimmed over the papers, his face remained stoic. "Shouldn't you be over at the Complex seeing if they need any help?"

"Um, no sir. It's my day off, actually. I'm just looking into some information about the William Mason case," Gabe said as he stood up.

"There *is* no Mason case, Detective," Chief Clutterbuck responded. "The case was closed as an accidental death, son. Nothing else to look into."

"Well, sir, I just recalled that there were several robberies at the shop where Mason was found, and I thought they might be linked to how he wound up in that—"

"Wilcox, *what* did I just say?" Gabe's burly boss leaned forward intensely, his eyes boring into the younger man's. I could feel the hostility from my hiding place behind a bookcase.

"I understand, sir, but—"

"Are you hard of hearing, son? I said the case is *closed*. Kid was presumably there when they pulled out the safe, he tripped, and fell into the wall. No one noticed because of how far he fell down, and someone accidentally bricked him up. Now, how tough is that to imagine?"

Considering Spike had a technicolor mohawk that stuck up feet in the air? Kind of hard.

"I understand, sir, but—"

"Haven't you heard about construction workers being entombed in concrete when building bridges and such?" Clutterbuck challenged. "Happens *all* the time. They just leave 'em there."

Pepper's face contorted in fury. I was tempted to peek into the flood of words that was likely rattling off in her head, but I bit my lip and remembered I *would* not do that to people. If they broadcast their thoughts, nothing I could do about that. But dig in? It wasn't right, and it wasn't honest.

Hell, *these* humans didn't even know it was *possible*. If I could control it, and I *could*, it was my responsibility to uphold people's privacy.

Even if I really, *really* wanted to know what she was thinking.

"Now, you let me have those papers, and you get on back to the work you're *supposed* to be doing," Chief Clutterbuck told Gabe with finality as he reached over and collected up the files.

Gabe hesitated and looked as if he wished to say more.

"Go on, *now*, Detective."

The files of papers clasped in Clutterbuck's meaty hand pointed Gabe toward the door.

"Yes, sir," Gabe gave in, and he thrust himself

up, spinning toward the door without looking at our hiding place at all.

The chief stood silently, papers still clutched in his hand, and watched Gabe walk out the enclosure door, and then down the stacks. Chief Clutterbuck did not turn away until he saw Gabe walk out of the front door of the library and into the afternoon sun.

"Damn nosy kid," he mumbled as he spun away from us.

Though we couldn't see what Chief Clutterbuck was doing, the sound of a paper shredder eating file after file was unmistakable.

TWENTY

"Who does he answer to?" I asked after we heard Irma scream her goodbyes to Chief Clutterbuck as he left the library. "I mean, cops can't just shred records, can they?"

"Legally? Probably not," Pepper said as she walked over to the plastic bin below the shredder and yanked it out. Digging in her purse, she pulled out a plastic bag, snapped it open, and began shoving shredded strips into it. "But who's gonna stop him?"

"State troopers? The FBI? I don't know, I mean, there has to be *someone*," I told her as I leaned against the table and watched. "It just seems like there should be someplace that you can make a complaint. If the police department is as corrupt as you say, anyway. Wouldn't someone above them be interested if all this is really that bad?"

Pepper stood up and sealed the bag, shoving it back in her purse. "If? You just saw the chief of police destroy four files related to the death of the citizen found in your wall," she said, her brows knitted together as she considered me. "You mean to tell me you need more than that to realize Clutterbuck is corrupt?"

"No, that's *not* what I mean. Pepper, stop putting words in my mouth," I told her a little more harshly than I intended. "You've asked me to help you, and so far I've gone along with everything, but I'm not some follower that just swallows everything someone tells me. If you could manage it, maybe just answer my questions without judging me for asking them. Can we try that?"

She looked a little startled by my abrupt statement, but I didn't really care. If Pepper wanted my help, she had to learn I needed to understand why I was doing things.

"Now, from what I understand regarding law enforcement in this state, you *have* a county sheriff, right? They're responsible for the entire county. That would include Mystic's End, clearly. Right?"

"Yeah," Pepper answered without enthusiasm.

"Have you ever gone to the Sheriff's Department to report this?" I asked her.

Irma walked in the cage and joined the two of us just as Pepper rolled her eyes at me.

"Of course I've reported the issues in this town, Fortuna," she told me, exasperation firing in her eyes. "I've reported the issues to three different elected Sheriffs. The chief of police doesn't report to the Sheriff's Department, though, he reports to the city managers. And the city managers? They're just as corrupt as everybody else."

"She's probably right, dear," Irma told me, nodding. "A complex that makes the kind of money those people make between the dog betting and the machine betting and the card betting—"

"There's a lot of money for bribes," Pepper cut Irma off.

"Well, yes, dear, that was the point I was trying to make," Irma said, slightly offended

"I just made it a little faster."

"Okay, back up a minute. You reported the corruption to the sheriff. What happened?" I asked Pepper.

"Nothing happened. Nothing *ever* happens."

I took a deep breath and exhaled, trying to muster up more patience. "I understand that you believe nothing has ever happened, that nothing came from it," I told Pepper slowly. "What I am trying to determine is *what* response you got regarding *why* nothing happens when you report corruption."

"Because everyone's on the take," Pepper responded.

"*Three successive sheriffs* have *told* you they are *on the take* and that's why they won't respond to the information or investigate your allegations?" I asked her incredulously. "All three just flat out told you that?"

"Well," Pepper shifted and crossed her arms. "Didn't say that in so many words but I knew what they meant."

"What *did* they say in so many words?"

Pepper looked uncomfortable.

"Just *tell* her, Pepper," Irma told her.

As much as Pepper normally ran her mouth, getting her to answer me was like pulling teeth.

"They said I didn't have any evidence," Pepper sighed as she looked down and smoothed her button-down top. "They said all I had were allegations, not evidence. And that they couldn't investigate the most powerful people in town just because I made an allegation. Or twenty."

"Thank you," I told her with a sour look. "That wasn't so hard, was it? Did you ask them about the abnormally high crime statistics?"

"With the thousands of people coming to the

complex every day, they didn't think it was abnormally high. Mystic's End is still considered a small town," she shrugged. "Even with the abnormally large Police Department, the sheriff figured high unsolved rates were par for the course with so many people passing through town."

"The population of the complex can be ten, even twenty, times that of the town," Irma added. "There may only be two thousand people in town, but if you add in the tourists, there could be twenty to twenty-five thousand people here on any given day."

"And more than half are probably drunk," I pointed out. "Okay, it looks like you have two choices, really," I told Pepper. "One, find hard and fast evidence of a crime. Evidence so rock solid that no one at the county level could question it. Address what you can. Take it step-by-step."

"Tell me something I *don't* know," she shook her head dubiously.

"Or two," I continued as if I hadn't heard her snarky response. "Run someone for Sheriff that understands what's going on in this town, and who wants to stop it."

"Like who?" Pepper demanded.

"What about your ex-boyfriend?" I asked.

"What about me?" Gabe said as he walked in the cage.

* * *

After Pepper explained my idea to Gabe, he paled.

"No," Gabe responded with a vigorous shake of his head. "Not a chance. I've barely been a detective for three years, I don't have the qualifications to run an entire county."

"Well, son, that's where you're wrong," Irma chuckled. "In this state, you just have to be a qualified elector and a resident of the county. You are *fully* qualified. Congratulations!"

"Um, thanks?" Gabe choked out, his eyes wide.

"I hate to put a hitch in y'all's get-a-long, though, but despite appearances?" Irma said, her expression growing serious. "Sheriffs are not the highest ranking law enforcement officer in the county."

"They're not?" Pepper asked with some surprise.

"No, ma'am, they are not. *That* would be the county coroner," the old woman explained. "He can conduct investigations into deaths, he has subpoena power, he can conduct inquests. The sheriff doesn't have any of those powers—other than investigative."

"Who's the county coroner?" I asked.

"Bobby Newsom," Gabe responded. "You met him when he and Ollie came to get Mason's body.

Well, I surely don't have the qualifications to run against him for the coroner job. I took no medical *anything* in school."

"My bet is he didn't, either. Are you eighteen years old? Never had a felony, have you?" Irma asked him. "Well, then, son, you, too, can be a county coroner in the *great* state of Arkansas."

"Are you telling me *Bobby Newsom* is the highest law enforcement officer in this county?" Gabe asked. I could practically see a green glow in his aura around his lower torso from the sick, sinking feeling in the pit of his stomach.

"Yes, Detective, I am," Irma nodded. "Frankly, I'm surprised you *didn't* know that. I would've thought they explained all that in your police training."

"I'm sure it was in some book somewhere," he responded absently, his eyes narrowed in thought.

"Doesn't your friend Ollie work for the coroner's office? The one with the long hair?" I asked Gabe. "Do you think he would know how Spike's death got classified as an accident?"

"Ollie, yeah. He would have to, wouldn't he?" the detective said as he fished out his phone from his pocket. "Let me call him. He should have a lunch coming up, maybe he can meet us at the diner."

"Not the diner," Pepper said. "Have him come

here. I don't want to talk to him in public. By the way, are you *helping* now?"

"If it keeps me from having the three of you push me to run for some electable position? Absolutely. As much help as I can proffer up," he told her as he hit the button on his phone and pulled it toward his ear. Pepper held up her hands in defeat, but as she turned to walk back to us a smile spread across her face.

"If I'd known it was *that* easy..." Pepper murmured to Irma and me.

* * *

"Hey, now, I haven't been here in years," Ollie said as he strode in. His old, faded blue jeans were torn in several places, and his County Coroner button-down shirt fitted loosely over a black Harley-Davidson t-shirt. "Not since elementary school, I would guess."

"Hey, we have some questions for you," Gabe said.

"Shoot," Ollie responded as he grabbed a chair and flipped it around so he was straddling it. He draped his arms over the back and smiled openly.

"We're curious about the coroner's office. What's your position, officially?"

"Officially?" he asked Gabe, still smiling.

"Assistant to the Arcadia County Coroner, I think. The job is I do whatever Bobby tells me, really. He and I are the only full-time folks at the office. There *are* other staff members, but they're not full time. We call them in if we need them. Not a huge number of murders in Arcadia County, really."

"Do you know why Will Mason's death was ruled accidental?" Pepper asked him.

"Bobby talked to Hoyt, and Hoyt said that Spike was helping him take out the safe early in the morning," Ollie explained, his head tilting. "Said Spike was pretty tired because he been at a concert the night before, and he was a little hung over. Hoyt went to the diner to pick up more coffee for them so they could finish, and when he got back, he said Spike was gone," Ollie shrugged. "Hoyt assumed Spike kept working while he ran to get the coffee, tripped because he was so tired, and fell into the wall. Well, after he was found, anyway."

"And Hoyt noticed nothing at all when he got back?" I pushed.

"Well, he noticed Spike was gone," Ollie said with a friendly smile. "But he didn't seem to think anything was out of place."

"That was good enough for Bobby?" Ollie nodded. "Even though twenty years ago no one looked for Spike because they assumed he never came back from Little Rock?" I asked.

Pepper shot up from the table and beelined toward a file cabinet Irma was excitedly pointing at. "It should be in the third drawer, dear," Irma said. "This is the first day anyone has come to look in the cage, so unless the chief just removed it, it should still be there."

"I got it," she announced, her voice expressing some surprise that the file was still there. She opened it and began scanning while she walked back to us. Gabe reached out gently and guided her back to her chair next to him since she was now oblivious to anything but Spike's disappearance file.

"They talked to him," she said. "Anyone want to guess what he said back then?"

"That Hoyt never saw Spike at night," I told her.

"You got it. One point for the new girl," Pepper frowned as she kept scanning. "And they never suspected him of anything at all. He had an alibi."

"Rowena Clutterbuck?" I asked as Pepper's head snapped up.

"Is she right?" Gabe asked. Pepper nodded, squinting at me suspiciously.

"Hoyt and Rowena claimed they were together all night, that their date ended at 2 AM on September 11, started at 7 PM on September 10, and that Hoyt dropped her off at her house. Then he went home to his."

"Well, that's kinda—" Ollie started, but Pepper cut him off.

"And they both claimed they were at the same concert that Spike attended in Little Rock. They saw him leave with four men they didn't recognize," she read, frowning. "And that Spike had told them he was running away."

The four of us sat, stunned.

"How did this file not get looked at before Bobby made the ruling on how Spike died?" I asked Ollie. "Isn't there some kind of standard practice that you all would pull the file?"

"Bobby kinda does what Bobby wants, if you get my drift," Ollie smiled and held his arms up. "He's the boss, and it's up to him how to investigate a death, know what I mean?"

"He's corrupt," Pepper told him.

Ollie smiled at her and shrugged. "Or he just doesn't care that much. I don't know, man. I just work here."

TWENTY-ONE

In my head, moving to Mystic's End would differ from my previous life at the circus. Sure, I knew it would take me time to make friends here, time to get involved with the rhythm of the town. When Gabe showed up in my shop to play twenty suspicious questions, I tempered my expectations even more.

But it would be a slower pace. Not as exciting. It would take me some time to find my place.

As Pepper, Gabe, and I pulled up in front of the police department, I had to at least admit that my desire to become a part of the fabric of Mystic's End probably should have come with a few more provisos—

"I can't believe you want to bring this to

Bobby!" Pepper protested at the top of her lungs. "He didn't even bother to look for it! He could have—"

"*He* ruled the death accidental," I replied, cutting her off. The three of us met Ollie, who had pulled in on his motorcycle and parked on the opposite side, at the double glass doors. "Unless he changes his ruling, they can do no further investigation, Pepper. So let's bring him the discrepancy and see what he says."

"I will leave you all here," Gabe said as we stepped onto the landing that led to the coroner's office. "Probably best if you two go in with Ollie to talk to Bobby. I wasn't supposed to be working on this case, and if this backfires, I don't want—"

"The chief saw you with these files," I pointed out.

"Not *those*. And you said you saw him *shred* the ones he saw me with. Which no one is supposed to know, by the way," Gabe told us, staring pointedly at Pepper and me. "I'd like to keep myself out of it if I can. For now."

"Who shredded what now?" Ollie asked, confused.

"Never mind," Pepper told him. She stepped forward and looked up into Gabe's face. "Why do you always book out just when it matters?"

"That's not fair—"

"Pepper, let him go. It doesn't help your crusade if the only police officer—"

"Detective," Gabe corrected me, still staring at Pepper.

"If the only detective on the police force that's agreed to help you gets fired, does it?" I asked her. Pepper and Gabe clearly had a lot of history I did not understand, but I could guess. Pepper's fiery personality and Gabe's conservative one had likely come into conflict before, and I had no doubt they would do so again.

"Fine, go. That's what you're good at," Pepper turned away from Gabe and began walking toward the coroner's office. Ollie hurried to catch up with her as Gabe stared at her walking away.

"You know, sometimes opposites can work," I told him. "You two don't seem to try very hard, though."

"You mean in a relationship? That ship has sailed, I promise. I still care about her, though, and I worry that she will stick her nose in something too far too fast and without thinking," Gabe sighed. "I just don't want to see her get hurt."

"If I hadn't convinced her to go to the coroner's office with the information, what would she have normally done?" I asked him quietly.

"She would've turned it in to the paper as a story," Gabe said. "The editor would've rejected it because it was just one piece of a puzzle, or because she didn't have enough proof, or because the proof she had was too inflammatory against someone else and he'd tell her he was worried about getting sued. Then she would've put it on her blog."

"Pepper has a blog?" I asked, surprised.

"Crooked Endz," he nodded. "Every conspiracy theory she's ever believed or come up with a shred of proof for. Half of it is about the corruption in this town."

"And the other half?"

"The supernatural, actually," Gabe said as he looked down at me, surprised, as if he had just put two and two together and realized it equaled ghosts. "I wonder if you were an entry there before she met you. She has a lot of stuff about hauntings, rumors of witches, creatures that can change into animals. All sorts of weird stuff."

"Corruption and the supernatural?" I asked him as I began walking toward Ollie and Pepper. "Sounds like my last job," I joked.

* * *

It shouldn't have been surprising, considering all we knew, that when we walked into the coroner's office, Hoyt Abernathy and Bobby Newsom were sitting at a metal table eating lunch together. It struck me as such a brazen response, though. They were eating on the autopsy table. The only autopsy table.

They were feasting where Spike's bones had lain just a few days before.

If I didn't dislike both of them before, that did it.

"Hey, Ollie, no guests in the office," Bobby gruffly barked to his assistant as he passed a bag of chips to Hoyt. "Especially not her," he said as he pointed to Pepper. "That woman never met something she didn't understand that she *couldn't* assign a bad meaning to."

"Actually, Mr. Newsom, we had a question for you," I said as I gently tugged the old police folder from Pepper's tight-fisted hand. "Pepper was doing some research at the library and came across this folder. It's from the original investigation into William Mason's disappearance."

"Yeah, so what?" he asked, mustard dribbling down his chin as he chewed open-mouthed. Hoyt, on the other hand, was staring at me warily. "Haven't you heard? The case was closed. Though I'm sure Stanford over there probably thinks a ghost body-snatched Willy and stuck him in the wall," the sloppy man laughed uproariously as he poked his dining companion. "Maybe on a full moon, right?"

"I'm new here, so I'm not exactly sure what you're talking about," I told him as I walked over and pushed the sandwich wrappers out of the way, opening the file up and pointing to the notes on Hoyt's interview. "But Ollie let us know that you ruled it accidental based on your friend's report of what happened that night," I smiled at Hoyt as Pepper stared, arms crossed. "Yet, years ago, Hoyt said something completely different."

"Yeah, well, he was a kid then," Bobby shrugged as he pushed the folder away and tugged the sandwich closer to him again. "Probably was a little drunk or a little stoned. Hoyt was a bit wild back in the day, if you know what I mean."

Another laugh with his mouth full, another slap on Hoyt's back.

Hoyt winced.

"Right, Mr. Newsom, I'm sure you're correct," I said as I moved the sandwich back from him once again and slipped the folder in front of him, pointing. "It seems like Mr. Abernathy—and forgive me, Mr. Abernathy, for talking about you as if you're not here—had a lot more to say back then. It seems like your friend, the one sitting here, might be hiding something. Don't you think?"

"Just who the hell do you think you are?" Hoyt kicked his chair up behind him and exploded in anger. "You want to talk about conspiracy theories?

How about some new girl moving to town, buying up the dog that wins more than anything, buying my father's building, and then accusing me of murder? How about that, Pepper?" he yelled as he looked back at her. "You don't think that's a conspiracy?"

"Well, maybe it *is*, Mr. Abernathy," I told him as I met his eyes as they returned to me. "So far, though, my buying a greyhound or the building hasn't resulted in a dead body."

"Well, that's not entirely true, now, is it? There wasn't a dead body in that building that anybody found until you showed up," Bobby Newsom pointed out as if he had suddenly discovered some great truths in the investigation. Ollie, Pepper and I glanced at one another in confusion. "Maybe you killed Will Mason years ago, and this is all some grand plot to cover it up? And now you're accusing Hoyt. See? I can spin a yarn myself, and I have just as much evidence of it."

"Are you *daft*?" I shot out before I could stop myself.

"I sure don't appreciate your tone," Bobby Newsom warned me as he pushed the file away again and violently snatched his sandwich. He pulled it toward him so violently that it wound up balancing on the top of his large belly. Seemingly unconcerned, he picked it up, tucked the meat back in with his finger, and took a bite. "Youf sholf kno—"

"Please wait until you've chewed your food, Mr. Newsom," I told him. "I can't understand a word you're saying at the moment, and I absolutely want to make sure I savor every pearl of wisdom you're about to utter."

"If you think your *fancy talk* will intimidate me, you got another thing coming," Hoyt advised me.

Ollie and Pepper stood near the door watching me intently. Ollie seemed gobsmacked that anyone was talking to his boss the way I was and was simply enjoying the show. Pepper...actually, I couldn't figure out what Pepper was thinking. And she had been quiet so long, it was a little unnerving, to tell you the truth.

"I said that you should know this is none of your business—"

"You are an *elected* official, Mr. Newsom. I live in this county now. I'm a taxpayer, I'm a resident, I'm a business owner," I told him as I ticked each thing off on my fingers. "You work for me, sir, and I have questions about how you handled the case that originated in my bedroom."

"Maybe Hoyt is right about you! Why would you have your bedroom on the third floor, anyway?" Bobby asked. "The second floor has all the plumbing and the high-grade insulation."

"What high-grade insulation?" I asked him, smiling.

"Dad wanted to test out some new insulation for construction," Hoyt said as if it should be obvious. "You open up a hole and just shoot it in there. It's foam, and we tested it out on that old building on the first and second floor," he told me.

"But not the third floor?" I asked.

"Well, no, because—" Hoyt stopped short, as if he just realized he had divulged too much.

"Because you knew there were bones in the third floor wall, and you didn't want them discovered," I finished for him.

"No! No, that's not why we didn't do the third floor," he looked me up and down disdainfully. "It was...it was to test the insulation! So we could have a basis for comparison!" he told me, but he spoke far too fast, as if the idea was being pushed out to push away any hint of his guilt.

"Did you insulate the roof?" I asked, but I already knew the answer. My inspector had commented on how odd it was that someone had put high-end insulation on the first two floors and the roof, but not the third floor outer walls. Anyone would've realized that the third floor walls remaining without insulation would mean the second floor insulation and the roof insulation's efficiency would be compromised.

Well, maybe not someone who thought *absolutely* was *fancy talk.*

"You're trying to trick me," Hoyt said.

"No, I'm trying to get you to confess," I leaned over the table and moved to the open folder in front of him. "I don't know whether you killed Will Mason, or whether your girlfriend Rowena did. Or maybe you both did. Or maybe *nobody* did, and it was an accident."

Hoyt looked at me angrily.

"What I *can* tell you is my next stop is to talk to Evangeline Leroux," I told him as I tapped his words in the folder. "I've met her, and forgive me for saying so, but she doesn't strike me as someone who thinks twice about throwing someone else under a bus to save her own rear."

Hoyt turned red with fury, and Bobby sighed. With a loud belch, he tossed his sandwich down and turned to examine his friend.

"Hoyt, *do* you know something about this?" Bobby Newsom asked seriously for the first time as he grabbed the open folder and pulled it away from his friend. "I can help you if you need it, but I can go to prison for covering up a crime. I ain't going to prison for you. I can't cover up what happened if you did something. But to know what I can do to help, I need to know the truth, here."

"Can you go to prison for being an incompetent idiot?" Pepper called from the side of the room.

"Actually, no, which is probably why I'm not in prison right now," Bobby called back to her with a chuckle. "Why don't you go get Detective Wilcox and ask him to come in here."

"It wasn't my fault!" Hoyt told Bobby.

"Let's just get the detective in here and sort out what's what, okay, Hoyt? I'm sure it's not as bad as all that," Bobby Newsom told his friend.

Bobby's friend didn't look so sure.

"Rowena and I met in high school, and boy, she was pretty," Hoyt said as he fidgeted in a chair in the corner. Gabe leaned against the autopsy table and watched the coroner's friend explain what happened that night in his father's shop. He had refused an attorney, even after Detective Wilcox read him his rights. "I had hopes that she would marry me, but I guess I always knew she wanted better than this town."

"What does that have to do with Will Mason?" I asked.

"Well, I'm getting to that, you nosy—"

"Hey," Gabe interrupted sternly. "Don't worry about her, just tell us what happened. Fortuna? How about you leave the questions to me, okay?"

Right. Gabe had asked Pepper and me to stay because we had more information about the case than *he* did, but *I* should sit down and be quiet? We were *literally* in here because the police didn't do their jobs. I glared at Gabe but turned back toward Hoyt.

"So, anyway, in July my father started storing a lot of cash at the shop," Hoyt explained. His face was tight with apprehension. "Rowena saw the stacks of money upstairs in the safe when she came with me at night."

"Came with you at night to do what?" I asked. Gabe glared.

"There were some beanbag chairs stored on the third floor, and it was a good place for us to get some privacy, if you know what I mean," Hoyt grinned lecherously at Bobby, who did not grin back. To the coroner's credit, he seemed to take this seriously. "Anyway," he continued, his grin falling. "After everybody would leave, Rowena and I would hang out here. That's when she saw the money."

"Was she the one that stole it?" I asked. Hoyt looked at me in surprise. "Pepper and I saw the records for the burglaries in August. Well, before they were...misplaced."

"It wasn't as simple as all that," Hoyt said. "Rowena and I were gonna run away together to Hollywood."

"Both of you?" Pepper asked, surprised.

"Well, yeah, we were in love. Rowena wound up with the money, sure, but it was supposed to be for both of us. It was for us to start our new lives in California, away from my father," he explained, the heartbreak and longing for that dream still palpable in the surrounding air. "I thought Rowena and I would be together forever. I would've done anything for her." His expression hardened. "And anything to get away from my father."

"Mason caught you and Rowena stealing the cash, didn't he?" Gabe asked as if he was a *real* detective with a badge and everything. "He came by the shop for something, and he realized what was happening."

"Yeah, well, I guess Rowena and I weren't as cagey as we thought," Hoyt told Gabe. "He figured out that the burglaries had to be happening late at night, and since he was on his way back late from Little Rock anyway, he stopped by the shop to check things out."

"Did he show up while you were up there?" Gabe asked.

"He heard us on the third floor when he came inside," Hoyt said, his voice growing quiet and his expression dark. "He didn't call out or anything, and we didn't hear him. I figure he crept up the stairs to peek over the landing to see who was there."

"Why didn't he just call the cops?" Pepper murmured.

"I couldn't tell you that. I almost wish he *had*," Hoyt looked down. "If we'd have gotten caught, Rowena would have never left me here alone. But he didn't. He creeped up the stairs all quiet-like, or we were so focused on what we were doin', we didn't hear him."

"What happened when he saw you?"

"He confronted us, started yelling at us," he explained. "See, the cops had suspected the money disappearing was an inside job, and Spike had been harassed for the whole month. Interview after interview. I guess they didn't bother Liz all that much because she was a girl," Hoyt shrugged. "But when Spike got up there and realized we were stealin' the money? Hoo boy, he was mad."

"What happened then?" Bobby asked.

Hoyt hesitated and looked his friend Bobby in the eye. "Spike fell down the stairs."

"What, did he lose his footing because he was yelling at you so animated-like? Perfectly healthy teenager just fell right down the stairs," Bobby said with incredulity. "Was his mohawk hair spray imbalanced? Too much in the back? Come on, now, Hoyt. What really happened?"

"I just told you. He found us, we were all surprised. Then he fell," Hoyt Abernathy repeated as he shifted in his chair. "Rowena ran out all scared like, and I didn't know what to do, so I hid the rest of the money and took the safe out and...well, you know," Hoyt said, shrugging.

"You were doing *really* well telling that story, right until the end. You did not stick the landing," I told him as Gabe poked me to be quiet.

I knew that Hoyt Abernathy had been telling the truth, right up to when Spike appeared on that landing. Sensing truths and lies? That was a type of telepathy and intuition that was very difficult to turn off. Hoyt had told the truth. And then he stopped.

"You still love her," I suggested, and Hoyt turned to look sharply at me. "Rowena. Evangeline. You're still in love with her."

"That has nothing to do with any of this," he snapped at me. "It was my father's store, I did it, what happened to Spike was an accident. That's it."

"If you were just going to take the fall for her, why were you worried that I would go talk to her?" I asked him, squinting. "You weren't worried that she was going to throw you under a bus," I guessed. "You were worried that she would think *you* didn't throw yourself under one to protect *her.*"

Images screamed in his mind, and I focused on

what he was mentally shouting. Opening myself up further to him for just a moment, I saw Spike reach the top of the landing. The three of them shouting at one another, arguing. Spike shaking his head no. Rowena thrusting bundles of cash at him, her face frightened, her eyes pleading with him not to turn them in. Spike steadfast at the top of the stairs, shaking his head no.

One more thrust of the cash, and Spike loses his footing. He comes to rest on the second floor landing, cash fluttering around his body even though he no longer moved.

I was grateful, at least, that it was quick. Spike didn't suffer.

Well, okay, he suffered some humiliation since they shoved his body in a wall. But his death was quick, clearly. It was no wonder he didn't know what happened to him.

"I think Rowena pushed him," Pepper said, her eyes narrowing.

I turned and stared at her. Had she just picked up on what I did?

"She didn't!" Hoyt shouted.

"I *bet* she did," Pepper disagreed. "That girl was always putting her hands on people in high school, pushing people out of her way. Heck, they think she killed her rich husband to get his money. Wait— what happened to the money?" Pepper asked him.

"Rowena used it to start her new life in Hollywood," Hoyt sighed. "She was afraid that my father would find out what we did, and so I had to stay here to cover."

"Does your father know? That Spike was in the wall?" I asked.

"I'm not gonna answer that," Hoyt told me.

"Why? What's the harm in it now?"

"I am not gonna answer that," Hoyt repeated evenly.

"It wouldn't matter if you did," Gabe said with a shrug. "I can't arrest you for anything you told me. Statute of limitations ran out a long time ago."

"Are you kidding me?" I asked him, shocked.

"There is no murder here, or if there is? I haven't heard evidence of it," Gabe explained. "Class A and Y felonies toll at six years, and it's been far longer than that. They've both been living openly all that time, didn't make any effort to hide—"

"They hid a body! Doesn't that mean the statute of limitations starts when the body is found?" I asked him, calling on my recent viewing of *Law & Order* to inform me. Which I believed (considering how lackadaisical the police department had been in handling this case) made me slightly more informed than Gabe.

"I *told* you," Pepper said as she leaned into me.

"Nothing ever happens here in Mystic's End. Somehow, the bad guys *always* seem to get away with things."

"I'm not a bad guy!" Hoyt protested hotly.

"Right, you just stole half a million dollars from your father, gave it to a *girl*, and then shoved a friend of yours in a wall and left him there for over twenty years to cover for it," Pepper shot back. "You're a prince among men, Abernathy."

He looked back at her, his face dangerous.

"State law is state law, Stanford," Bobby Newsom told her as Gabe looked on, troubled. "We could keep digging, but you said some case files are missing, and Hoyt here wouldn't turn on Rowena if you yanked out his fingernails with pliers. Now, *she* might turn on *him* and make up some story just to make sure she doesn't take the rap for nothin'," Bobby said as he scratched his stubble. "But with so much evidence gone? We'll just be running around in circles. I, for one, enjoy my leisure time more than that."

"Unbelievable," I said to the highest ranking law enforcement officer in the county. He shrugged and smiled at me.

"Welcome to Mystic's End," Pepper said standing up. She then turned to Gabe. "Are you going to at least record this somewhere so people know what happened to Spike? And tell his father? I mean, that seems like the *least* you could do."

"I will," Gabe told her through clenched teeth.

"Well, I'm glad we got that all sorted out," the county coroner said as he stood up. "And I would like to point out that while it's nice to have a story, the cause of death? It was *accurate*. At least as far as any of us will *ever* know," Bobby smiled.

Based on what I saw in Hoyt's head, the infuriating coroner was right. It was *technically* an accident. It didn't *seem* like Rowena had meant to push Spike down the stairs. It looked to me like she was excited, kept trying to bribe him, and she pushed harder and harder the more he said no.

But still, nothing about this seemed right.

TWENTY-THREE

"I caught them?" Spike asked, his face contorted with the effort of trying to call up a memory buried by twenty years and a death. The ghost was less concerned with the details of his death than I predicted he would be, but I still assumed at the end of the story, Spike would be able to leave the building. "They were stealing?"

"Yes, money for Rowena—Evangeline—to move to Hollywood," I explained. "Originally, they were both supposed to move together. After your mishap, she took off with the money and Hoyt remained here."

"How's he taking it?" Pepper asked as she glanced up from her pad, pen poised in the air. "Is he upset, mad, sad?"

"What are you writing?" Gabe asked skeptically as he wandered over toward her perch on the couch. "You're not going to put this in your blog, are you?"

"Of *course* I am," she told him defiantly. Now it was Gabe's face twisting with the effort it was taking him not to rip the notebook from his ex-girlfriend's hand. "The people in this town deserve to know what happened."

"Why?" I challenged her.

"What do you mean? How is that *even* a question?" Pepper asked clutching the pad to her chest as Gabe tried to get a peek at what she was writing. "Truth should always be disclosed. Anything else is a corruption."

"The world isn't so black and white, Pepper," I told her with a sigh. "Sometimes, there's a *reason* that secrets are secrets, and it's better for everyone that they stay that way. There's a wisdom in knowing which truth should be brought to light and which ones should be kept in the dark."

"That's preposterous," Pepper scoffed at me as she lowered her notepad and began writing again. "Truth is truth, Fortuna," she muttered as she began furiously scribbling again.

"I know a whole host of theorists that might disagree with you." Gideon barked and wagged his tail happily.

"I took a theory course in college once," Pepper told me, looking up. "I dropped it within three weeks when I realized none of the tests would have multiple choice answers."

"Man, is she color blind?" Spike asked. "I don't think she even *sees* gray."

I chuckled. Gabe, who was over by the coffee and tea station, looked up curiously. "Spike is tickled by Pepper's rigid belief that there is a right and wrong answer for everything. What *are* you writing about, Pepper?"

"Spike," she said. "And you."

I halted and turned. "What do you mean, you're writing about me?"

"You can talk to the dead," she told me without looking up. "And now I've witnessed it. It will be a great follow up to the original blog post that I wrote about you and your history when you came to town."

"What original blog post?" I asked cautiously.

Pepper rolled her eyes and reached into her messenger bag. After searching around, she pulled out a tablet. With a few taps of her finger, she turned the screen around to me and held it out.

Mysterious Fortune Telling Artist Moves to Mystic's End

I winced.

As I read, though, I had to admit as things go, the story could have been worse.

Pepper had dug up my adoptive family, original name, the boarding school I attended, and the two circuses I had traveled with. She did a study of my *stage name* and its origins. There were hazy images of me and Charlotte, rumors of witchery never proven, and links to a forum where the Magical Midway's ability to move quickly over vast distances was hotly debated.

"The two of you really don't have any respect for anyone's privacy whatsoever, do you?" I said as I scrolled through the hypotheticals, rumors, gossip and hearsay.

"I'm a police officer," Gabe protested. "I was just—"

"Right, and she's a journalist," I pointed at Pepper. "You guys, both of you, dug into me before you even *introduced* yourselves. Jeez, it's no *wonder* the two of you are both single."

"Hey!" Pepper protested indignantly and suddenly paused. Shrugging, she declared "Yeah, okay, that's fair."

* * *

Hours later, after Gabe and Pepper left (both arguing about how Spike's murder could have been better handled), I sat with my feet folded under me reading through *Crooked Endz* on the tablet Pepper let me use.

"Slow down," Spike murmured as he hovered over my shoulder. I stopped scrolling and reached over to scratch Gideon's head. The sleeping greyhound was curled up next to me, his head resting against my side. "Is that true?" Spike asked me. "Is there really such a thing as a Witches' Council?"

"There was," I told him. "The whole thing changed right before I got here. But yep, once there was."

"You were part of all this?" Spike asked me as he floated down to look at me face to face. I nodded. "Why would you leave something magical and...I mean...you had werebears!"

"I didn't *have* werebears, Spike. They're people, not pets."

"What I mean is Mystic's End must seem completely *boring* to you now. Why would you even come here?"

I paused and got up to look down from the second floor to the steps of the old jailhouse. It seemed impossible that anyone could leave an infant on those steps and not be seen, and yet my mother did. "You see those steps?" I asked him.

"Yeah, what about them?"

"Someone left me there just after I was born," I told him as we both stared down at the square, the sunset painting the old bricks orange. "I don't know who, or why. After watching Charlotte and Gunther try to figure out what the paranormal world actually was, I realized I didn't know who I was. So, I came here to find out where I came from."

The ghost and I looked quietly out the window toward the steps as a Lincoln Town Car pulled up in front of it, blocking my view. A dark window rolled down, and a platinum-headed woman emerged from the blackness, her face upturned as she stared at my building.

"I bet *she's* not happy with you," Spike said.

"It looks like everyone beat all the statute of limitations on whatever crimes may have been committed," I told him as Evangeline Laroux stared up at me. "Why would she be annoyed at me for helping Pepper figure out what happened? I didn't know where that story was going."

"I'm sure she didn't want anyone to know, and I'm also sure Pepper will write an exposé about it on her blog so everyone will know. Anyway, you do know that she's got a *huge* crush on Martin Salvi, right?"

"How would *you* know?" I asked him, startled.

"Gideon," Spike pointed at the dog. "Apparently, I can see the pictures in his head, too."

Gideon opened one eye on the couch and thudded his tail once, then twice. Then he closed his eye and went back to sleep.

"Well, whether she has a crush on Martin has nothing to do with me," I replied as her window rolled back up and the car drove away.

"It does if she thinks *you're* competition," Spike said as we turned away from the window and went back to reading *Crooked Endz*.

* * *

After all the drama of the past few days, the building seemed quiet. Okay, as quiet as it could be with a punk ghost and an unusually vocal greyhound running up and down three flights of stairs after one another.

I came to the third landing and leaned down to take out the small communication cauldron Charlotte had given me. Tapping the side to wake it up, the block of gel in the center melted into a steaming lump of rainbow-tinted goop.

Once it was a bubbling liquid, I called Charlotte.

"Hey," I told her as I carried the mini-cauldron. "I need to fix this wall. Can you tell me how to do it or give me a spell or something?"

"What are you asking *me* for?" she asked,

rolling her eyes. "I don't have the ringmaster super power anymore and, anyway, it wouldn't have worked outside the fairgrounds. Let me get Gunther. I bet he knows some repair spell."

I planted the small cauldron in front of the hole in the wall and waited until Gunther, a tiny Gunther, showed up in the mist.

"You want to brick up that hole?" he asked me, squinting.

"Yep. Can you teach me?"

"Sure, watch," he said, and a normal-sized arm jutted out from the misty mini-Gunther into my bedroom and solidified. He reached up to the wall and touched an undamaged brick. "The easiest way is just to write it in Theban," he explained as he wrote REPAIR in the ancient witch alphabet with his index finger. Gunther's sort-of disembodied hand snapped, and the brick began to clone itself, slowly covering the hole.

"Neat, what can I use that with? Bricks, wood?"

"Anything that's damaged, but built by building blocks of some kind that are uniform. So, a fence or a wall. Even broken glass. As long as it's uniform, that'll do it," Gunther explained as his hand withdrew back to Mickwac.

"You *are* a witch," Pepper whispered from the third floor landing.

I kicked over the cauldron, sending the rainbow

liquid flying everywhere. After it splashed, it crawled together and reformed itself into the gel cube as the wall continued to brick itself up.

Great.

"How did you get in here? Oh, forget it, look, I can explain—" I said, but I stopped as the micro-cassette recorder clicked on. I glowered. "Turn it off."

"No," Pepper looked at me defiantly, the recorder held out in front of her. Shaking.

"Pepper, I mean it. Turn that thing off."

"No! People deserve to know what's going— hey! Dog!"

Gideon leaped off the couch and seized the recorder from Pepper's outstretched hand. The greyhound's claws skittered against the floor as he dashed around the couch. Pepper chased him.

"He's a greyhound, Pepper. You won't catch him," I told her as the dog paused and waited for the reporter, then raced away at breakneck speed just as her hand outstretched to grab him. "Sit down. Let's talk."

"You're a *witch*!" she shouted, pivoting on me. "I've read about you people. You can wipe minds with a wave of your hand. I need that recorder! I need to remind myself this took place when you do your Vulcan mind wipe on me!"

"It's a mind meld. A *Vulcan mind meld*. Not a

mind wipe. And you suspected I was a witch already," I told her as I leaned against the wall and crossed my arms. "Why are you now, suddenly, freaking out over the concept?"

"*Because there was a disembodied arm in the middle of your bedroom!*" Pepper screamed. "And there was rainbow goop and some guy's voice coming out of a bowl, and the bricks were *moving all on their own!*"

Humans weren't alarmed by telepathy, or fortune telling. In fact, I'd always found that almost everyone seems to fancy themselves just a bit psychic. Whether it's a killer instinct in business, a mother's intuition, it didn't matter. It was easy to understand. Human beings can deal with the notion of mental metaphysics.

Start throwing anything undead into the mix, like ghosts or vampires, and they get a little shaky.

Upend the laws of physics?

They're close to a hysterical breakdown.

Whatever Pepper Stanford *believed*, whatever she had reported about, it occurred to me as I watched that she had clearly never *seen* the supernatural, the real supernatural, with her own eyes.

Now she had, and her human mind was experiencing trouble handling it.

"Pepper," I told her in as calming a voice I could muster. "Sit down."

"No!"

"Sit down before I turn you into a toad!" I roared as I pointed to the chair in front of my make-up mirror.

Pepper sat.

TWENTY-FOUR

"Fine, yes—I'm a witch," I told her as she perched on the small chair and inspected the newly bricked up wall cautiously. "I suppose there's no point in refuting it. You saw with your own eyes that I have skills that are—"

"You're going to murder me, aren't you?" Pepper whispered.

Spike laughed out loud behind me, and I shifted to glower at him.

"I'm not going to kill you, Pepper," I told her as I sat down on my bed.

"I think you are," she countered, her voice high-pitched.

"I'm not going to kill you, Pepper."

"You just threatened to turn me into a toad!"

"You can be especially frustrating, you know that?"

"I *do* know that! That's why I think you're going to kill me!" Pepper exclaimed emphatically, her eyes wide as she gawked at me. "I think half the town would kill me if they could do it with a wave of their hand and a little effort, you know!"

"Stop, just stop," I said, and I seized her hands. "Here's the deal—I don't really want it spread around town that I'm a witch. It's not *forbidden* for humans to know about witches anymore, but it's not something that I want to wave a flag about. You understand?"

"But people have the right—"

"I have the right to my *privacy*," I said, cutting her off. "It's something you and Gabe seem to struggle with a great deal, but if you don't want me to pluck the awareness of this right out of your head," I told Pepper with far more certainty than I felt at being able to do the thing I was threatening. "Well, then, agree to keep my confidence. Full stop. No writing about me. No blogging about what we talk about. And the blogs about me come down."

"That's censorship!" Pepper stood up and pointed her finger at me. I raised an eyebrow at it, but she continued her combative stance. "You can't do that! I have freedom of the press!"

"You do," I acknowledged. "And you have a

choice to make. Be my friend and respect my privacy, or don't be my friend and write about me. That's your choice."

Pepper let out some kind of groan of frustration that sounded more like an injured animal in the woods that had just been charged by a werewolf. She turned away from me and began pacing while complaining to herself. Turning, she raised an eyebrow toward me. "How long do I have to make this choice?" she demanded.

"Sixty seconds," I told her, being more generous than I felt like being.

"Oh, come on!" she lamented and began pacing again. Then, suddenly, she stopped. "If I'm your friend, you won't hide your witchy stuff from me? You'll answer questions about it?"

"If they're appropriate questions, sure. *If* you don't write about it."

"If I can't write about it, I'm giving up an *awful* lot here. What do I get in return?" she asked as she studied me, her brows furrowed. "I've spent the past several years trying to find proof of the supernatural, and now that I have it, I can't tell anyone? That'll be absolute misery."

"If you decide to write about it, you'll give up knowing," I told her, shrugging. "So, maybe we *shouldn't* be friends. To be frank, I've noticed you're a little challenged in the self-discipline department."

"The hell I am!" Pepper protested. "I don't have a problem with self-discipline. I have a problem controlling myself in the face of evil."

I stared at her. "Um. That's...that's a self-discipline—"

"If I don't write about you, *you'll* help me," Pepper said as she strode up and stared into my eyes. "That's what I'll get out of it. You'll answer *my* questions about what you can do, but you'll put your signature talents to work making this town better. Deal?"

"Are we *negotiating* for friendship?" I asked. I had gone into this discussion feeling pretty much like I was in the catbird seat, here, and somehow Pepper Stanford had turned the whole debate around in a few short moments. "Like, making a deal to be *friends*? I swear, Pepper, you missed your calling. You should have been a lawyer."

"I didn't miss my calling, but maybe *you* did," she told me, crossing her arms. "Sure, art is important. It makes people happy. And what you did for the dog, that was nice," Pepper said as she waved her hand in Gideon's direction. "But you can do *so much more* with your gifts. You could make things better for all the dogs at the track, not just take one out of it. You could catch the people that are *wrecking* this town. You could—"

"You don't know my powers, and I barely know anything about this town—"

"I know *everything* about this town," Pepper told me. "If we team up together—I mean, do you honestly think Spike would have been unburied, unmourned, and stuck in a wall for twenty years if you and I had explored that case when it took place?"

She had a point. Spike may not have known what happened to him, but he knew enough to let me know that his body was in the wall. "That's true," I admitted to Pepper. "I can't argue with you there."

"And if we *had*, the statute of limitations *wouldn't* have run out, and Hoyt Abernathy would be in jail," Pepper insisted, her eyes flashing. "At the *very* least, he would have gotten a fair trial. Evangeline, too."

"And I wouldn't have been stuck in this building," Spike added as he drifted over to Pepper. "I think you should do it. Team up with her."

I stood up and walked over to the window. Looking down at the steps where I started my known life, I wondered if everything was an accident or if I was meant to meet Charlotte. Was I rejected and then tossed carelessly into the Addington household, then the circuses?

Or was I meant, from the beginning, to go on that journey so I could come full circle here, a newly cemented *real* witch? What did being the mystic of Mystic's End really mean, if anything?

I turned and studied Pepper.

"*If* we do this," I said as a smile spread across her face. "*You* have to stop bumbling into everything without a care in the world in full view of the entire town."

"I...can *try*. To be honest, I'm not so good at that sometimes," she conceded.

"You don't say. And no writing about anything supernatural you learn from me. Nothing. Not a *single* word."

Pepper nodded firmly.

"Oh, wow," Pepper blinked, and suddenly she shrieked. "You're a *real* witch. That's just *crazy*. I'm friends with a real, honest to goodness *witch*."

"Yep," I nodded, grinning.

"Wait until I tell Gabe!" she chuckled.

"Pepper!" I shouted.

"What? You said I couldn't write about you! You said *nothing* about verbally *telling* people things," she pointed out.

I took a deep breath and re-explained the

notion of privacy to Pepper while wondering what, specifically, I had gotten myself into.

* * *

THANK YOU FOR READING!

I hope you enjoyed Mystic's End! Please think about leaving a review! Fortuna and Gideon's adventures continue in Book 2, Angel in Demise!

KEEP UP WITH LEANNE LEEDS

Thanks so much for reading! I hope you liked it! Want to keep up with me? Text me at 1-512-359-3123 to get updates, info, or to shoot me a question!

You can also visit leanneleeds.com to:

Find all my books...

Sign up for my newsletter...

Like me on Facebook...

Follow me on Twitter...

Follow me on Instagram...

Thanks again for reading!

Leanne Leeds

FIND A TYPO? LET US KNOW!

Typos happen. It's sad, but true.

Though we go over the manuscript multiple times, have editors, have beta readers, and advance readers it's inevitable that determined typos and mistakes sometimes find their way into a published book.

Did you find one? If you did, think about reporting it on leanneleeds.com so we can get it corrected.

www.ingramcontent.com/pod-product-compliance
Lightning Source LLC
Chambersburg PA
CBHW031601240626
47153CB00002B/595